A Place to Belong

Cathy Mansell was born in Ireland and, although she now lives in Leicester, her Irish heritage plays a significant role in her fiction. Hailing from a family of writers, she says it was inevitable that she too would become one. She has had five novels published by Tirgearr Publishing. *A Place to Belong* is her first with Headline.

To find out more about Cathy, visit her website: **cathymansell.com,** find her on Facebook: **facebook.com/CathyMansell12** and follow her on Twitter: **@cathymansell3.**

By Cathy Mansell

Shadow Across the Liffey
Her Father's Daughter
Where the Shamrocks Grow
Galway Girl
Dublin's Fair City
A Place to Belong

A Place *to* Belong

CATHY MANSELL

REVIEW

HEADLINE PUBLISHING GROUP
An Hachette UK Company
Carmelite House
50 Victoria Embankment
London EC4Y 0DZ

www.headline.co.uk
www.hachette.co.uk

I'd like to dedicate *A Place to Belong* to my incredibly courageous daughter, Samantha Russell. Having faced and conquered the devastating news she had breast cancer in 2016, she has inspired everyone with her spirited attitude. She is involved in various charity events and hosted a race evening to raise money for the Willow foundation, a charity working with young adult cancer sufferers aged 16–40. Samantha has recently undergone breast reconstruction; the operation proved problematic but throughout her ordeal she continued to encourage others going through the same thing.

I'm thankful to God that Samantha is back teaching full time. She never slows down, living life to the full, enjoying every moment with her husband Mark and her two precious boys, Harrison and Alfie.

Chapter One

1943

Someone shouting woke her. She strained to listen. No one was calling her at this hour, she must have been dreaming. Closing her eyes, she lay back. The orphanage faced on to the street, busy by day, but in the dead of night she was often disturbed by a door slamming and the odd drunk cursing his way home. How she hated this place! Her attempts to escape had failed. Even after ten years, she had never accepted the harsh regime of the institution. A yearning for love and one day a family of her own kept her going.

A faint smell of fumes shook her out of her reverie. She sat up and glanced along the row of sleeping girls, their white nightgowns visible in the darkened room. It was a cold February night, and she had no idea what time it was. Reluctant to wake the others only to be rebuked for disrupting their sleep, she threw off the blanket and drew her shawl around her. Her toes touched the icy floorboards as she slipped her feet into her boots. Her bed was closest to the door, and she crept towards it. She had to find out what was going on even at the risk of being caught and told off by the night attendant. The door closed behind her as she tip-toed down the corridor. Something was burning. The fumes grew stronger, catching the back of her throat as she groped her way down the stairs. In the dim light smoke curled up the wooden staircase. She heard voices coming from the rear of the building and someone hurried towards her.

'Get back upstairs and stay there.'

'What's happening? Are we going to die?'

'Do as you're told, girl! Wait in your dormitory and keep the door closed.'

She knew the place well and yet it was hard to say where the smoke was coming from. She stayed where she was on the first floor, listening to the sound of coughing and the shuffling of feet. Her eyes were streaming as she struggled to see in the darkness. Someone holding a lighted candle gripped her arm, pushing her towards the stairs. She covered her mouth with her shawl, but she had no intention of going back. Some of the children were already making their way down through a haze of smoke, crying, confused and frightened.

'Go back and wait until you're instructed.' It was the night supervisor.

Some attempted to obey but were forced back by fumes. Coughing, she made her way along a corridor to a doorway that opened out on to the forecourt. It was locked. A few girls huddled behind her.

'What are we going to do?' one girl cried.

'I'm not staying to be burned alive. If you help me, we'll get out.' With the heel of her boot, she broke a window, climbed on to the ledge and jumped down into the yard. Others followed and they held on to each other, choking and trying to catch their breath.

'Listen!'

Angry voices were yelling, 'Open the gate.' The bell kept on ringing.

'Someone's here! They'll get us out.' But she knew the Mother Abbess would not unlock the doors, or let anyone in, until the sisters were up and dressed, and that might be too late.

Minutes passed. The shouting and knocking continued until someone finally unlocked the entrance, and men from the neighbourhood rushed in. Her eyes stinging, she made a dash for freedom. Traumatised girls escaped alongside her, some ran screaming for help. Others less capable were dragged back inside.

The street, now empty of traffic, was filled with the sound of crashing glass and shouts of panic. Residents and shopkeepers hurried towards the burning building, some carrying buckets of water. Pausing for breath, she inhaled the night air, before continuing to run until her lungs gave up and she slid down on to the pavement, gasping. The cold penetrated her thin clothes, and she wrapped her arms around her knees to keep warm while chaos erupted.

When she looked up, flames licked the front of the building. Tormented screams filled her ears. With a desperate need to do something, she jumped to her feet, and ran alongside others to fetch and carry buckets of water. Men placed extended ladders to the upper floors and sprayed water from a hose; it was useless against the blaze now raging. Small faces pressed up against the windowpanes tore at her heart. Children wept in the arms of neighbours.

Women called on the names of Jesus and His Holy Mother to save the children. When she could no longer feel her hands, exhausted, she dropped to her knees. She looked towards the heavens, tears streaming down her face. She knew it would take a miracle to get everyone out alive. A gentle hand touched her arm, and she glanced up. An older woman wearing dark clothes, a shawl covering her head, glanced down at her. She put a thick blanket around her shoulders.

'Come away now, me dear. Ye'll freeze to death out here. There's nothing more ye can do. Leave it to the men.' She helped her to her feet and guided her down the street and inside a cottage. It was cosy and inviting. 'Ah, sure, sit ye down, ye poor wee creature.' She removed the clothes horse, where undergarments were airing around the stove, and stoked the smouldering embers. 'Aren't ye the lucky one to have got out of there alive.'

She felt unable to speak, as if her tongue had frozen along with the rest of her.

The woman placed peat on the hot ash and lifted the heavy black kettle from the hob. 'Sure, once ye wash the dirt and grime from yer face you'll feel better, so ye will.' She poured warm water into an enamel basin and handed the girl a used bar of Sunlight soap.

Her hair reeked, and no one would guess she was anything other than a street urchin. She soaped her face and hands; the soft bubbles felt luxurious after the harsh carbolic the nuns issued at the orphanage.

She stared at the black cooking range fitted into the chimney breast with a fireplace on one side and a cast-iron oven on the other. An ash rake and tongs hung by the side, and the heat radiating from the range sent out a warm, comforting glow that took the chill from her bones. The woman thrust a warm drink into her hand. 'Sup this.'

Her hands shook as she wrapped them around the mug and sipped the drink. She wasn't sure what it was, it tasted so creamy. 'Will . . . will . . . the little ones be okay? I should have stayed to help them,' she cried.

'Don't fret now. Those poor wee babies are not your responsibility.' She saw pity in the woman's eyes. 'I'm Ma Scully. My nephew's out there alongside the military and the constabulary, and if anyone can save those wee childer, he will. What are we to call ye?'

For a second, she had to think. The name her parents had given her was considered too fancy for the orphanage and replaced with Bridget. But she would never forget her real name. 'Eva, Eva Fallon.'

'Is that a Dublin name then?'

'I don't know.' She barely remembered her life before the orphanage. Discouraged from talking about it, she had eventually stopped asking.

'How old are ye, Eva?'

'It's my birthday today; I'm seventeen.' She was one of the oldest girls in the orphanage, and she had been on errands to the local store many times. But now, she could never go back.

'Well, sure it's a day ye won't forget in a hurry.' The woman shook her head. 'When ye finish yer cocoa, ye can sleep on the settle bed, and when Cathal gets back, we'll see what's to be done.' She lit a lamp, placed it next to Eva and handed her an extra blanket. 'I'm away to me bed; the dawn's not yet risen. Sure, there'll be a lot to do the morra so there will.'

Eva thanked her and climbed into the chair bed alongside

the wall. It was like a bench with a high wooden back. Grateful, she lay down, pulled up the cover and wept. Each time she closed her eyes, she could see flames devouring the building.

Outside, she could hear a cacophony of bells clanging; wagons clattering past at speed increased her anxiety. 'Oh, dear God! Please save those poor wee children.'

A pungent smell from the peat fire woke her. She glanced across to where a man was sitting at the table, his head in his hands. She stiffened. He glanced up, his dark eyes bright in the firelight. Smudges of ash lined his face, his hands red and blistered. He appeared oblivious to her in a darkened corner of the room. His chair scraped the floor, and he stood up. The latch on the door lifted as he went outside. With the blanket surrounding her she padded over to the window. A mist hung over the street and her heartbeat quickened. She felt ashamed to have slept while the place she had lived in for most of her life was burning. She needed the privy but, too nervous to go out to the yard, she lingered in the doorway. He was in the lean-to, stripped to the waist. He scooped cold water from a barrel, and poured it over his head, face and around the back of his neck. He shuddered as the water dripped over his shoulders. Eva, flushed with embarrassment to have watched while he performed his ablutions, turned and moved back into the room. He must have been out all night saving the children. Dear God! It made her all the more aware of how lucky she was to be alive.

When he came in, she didn't know what to say, or do.

He glared at her, a mystified look on his face. 'Who? Where? Who are you?'

Eva took a deep breath and swallowed. 'I'm . . . I'm sorry. I'm looking for Ma Scully.' She fidgeted with her hands and glanced around her.

'She's still sleeping.'

'It . . . it was good of her to take me in last night.'

'Are you one of the orphanage kids?' His wet, wavy black hair fell over his eyes, and he brushed it back with the towel.

She nodded. He sat down by the hearth and leant forward, his elbows on his knees. She resented being called a kid, today, but when she glanced down at her grubby nightgown, it was all too obvious. 'Please, sir, do you know if all the children got out?'

He raised his head. 'Some have already been taken to the tuberculosis hospital. You should go too. You'll be okay there. I'll take you if you like?'

Wishing Ma Scully was here, she lowered her head. She wasn't going anywhere to be sent away to another orphanage, God only knew where. If only she had any family, somewhere she belonged. Apart from the nuns, she knew no one in the town.

The man stood up and pulled on his jersey. He was tall, with broad shoulders and strong muscles. 'You must be hungry. There's stirabout on the hob if you'd like some.'

She thanked him, unable to stop her shaking limbs. It was the first time she had been alone with a man and she tightened her grip on the blanket, wrapping it around her body. Her stomach rumbled but she couldn't eat, so she sat down on the bed, resting her feet on the floor.

'How on earth did you manage to escape that place with your life?' He looked at her. 'Do you know what happened in there?'

7

She shook her head and bit her lip to stop it trembling, feeling hot tears rush down her face.

'It's all right,' he said kindly. 'Don't be nervous. I guess you're still in shock. Sure, I'm just grateful I was here at the time and able to help.' He sighed. 'The worst bit is still to come.'

Eva got down from the settle. 'I should go down and see what I can do to help.'

He put his hand up to stop her. 'I wouldn't do that, miss.'

She caught a glimpse of herself in the mirror. She looked scruffy – and with no other clothes to her name, what could she do? Her black hair was matted and the smudges around her pale green eyes gave her a startled look. She glanced round as Ma Scully entered the room.

'You're not going anywhere dressed like that. You'll freeze to death.' Ma Scully was a formidable woman. Her thick, wiry hair was swept back from her forehead and curled over her ears. She wore a black woollen dress with a white lacy collar and a warm knitted cardigan that buttoned down the front. A silver cross hung round her neck. The determined angle of her jaw gave Eva the impression that nothing was about to faze this woman.

Relieved to see her, Eva's shoulders relaxed and she sat at the table.

Ma Scully turned to her nephew. 'Have ye eaten, Cathal?'

'I can't stomach it, Ma.'

'That bad, eh?'

He unhooked an oilskin coat from the door. 'I'm going back down. There's still a lot of work to be done.'

'Terrible business, so it is. I see you've already met Eva.' She began to cut and butter slices of soda bread.

He nodded.

'I'll be along soon to give a hand.'

He shifted his stance. 'Look, Ma. It won't be pleasant.' He put a hand on his aunt's shoulder. 'We, we didn't manage to save everyone.'

Eva's eyes widened, and she blinked back tears. 'You can't mean that. Sure the men came to save them.'

'Ah, the poor wee blithers,' Ma said.

'We did our best.'

'Is the fire under control now?' Ma asked, scooping porridge into bowls.

'It's still smouldering. Trying to fight a fire of that size with water buckets and ladders . . .' He shook his head. 'By the time the fire brigade arrived from Dundalk, the place was already ablaze.'

'I want to go and see my friends,' Eva said, her eyes brimming with tears.

'Sure, I'll come down with ye later.'

'I wouldn't advise it, Ma. Not with the girl.' He finished pulling on his heavy-duty boots and picked up his hard hat. At the door he turned round. 'If you insist on going down there, you'll have to stay well clear of the building. It won't be safe.'

'You be careful, Cathal,' Ma called after him as he left.

Eva rushed towards the back door.

'If you're looking for the privy, it's the red-brick building at the far end of the yard.'

Chapter Two

Buttoned into a dark, oversized coat, her hands snug inside
a pair of knitted gloves, Eva walked down the street accompanied by the older woman. Her stomach felt knotted, but
she had to see for herself. Ma Scully carried a bag of supplies
including flasks of hot tea and sandwiches. In spite of the
early hour the sky was brightening, but Eva shivered, her
head ached, and a vein pulsed in her temple. Cathal was
chatting with the military. Clouds of dust rose from mounds
of rubble and bricks, and a gassy smell made her cough. The
room where she had slept the night before was now a pile of
smouldering debris. The town buzzed with speculation,
and some people looked on in stunned silence. She saw tears
in grown men's eyes. A group of women in shawls, their
heads nodding in disbelief, were looking up at the burned-
out building.

'Why in the name of God didn't them holy sisters let
them childer out?'

'It's a damn shame, if ye ask me,' one man bellowed.

Eva wondered if they were right. The nuns had taken an age before opening the gate. An overpowering sense of sadness swamped her, and she watched Cathal place a mask over his mouth before walking into the gaping building. She was about to follow him but the military held her back.

'It's not a sight for a young girl's eyes.'

She pulled away to move in closer. There was a large opening where the heavy convent doors once stood and she could see through to the forecourt. A row of bodies lay side by side, covered in sacks and blankets, their blackened feet sticking out. The overpowering stench of burned flesh made her retch, and she vomited on to the pavement.

A woman in uniform with the Red Cross emblem on the sleeve of her coat walked towards her. 'Come away from there, before you get hurt.'

Eva couldn't answer, and the lady helped her across the street. She placed her next to a group of stunned children, still in their nightclothes, with blankets over their shoulders. Eva tried speaking to them, addressing them by name, hugging each one. There was no response, no recognition, just blank stares. Some had minor injuries and burns, and she hoped that they had also spent the night with some kind family. She glanced around for Ma Scully who was busy consoling two distressed women, pouring them tea from her flask.

The woman from the Red Cross came back with a young girl, then she turned to Eva. 'Do you have any relatives, child?'

'Relatives?'

'Anyone in the area with whom you can stay?'

She shook her head; she doubted Ma Scully would want her to stay another night. Ambulances were now arriving in quick succession.

'Don't worry,' the woman said. 'We'll take you along with the rest of the children, to hospital, where you'll be given food and looked after.'

Eva drew the collar of the coat closer around her neck. Thoughts of food were enticing but she couldn't take the risk. She looked across the street. One shop had a ginnel that backed on to a field full of black and white cows.

Frightened of being taken into care again, she edged away from the thickening crowd. She escaped unnoticed into the fields, where she took refuge inside an empty barn. She snatched up a fistful of straw and stuffed it into her boots to keep her feet warm. Then she lay down on the dry hay and sobbed.

She must have slept, for when she woke it was raining. She jumped to her feet. Outside, the street appeared quieter. The farmer would be out any minute to herd the cattle inside. She had to get out of here! In her haste, she stumbled and fell into a ditch. It was waterlogged and the icy chill took her breath away. The intense scream of a vixen sent a shiver down her spine.

Drizzle wet her face as she ran, her boots squelching with mud, until she was at the back entrance to Ma Scully's cottage. She squeezed through a gap in the hedge, darted into the yard, ran inside the privy and bolted the door. She sat on the wooden toilet seat, shivering, and drew her knees up to her chest. She felt sick from worry. What if Ma refused to take her in? Where would she go? Her life at the orphanage had been bad, but the uncertainty of being alone in the world, with no one to turn to, was far worse. With hindsight, she wished she had gone in the ambulance with the rest of the orphans.

Her legs felt numb, her stomach rumbled and her teeth chattered by the time she saw a light come on in Ma's window.

'Ma, it's me, Eva.' She hammered on the door.

It flew open and Ma glared at her.

'God and His Holy Mother! Look at the cut of ye. What are ye doing here? I thought ye'd gone with the rest of the childer in the ambulance.'

A sudden cramp made her legs buckle. Ma helped her inside and put her to sit next to the range.

'Please don't send me away. I won't go!'

'Well now, ye'd rather run away and freeze to death, would ye? Drink this.'

Eva removed her soggy mittens and warmed her hands around the bowl of thick broth, drinking hungrily from the bowl.

'Thank you.'

'If yer seventeen, like ye say, ye can get work and take care of yourself.' Ma shook her head. 'But in your present state, God alone knows how.'

'Who'll employ me when they find out I'm from the orphanage?'

'That's hardly your fault, now is it?' Ma sighed. 'As long as ye can prove you're honest, I might be able to help.' She chuckled. 'Look at the cut of ye,' she said again. 'We're going to do something about that right away.' She clicked her tongue. 'Help me to bring in the tin bath from the yard. You can have a wee soak here in front of the stove.'

Ashamed, Eva glanced down at her dirty, smelly clothes. The nuns were so particular about cleanliness. Thoughts of a bath sounded wonderful. But could she trust Ma not to let anyone in, or to have her sent away? Eva placed the empty bowl on the table, followed Ma outside and helped her to unhook the tin bath from the wall. She had never washed in a tin bath before, and she didn't want to now.

'It's all right. I'll just wash my face and hands and go to the public baths tomorrow,' she said, in spite of not having a penny to her name.

'So, ye'd stay in those filthy clothes till then, would ye? Sure, yer not sleeping in a bed of mine like that.' Ma nodded towards the bath. 'Come on now, let's get this thing inside.'

'What if someone comes in?'

'Oh, you needn't worry about that. As for Cathal, sure he won't be back for ages yet. He's down the Farnham Arms with the rest of the men. After the day they've had, I doubt any of them will sleep without a belly full of ale inside them.'

At the orphanage, they had cubicles when they took a bath. And Eva hardly knew the woman who had taken her under her wing. A frown puckered her forehead.

'I'll bolt the door if it'll make ye less nervous.'

Chapter Three

The bath was full, the kitchen filled with steam, the fire crackled, and Eva couldn't wait to get out of her dirty clothes. Ma retreated to her bedroom, leaving her with a new bar of Sunlight soap and a large towel. She peeled off her clothes and placed them in a bundle, then dipped her toe into the water before easing herself down into the tub.

Later, dressed in one of Ma's long nightgowns, Eva helped to empty the bath and then dried her jet-black hair, letting it fall around her shoulders. She couldn't remember a time when she had been this warm. How lucky she was to have met this kind woman. Without her, she would have frozen to death in a ditch, with nowhere to go. Her anxiety returned. What would happen to her now? She was fortunate, while her friends had perished. What right did she have to feel sorry for herself?

Ma came back with clothes over her arm. 'I've a trunk full of good-quality second-hand clothes I keep for emergencies such as this. You should find something to fit in this lot.' She placed the clothes on the table. 'How is your needlework?'

'Okay, I think.'

'Grand! I'll get the darning box.' Eva sorted through the clothes and picked out two skirts, a blouse and a dress. She held a long navy skirt against her and a smile lit her face.

'Why don't ye try it on?'

'Can I?' In a recessed corner of the room, she pulled a jumper on and stepped into the skirt. It fell down over her hips and she held it up with one hand.

'Come here, child!'

Eva walked towards her.

'A few tucks here and there and you can wear it the morra.' Ma took pins from a tin box and stuck them down the length of the skirt to fit Eva's thin frame. 'Now all you have to do is get sewing. You'll find everything you need in here.' She tapped the top of the needle box.

Eva had no memory of wearing anything other than the dull grey, striped dress issued to all the girls, and she was delighted to have proper clothes to wear. 'I don't deserve your kindness.'

'Why's that then?' Ma pulled a chair over and sat down. 'Those kiddies' deaths are not your fault. Unless there's something you're not telling me.' Her face took on a stern expression, like the nuns when they wanted her to admit to something she hadn't done. 'Is there?'

'No!'

'Right so! I'll leave you to make the alterations, then you had better get yourself to bed. The morra, you and me need to have a serious talk.' She stood with arms akimbo. 'I need to know everything about you if I'm to help you find work. Is that understood?'

She nodded and wondered what Ma wanted to know about her. Did she think she was lying and that the tragedy at the orphanage was her fault? She went over it all again in her head as she sewed. The guilt to have left the little ones to fend for themselves niggled at her conscience. When she had finished sewing, she removed all the pins and tried the skirt on. It was a good fit, and she ran her hands over its length. You could hardly see the stitching. Invisible mending, the nuns called it. She had won a certificate for her sewing and embroidery. The nuns had entrusted her with all kinds of delicate garments and vestments that needed repair. It was a job she enjoyed. However, she still had to scrub floors until her fingers blistered, polish brasses, wash and peel vege-tables, as well as take care of the nursery children during the day. As a consequence her education had suffered when she could not keep awake.

She took off the skirt, placed it at the end of the bed, and climbed in. She felt lonely and afraid for her future – whatever that might be. Somehow, she had to convince Ma Scully that she had no hidden secrets, nor was she a liar. If Ma Scully was to find her employment, what would it be and how far would she have to travel? On that thought, she fell asleep.

The sound of men's voices, bidding each other goodnight outside the window, woke her. She kept her eyes closed as Cathal came in; she listened as he raked the embers and banked up the fire. She watched him stretch his broad shoulders, saw his gaze flicker across the room to where she was. Then he paused in the doorway to his bedroom before going in and closing the door behind him. Eva knew little of men, but there was something good about this man. Just like his aunt, he had shown her kindness, something she had experienced little of in the past.

Next morning, Eva was last to waken. Ma and her nephew were sitting by the hearth talking, and she assumed it was about her.

'Oh, you're awake then, sleepy head?' Ma said.

'I'm sorry. I rarely sleep this late. What's the time?' She sat up, pulling the blanket around her.

'It's eight o'clock. Cathal's away to Dublin and has a train to catch. Will you be all right on your own while I take him to the station?'

'I'll be grand.' Being left alone in the house made her feel trusted, or maybe she was being tested. 'Is there anything I can do while you're gone?'

'Keep the fire in and tidy up. When I get back, I have a proposition for you.'

Eva nodded.

Cathal slipped on his jacket and threw a waterproof over his shoulder. 'Well,' he said, looking across at her, 'it was nice meeting you, Eva.' His handshake was warm. 'I hope things work out for you. If you follow my aunt's advice it'll keep you from the workhouse.'

Then they were gone out the door. She climbed down from the bed and ran to the window. Ma got into the cart next to Cathal, and Eva watched him wrap a rug around his aunt's knees before taking the reins and guiding the reluctant horse forward. He was so handsome. Everything about him radiated confidence; she had seen that same conviction in the Mother Abbess. But unlike her, he had shown her compassion, and she was sad to see him go. She had hoped he would see her dressed in proper women's clothes with her hair clean and arranged in a chignon. He might then have gone away with a different image of her. She sat down at the table and ate a little of the bread Ma had left her, and sipped the tea. She wondered what 'proposition' meant. If she had a dictionary, she could find out.

She got dressed in the skirt she had stayed up late to alter, and added a white polka-dot blouse. She pulled a navy cardigan from the pile Ma had left out and put it on. It was far too big, but she rolled up the sleeves, then she tied one of Ma's aprons around her waist and began the washing-up. She ladled water from the large earthenware pot into a basin and washed and dried each piece of crockery before placing it back on the dresser. She swept and washed the floor, then placed a few pieces of peat on the fire like she'd seen Ma do. When she had finished, she surveyed the room, making sure it was neat and tidy before sitting by the fire to wait. Why was it taking so long? Was the station that far away?

Bored of waiting, she couldn't help her curiosity and opened the cupboard underneath the dresser where Ma kept oatmeal flour and other foodstuff. Eva didn't know how to make bread so she decided it was best not to try. She opened the door to the room where Cathal had slept. The single bed had a white candlewick bedspread brightening the dark oak furniture. A rolled-up copy of *The Anglo-Celt* rested on the bedside table. She picked it up. The front page was all about the war in Europe but nothing yet about the fire at the orphanage.

A picture of Mary holding baby Jesus had a brown scapular hung across it and on the other wall was a picture of an elderly man with a moustache. She opened the large oak wardrobe, hoping to find a garment belonging to Cathal that she could touch. It was empty. She fingered the loose change in a dish on top of the chest of drawers, moving the

shilling, sixpence and two pennies around with her index
finger. Why had he not taken it with him? At the back of a
drawer, her eye was drawn to a man's gold-plated wrist-
watch. She had seen nothing like it before. She brought it to
her ear. It had stopped ticking, and she fought the urge to
wind it. She wondered who it belonged to. She placed the
wide strap around her wrist, pulling it tight to fit. 'Swiss'
was written in small gold lettering across the face. She had
never seen a watch close up. Still wearing it, she wondered
what it would be like to own something so precious. She
had possessed nothing of her own at the orphanage except
for a miraculous medal on a blue ribbon that each girl wore
around her neck. Daydreaming, she didn't hear Ma Scully
return.

'You thieving young wench.'

Startled, she turned round.

Ma Scully was in the doorway, her arms folded across
her ample chest.

'I . . . I was just looking.' She removed the watch from
around her wrist and placed it down on the chest of drawers. Tears welled in her eyes. 'I wasn't stealing, honest to
God, I wasn't. Please believe me.'

Chapter Four

She stood rigid while her apron was searched and tossed to the ground. Ma Scully probed the pockets of Eva's skirt, a grave expression on her face. 'Take it off.'

Eva unzipped the skirt. 'I've taken nothing.'

'Now yer underwear.'

'Why won't you believe me?' Her eyes watered.

Ma raised an eyebrow. 'Don't make this harder than it is.'

Eva flushed with embarrassment as she undid the safety pin that held up her knickers. They dropped to the floor. Humiliated, she crossed her arms over her nakedness. This was worse than anything she had experienced at the orphanage.

'Okay, get dressed. What were ye doing in that room handling stuff that doesn't belong to you?' Ma straightened her shoulders. 'You had no right to go snooping around my house.'

'I'm sorry.' She sniffed and pulled on her clothes. 'I meant no harm.'

'Nosy, more like.' Ma disappeared into her bedroom and closed the door. Was she checking for missing items? When she came out she said, 'I guess you hadn't got as far as my room then.'

Shocked at her accusing tone, Eva couldn't speak.

Ma's mood remained distant, and Eva was at a loss how to reassure her she wasn't a thief.

Later, Ma unhooked a rabbit from the lean-to, slapped it down on the table and skinned it, as if she was taking her frustrations out on the dead animal.

'Please, let me help?'

'No! Sit over there, where I can keep me eye on ye.' She pointed to a chair in the corner. 'I need to think.'

Sick with uncertainty, Eva fidgeted with her hands. Wasn't the truth enough? If only she knew what Ma was thinking. Would she send her away to another institution – or even worse, to the workhouse? Eva watched her wash and dry the rabbit. Then she made a thick paste of cornflour, milk and spices and rubbed it into the pink flesh before placing it into the pot hooked over a bar above the fire. The silence unnerved her. Being mistrusted made her stomach ache. With hindsight, she wished she hadn't let her curiosity get the better of her. She felt wretched. Should she leave? A foolish thought. Where would she go?

The longer Ma stayed silent, the more uncomfortable Eva became. Her voice muffled with unshed tears, she asked, 'What would you like me to do?'

The older woman sat staring into the fire. And Eva pondered what to say next. Relief washed over her when, at last, Ma turned to face her. 'Come over here.'

She moved closer.

'Now look here. I will ask you something – and please

don't insult me by lying, because I have ways of getting at the truth.'

She nodded.

'Have you ever stolen what doesn't belong to you? Think before you reply.'

She glanced at her hands, fingers intertwined.

'Well?' Ma prompted.

'I've never robbed anything in my life.'

'Are you sure about that?'

'Yes, I am—'

There was a hissing sound and the lid on the pot rattled. Ma lifted it from the hob and moved it to the side. The smell of the rabbit stew wafted around the room.

'Okay. What choice have I but to believe ye? Let me down and it'll be my integrity that's in doubt. Do you understand?'

She nodded, not sure she did. 'I won't let you down, I promise.'

Ma rocked back and forth in her chair, then she gave Eva a lopsided smile. 'Oh, go on, put the cups out and wet the tea. While you're at it, cut up that tasteless brown loaf. The sooner this war is over the better, and we'll get proper flour.' At least Ma hadn't thrown her out. 'But I need to know everything about you and what work you did at the orphanage.'

Eva nodded. She had nothing to hide. Trusted with a menial task, she hoped Ma Scully now believed her. When the meal was ready, she moved across to the table.

'Eat something, there's not a pick on ye. Didn't they feed you in that place?'

'None of us got enough, and the porridge was watery.'

'Oh, I can believe it all right. We're going through hard times. That's why I have to think hard about your future.'

Eva nodded. At least Ma was talking to her. 'Thank you.'

'What was it like living with the nuns? Were you happy?'

'Yes, sometimes. I had to learn to look after myself. At first, I was rebellious and ran away twice ...' She paused, wondering if she should have admitted to that.

'Where did you go?'

'I hid in the fields until I was brought back, kicking and screaming, then locked in a room with no food until I repented. The second time I was so furious, I pulled the nun's bonnet from her head and got a longer detention.'

Ma smothered a giggle. 'Sure, I'm glad it hasn't crushed yer spirit. All the same, ye can't be running away when things get tough. Most folk in these parts find it hard to earn a crust. I hope you realise that.'

'I do.'

'What kind of jobs have you done? Can ye count numbers, read and write?'

'Yes, I love reading, but there wasn't much time for that. I enjoyed making smocks for the children, embroidered table mats, linen and bedding that the nuns sold.'

'Aye, I've seen how ye use a sewing needle. You did a grand job on that skirt. What about the domestic stuff?'

'I got plenty of experience at the orphanage.'

'How did you come to be there, Eva? Do you remember your parents?'

The question sent a stab of sadness through her. For years she had wanted to know more about them but, forbidden to ask questions, she knew very little. To prevent Ma from seeing her distress, she stood up, picked up the cups and placed them into the large basin.

'They died when I was young. Gas leaked into the room while they slept. I have no memory of being rescued.

Afterwards I couldn't speak for a long time. But I remember arriving at the orphanage by cart. I had my favourite doll, Lilly, with me. Terrified, I clung to her. The woman who took me there gave the nun a pile of rolled-up notes. When she left, she told me to behave myself. The nun took my doll and said the other girls would be jealous, so I never saw Lilly again.'

'Your family had means, so?'

'I don't know. My father was an accountant at a shoe factory and my mother ran a dress shop. She read me picture books and when she had to go to work, a kind lady looked after me.'

'Was she the woman who left you at the orphanage?'

'I don't think so . . . that's all I remember.'

'Did anyone ever come visit you?'

'No.'

Ma Scully had peeled her back, a layer at a time, and was the only person to question her about her past. It saddened her that she couldn't remember. She had finished drying the dishes when Ma placed a gentle hand on her shoulder.

'Life hasn't treated ye well, has it? And it won't get much better.'

'What do you mean? You're not sending me to the workhouse, are you? I won't go!'

'Sure, give over. Come and sit down.'

She dried her hands and sat at the table opposite Ma. 'Now, Eva, love. You might think I was hard on you earlier, but wherever you work, your employer will expect honesty.'

Her eyes widened. 'Have you found me somewhere?'

'Well, after I dropped Cathal at the train station, I called in at Blackstock's farm and spoke to the owner. He's willing to see you the morra morning, so he is. He lost his good wife and needs someone capable of doing the chores. I believe his mother-in-law lives there too. Never met her, but heard tell, she's as sour as an old grape. And from what I've seen of the place it looks neglected.' She looked at Eva. 'That's the best I can do fer now.' She pursed her lips. 'I can't promise it'll be easy.'

'I don't mind hard work.'

'It's an opportunity and if you behave yourself, it might be the making of ye. He uses stable lads and field workers.' She placed both hands on the table and got to her feet.

Eva wanted to hug her in gratitude. 'That's grand, so it is. Am I living in?'

'Sure, they'll arrange that with you.'

'Does . . . does he know I'm from the orphanage?'

Ma nodded. 'He's prepared to give you a chance.'

Chapter Five

She rose at five o'clock and made herself useful by laying the
fire and cooking the porridge. It was the least she could do
to express her thanks. After she had eaten, she dressed in
warm underwear and stockings. It was the first time she
had worn a petticoat and she couldn't resist running her
hands down the silky material. She had enough practical
clothes to wear, picked up at the Town Hall from donations
to the orphaned children – Eva had never seen such an array
of garments. She slipped on a black pleated skirt that came
to below her knees and pulled on a pink woollen jumper.
Then she pushed her small feet into a pair of second-hand
boots that laced up the front. She smiled, pleased with how
she looked. No one could mistake her for an orphan now.
She combed her long hair, drawing it back with a ribbon,
and dabbed powder on her face, wishing she had a smear of
red to colour her lips. The nuns would consider that a sin.
Those rules didn't apply to her any more. Satisfied, she
turned away from the mirror and set the table for Ma's

breakfast of porridge and a boiled egg. Too jittery to sit, she remained standing. The clock above the mantel struck six as Ma stood in the doorway.

'Ye look too grand for working on a farm, so you do.'

Eva's heart sank. 'Shall I change?'

'Ah, sure, there's no shame in looking your best.' She sat at the table and Eva placed the food in front of her. 'I could get used to this.' She smeared a thin layer of butter on her bread and dipped it into the egg yolk. 'Have you packed everything ye need?'

Eva nodded and looked over at two cases by the door. She threw a warm cape with a hood around her shoulders; she couldn't wait to get going. Not that she wanted to leave Ma Scully or the security of the cottage. It was more a habit instilled in her at the convent about being punctual.

It was still dark. The street was damp, as if it had rained during the night, and a low mist settled over the fields as they made their way to the livery where Ma stabled her horse. This was Eva's second time riding in a cart and she was as nervous now as she had been ten years ago. She sat up front next to Ma. There was space at the back for provisions. Ma wrapped a rug across her knees. As they moved out of the town, the clip clop of the horse's hooves echoed along the country lanes. Eva who had never seen the countryside watched it roll by, and in the distance the beautiful landscape lifted her spirits. They passed farms and pastureland with cattle grazing, fields with crops of wheat and vegetables. Ma had told her times were hard, and it was understandable that people with smallholdings were growing their own food. They were crossing Butler's Bridge when she asked, 'Is it far now?'

'A wee few miles, that's all.' Ma stopped by the roadside, allowing the horse to drink from a trough and empty himself leaving a pile of horse dung by the side of the road, while Eva wrinkled her nose. 'Two journeys in one day is a bit much for old Paddy.'

The trees on one side of the road parted, revealing an expanse of water. A hazy mist shimmered across the surface.

'Isn't that a grand sight to be sure?' Eva declared.

'Sure, there's a lake around these parts for everyday of the year.' Ma took the reins again. 'Come on, boy, we must keep going. It's almost seven thirty.' She glanced up at the brightening sky and Eva wondered how she could tell the time with no clock.

Mesmerised by the mountains and the scenery surrounding her, Eva wondered if living in the country might not be so bad.

'Bawnboy has lovely lakes too, but I guess you'll be too busy to see them.'

Ma's words brought Eva back to earth, and butterflies formed in her stomach.

When they arrived, shopkeepers were setting up their wares and bid them good morning as they drove through the quiet village. Smoke curled from the chimneys of small cottages. Eva thought it was the middle of nowhere, and a loneliness she hadn't expected enveloped her.

They turned up a stony dirt track full of potholes. The wheels of the cart wobbled, throwing her against Ma as she steered the horse forward then pulled up outside a lopsided gate that opened on to a muddy yard. Inside, old farming implements left to rust were sprouting weeds. The farm comprised a grey single-storey house surrounded by several acres of land. The place sent a shiver through Eva's body. Two men shovelling silage into barrows glanced up. The sour, putrid smell made her want to heave. She hesitated, feeling silly in her posh clothes. Ma was right, she would be more at home in an old pair of wellington boots.

'Well, go on.'

'You're . . . you're not coming in then?'

'No, I'm not. You'll be grand, so ye will.'

She took a deep breath and climbed down from the cart, dragging her heavy suitcases. Ma whipped the horse, and as it turned round, Eva's heartbeat quickened.

'Now, go on,' Ma said again. 'Don't keep Mr Blackstock waiting.'

As soon as Eva stepped through the gate her feet sank into the earth. Her limbs shook as she picked her way across the filthy yard. A young man came towards her, his black wellington boots squelching in the mud.

'Can I help?' He took her cases, smiling at her discomfort. 'If you will work here, miss, you must get used to it.'

She shrugged, wishing she had gone back with Ma. Then, straightening her shoulders, she said, 'I'm here to see Mr Blackstock.'

'This way.' He walked ahead of her past a hay barn and a row of sheds with corrugated roofs that looked like they were ready to collapse. What she assumed to be the privy was a wooden hut with a sloping roof that faced the back door of the farmhouse. Ducks and hens clucked on the cobbles outside as the lad showed her into the kitchen.

Eva stood on the stone floor of the large kitchen, her luggage by her feet, wondering if she should have removed her boots, even though the floor had mud-spattered footprints all over it. It was colder in than out. The walls held no warmth or colour apart from a religious picture of Jesus in the Garden of Gethsemane.

'I'm sorry about the mess,' she said, glancing down at her feet, as a tall thin man walked in.

He looked old to Eva, with a moustache and a swat of grey at his temples. His hair stuck up at the back, as if he had just got out of bed.

'I shouldn't worry as you'll be the one cleaning it up!' He sat at the table and ran his hand over his face. He was wearing a black armband.

She wondered how long his wife had been dead.

'You're the kid from the orphanage. How old are you?'

She was furious at, yet again, being called a child, and she sucked in her breath. 'I'm seventeen, sir.'

'Seventeen, eh? Well, tell me, are you honest?'

'I am, sir.'

He was silent for a few seconds. 'I was hoping for someone with more meat on them. How will you cope with farm life?'

In spite of her doubts about working here, she said, 'Oh, I'll be fine. I can do most things and I learn fast.'

He stood up and paced a few steps, then turned to face her. 'Aye, I see you're a plucky wee lass. Your wage is six shillings a week including your keep. But not until I'm satisfied with what I'm getting for my money.' He cleared his throat. 'Aye! And a grand wee girl an all. However, I won't tolerate any shenanigans.'

'Sorry, sir . . .' She frowned. 'I don't understand.'

He laughed. 'You needn't pretend with me. I know what you convent girls get up to.'

Her face reddened, and she was at a loss for words. Whatever did he mean?

While she was pondering her reply, he said, 'The mother-in-law, Aggie, will oversee your work and report on your progress after one week. Do you understand that?'

'Yes, thank you, sir.'

His abrupt manner made her uneasy. He turned to leave and then glanced over his shoulder.

'What are we to call you?'

'Eva, sir.'

'Well, Eva. We are a church-going family and I expect my workers to attend Sunday service. You'll be joining us, will ye not?'

The question surprised her. Didn't everyone? It was a holy day of obligation!

'Yes, sir.'

He raised his eyebrows. 'I'll get Aggie to show you what wants doing.'

She relaxed her shoulders. Although meeting her employer hadn't been as terrifying as she had expected, his remarks about shenanigans puzzled her. She'd ask Ma Scully when she saw her again.

As she stood there, she looked around her. A basket of washing sat next to a large earthenware sink and a sack of potatoes stood in the corner. Dirty dishes stacked on the table and around the hearth deflated her spirits. Cobwebs hung from the four corners of the ceiling. A man walked in, traipsing more dirt in his wake. He humped a galvanised bucket on to a worktop, the creamy milk slopped on the floor. He placed a piece of gauze over the top, tipped his hat, gave her a lopsided smile and left. Her stomach rumbled, and she wondered how long she would have to stand here?

The ticking of the mantel clock unnerved her, and she jumped when it struck the hour.

Being made to wait like this was unbearable. If someone didn't come soon and tell her what to do, she would have to find the privy.

Chapter Six

A woman in dark clothes, her peppered hair in a tight bun, with features sharper than the Mother Abbess's, sauntered into the kitchen. The scowl on her face left Eva in no doubt she would show her no mercy, and she wasn't sure whether to laugh or cry.

'Right, ye'd better come with me.'

Eva took a step after her.

'Take them filthy boots off first. I'm sick to death of trying to keep this place clean.'

Eva stiffened, then bent to remove the offending boots. Holding them aloft, she glanced around for somewhere to put them.

'Oh, leave them there!' the woman bellowed.

For a second she could have been back at the orphanage. She followed the woman along the corridor with doors on either side until she stopped by a cupboard that opened on to shelves, filled with linen, overalls and indoor shoes.

'Well, ye can't work in them clothes. You're working in

the kitchen, and ye better pull yer weight, or ye'll be back where you came from.' She wrinkled her nose. 'Oh, I forgot. The place burned down, didn't it?' She sniggered, then plucked a nondescript dress and apron from the cupboard and pushed them towards her. Her flippant remark sent a shiver through Eva's body. 'The closet's outside, and this is your room.' She unlocked it. 'Not that you'll be spending much time in it.' She nudged her inside. 'Now, get dressed and don't be all day. You're a scullery maid not a parlour maid.' She sniffed. 'And a foundling at that.'

Why was she being so horrible? Suppressing the anger coursing through her, she bit back her frustration. In spite of the woman's insults, Eva wasn't sure how to address her.

The stone floor was cold. Her bed had a flat straw mattress next to a low cupboard with a ticking clock on top. An aluminium bowl and jug sat on a dressing table with a rimless mirror. A ladies' bicycle, with a basket on the front, resting against the other wall surprised her. Through the window she could see men and boys working on the land. She pulled the flimsy curtains together and dressed in the faded brown frock that hung like a tent, tied the long white apron around her thin body, fixed her hair and shoved her feet into shoes without laces. They slipped up and down as she walked towards the kitchen.

'Afore ye start on the messy jobs we've butter to make. Have ye done any churning?'

The unexpected question threw her, and she wished she could say yes. But the woman might ask her to get on with it and then she'd be in a right pickle, so she shook her head. 'No, missus.'

'It's mistress, to you. Why he took on the likes of you,

I'll never understand. Ye don't look as if you've ever done a day's work.'

Eva sucked in her breath, unsure how to respond. She didn't want to lose the job before she got started, but this woman knew nothing about her life. 'That's not true. I've worked hard at the orphanage.' She held out her hands, red and sore with blisters healing over.

'Found yer tongue, have ye?'

'Just never churned butter before, mistress.'

'Don't be clever with me. Get that cream into the churn and be quick about it.'

It was on a table next to the dresser. The round wooden structure, held together with metal rings, had a hole in the centre where the handle came through. Eva carried the milk across and poured it into the container, careful not to spill a drop in spite of her trembling fingers.

'Ye'd better watch how it's done then.'

Eva stood aside, holding her hands in front of her to stop them shaking.

The mistress added salt, turned the handle twice. 'Now keep it going until ye see lumps of butter floating on the top.' She went into the yard, leaving Eva alone.

This was hard work and seemed to take forever. Each time she took a peek all she saw was liquid, and she prayed that the yellow substance would appear soon. She turned the handle faster, but it made no difference. Half an hour had passed and her arm ached. When she lifted the lid, small mounds of creamy bits were forming, and her face brightened. It smelt good, and she dipped her finger in to taste it. It was delicious. She wiped her hands on her apron and glanced around for something else to do; there was no shortage of jobs.

The mistress came back. 'Right, you. Light the fire.' She pointed towards the black, empty hearth. Above it was a stout iron bar which held several black pots and skillets, and a small oven to the side. 'Look lively, girl. Skin and wash the rabbits and cook them. Put on enough for the men.' She straightened her shoulders. 'And ye'll need a bigger pot for the washing. The mangle's outside.'

Eva set about her tasks, but she was curious to see what happened to the butter. As she worked, she watched the mistress scoop it out and place it in a colander before rinsing it underneath the cold tap. Amazed at the amount of creamy substance coming out of the churn, she stopped to look. 'You can stop drooling, it's not for the likes of you.' The mistress placed the mound of butter on a slab and with a wooden spatula she patted and shaped it into square blocks. Then she wrapped it in greaseproof paper and locked it away in a cupboard.

Eva was using the scrubbing board, rubbing carbolic soap into the clothes, when the mistress said, 'Make sure you get all the stains out and peg that lot out on the washing line before it rains.'

The wind blew at her hair and it came undone, falling around her shoulders as she hung out the washing. The whiff of manure took her breath away. Hens ran towards her and she stiffened, unsure how to react when they clucked and pecked the ground by her feet. Working here would take some getting used to, and she'd have to grin and bear it until then. Two men were standing nearby, one cutting up turnips and the other throwing them into a machine and turning the crank handle. The younger one glanced up; it was the same lad who had carried her cases that morning.

'You from the orphanage then?'

News travelled fast.

Heat flushed her face. 'I . . . I was, but not any more.'

He walked across to where she was pegging out the washing and removed his cap.

'What's yer name?'

'Eva.'

'That's grand. I'm plain old John.' He had a warm smile. 'You know, I spent time in the workhouse, when me mam was sick like, but it bothered me none. Whatever you're cooking smells appetising. We've not had many hot meals since the missus died. God bless her.'

Eva was pleased to see a friendly face and have a normal conversation. She was about to respond when she saw Mr Blackstock trudging across the muddy yard.

'Get back to work, lad. I don't pay you to stand around gossiping.'

John gave her a sheepish smile before sauntering away.

Holding the empty basket, she turned to go when Mr Blackstock said, 'How are you getting on?'

'Grand, thank you, sir.'

He shook his head. 'Aye, 'tis nice to see the washing blowing on the line again. I'll be in at one o'clock. Make sure the dinner's ready.'

'Yes, sir.'

With no time to spare, she prepared the vegetables and put them on to cook. When she checked the rabbit by sticking a fork into the flesh, it came away from the bone. She scrubbed the table, washed the dirty dishes and the stains from the floor. Her face flushed, she hooked a dangling lock of her hair behind her ear and set two places for the boss and the mistress – and on a separate table, by the door, plates for the men. The place filled with the smell of cooking and her stomach rumbled. It was lunchtime, and she expected Mr Blackstock to walk in any minute. She hoped her efforts would please him. Hunger made her stomach cramp and her throat was parched. Nobody told her what time she was to eat, and the food was so tempting. She reached for the bread when the mistress's back was turned and popped a small piece into her mouth.

'If everything's ready, you can clear off until we've finished eating.'

Eva was rendered mute.

'Well, don't stand there. Clean the privy.'

It wasn't a job she relished doing, but it was better than staying and watching them eat.

Chapter Seven

When she heard Mr Blackstock shouting at the men to return to work, she made her way inside. She washed her hands. The mistress scraped back her chair and stood up.

'Ye can have a drink and get your dinner. And don't take all day about it, there's plenty to do.'

Ravenous by now, Eva sat down at the table and poured the stewed tea into the jam jar for her use. She wasn't considered good enough for a proper mug, but she was too hungry to care. She put the milk in and took a sip. It was cold. Grateful for small mercies, she didn't complain. However, when she lifted the lid from the cooking pot, she could have cried. Nothing remained but the dregs of the stew and a piece of carrot. They couldn't have eaten it all! She'd cooked enough to feed an army. Did they expect her to work on an empty stomach? Annoyed and humiliated, she scraped out what was left on to a tin plate similar to the one used for the yard cat. She snatched up the last slice of bread and used it to soak up every morsel.

With an empty feeling gnawing at her stomach, she took the dirty dishes to the sink while glancing down at the floor, covered in footprints, and wondered why she had bothered to put so much effort into cleaning it earlier.

That afternoon Eva was working in the yard. Hens clucked around her as she scooped up at least a dozen eggs into her apron. She enjoyed the task and soon realised that the chickens were harmless and not interested in pecking her toes. She took the eggs inside and placed them into a cracked ceramic dish on the dresser.

Both log and peat baskets were empty. So she went back out. In spite of having been covered, the sods of turf were coated in frost. Once the baskets were full, she carried them in, placing them by the hearth. Straightening up, she stretched her shoulders. Her mouth was dry; she glanced at the jug of buttermilk on the table. How she longed to taste it.

Before she gave in to temptation, Aggie yelled, 'Get that filled!' She pointed at the potato sack sagging in the corner.

'Where are they kept?'

'In the ground. Where do you think?' came the caustic reply.

Her job at the farm was confusing. She wasn't sure what her duties were. Was she expected to dig up potatoes, or was Aggie determined to break her? She walked past the sheds where the men were dealing cards on an upturned wooden crate.

John jumped up when he saw her. 'You won't tell the boss ye saw us playing penny poker, will ye?'

Eva frowned, glancing down at the row of coins. She didn't have a clue what they were on about. 'Not if you show me where the potatoes grow.'

The lads put the coppers into their pockets; the older one shuffled the cards, then hid them underneath a crate. 'I'm Mick,' he said. 'How ye getting on with old Aggie?'

'Not too grand.' A flush coloured her cheeks, in spite of the cold wind, and she pushed her hands up the sleeves of her cardigan.

'Why didn't she ask us?'

Eva shrugged.

'Sure, ye'll need to wear something warmer and I'll show you where to dig.'

She went with Mick towards the back of the farmhouse where she could see a vegetable plot.

'Don't worry,' he said, 'I'll help ye. Put this on.'

He handed her a large waterproof coat. It was stiff from being left outdoors. It smelt damp, was icy cold and made her shiver. He lifted a spade and a pick, placing them into a wheelbarrow, and she followed him down the frosted pathway along rows of vegetables, turnips and onions until they came to the potato patch.

As Mick hacked at the frozen earth, she dug into the soil as best she could. Then with her bare hands she unearthed the spuds, shaking off the surplus clay before throwing them into the barrow. John had joined them and was digging up the carrots. It was back-breaking work. Would she have to do this every day along with all the other chores?

Just as she thought it, John said, 'Dominic's off sick today. It's his job.'

'The old crow,' Mick said. 'If she asks ye again, come and see one of us.'

She thanked them in spite of her rising anger towards Aggie. Why did the woman hate her so much?

'Right,' John said, pulling up a few more carrots. 'This

should keep ye going for a while. Let's get this lot back to the yard. We'll leave it outside the kitchen door and ye can take what ye want from there.' He smiled.

'Thank you, thank you both.' She lowered her gaze.

'And ye won't mention . . . ye know.' John fidgeted with his coat sleeve. 'The boss would sack us if he found out we were gambling.'

'Haven't I said I wouldn't?' She blew into her hands, her nails blackened with mud.

'We heard about the Cavan fire down the local. Were you there then?'

Her guilt at being a survivor brought a lump that almost choked in her throat. 'I can't bear to think about it. It makes me sad.'

'I'm sorry,' John said quietly.

There was little light left in the sky as they turned into the yard. Eva, weak from the cold and hunger, picked up a carrot and placed it into the pocket of her apron.

Mr Blackstock met them by the door, his boots caked in mud. 'What's going on here?'

The men stopped in their tracks, lowering the barrow, full of produce.

'Is this what goes on behind my back?' He glared at John and Mick. 'I'll deal with you two later. Eva, inside and do what you're paid to do.'

She sat down to stop herself from shaking.

Mr Blackstock stood glaring at her. 'Cavorting with the lads, is it? So, it's right what they say, and I'd hoped you might be different.'

'I . . . I don't know what you mean.'

'Course you bloody well do. And stand up when I'm talking to you.'

She got to her feet, gripping the side of the table for support. 'I did nothing wrong, sir.' She fidgeted with her hands. 'They were just helping me to dig up the potatoes. I . . .'

'What are you gabbling about, girl? Why were you digging up potatoes?'

'It was what the mistress asked me to do.' She swallowed.

He reached for his pipe, lit it and took a few puffs. 'Now listen here, Eva. I hired you to do household chores. Is that clear?'

She looked up, tears brimming in her eyes. 'Yes, sir.' Her body swayed, and she gripped the table.

'What's the matter with you? If you're not up to the job, you'll be no use to me.'

'If I could have something to eat, sir, I'd be grand.' She dared to ask. 'I mean . . . can I make myself tea? I'm so hungry.' There, she'd said it, and if he sacked her for her insolence, there was nothing she could do.

His brow puckered, and she feared she had spoken out of turn. 'Haven't you eaten today?'

'There was nothing left in the pot, sir.'

He shuffled his muddy feet towards the mantel, took a key from behind the clock and handed it to her. 'Wash the dirt from your hands and you'll find bread and bacon in the cupboard. Tea is on ration, so go easy with it.'

'Thank you, sir.'

'Lock it after you and keep it safe for me.' He cleared his throat. 'I'll speak with Aggie.' He removed his boots and went down the corridor towards the parlour.

Eva wasted no time in making herself a satisfying sandwich. She put two rashers into the pan with dripping. She couldn't wait for it to cook, and the smell made her drool. When it was ready, she placed it on a tin plate by the inglenook and fried slices of bread, then sandwiched them together with the rashers. It was delicious, and she licked her fingers. After quenching her thirst, she felt satisfied. The boss seemed a good sort and she would take no notice of what Aggie said in future. Locking the cupboard, she put the key into her pocket. Feeling a rush of energy, she mended the fire. When the potato and vegetable sacks were full, she mopped over the floor again, and set a light supper for her boss of bread and cheese. She glanced around, making sure everything was in order before retiring, when Mr Blackstock appeared in the doorway.

He shook his head. Then he looked down at the hearth. 'Good, you've banked it up.'

She nodded and handed him back the key.

'You get yourself off to bed. You've worked hard.'

'Thanks, sir. What time do I start tomorrow?'

'Have my breakfast ready for six.'

That night, her body ached. This was nothing new to her – but at least, at the orphanage, the work was clean. She lit the candle placed for her use. It was nine thirty. She took off her clothes, washed and got into bed. Her hair would have to stay with the smell of farm dust.

Alone in the room, she felt vulnerable. She never expected to miss the chatter and companionship of her friends, but she did: their snippets of conversation, whispered around the room before the attendant came in to extinguish their candles. Angry tears choked her when she recalled the day she had just endured. But she drifted off to sleep, determined she would not let Aggie break her.

Angry voices woke her. She sat up and listened.

What were they arguing about?

The exchange grew louder until it was impossible not to hear.

'Be very careful what you're implying. She's but a child.'

'It never stopped ye afore,' came the reply.

'If I slipped up, it was only once, years ago. Mary forgave me.'

'Aye! Well, I'll not forget. And now you've taken on a young one from the orphanage instead of hiring a proper housekeeper. Ye can't expect me to run this place single-handed.'

'And pray, when did you do a day's work around here? That girl is worth ten of you.'

'Sure, have it your own way, and don't say I didn't warn ye when you're the talk of the village.'

Chapter Eight

Eva went about her chores with the argument still on her mind, making her head ache. John brought in *The Anglo-Celt* newspaper and placed it down on the table.

'For the boss.' He fidgeted with his hands. 'Sure, look, I'm sorry if we caused ye to get into trouble yesterday.'

Eva felt a flush to her cheeks.

'Mr Blackstock's a strict religious man,' John continued. 'That sort will always jump to conclusions.' He smiled.

'It's okay.' She picked up the spoon and gave the porridge a stir. The argument she had overheard, still playing inside her head, was of more concern to her.

He turned to go, then looked back. 'Eva, did you know we've to eat outside from now on?'

'No. But why?'

'Doo no.'

'Who said?'

'The boss.'

'Has it anything to do with you helping me?'

He shrugged and hurried out.

What was she to think? The whole business filled her with uncertainty. Her life was about to become even more isolated. She was placing cutlery on the table when Mr Blackstock walked in, yawning and scratching his head.

'Aggie's away to Cavan town on some errands this morning. Will you be okay on your own?' He picked up the newspaper.

'Yes, sir.' She swallowed. At least the mistress wouldn't be hovering around watching her every move. Lowering her eyes, she placed a large bowl of porridge before him with cream and a measure of sugar before frying his rashers and eggs.

He continued reading, then he cleared his throat. 'The fire in the town has pushed the war efforts off the front page,' he said without looking up.

She didn't want reminding about the tragedy and did her best to act normal. She sliced bread, then busied herself cooking his breakfast. He read in silence and when his food was ready she placed the bacon and egg between two pieces of fried bread, like he'd asked. He was eating and reading at the same time while she got on with preparing the vege-tables for dinner. She wondered why he had ordered the men to eat outside. She had thought him a kind man, but doubts now clouded her judgement. After what she had heard Aggie say about him, she was nervous around him.

When he scraped back his chair and stood up, relief flooded through her. She was clearing the table when he spoke.

'Well, Eva.'

She paused with the plates in her hand, her heart beating fast.

'Are you pleased to be out of the institution, then?'

She glanced down, not sure she was.

'Well?' he said.

'I think so, sir. I miss the friends I made there.'

He nodded. 'Shocking thing to have happened. From what I've heard, you were fortunate to get out alive.' He shook his head. 'Someone will be held responsible.'

'Yes, sir.' She continued to place the dishes on a tray before immersing them in soapy water.

'Can you read, girl?'

'Yes, sir.'

He smiled. 'Well, then. I'll leave the newspaper. I'm in the top field if there's anything urgent, and I'll be down for dinner at the same time.'

When he left, she blew out her lips. She had no reason to dislike him, but she couldn't help her feelings of anxiety around him. She was also wary of trusting him. The nuns had said most men were unreliable unless they put a ring on your finger. But she wasn't getting wed, not that she thought anyone would ask her. She hadn't even explored her surroundings. Besides, she didn't know what love was yet.

With the dinner cooking and the kitchen tidied, the washing blowing on the line, she sat down with a drink and the newspaper. Details of the tragedy brought it all back, and she was mopping her eyes when Aggie stalked in.

'What's up with you, then? Work getting too much for you already, is it?' She removed her hat and gloves, and slung her coat across a chair.

'I'm grand, mistress, and no, it's not too much for me.'

'We'll soon see about that!' She scowled. 'Make yourself useful and get me something to eat, I'm famished.'

Eva paused by the cupboard, then she remembered that Mr Blackstock had the key.

'Well, what are you waiting for?'

'The cupboard's locked.'

'If it wasn't for the likes of you, we wouldn't have to lock it.'

The accusation niggled. 'I'm not a thief.'

'That lip of yours will be your downfall one of these days, my girl.'

Eva made a sandwich of cheese and pickle sauce and plated it up with a pot of tea and left Aggie to eat. Eva felt the woman's eyes boring into her as she put the filthy net curtains to soak. She was standing on a wooden chair to clean the grime from the kitchen window when Aggie's next words astounded her.

'If your plan is to take my daughter's place, you can think again, missy. My son-in-law may need a new wife, but over my dead body . . . it won't be you.'

Aggie's grating voice sliced through her nerves and she stumbled, almost falling off the chair in her haste to get down. She stood in front of Aggie, the dusty cloth dangling from her fingers. 'That's a terrible thing to say. I don't want to take anyone's place. I'm here to work and save money for my future.'

'Oh, you would say that! I know your sort. It's written all over ye. That's why that Ma Scully woman brought ye here, isn't it?'

Eva felt her face redden. 'I think you should stop saying wicked things. I don't know what you're talking about.' Her body shook and she took a long breath, for if she continued she would lose her temper. Struggling to hold back her anger, she returned to the task in hand. 'If you've finished insulting me, I have work to do, and I'd like to get on with it.'

'Ye cheeky young beggar, you. I'll see your name in ruins, that's if it isn't already. You see if I don't.' She stood up, snatched up the newspaper and left.

Eva sat down, her limbs shaking. Why was Aggie saying bad things about her and Ma Scully? Thinking her short time working at the farm was at an end, she sniffed back tears.

At one o'clock sharp, Mr Blackstock tramped in trailing mud in his wake. It was ill breeding, she knew. But hadn't she done the same thing herself the first day she arrived?

'That smells good,' he said, removing his outdoor coat.

Aggie appeared behind Eva, holding the plates, then she placed them down on the scrubbed table and fussed about as if she had had a hand in preparing it all. 'Well, sit down, Jacob and get stuck in.' She beckoned to Eva to fill his plate with meat and vegetable stew.

As they ate theirs, the smell made Eva's stomach rumble. She was standing by the hearth, wondering what to do about the men's dinner, when she saw the conspiratorial look that passed between Aggie and Mr Blackstock.

He put down his knife and fork. 'Eva, the men will eat in the yard from now on. Can't have them making free.'

'Why? What's wrong?'

'Nothing for you to concern yourself over.' He cut his meat and ate.

Eva bit back her anger and piled two enamel plates with food. John and Mick were being punished for helping her yesterday, made to have their meals outside like the animals, and it riled her. If only she didn't have to rely on him for her living, she would insist on a proper answer. When the men knocked, Eva passed over the hot dinners, knowing the food would be cold by the time it reached the barn.

'Thanks, miss,' Mick said, and John gave her a cheeky

wink before she closed the door as a gust of wind swept in across the floor.

That evening, Mr Blackstock went out, and Aggie retired early. With the place to herself, and the kitchen tidy, Eva thought she would use the indoor closet, maybe have a bath.

The parlour was at the far end of the corridor. Aggie had never asked her to clean that room, and she hesitated by the door, recalling how her curiosity had got her into trouble at Ma Scully's. However, she couldn't resist the urge to look inside. She was surprised to see how grand it was; she could have been standing in the Mother Abbess's sitting room, with the distinct smell of lavender polish. It was a lovely room in contrast to the rest of the house. She imagined the family entertaining in here with friends when Mrs Blackstock was alive. Moving further in, she inspected the gramophone and wondered when it was last played. The square dining table had a cream crocheted tablecloth, the pattern so delicate she lifted the folds and felt the silky threads. The empty fireplace had candelabras on either side of the mantel with a clock in the shape of a dog. And underneath the large window that overlooked trees, fields and pastureland was a mahogany desk. There was a piano against the wall with silver framed photos on the top. One was of a much younger Mr Blackstock, and she assumed the young lady with dark hair was his wife. The other was a framed photo of two small boys dressed as altar servers. She raised the lid and her fingers touched the ivory keys. How she would love to play. Deep in thought, she didn't hear footsteps behind her until someone shut the lid with such force it almost trapped her hand.

Startled, she swung round. Tongue-tied, she regretted giving in to her inquisitiveness. 'I'm—'

'How dare you come sneaking around in here? Get out, now!'

'I'm sorry, I . . . I was looking for the bathtub.'

'Bathtub! Baths are not for the likes of you. Get out of here.'

Eva bit down hard on her lip and turned away. Aggie was trying to humiliate her, goad her into a fight so she could sack her. Well, she wouldn't give her the satisfaction.

She hurried out, and the door swung shut behind her. Eva stood in the corridor to recover from Aggie's onslaught. A strip-wash in her room would have to do for now. She was about to enter the kitchen when she heard the boss return and kick off his wellingtons. She felt relieved she hadn't been in the bath tub. He was back early, and she was glad she had prepared his supper earlier.

She thought it only polite to bid him good night, but didn't want to be alone with him.

'Aye! Don't forget it's Sunday tomorrow.'

How could she? 'Is the church far from here, sir?'

'Only a short walk from the village.' He coughed. 'I'll be up to milk the cows as usual and let them out to pasture. So, I'll expect my breakfast.'

She nodded. 'If there's nothing else, sir.'

He sat at the table, his arms outstretched.

She turned to go.

'Just a minute, Eva.'

Her pulse quickened.

'You may have thought me unkind to the men today. You'll come to realise that whatever I do is for your safety.' She was opening her mouth to protest when he continued. 'Well, good night now. I hope you'll settle here with us.'

Chapter Nine

After breakfast, Eva was clearing the table, and about to wash the dishes when the boss said, 'Do that later, we don't want to be late for church now, do we?' He had on a charcoal suit and a red woollen jersey underneath his beige overcoat. He held a grey trilby between his fingers.

Aggie walked in, dressed in a smart tweed outfit that was buckled at the waist, with matching hat, gloves and handbag. Eva removed her apron and glanced down at her brown dress and black boots, then she hurried to her room, tidied her hair and pulled on her coat. When she came back, Aggie pounced.

'You can't go looking like that. Even *you* know you have to cover your head.'

Eva's face flushed bright red. At the convent, the girls wore shawls over their heads. 'I'm sorry, I . . .' She hadn't been to church since the fire and she felt nervous about going to a service where she knew no one.

'Oh, here, use this!' Aggie clicked her tongue and pulled

a dowdy brown headscarf from her handbag. 'I want it back, mind, after you've washed it.'

Eva placed it over her hair, tying it under her chin, and followed the others out of the front door, which was only used on Sundays. The gravelled driveway had a grass lawn on either side and led down to the main entrance with two stone gateposts, minus the gate. Mr Blackstock was sitting in the trap and Aggie climbed up on to the platform. Eva hurried past them. The morning was crisp. As she walked, she could hear church bells and for a second she could have been back at the convent.

When they drew level with her, Mr Blackstock stopped. 'There's plenty of room for the girl!'

'Are you mad, Jacob? She's a servant, and a waif at that. Do you want to start tongues wagging?' She patted her hair and straightened her shoulders.

On hearing the exchange, Eva continued along the lane. When they overtook her, her boss raised his hat. She smiled but the miserable grimace on Aggie's face didn't go unnoticed. She walked through the village, with cottages and shops on either side. The general store had a petrol pump outside and a 'closed' sign hanging on the door. People were leaving home and joining their neighbours, wishing each other good morning. Eva, aware of the curious glances coming in her direction, lowered her head. She was a stranger, and it was natural for them to wonder who she was, and why she was walking alone, yet no one spoke to her. They were family groups, all of them making their way towards the church in Kildoagh.

It was quiet, apart from the sound of men's steel boots pounding the road and the low reverential chatter of the women. She followed behind, keeping her distance, until she arrived at Holy Trinity. Unsure, she paused. She had never seen a church like this before, and she hoped she'd come to the right place. It was nothing like the convent church. Shaped like a barn, the solid grey structure was rendered in lime plaster, with a small stone cross at the gabled end. Bicycles leant against the side wall and other forms of transport were parked at the front. The pointed glass windows had elaborate decorations and also formed a fanlight above the two wooden doorways. The windows enhanced an otherwise dull exterior.

Then she saw Mr Blackstock make his way towards the entrance. Forcing a smile, she joined the crowd and wondered how they would all fit into the small church, when a vice-like grip on her arm made her jerk round. A man with a serious expression pointed her towards the other door. Red-faced, she moved across to where a large group of ladies had gathered. She saw Aggie up ahead and dawdled behind.

She followed the women inside and sniffed the familiar smell of incense and lighted candles. It was then she discovered that men and women sat in separate galleries at opposite ends of the church. She climbed the steps to the women's gallery and genuflected before taking her seat. The unfriendly attitude of the women – coughing, sniffing and turning their heads away – made her uncomfortable, until someone tapped her on the shoulder to show her she was occupying the pew reserved for the ladies' choir. Apologising, she vacated the bench and moved to the back row. She didn't like it here. Never before had she felt an outcast in God's house.

She glanced across to the men's gallery as John and Mick shuffled on to the end of a pew, and she relaxed. From the expressions on both their faces they were feeling the same as she was. She wished to be anywhere but sitting here amongst people whom she considered hypocrites.

Just before the last hymn, she excused herself to God and slipped out, to the sound of disgruntled mutters from the women. She inhaled fresh air and looked towards the craggy hills of Slieve Rushen mountain. Even in its winter coat of misty grey and purple, it looked beautiful. A noisy sparrowhawk soared high across the mountain top. She walked along the lane. Was it only a few days ago that Ma Scully had brought her here? It seemed longer. She continued walking, surprised when a lake came into view. She stood and stared at the scene before her, refreshing after the stifling confines of the church and the hostility of the women. The winter sun shimmered over the water and clusters of snowdrops fringed the edge of the lake where swans were busy building their nests. She had missed so much, seen so little.

The heavy footsteps of someone running towards her made her jump. Was she on private land? Her heart pounded until she saw John's smiling face, and her shoulders relaxed.

She hadn't recognised him in his Sunday best coat, clean white shirt and shiny boots. She felt dull in her work clothes and wished she'd had time to dress up. 'Sorry if I startled ye.'

'I thought I was in big trouble.' She smiled. 'Isn't it lovely here?'

'Sure, 'tis grand. I spent time here as a boy, still do.' He dug his hands into his trouser pockets and looked out across the lake.

'Can anyone come here, then?'

'Course.' He laughed. 'It's Templeport. In the week it's busy with boats and fishermen.' They walked further along.

'See that island out there in the middle?' He pointed. 'That's the oldest cemetery in Ireland.'

'Do they bury people there?'

'Yes, the ground is consecrated.'

'It is?'

'But don't worry, there won't be any burials today.'

'John, are you going back to work?'

He shook his head. 'I have the whole day off on condition I attend church. It makes the boss look good in the eyes of the community. We catch mass at the workhouse. It's nicer there.'

She lowered her gaze. 'Why'd you come here then?'

'Ah, sure I thought you might need moral support.'

She smiled. 'That's kind of you. I felt out of place.'

'We're not all snobs in Bawnboy.'

'I hope not.' She tightened the belt on her coat.

'Do you think ye'll stay on then? I mean, at the farm.'

'I don't know. Not sure Aggie wants me to.'

'They'd be mad not to keep you.'

'Oh, I hope you're right. They didn't say what time to be back.'

He nodded. 'Sure, you must cook their dinner. I can't see Aggie doing any work today.' He sucked in fresh air and straightened his shoulders. 'I was about to take a stroll ... but if you have to go, I'll walk along with ye. That's if ye won't mind, like?'

'I'd be glad of the company.' Smiling, she pushed her cold hands inside her coat pockets. John was the first boy she had spoken to and being alone with him didn't scare her at all; they soon fell into step. He wasn't what she would call nice looking, at least, not in the way Cathal was. But John was a friend, of similar age.

'Can I ask you something?'

He paused, ran his hand over his mop of fair hair. 'Fire away.'

'Well, I wondered what you thought about Mr Blackstock? Do you think he's a good man?'

'That's a strange question, Eva.' He shook his head. 'He's all right. Bit on the strict side, but I guess he's like most.'

They continued walking.

'His missus, now she was a kind woman. Not like Aggie, the dragon.'

Eva laughed. 'Did they have any children?'

'Aye! Two sons. Both lads helped on the farm – before I came to work here, mind. The older one died of some disease or other, and the younger one joined up.'

'That's sad. What do you mean, joined up?'

'He went in the British army to fight them Germans. They say it's what killed his mother. I'd a gone an' all, only me dad hates the British, you know. But what does it matter who kills them Jerries? It's kill, or be killed, I'd say.'

Eva frowned. She knew nothing at all about politics, and little of the war going on in Europe. In spite of her curiosity it had been a closed discussion inside the orphanage. Ireland had remained neutral, and she wasn't sure how she felt about that either. As they approached the village, a woman stood at her door watching them.

'What have you two been up to then? It doesn't take a genius to guess.'

Eva's shoulders stiffened, and she was about to give the woman a piece of her mind when John touched her arm. He was gentle, unlike the man who'd grabbed her arm outside the church earlier.

'Just ignore the small-minded old biddy,' he said. 'She's

another dragon.' With his hand on her back, he steered her firmly towards the dirt track and the farm. 'I'll see you tomorrow.' He shuffled his feet, making patterns on the dusty path.

'Yes,' she smiled.

Mr Blackstock was standing in the doorway smoking his pipe. He watched her side-step through the muddy yard. How long had he been stood there?

'So, there you are, Eva. We thought you'd got lost. Can you get started on the dinner? And Eva. I'd like a word with you later.'

'Yes . . . yes, sir.'

He pulled on his wellingtons and walked towards the barn.

Chapter Ten

With hindsight, she wished she had returned straight after church. But had she done so, she would have missed that unexpected chat with John. Now she hoped she hadn't displeased Mr Blackstock. What did he want to speak to her about?

Inside, vegetables were spread out on the kitchen table and the smell of chicken cooking in the big black pot surprised her. Removing her coat, she folded Aggie's scarf and shoved it inside her pocket to wash later, then pulled her apron on. She was halfway through scraping the carrots when Aggie burst in, clutching eggs to her chest.

'Oh, you're back, are ye?' She put the eggs into a bowl on the dresser. 'I said to Mr Blackstock, give that girl an inch and she'll take a yard.'

'Sorry, mistress. You didn't say you wanted me back.' She took the cabbage to the sink to wash. 'Half the time I don't know what's expected of me,' she muttered.

'Cheeky young bugger, you, I've told ye afore to watch that tongue of yours, or ye won't have a job.'

Eva tried to ignore Aggie's remark and got on with chopping the cabbage. Now wasn't a good time to ask if she was being kept on.

Later, with the meal over, Aggie went to her room and Eva put a leg of chicken on to a plate. The vegetable pot was empty, and she poured the remaining gravy over her chicken and ate it at the table. Mr Blackstock sat by the hearth smoking his pipe, his eyes closed. As she ate, anticipation churned her insides. What was it he wanted to say to her? Aggie came back into the kitchen wearing her hat and coat. Eva braced herself for another onslaught. But instead, she smiled towards Mr Blackstock. 'I'm off to me sister's, Jacob. Will ye be okay on your own with this one?' She glared at Eva.

'Oh, I'm sure I can cope. You get off now while it's still dry.'

Eva was glad to see the back of the mistress but she was nervous being alone with her boss. The argument she had overheard wouldn't go away, and she felt uneasy around him. She had tried so hard to please her employers and she didn't want to let Ma Scully down. If Aggie had any say in it, she would be in search of a new job tomorrow.

She finished eating, and washed up. No other form of domestic work was permitted on Sunday and she wondered what to do with herself. With the yard quiet, the only sound came from the crackling of the peat burning in the grate and the odd spark that shot up the chimney. The silence unnerved her; each time she glanced over at him, his eyes were closed, and she was desperate to know what he had to say to her. A spider scuttled from a pile of logs by the hearth and she watched its progress to freedom as it scampered across the kitchen floor and underneath the back door. She cleared her throat twice, but he didn't appear to notice. Just as she thought about going to her room, he puffed on his pipe and smoke drifted across the room. He shifted and sat upright.

Eva hung the wet tea towel on the rack and fidgeted with the corners of her apron. 'Would . . . would you like something to drink, Mr Blackstock?'

He cleared his throat. 'Yes, sure I never say no to a brew. The provision cupboard is open.'

An oversight on Aggie's part, she thought, picking up the kettle from the hob and warming the pot. He liked his tea strong. Opening the tea caddy, she spooned in the correct amount and poured on the boiling water. When it was ready, she placed a slice of Aggie's shop-bought fruit cake on to a plate.

He moved over to the table. 'Will you join me in a cup, Eva?'

Surprised to be asked, she hesitated. 'I'm not sure I should, sir.'

'It's okay. I've something to say to you.'

Her heart pounding, she placed her jam jar down. 'Oh, bring out the best cups.' He gesticulated towards the dresser. 'It's Sunday.'

She swallowed. What if Aggie came back? Her hands shook as she lifted down the best china and poured the tea, trying not to spill it into the saucer.

'Sit down, Eva.'

She had questions of her own, but her nerve left her.

'Well now, are you happy working here?'

She lowered her eyes, frightened to look at him across the table. 'Yes, I am, sir.' She picked around the edges of her thumbnail. 'Are . . . are you keeping me on, then?'

He leant back and studied her, doused his pipe and placed it inside his pocket. 'I'm guessing Aggie hasn't spoken to you yet?'

'No, she hasn't, sir.'

'Well, if the last few days are anything to go by, I'd like to keep you on.' He played with his moustache. 'However, there's a problem.' He leant forward, looking at her.

She edged backwards.

'I know Aggie's not the easiest of people to get along with, and I have to be sure you can cope with that. Voicing your opinion will only make matters worse, and I need harmony in this household.'

Eva gave her answer careful consideration. 'I'll try, sir, but I . . . I'm doing my best.'

He smiled. 'If Aggie were to leave, I'd have to let you go.'

Eva sipped her tea and placed the cup back on the saucer. Why would Aggie leave?

'Sure, it would be unethical for me to have you living here under the same roof without her, and set the tongues of the gossips and hypocrites wagging.' He paused. 'Do you understand?'

'Yes,' she swallowed. 'I think so.'

'It's been a difficult time since my wife, Mary, passed away. She was the only one who understood Aggie's ways and could put a smile on the woman's face.' He rubbed his fingers across the stubble on his chin.

'I'm sorry, sir. I mean, about your wife.'

He shrugged. 'Sure, that's the way of things.' He finished his tea, and she poured him another. 'Well, now that's settled. I'll pay you six shillings plus your board. Your hours are from six a.m. until nine p.m., Monday to Saturday. You'll have time off for church on Sunday, and then again from three p.m. until six the following morning.' He cleared his throat. 'Is that agreeable to you?'

'Oh, yes, sir. That sounds grand. Thank you. I won't let you down, and I'll try extra hard with the mistress.'

'Righty-ho then.' He counted out what was due to her, placing the coins on the table. 'You're free now until tomorrow.'

Eva's spirits soared and she couldn't wait to tell Ma Scully. She picked up the silver shillings and hurried to her room. Perhaps she should pay Ma a visit? She brushed her hair, leaving it loose around her shoulders, pulled out a case from under the bed – full of clothes she hadn't time to look at, let alone wear – and rummaged through. Selecting a white blouse and a warm, grey striped jacket and matching skirt with a large pleat at the front, she placed them on the bed. The jacket was a good fit, but the skirt was loose around the waist so she used a safety pin to secure it. She slipped off her house shoes and pulled on her black ankle boots. Feeling happier than she had done in a long while, she glanced in the mirror. What would Sister Catherine think of her now? She was the only nun at the convent that Eva had got on with. It was she who had consoled her when she got into trouble. 'You're a good girl, Bridget,' she would say. 'If you'd only stop antagonising Sister Louise, life would be easier.'

Mr Blackstock had asked her to try harder to get on with Aggie. She had no choice but to swallow the woman's insults or lose her job.

Now she had enough money in her purse to catch the train to Cavan. And with hours yet before she had to be back, she would not waste a minute of it. Straightening her shoulders, excitement bubbling inside her, she walked through the kitchen. She hadn't expected to see Mr Blackstock still sitting at the table.

'You're a fine wee colleen, Eva, if you don't mind me saying.'

Unsure how to respond, she smiled.

He got up, went across to the window and looked outside. Then he turned to her, his eyebrows raised. 'I hope you're not meeting that yard lad, John, are you?'

A flush coloured her face. It hadn't entered her head. Puzzled why he should ask, she shook her head. 'No. I'm going to see Ma Scully.' She lowered her gaze, embarrassed by the way he was looking at her.

'That's grand so. How're you getting there?'

'By train, sir.'

'I'm not sure if there's a Sunday service.'

She hadn't thought of that.

'Besides,' he said, 'the narrow gauge only takes you as far as Belturbet.'

'Oh, no. Are there no other trains at all today, sir?'

'You might catch one from Killeshandra, but it's a good wee walk to get there.'

'I didn't think.' Her high spirits ebbed. This would not be as easy as she had first thought.

He scratched the side of his face. 'I suppose I could take you in the trap, but,' he knocked the contents of his pipe out on the stone fireplace and refilled it, 'you'd have to promise not to tell Aggie. She might get the wrong impression.'

In spite of the temptation to say yes, the row she had overheard the other night made her wary. She swallowed. 'That's kind of you, sir. I'd rather not.'

He sighed. 'Aye, happen you're right.' He shook his head.

Eva moved towards the door.

'Can you ride a bike?'

Although she had never ridden one in her life, she nodded. How hard could it be?

'It's up to you. Sure, if you'd like to, you can borrow Mary's. It's in good order, but the wheels might need pumping up. If you bring it into the kitchen, I'll take a look for you.'

Mr Blackstock was waiting with the bicycle pump in his hand. He pressed the tyres with his fingers. The back tyre was a little flat, so he undid the cap and pumped it full of air. The sound was like the bellows she sometimes used to get the fire going in the morning. She didn't like being alone with him, and was eager to be on her way.

'That should do you.' He fixed the pump to the bike. 'Just in case you need it.' He smiled. 'Well, you'd better be off – and don't be late tomorrow.'

Thanking him, she hurried outside. The hens ran towards her, clucking around her feet as she carried the bike over the mud and then wheeled it down the track. She could feel his eyes watching her from the back door and she waited until she was on the lane and out of sight before trying to get on the bike.

After a shaky start, she knew it would not be easy. As she tried to steer the handlebars in a straight line, the front wheel buckled and she fell into the grass verge. Embarrassed, she dusted herself off and smiled at people she met; some responded, while others glared and whispered behind their hands. She walked a short distance, then attempted to ride the bike again. Just as she thought she had gotten the hang of it, a bump in the road threw her off balance and she landed on the ground, grazing her knee and elbow. With a hole now in her black stockings, she would look a sight by the time she got to Ma's. At one point she almost left the bike by the roadside, but then it wasn't hers to abandon, so she persevered.

Eventually she was riding along with the wind in her hair, dodging potholes, feeling a sense of freedom. In spite of her bruised knee and grazed elbow, this was a Sunday she wouldn't forget. When she arrived at Killeshandra railway station, her legs ached but she had made it. Excitement mounting, she bought a ticket and paid to take the bike on board. It was the first time she had travelled alone, and it felt good. It was late afternoon, and the train was half empty. She took a seat by the window and stared out, looking at nothing specific.

Her mind went back to the last few hours with Mr Blackstock. Apart from the strange way he had looked at her, she had no reason to dislike him. He had shown her kindness and perhaps she had misjudged him. But there was still the question of the way he had treated the yard men, and John in particular. She was glad he hadn't insisted on taking her in the trap. There would be more than Aggie to jump to the wrong conclusion. Why, she wondered, was he being so nice to her?

Chapter Eleven

When Eva arrived in the street, the sky had clouded over and she hoped it wouldn't rain before she got back. She picked up a newspaper from the young boy on the corner and read the headlines. The war was still raging, with no end in sight. People here kept abreast of what was happening but they were unhappy about the Irish men and boys who had left the country to join in the fighting. Apart from a bomb dropped on Dublin two years ago, Ireland was untouched. Folding the paper carefully, she placed it into the basket on the front of the bicycle.

Teary-eyed, she cycled past what remained of the orphanage, with the convent still intact, and wondered if any of the children had returned there. How she would love to see Ma's nephew again and thank him for all he had done to help save the children. Something had stirred in her the first time she saw him, sitting at the table in Ma's the morning after, and she wondered if he would be here today.

Outside the cottage, she placed the bike against the wall and lifted her bag along with the newspaper from the basket. She ran her hand over her hair, adjusted the safety pin in her skirt, and rapped on the door.

The shock that registered on Ma's face took her by surprise. 'Have I called at a bad time?'

'No, of course not. I wasn't expecting ye, that's all.' She glanced round at the bike. 'Where'd that come from?'

'It belonged to Mr Blackstock's late wife.'

'You must be in his good books then. Come in.'

Smiling, she stepped inside. A clothes rack surrounded the hob and Ma moved it to the side.

'I've just taken me washing in as it looks like rain.' She turned to Eva. 'What brings ye today? You've only been gone a few days. You've not run . . . ?'

'No. It's my afternoon off.' She smiled. 'So, I thought I'd come and see you. I would have brought a cake, only the shop was closed.'

'Well, now, ye don't have to bring me cakes, I'd prefer to bake me own. Sit down.' Ma ran the poker through the bars and ash fell into the pan. Joining Eva at the table, she asked, 'How ye getting on then?'

'Okay! Mr Blackstock seems pleased with my work. There's just one problem.'

'Aye, go on. Out with it.' Ma shook her head.

Eva lowered hers. 'I've not brought any bad news.'

'What is it then?'

'It's the mistress. I can't do right for doing wrong. Mr Blackstock says he'll keep me on if I can keep peace with her.' She took a breath. 'I heard them rowing about me, the other night. And later she accused me of trying to take her daughter's place. She said terrible things and it's hard not to answer back.' She paused. 'I try, honest I do, but she hates me. I don't know why.'

'Aye! She's jealous. Jealous of your youth and bonny looks.'

Eva felt her face redden and fidgeted with the buttons on her jacket.

'Has he been okay with ye?'

'Yes, Ma.'

'And he's keeping ye on?'

'I've a room of my own and six bob a week,' she rattled on, 'with most of Sunday off.' She paused. 'So, I thought I'd come and give you the good news.'

'Well, that's grand to be sure. Six shillin', eh? You'll soon be buying your own clothes then.'

'I'm pleased at that, Ma.'

'Stand up and let me look at you.'

Eva stood and did a twirl.

'That skirt's big.'

'I didn't have time to alter it around the waist, but I will.'

'It suits ye, so it does.' Ma stood up and set the table. 'I've made soda bread and scones. The flour's rubbish but with some strawberry jam, they'll not taste too bad. I bet you could murder a cup of tea?'

It sounded good to Eva, for she was thirsty after her long journey.

'I want to hear all about your work at the farm, so I do, and don't let Aggie get your goat. I'd hazard a guess there's not a soul in the whole of Cavan could get on with that woman. How Jacob's put up with her all these years is anyone's guess, so it is.'

* * *

After they finished their tea, and Eva had licked the jam from her fingers, she helped to clear the table and wash up. Outside it was getting dark. Had she been foolish to come all this way when she had to go back the same day?

They were sitting together by the hearth when Ma said, 'Tell me, Eva. Do you find it lonely? Have ye made any friends in the village?'

'I don't have time to be lonely, Ma, but I miss the girls from the orphanage. There's two lads who work in the yard. You saw them when I arrived. John, the younger one, walked me home from church on Sunday.' She lowered her head. 'And now Mr Blackstock's banned him from coming in the kitchen.'

'Why's that?'

'I don't know.'

'Has he done, or said, anything improper, this John?'

'No. He's nice and we talk sometimes.'

'Has *he* seen you with him?'

'Well, yes. So has Aggie.'

'Have ye asked Blackstock why?'

'He said it was just trying to keep me safe. But I don't know why.'

'Well, he's very high-minded, but let me know if it continues. He can't stop ye talking.' She bent to stoke the fire. 'Cathal was here yesterday, he asked about ye, so he did.'

At the mention of his name, Eva's heartbeat quickened. 'How . . . how is he? His hands were burned in the rescue.' She tried to hide her concern.

'Oh, he's fine. He rushed in without thinking. It was that kind of situation. A few blisters won't bother him. We were fortunate he was here.'

'He's a hero. He saved a lot of the children.' Eva couldn't

bear to think about the ones who died. It brought on a dull ache in her stomach.

'Try to put it behind ye. Sure, no one could have done more.'

Eva nodded.

Ma stood up and went to the window. She glanced out before closing the curtains. 'The day is already curling inwards, soon the night will take down the last of the light.' She turned back. 'You might as well stay the night and make an early start the morra. You can sleep in Cathal's room. Besides, the trains are slow at this time of a Sunday. I'd take ye in the rattletrap only me eyes are not good in the dark. Anyhow, I saw no lamp on that bike.'

'I didn't think. Are you sure you don't mind?'

'Not at all. I'd not get a wink thinking of ye riding them dark lanes at this hour.'

Relieved that she could stay, Eva gave Ma a grateful smile.

'Look, you'd better bring that contraption through to the back.'

The wheels were muddy, and Eva carried the bike across the room and out the back. The image of Cathal splashing water over his rugged face flashed through her mind; the sight of his black hair dripping wet would remain with her always.

When she came in, Ma was reaching inside the cupboard. She brought out a bottle and held it up. 'I've been looking for an excuse to open this.'

Eva frowned. 'What is it?'

'It's me elderberry wine. Been fermenting for the past six months.' Smiling, she took glasses from the dresser and poured two generous portions. 'Here's to yer new life.'

Cathy Mansell

They both sat down by the fire.

Eva brought the glass to her lips and sipped. 'It needs more sugar.'

Ma's eyebrows shot up. 'You've tasted it before then?'

'The nuns have it sent to the convent. I sampled a drop once when I was in the sick bay.'

Ma shook her head and they both laughed.

'Now, I want to hear more about the farm.'

Eva told her everything, even about the butter churning.

'It's hard work that, so it is. I used to make it years ago, before me fingers became crooked.' She put down her glass to show Eva her fingers.

'They look sore. Are they painful?'

'Sometimes. I always know when it will rain.' She sipped more wine. 'Enough about me. So, all the produce at the farm is home grown then.'

'Aggie had me digging up potatoes. Mr Blackstock went mad, and then told John off for helping me.'

'They seem to expect a lot of ye for six bob. I hope it won't get too much.'

'I can manage. With every Sunday off, it's not too bad.'

They sat sipping their drinks when Ma said, 'Did them nuns ever talk to you, ye know, about when you left the orphanage? Looking after yourself.'

Eva laughed. 'Are you kidding me?' She was feeling relaxed with the wine and the warmth coming from the stove. 'Whenever I tried reading a book sneaked in by one of the other girls, I got caught and told off.'

'You like books then?' Ma poured herself another glass.

'I could read before I entered the orphanage.'

'Well, get in the habit of buying a newspaper. You'll learn more about the world that way, so ye will.'

While Ma Scully snored in her rocking chair, having consumed too much elderberry wine, Eva roused herself from her comfortable position to put peat on the fire, then she covered it with hot ash to keep it in through the night. She made a pot of stirabout and placed it on the hob. She hadn't the heart to disturb Ma, yet how could she go to bed and leave her?

Thankfully, Ma stirred. Rubbing her eyes, she glanced up. 'Oh, Eva, I'm sorry. I've slept a good wee while then?'

'That's okay.' Eva smiled. 'I've had a lovely afternoon. Thank you.'

'Aye indeed. Isn't yourself after giving me a lovely day too.' She got to her feet. 'Anyone with a bed is in it; besides, you'll sleep like a top after me elderberry wine.' She padded towards her room. 'Good night, lovie. You'll find matches and a lamp by the bed.'

'I promise I won't disturb anything.'

'Get away with ye.' Ma smiled. 'You're okay, Eva Fallon.'

'Ma, when you see Cathal, will you tell him I said . . .' She paused, hoping Ma hadn't seen the flush that coloured her face. And it wasn't from the heat of the fire.

'Sure, whatever it is, ye can tell him yourself when he comes back down for the memorial service next month.'

Chapter Twelve

The last time she had been in Cathal's bedroom, she ended up being accused of stealing. It felt comforting to have been invited. She struck a match and lit the lamp. This was luxury compared to her room at the farm. She undressed, laying her clothes across the chair, not daring to open any drawers, and washed in the ceramic basin. The soap had a masculine smell when she held it to her nose. The brown scapular had gone but the picture of the gentleman with the moustache was still hanging on the wall and she wondered again who he was. Could it be Ma Scully's husband? She knew little about Ma, and even less about her own life. The white bedspread had been changed for a blue one and she ran her hand over its softness before slipping in between the cold cotton sheets. Pulling the covers around her, she fell into a deep sleep.

She woke to torrential rain blocking gullies along the street. She wished she had made the effort to go back the previous evening, and an anxious feeling settled in her stomach. Mr Blackstock expected her at the farm by six.

'Will ye look at that downpour,' Ma said. 'I guessed it might rain, as me fingers were giving me gip in the night. You'll be wet through afore ye get to the train. I'll bring round the jalopy.'

'No, you'll get soaked. I'll be grand.'

'Sure, I'm well padded with a waterproof, and there's a big umbrella out the back, so you can hold it over the both of us as far as the station.' Eva hated to trouble her, but if she didn't get going, she'd miss the train. Ma pulled on her rainwear and handed Eva a spare waterproof. 'Ye can borrow this. It'll swamp ye, but at least it'll keep ye dry.'

Eva struggled to lift the heavy bike on to the cart. Rain ran down her face and wet her hair as she stepped up next to Ma, who held the umbrella over her. Then it was Eva's turn to hold it steady against the wind. It proved difficult, with the rain beating down and dripping on to their feet. But Ma urged the horse relentlessly on.

No sooner had they arrived at the station when the rain ceased.

'That was bad timing,' Ma said, glancing up at the grey sky.

Eva shook the brolly, folded it and placed it down by the side of the cart. Then, on impulse, she reached over and hugged Ma.

'What's that for?' the older woman chuckled.

'For everything.' She stepped down and unbuttoned the waterproof.

'Hang on to it. Sure, you might need it the other end.'

'Can I come and see you again?'

'Course ye can. And afore ye go,' she reached down the

side of the cart, 'take this wine to Mr Blackstock. Tell him it's from me.'

Eva was about to lift the bike down when the station porter came to her aid as the train chugged into the station. 'You'd better hurry, miss.' He glanced at her ticket and placed the bike in the luggage van.

Eva waved goodbye to Ma and climbed on board. Consumed with thoughts of getting back on time, she took no notice of her surroundings.

At Killeshandra, she retrieved the bike. After a few wobbles, and almost falling off when her raincoat caught in the wheel, she steadied herself; she pulled off the offending coat, placing it in the basket. Then she pedalled as fast as she could without stopping, careful not to spill the wine. If the boss changed his mind about keeping her on, she only had herself to blame.

Most villagers were still asleep. She saw no one, apart from the milk cart making its way around the various farms. Exhausted, her legs aching and mud-splashed, she entered the yard as the cock crowed. Gasping for breath, she wheeled the bike into the kitchen and left it inside the door. She placed the wine on the table and removed her outer clothes. With less than half an hour to get the boss's breakfast, there was no time to wash the dirt from her legs. The fire hadn't been banked so, working fast, she raked yesterday's ashes, using kindling and the bellows to get the fire going. The porridge made, she left it to the side before cooking sausage, egg and crispy rashers the way he liked them. John and Mick passed through to the sheds. Both men gave her a nod.

Mr Blackstock walked in, yawning, and sat down. He

ran his fingers through his thinning hair. Eva placed his breakfast in front of him. The smell of the rashers made her mouth water.

'You got back okay then?' he asked.

'Yes.'

She wondered if he realised she had just arrived, when he said, 'How was the bike?'

'It was grand, thank you, sir.'

'What's this?' He picked up the bottle and studied it. 'Is this alcohol?'

'No! I don't think so, sir. Ma Scully sent it for you. It's one of her home-made elderberry wines. And she hopes you enjoy it.'

He nodded. 'Wouldn't do for you to fall into bad habits. Elderberry, eh? It's a while since I tasted any. The wife used to make it before she took ill. Thank Ma Scully the next time you see her.'

Then he tucked in to his breakfast, and Eva busied herself with her chores.

Before he left, he told her he and Aggie had business in Cavan town later that morning and if she wanted anything bringing back, it was a good opportunity to ask.

It was eight o'clock when Aggie put in an appearance. She piled a heap of washing into the basket while Eva served her breakfast.

It didn't seem right to be asking a woman who disliked her to buy her personal items. Far better if she could get them herself, but a whole week was a long time to be without soap. As she wasn't allowed to leave the farm, except on her day off, she had little choice. The nuns ordered everything they needed at the convent, and she didn't know how much things cost. She still had a florin and six pennies in her purse.

'What are you daydreaming about, girl?'

'Sorry, mistress. I was wondering if you wouldn't mind bringing me back a few bits from the chemist in Cavan this morning?'

'As long as I get the money. And let me tell ye, I'm not paying for your vanities. A girl your age shouldn't be wearing lipstick.'

Eva smiled. 'I'm not asking for lipstick, mistress. Just soap, tooth powder and Pond's cold cream; that kind of thing.'

'Jot it down, that's if ye can write. And make sure you give me enough,' Aggie snapped.

Eva ignored the remark and scribbled the items down on a paper bag. Opening her purse, she handed Aggie a florin. 'Is that enough?'

'It had better be.'

Monday had started busy and continued throughout the day. Eva had no time to think between chores. Keeping the kitchen floor clean was her biggest nightmare. However, the rest of the week flew by, and she only had two run-ins with Aggie. Eva had grown fond of the tom cat, and as no one had bothered to give it a name, she called it Lucky and made a fuss of it whenever she went out to the yard. The cat purred and rubbed against her legs. Trouble started when Aggie spotted her giving it a saucer of milk.

'The bloody cat's not here as a pet. Its job is to kill vermin. Left to you, we'd be overrun with the blithers.'

If it wasn't one thing it was another. The spuds, according to Aggie, were soapy. 'You stupid girl. You should have left them in the pot a wee while after you'd drained off the water.'

Eva was about to answer, when Mr Blackstock came to her rescue.

'The girl's allowed a few mistakes.'

'Even an idiot knows how to get taters floury,' she snapped.

'That's enough. I want to eat my dinner in peace.'

Silence descended but Aggie continued to goad Eva, finding fault with everything she did. Each time Eva was about to retaliate she recalled Mr Blackstock's request for harmony.

Later, she went to the yard to bring in the washing. It had been breezy, and the clothes were right for ironing. John's cheerful smile appeared from behind a pillow case, making her jump. He made a funny face and she couldn't help laughing.

'I hope you've not soiled the clean clothes with your dirty hands. The mistress will have me wash them all again,' she said, examining the laundry before putting it into the basket.

He held up his hands. 'Now, would I do a thing like that?'

She shook her head and lifted the laundry on to her hip. John lingered, making circles with the toe of his boot. 'Eva, I was wondering like . . . erm . . . would you, I mean . . . can I take you to the St Patrick's Day dance?'

His question surprised and delighted her. She wanted to say yes, even though she wasn't sure she could dance. 'I . . . well . . . I.'

He shrugged. A flush coloured his already ruddy complexion. 'I guess you're going with someone else?'

'No. It's just. I'll be working and . . .'

'Don't you know? It's a holiday.'

Apart from mass at the convent on St Patrick's Day, it had been like any other day. And she doubted Mr Blackstock would give her a day off.

'Where's the dance held?'

'In the hall at the workhouse. So, you'll come then?'

She felt a fluttering of excitement. 'Yes, all right. But I must make sure it's okay, you know, with Mr Blackstock.'

John chuckled. 'Sure, haven't I told ye no one works on Paddy's Day.'

Aggie had been standing in the doorway watching them, and her eyes narrowed as Eva passed through to the kitchen. But Eva didn't let it bother her, and a smile brightened her face. Now, she had something to look forward to.

Chapter Thirteen

It was nine thirty before she finished her chores. Aggie, who never stayed up late, was sitting at the table, a stony expression on her face, the newspaper spread out in front of her. Eva was about to bid her good night when Mr Blackstock came down the passage holding a shirt over his arm.

'The collar's frayed on this, Eva. I wouldn't ask, only I need it tomorrow.'

Aggie glanced up. 'Sure, what's going off tomorrow, Jacob?'

'Oh, just business, nothing for you to worry your head about.' He sat by the fire and sucked his pipe.

Aggie folded the paper and passed it to him, then she moved her chair closer. Eva saw the way her eyes glinted and narrowed; her son-in-law's answer hadn't satisfied her. Eva sat at the table, the sewing box open in front of her.

'Stop squinting and get on with that shirt.'

'The light's bad, mistress.'

They were using candles to save what little oil they had.

Eva moved the candle from the dresser on to the table. She worked as fast as she could, knowing Aggie wanted her out of the way. Was she going to tell the boss she'd caught her talking to John? She wouldn't put it past her. Eva did her best turning the collar, pricking her finger and sucking the blood up in case it stained the cloth.

'Aren't you finished with that yet?'

Being pressured like this annoyed her; she liked to do things well. And with more time and light she might have done a better job. She bit the thread with her teeth, returned the needle and cotton to the OXO box, got to her feet and hung the shirt over the back of a chair.

'Good night, sir, mistress.'

Mr Blackstock muttered good night, and Eva hurried to her room.

She lit the candle and drew the curtains across. It was freezing. Too cold to undress, she lay on the bed thinking about John's invitation. What would she wear? She reached under the bed and pulled out one of the suitcases she had brought with her, lifting it on to the bed. Amazed at all the stuff Ma had packed inside, she held up a green dress with a white lace collar. A few alterations were needed before the dance, but it was green and just the right shade. She pulled out a woolly jumper the colour of oatmeal, got undressed and put it on over her nightgown, doused the candle and got into bed.

She hadn't been asleep long when loud voices coming from the kitchen woke her. Aggie was ranting. She got up and put her ear to the door.

'Are you losing your marbles, Jacob Blackstock? You should talk to that woman, Ma Scully!'

'Enough, Aggie. This is my farm. Stay out of my affairs.'

She flinched when a door slammed, and got back into bed. Why were they talking about Ma? Were they planning on sending her back? She didn't know what to think and found it hard to get back to sleep.

Next morning, Eva convinced herself that their argument had nothing at all to do with her, and she got on with her work. Mr Blackstock never spoke at breakfast, and left soon after. It was butter day, and Aggie was in the kitchen for most of the day. She was quiet, and her tight-lipped expression made Eva tense around her.

Eva's arm ached from churning but each time she stopped to check inside, Aggie screamed at her to get on with it. At last, large clumps of butter appeared and Aggie took over. Eva got on with yesterday's ironing, and when she glanced over at the older woman, it was obvious something had upset her; she looked like she had sucked on a lemon. Instead of patting the butter into shape, she was pounding it so hard that Eva expected it to slide from the board on to the floor. When she had wrapped it in greaseproof paper and put it under lock and key, she ordered, 'Make me a mug of tea. I'm parched.'

Eva put the ironing away in the linen cupboard and did her bidding. She cut a slice of currant bread and made a fresh pot of Lipton's, hoping to appease the woman. Aggie insisted on three spoons of sugar, in spite of the rationing. She lingered over her drink, her tight expression remaining. At last she stood up, brushed the crumbs on to the clean floor and stomped towards the parlour. Eva heaved a sigh, and the tension left her body.

At the first opportunity, she slipped on her outdoor shoes. She needed a change of scenery and was looking forward to a chat with John. She couldn't see him so, after collecting the eggs, she walked to the sheds. He was chopping logs, throwing them into a heap in the corner. He glanced up as she called his name but he didn't speak. There was no welcoming smile.

'What's up?'

He turned his back and continued to wield the hatchet.

'John, what's wrong?'

With no response, her happy mood faded. Heat flushed her face. 'What about the dance; don't you want to take me now?'

He looked round. 'I'll be in trouble if I'm seen talking to ye.'

'Why? What have I done?'

'Leave me alone, will you?'

Eva, her limbs shaking, hurried away. This was so unlike John. Who, or what, had caused him to change? A lonely, wretched feeling enveloped her.

Chapter Fourteen

Blackstock left the farm by horse and trap and made his way to Cavan town. He had a meeting with the manager at the bank. But there was something more pressing on his mind and he wanted to see what reaction he got when he called on Ma Scully. He was well acquainted with the woman and the good deeds she was renowned for at the hospital, as well as helping out with the Red Cross.

His business finished, he popped into the local pub on Main Street. It wasn't something he did often; it went against the grain. He hated the demon drink, he'd seen how it could destroy a man's soul. However, today of all days, he needed a crutch. With a glass of Guinness in his hand he sat in a quiet corner to contemplate his motives.

A short time later, he passed what remained of the orphanage, shuddered and pulled the collar of his overcoat up around his neck. Men were securing a scaffold to the area, and he wondered if they were going to rebuild. It wasn't difficult to find out Ma Scully's address, as her reputation preceded her. Outside the neat cottage, with its shiny brass door knocker, he paused and glanced along the pavement. Women in shawls gossiped at their doors, then huddled closer in hushed whispers. He took a deep breath and knocked.

'Sure, why don't ye come on in, Mrs Keogh? The door's on the latch.'

'Drat!' She was expecting someone. Unsure about walking in, he knocked again.

'Who the dickens is it?' Muttering, Ma pulled the door open. 'Jacob Blackstock! What brings you to my door? Nothing wrong, is there?'

'No, not a wee bit of it.'

'Come in, come in.' She stood back, allowing him access.

He removed his hat. 'I'm sorry to call unannounced, but I had business in town and wanted to thank you for the elderberry wine.' He smiled.

'Aye! Sure, ye needn't a done that. I thought ye'd changed yer mind about Eva?'

He played with the rim of his hat. 'Ah, no, not at all.'

'Look, sit down, will ye?' She pulled out a chair. 'I'll get you a cup of tea.'

While she busied herself at the stove, he glanced around at the tidy cottage, the cosy fire, the smell of bread cooking in the oven. 'I hope I'm not intruding. Are you expecting someone?'

'Ah, sure, there's always bodies coming in and out. It's what keeps me ticking, so it does.' She brought the tea tray in with slices of cake.

He placed his hat on the table and stretched his legs. Ma Scully was a similar age to himself, with traces of grey in her wavy hair swept back from her forehead.

'Now, if ye've not come to complain about Eva, what brings yer here?'

'Sure, can't an old neighbour pay a visit any more?'

'My door's open to a good neighbour any day of the week, sure don't ye know.' She poured his tea. 'It can't be easy for ye with poor Mary gone.'

He shook his head. 'No indeed, it's not.'

'Now, how do ye like your tea?'

'Milky with sugar, if you can spare it.'

'Just how I like me own. But, ye'll have to do with a pinch.' She stirred the tea and settled in her chair. 'I guess you've not come all this way just to thank me for me elderberry wine.'

He took a sip and placed the cup back on the saucer. There were no flies on this lady. She was as sharp as the knife she used to cut the home-made cake. Her floral dress with a shiny brooch on the lapel masked the power that emanated from her, and he was cautious of upsetting her.

He cleared his throat. 'The girl Eva's a real treasure. I'd like to thank you for bringing her to me. And what happened at the home is a tragedy. I can take her off your hands. I'm here to ask your permission to marry her.'

'What? Are ye kidding me? She's just a child, an orphan.' Ma stood up. 'Eva knows nothing of men, or the world they inhabit. She's an innocent.'

He had given little consideration to any of that. 'She's seventeen, hardly a child.'

She glared at him, one hand on her hip.

'I'd treat her fair, make sure she doesn't want for anything. It's just that the mother-in-law, well, she's getting on, and an irritable soul at the best of times.' He shifted, picked up his hat and placed it down again. 'If she was to up and go to live with her sister in Leitrim, I'd have to let Eva go. My reputation would be at stake. You understand!'

'Aye! I understand all right. That woman has no intention of leaving, and you know it, Jacob Blackstock. If Aggie ever leaves, I'll find somewhere else for Eva. She is, after all, an accomplished young girl.'

'Sure, it makes sense. Can't you see? The girl will make an ideal wife and help me run the farm.'

'Now, you listen. Eva's not my ward, nor even my responsibility. But she's far too young to marry anyone, let alone an old goat like you.' She swallowed, her chest heaving, and sat down again.

'There's no need for insults. I'm a God-fearing man. And if you're not her guardian, then it will be up to the girl herself.' He stood up. 'It was a mistake to come here.'

Ma laughed. 'Elderberry wine, my eye! I'll never give my blessing for you to marry Eva, and if she takes ye on, that'll be up to her.' She straightened her shoulders. 'But if you take my advice, Jacob Blackstock, you'll leave that girl alone or you'll have me to deal with. Now, if you'll excuse me, I've other folk to see.' She held the door wide and handed him his hat.

Chapter Fifteen

On Sunday, the two men from the yard were not at church. When the service was over, Eva hurried towards the lake. If John wanted to talk to her, away from prying eyes, this was where he would be, and she wanted answers from him. There was no sign of him, and no telling if he would turn up. She sat down on a bench to wait a while.

Daffodils were showing their heads above the grass verges and swans floated past. She was lonely and in no hurry to return to the farm. Still pondering John's sudden change of attitude, she had no choice but to make her way back.

The last of the worshippers were just disappearing inside their homes, and she wondered how it would feel to be part of a real family. At the edge of the village she stopped by the bridge, watching small children playing hopscotch in the lane. She took deep breaths before turning towards the farm and the stagnant smell of horse manure that would greet her once she stepped into the yard.

It was then she saw him, leaning over a gatepost, looking into the distance. She hurried towards him. As she approached him, he didn't move, but nor did he glance in her direction

'Hello, John. I was hoping to catch you.' She rested her arms on top of the wooden gate, looking across the same stretch of land, a green blanket of hills and valleys. He looked as lonely as she felt. 'Why are you avoiding me?'

'I'm sorry, Eva,' he said, without turning round. 'Things are tough at home. I can't lose me job.'

'I don't understand. How can talking to me make that happen?'

'Look, I can't say. Sure, leave me alone?'

'Why are you being like this? Has Aggie said something?'

'You'll find out soon enough, if you don't already know. It's ... oh, just go, will ye?' He glanced around. There was no one in sight along the country road. He shuffled his feet.

'I don't know what you're talking about. Please, tell me?' She swallowed. 'I thought we were friends. Friends talk to each other.'

'I can't. Now leave me be, will ye? Just be careful.'

'Careful! Of what? For God's sake, tell me?'

'Go away. I've already said too much.' He jumped over the gate and plodded off across the field.

Eva stared after him, a sinking feeling in her stomach.

Aggie wore her usual gloomy expression and Mr Blackstock did not speak at all during Sunday dinner. Afterwards, he took himself off to the parlour, his rolled-up newspaper under his arm.

Aggie jumped up from the table. 'I knew you'd be trouble right from the start.'

Eva lifted her hands out of the sink, dripping soapy water on to the floor. 'What have I done now, mistress?'

'Don't act the innocent with me.' With that Aggie flounced out, banging the door behind her.

Thank the Lord it was her afternoon off and whatever ailed the pair of them could have nothing to do with her. In her room, her heart weighed heavy. She changed her clothes, picked up her bag with her wages tucked inside, and set off on the bike.

Ma Scully was the only one who might make sense of it all.

On the long journey into Cavan her mind was full of questions she had no answers to. It didn't take much to displease Aggie, but John keeping quiet annoyed her. Cold and weary, she dismounted outside Ma's cottage, and the door opened before she knocked.

'Ah, Eva. Come in, come in. I saw ye coming from the winder.' Smiling, Ma stepped back inside. 'Sure, ye must have better things to do on your day off. All the same, it's lovely to see you.' She took Eva's coat and hung it up. 'You're perished, so ye are. Move over to the stove.'

Eva rubbed her hands together. The smell of baking made her mouth water. Ma's knitting was on the table alongside a cup of tea. She loved coming here. It was always welcoming, warm and cosy.

'I'm not disturbing you, am I? Only I have to talk to you.'

'Sit down. What's wrong?'

'I'm not sure.'

'We'll leave the tea till later so.' Her forehead creased into a frown. 'Go on. I'm all ears.'

Eva sat down, straightened her skirt and took a deep breath. 'The mister and Aggie are acting right queer, so they are, and John still won't talk. What do you think's going on, Ma?'

'I don't know, pet.'

'You don't think Mr Blackstock has changed his mind about me working at the farm, do you?'

'Why? What has he said?'

'Nothing. But I overheard him and Aggie arguing again, and your name was mentioned. I'm convinced he'll ask you to take me back.'

'No. It won't be that.' Ma fingered the pearls around her neck. 'Did this John say who told him to back off?'

'No. He won't say, but I believe it was Aggie. She hates me.'

'And what about Blackstock? Does he treat ye okay?'

'Doesn't say much, as long as he gets his meals on time.'

'Aye! Typical man. Ye have to watch yourself around men like him. And tell me if he gives ye the eye?'

'Ma, what are you saying?'

'Eva, you might not think so, but you're a bonny wee girl and, well, mind yourself, that's all. You're not schooled in the ways of the world, and there's some who'd take advantage of a good-looking lass.'

A worry wrinkled Eva's brow. John had told her to be careful and now Ma was talking like this. Reaching out, she touched the older woman's arm. 'I don't understand. What have I done wrong?'

'Nothing, nothing at all, Eva. It's not you, it's the others. And as for Aggie, she's always been odd, that one. She'd fall out with her own shadow. Let's forget about that lot.' She whipped the scones from the oven and put them on a rack.

A letter sat on the mantel shelf addressed to Cathal

Burke, with a Dublin address. Eva's heart somersaulted just reading his name. How, she wondered, was it possible for someone to induce a happy feeling even though they were miles away?

'You must be hungry,' Ma said.

Eva was famished. However, when she noticed Ma's swollen ankles over her black lace-up shoes, she said, 'I'll make the tea.'

'Aye, that would be grand. Afore I forget. It says in the newspaper, there'll be a requiem mass for the wee childer, at the end of March.'

'Oh, where will it be held, Ma?'

'I believe it said the convent, now they've made safe the entrance.'

Eva looked up from spreading raspberry jam on her scone. 'Will the nuns be there?'

'Now ye've got me. I'll find out.' Ma pursed her lips. 'It'll be a sad day for them sisters all the same.'

Eva was thinking how nice it would be to see some of the girls again, in spite of the occasion. She hadn't visited the town's graveyard yet because she couldn't bear to see the mass grave where the children were buried with no identity. Unhappy memories of her life at the orphanage came flooding back. The silly rules – like running in the corridor – that warranted a detention. How hard she'd worked looking after the infants, being wakened at night to attend to them. And being told off for falling asleep during lessons. Apart from Sister Catherine, she didn't think the nuns were holy; some of them were cruel, the way they punished her for the smallest demeanour. The hours spent kneeling, praying for forgiveness, when she had done nothing wrong. No matter how bad things got, she would miss none of that.

'Eva.'

'Sorry, Ma. I was somewhere else.'

'You've no need to worry about them nuns. They have no power over ye any more.'

She smiled. 'Yes, I know. Is Cathal still attending the service?'

'Oh, yes.' Ma's eyes brightened. 'And the chief superintendent of the Dublin fire brigade is coming with him.'

Ma's smile stayed with Eva on the long journey back to the farm. Her spirits lifted; Ma had doused most of her worries. And surely she didn't have to mind herself around Mr Blackstock? He was an old man.

Chapter Sixteen

Whenever Mr Blackstock walked in, Eva was at sixes and sevens. At one point she dropped eggs on the floor. What if he made advances; what would she do? Knowing what she did, Ma's warning left her anxious around him. Few words passed between himself and Aggie, but the woman's snide remarks towards Eva continued, once they were alone.

On the morning of 17th March, everyone attended church wearing green and sang with gusto the hymn 'Hail, Glorious St Patrick'. Eva was dreading the holiday. Villagers went about with happy faces, no doubt planning a family fun day. Ma Scully was visiting a close friend in Enniskillen, so she couldn't visit her.

At the farm, the meal of chicken, cabbage and mashed potato with gravy was eaten in awkward silence. The yard was quiet, even the hens seemed to have gone on strike.

Later, in her room, she changed her clothes. The green woollen dress with long sleeves she had planned to wear to the dance fitted, showing curves she did not know she had, as she checked herself in the mirror. The nuns would say she was vain. No one would see her anyhow. How she wished for a family of her own. At the convent she'd had friends, but here she was like Cinderella while everyone else enjoyed the St Patrick's Day celebrations. A blanket of loneliness closed around her.

She spent the rest of the afternoon sewing, making alterations to the clothes Ma Scully had given her, surprised her employers didn't disturb her for something. Later, she stood by her bedroom window. The evenings were drawing out but a grey and black cloud hovered overhead like a bruise. It reminded her of the time she had dodged a swipe of the nun's hand only to slip and fall against the edge of the workbench, hurting her shoulder.

Her head throbbed, and she was in need of fresh air. But embarrassment to be seen out walking alone stopped her. Besides, where could she go? She hated sitting about doing nothing; it wasn't in her nature. It felt like the walls were closing in on her until she had to get out. She slipped on her warm tweed coat with large lapels, and tied the belt.

Outside, the wind wound itself around her legs and whipped her hair. It would be just her luck to get caught in a downpour. Everywhere looked different at night. Along the lane her heels echoed, and as she approached the village, she could hear excited voices and merriment as families celebrated inside their homes. She thought about Cathal marching in the Dublin parade and wished she had been there. By the time she reached the corner the sound of toe-tapping Irish music spilled out from the workhouse. It made her want to dance. She did a few shuffles on her toes and did a twirl until she felt silly dancing on her own in the dark. Was John at the dance with another girl?

The shadow of a man in a black coat and trilby came towards her, battling against the wind. Mr Blackstock! Too late now to avoid him. Anxiety knotted her stomach. Her head down, she braced herself for what he might say.

He tipped his hat, then paused. 'Eva! Bless my soul, I didn't recognise you. You look, well . . . never mind. What are you doing out on such a wild night?'

'Just taking the air, sir.'

He cleared his throat. 'I thought you'd gone to celebrate in Cavan town.'

She shook her head, and her heart raced. Would he insist she went back to the farm with him? Well, she wasn't going anywhere with him!

'I wouldn't advise you to stay out too long. Even in these parts it can get rowdy on St Patrick's night.' To her relief, he tipped his hat again as he moved on.

She pulled her collar up around her neck, shoved her hands deep into her pockets and looked up. The wind, now stronger, blew at her hair. Leaves rustled and tree branches creaked and swayed. She was about to return to the farm when she heard what sounded like the drone of an engine. It grew louder, causing her to look up. The flashing lights of a plane circling in the sky were rare in these parts, and she thought of the war. Would it drop bombs? Her heartbeat quickened and she ducked down, covering her head. It was low over the village now and appeared to be struggling to stay in the air. Was it going to crash?

Frightened, she hurried back towards the workhouse. She had to warn them. When she glanced back, the aircraft was still circling above as if it was lost, its lights visible. She lowered her head a few times as the plane dipped, almost touching the houses and trees. Panicked, she couldn't move fast enough as she ran up the dirt track to the workhouse. Out of breath, trembling and without thinking, she went inside. The music was deafening. The celebrations were in full swing. Couples were dancing and swinging each other around while the fiddlers played Irish jigs.

Eva stood up on a chair, waving her arms and shouting at the top of her voice. No one took any notice. She marched up on to the makeshift stage. Musicians glared at her. Her heart hammered as she pushed to the front.

'Who is she?' a woman asked. 'Is she going to sing?'

Taking a deep breath, Eva hollered as loud as she could. 'There's an aeroplane circling around the village. It might be a German bomber. It looks like it will crash.' Her voice sounded shaky in her ears. The place fell silent. All eyes turned towards her. Her face went hot. She took a breath to calm her racing heart.

An explosion echoed through the building. Within seconds, men, women and children were running outside. Craning their necks, they followed the trail of smoke that led across the fields towards the lake. There was another loud bang and Eva thought they must have heard it in Dublin. A strong smell of burning metal filtered up through the village. A stunned crowd made the sign of the cross and muttered prayers. Husbands and boys abandoned wives and girlfriends and went in search of this strange happening, while mothers with children hurried to their homes. Still in shock, Eva had to restrain herself from following to see for herself what had fallen from the sky. Instead, she ran as fast as she could back to the farm. Breathless, she approached the gate, almost colliding with Mr Blackstock's pony and trap as he came out of the drive. He pulled to a stop.

'Eva. Thank God you're safe. Do you know what's happened? Is it a bomber?'

'Not sure. A plane has crashed, sir.'

'I thought as much. It flew over the farm. Stay with Aggie, will you, please? This is very distressing for her.'

'Yes, sir.'

'Thanks. I'll see what I can find out.'

Eva felt at ease with him for the first time in days. For a few seconds, she stood looking down towards the village. In the distance she saw flames, like a huge bonfire, and a line of torches and lamps making their way to the lake.

Chapter Seventeen

In the kitchen, Eva stiffened to find the woman who had made her life miserable from the day she arrived at the farm crouched underneath the table, trembling and with a look of fear on her face.

'It's all right, mistress.' Eva bent down and held out her hand. 'You can come out. It's safe.'

Aggie brushed away the proffered hand. 'How do you know? There could be more of them coming to bomb us out of our beds.'

'We're not at war, mistress. A plane crashed.'

'You can't be sure of that. I'm staying here. Get me a pillow and a blanket, and be quick about it. Then make me a hot drink.'

When Eva returned, Aggie was as white as a sheet, and in spite of the way she had treated her, Eva wanted to help her. It was the first time she had seen Aggie vulnerable; a woman who felt in control was now looking terrified, and she pitied her. The plane crash had shocked everyone, and she didn't feel too good herself.

She made cocoa with milk for Aggie and another with water for herself. She was about to drink it when she heard the clanging bell of the emergency service, and she rushed outside. Aggie screamed at her to come indoors. The putrid smell of smoke lingered in the air as she hurried back in. If only they had been as quick when the orphanage burned down! The memory of how the fire had taken hold overwhelmed her, and her lucky escape sent a shudder through her body. It was a night she would never forget to her dying day: Cathal saving the children, and the friends she had lost. This time she hoped there had been no loss of life.

She placed more logs on the fire and sat down. Aggie stayed where she was, now more comfortable but still grumbling, asking when her son-in-law would be home. 'He should not have left me.'

Eva had wondered that herself. He'd been gone for over an hour. Where could he be? Her anxiety mounted as she coaxed Aggie to sit by the fire. 'You'll be much warmer, mistress.' Pushing her feelings to one side, Eva had no choice but to look after the woman until Mr Blackstock returned. She placed the blanket across Aggie's knees. It was flung aside.

'Leave me be, will ye?'

But when Eva handed her a bowl of warmed-up stew, she grasped it with trembling hands. Then, helping herself, she sat by the table.

Eva's head throbbed; being left with Aggie for company wasn't how she had imagined spending St Patrick's night. Frightened of leaving her alone, she took the dishes to the sink. 'Shall I put a hot jar in your bed, mistress?'

'I'm going nowhere until Jacob's home.'

When, at last, Aggie's eyes drooped, Eva rushed outside to the privy. When she came back, Aggie was fast asleep and spittle dribbled on to her chin. The evening had turned into the most unexpected of happenings, and she doubted anyone in the village would sleep. Her own curiosity was enough to keep her awake until she knew more.

Mr Blackstock arrived home, accompanied by an old farmer whom he introduced as Big Finn. He was barely through the door when Aggie, woken by the gust of wind that swept in and around the kitchen, pounced.

'Where in the name of Jaysus have ye been? Anything could have happened.'

'It's all right, Aggie.' He rested his hand on her shoulder. 'Once I knew the village was in no danger, I went to see what I could do to help. That's when I came across Big Finn here.'

Turning away, Aggie clicked her tongue.

Eva, intrigued by the old man, watched. He removed his battered trilby with a wilting sprig of shamrock tucked underneath the band. A flurry of white hair covered his face and chin. He dropped his heavy overcoat on to a chair, then removed two more before loosening his waistcoat. Eva glimpsed a bright green jersey with stains down the front. Not surprisingly, his boots were muddy. She had seen no one wear so many layers, and was unaware she was staring until he said, 'Ah, sure, I'm like an onion when peeled.' Heat burned her cheeks, and she looked away and set about making a hot drink for both men.

Aggie grimaced, glaring at Big Finn. 'Did ye have to bring him here?'

Eva took a breath and Mr Blackstock said, 'Where's your Christian charity?'

The farmer appeared unfazed by the remark. He stretched out his hands to the fire, rubbing them together and beating them against his forearms.

'Big Finn's place is the cause of investigation and the Gardaí are there. Sure, the force of the plane crash brought down a tree that smashed through his roof.'

Aggie shrugged. 'Do ye know why the damn thing crashed down here? Were there any survivors?'

'Rumour has it, it was the pilot's error,' Mr Blackstock said, pulling a chair to the fire next to Finn. 'They found no one at the crash site.'

'Well, sure I was in the scullery like, and I thought the world had ended when I heard the explosion,' Big Finn said. 'It sounded like a bomb, so it did.' He scratched his head. 'There was a knock on me door and this chap in an RAF uniform stood afore me. The poor fella looked a wee bit disoriented. He told me he and his co-pilot were on a trial run to the North in the Bristol Beaufighter when they ran into bad weather and went off track.'

'Did you tell him to scarper?' Aggie asked.

'Ah no! Sure, I gave him a square of bread and a drink and some wellingtons, so I did.' He chuckled. 'He had no shoes on. Nice fellow. Australian he was. Said he and his co-pilot bailed out when they knew the plane was out of control. They're still looking for the other fella.'

'He'll turn up somewhere,' said Mr Blackstock.

'They'd flown all that way from some Scottish port or other, only to crash into Templeport lake. Can ye believe that, now Jacob?'

Jacob Blackstock sucked on his pipe. 'Sure, stranger things have happened, Finn.'

Eva was at the table, cutting bread and pouring poteen the visitor had brought with him.

'And who is this wee girl you have here?' The farmer narrowed his eyes. 'Bit of a dark horse now, so ye are?'

'Not at all. This is Eva. She's been working here for a few weeks.' Jacob smiled. 'And I don't know what we'd do without her.'

Aggie glared at him. 'I wouldn't go that far.'

'Aye, she looks a bonny wee girl.'

Eva lowered her gaze as she passed them their drinks. This eccentric individual should frighten her. Instead, she delighted in his storytelling and his unique character.

'So,' Aggie said, turning to Big Finn. 'Was he arrested, this pilot fella?'

'Ah, sure, Father Doolan is having him smuggled across the border to avoid internment, with the Republic being neutral an' all.'

'Well, I guess the priest would know best,' Mr Blackstock said.

Big Finn opened his canvas bag. 'Look here. The young pilot, he gave me all these cigarettes. You know they're still on ration.'

'Well,' Mr Blackstock smiled. 'One good turn deserves another, I suppose. But you don't smoke cigarettes, do you?'

'I'll get a shilling a packet on the black market, it'll help pay for the hole in me roof.'

'Why couldn't it have been something more useful,' Aggie grumbled. 'How long will he be staying?'

'As long as needs be, Aggie. Eva, would you mind making a bed up in the spare room?'

Aggie was on her feet. 'But that's Matthew's. I won't hear of it.'

'Matthew's not here, now is he?' He gestured to Eva to go ahead.

The bedroom had always been out of bounds to her and

she hesitated, then followed Aggie who was muttering her disapproval.

'This is my grandson's room and I don't want any old Tom, Dick or Harry sleeping in it.'

Eva, feeling a sense of unease, stood while Aggie reached for the key and unlocked the door. Inside, Eva looked on as Aggie whipped off the blue eiderdown, pillow, sheets and blanket, leaving a bare mattress. Amazed, Eva watched her empty the chest of drawers, lifting out a hair brush, hair cream and other possessions belonging to her grandson. She even removed a shirt and jersey from the single wardrobe and lifted the colourful handmade rug from the floor. The room was now as sparse as Eva's.

'Well, what are you gawping at?' She pressed everything into Eva's arms. 'Fold these and put them away. Then get an old blanket.'

Eva couldn't believe what she had seen. Didn't Aggie trust anyone, even a neighbour whom she had known for years? The woman went out and on her return, she removed the oil lamp and replaced it with a candle.

Eva put the bedding away and picked up a straw-filled pillow Aggie had left by the door, then went to find blankets. She thought it was mean to treat an old gentleman in this way. The farmer would have to sleep in his clothes if he were to keep warm.

When she had finished making up the bed, she returned to the kitchen. Aggie had gone to her room, and she knew she should too. Tiredness had deserted her, and she was keen to stay and listen to Big Finn's stories. The two men were sitting together smoking their pipes, talking about the war and disputing whether De Valera was right to keep them from joining in the war against Germany.

'Our lads would at least have saved us the shame,' Finn said.

Eva tidied away the dishes and pretended at being busy so she could hear more. Soon the smell of tobacco hung heavy; it caught the back of her throat, making her cough.

'I don't hold with war, it's wrong,' Mr Blackstock was saying. 'Have you heard from that grandson of yours?'

'Not a wee word from him since he left.' Finn sucked his pipe. 'You heard from your Matthew then?'

Mr Blackstock shook his head.

'Traitors, the both of them, and a disgrace to their country.'

Eva wanted to know more. But as she put away the last of the dishes, Mr Blackstock turned towards her.

'You had better get yourself off to bed now, Eva.'

He didn't want her to hear any more of their conversation. Nodding, she removed her apron. Come tomorrow, the village and the whole of Cavan would buzz with news of the crashed plane.

Chapter Eighteen

The following morning, the old farmer was the last person Eva expected to see so early, sitting by the empty fireplace, a blanket covering his shoulders.

'Oh, couldn't you sleep, sir?'

'Sure that room's like an ice house, child. Don't ye have any warm bedding or water jars in the place?' He scratched his head. 'At this rate, I'd be better off at me own abode, even with half a roof.'

Eva rushed to mend the fire. 'I'm sorry, sir. I'll get this going. Sure, it won't take me long.'

She had to start from scratch and felt awkward working around him. His eyes followed her as she attended to her duties. Once the fire crackled into life, she hung the kettle over the blaze. She was glad now she had prepared the stir-about before going to bed, and when it was ready she handed him a bowlful.

'This will warm you up, sir.'

Aggie had treated him no better than she would a dog,

and Eva wasn't surprised that the old man had complained of the cold.

'No need to call me sir.' He scooped the porridge into his mouth. 'Most people call me Big Finn – although, mind you, it's not me real name, so it's not.' He lifted another spoonful of the thick substance and swallowed it, drawing the spoon across his mouth and licking his lips. 'Sure, I was baptised Finbar.'

'Oh, that's nice.' Eva carried on slicing bread then beating eggs to make pancakes. She didn't want to fall behind, as Mr Blackstock would be in any minute for his breakfast. But she was interested to hear more about the old farmer. 'How did you get the name Big Finn?'

'Well, when I was a lad, I spent me days fishing by the lake. I only had a makeshift rod, like, and never caught much. Then I made a big net and dropped it into the water. Lo and behold, I couldn't pull it up. It was heavy, so it was. I struggled. But I hauled it up.'

Eva smiled and felt at ease around the old man; she liked that he shared stories with her. 'What happened then?'

'I'd only caught the biggest pike you ever saw.' He put down his bowl, stretched his arms to show its size. 'It thrashed about and slipped back into the water. I bawled me eyes out.'

'Was that unusual then, to catch one that big?'

'Sure it was, but ye see, they wouldn't believe me. They said it wasn't possible. But I swear to the Almighty, it was a corker.' He picked up his bowl and scraped the spoon around the edge before placing it back down.

'Who did you tell?'

'The anglers from England who were fishing that summer, but they wanted proof. Even the boatmen who fished on the lake every day didn't believe me. Sure, they'd only caught fish a quarter of the size. After that everyone called me Big Finn, and the name stuck.'

Eva liked the old man, and hoped he would stay a while. 'Would you like more porridge?'

'I wouldn't say no to some of them pancakes.'

Mr Blackstock walked in, rolling down the sleeves of his shirt. 'Ah, Finn. What are you doing up at this hour? I thought you'd be still snoring your head off.'

'Snoring, me. Sure, I never got a wink of sleep. The cold in that room made me shiver, so it did. I've been sitting here most of the night.'

'I'm sorry.' He looked at Eva. 'Didn't you put a hot jar in the bed?'

'No, sir.'

He sat down at the table and Eva placed his breakfast in front of him.

'Put one in tonight then.'

'Yes, I will, sir.'

'I've a few things to attend to on the farm, Finn. Sure, if you like I'll drop you back at the lake so you can see what's been happening.' He got stuck into his breakfast while Eva poured more mixture into the pan for the farmer.

Aggie had yet to put in an appearance, and Eva hoped she would stay asleep for a while longer.

'Aren't ye going to the Ballyconnell fair, Jacob? I bet the young 'un here would like it.'

Eva knew all about the fair. Last year she'd been one of the selected few to be taken there by one of the orphanage attendants. Afterwards, she got into trouble for running away, and ended up locked in a room with neither food nor water.

111

'Sure, I doubt it'll go ahead after what's happened,' Mr Blackstock said, shoving a forkful of pancake into his mouth.

'Devil it will. 'Tis a crowd puller. A plane crash at the lake won't stop a tradition that has gone on for years, Jacob. Besides, curiosity to see where the plane came down will bring them in from far and wide.'

'Well, I won't be going. Sure, I'm too busy here. I've two cows about to drop.' He scraped back his chair, pulled on his yard coat and pushed his feet into wellingtons.

The old farmer did not try to get up, and Eva cleared the table and set a place for Aggie. The yard man brought in the fresh milk and filled the jug on the dresser. It was butter-making day, and although Aggie had plenty in the locked cupboard, Eva wondered if she should get the churn out and make a start. Besides, there was enough washing to keep her busy all morning.

Big Finn got up and stretched his arms above his head. 'I suppose the lavvy's outside, is it?'

Eva nodded.

The old man trotted out, leaving an unsavoury smell behind. As if on cue, Aggie walked in.

'What's that horrible stink?' She wrinkled her nose. 'Has that old scarecrow gone?'

Eva placed her porridge on the table. 'He's out the back, mistress,' she said while keeping her eye on the poached eggs. If they weren't cooked to Aggie's liking, with a thin white coating on top, she would refuse to eat them.

'Let's hope he clears off when he comes back.'

Eva looked up. 'Mr Blackstock's asked me to put a jar in the man's bed tonight.'

'Did he now?' Her lips tightened into a narrow line.

'Well, don't make him too comfortable, otherwise we'll never get rid of him.'

'Are we making butter today, mistress?'

'Not while he's still here. There'll be no butter-making in my kitchen.'

Eva brought the cooked eggs to the table and then went back to the sink, rolled up her sleeves, placed the pile of washing into the soapy water, and started scrubbing the clothes.

Big Finn came back, pulling his braces up over his shoulders. 'It's a grand day outside to be sure, missus. But last night in that room, it was bitter cold.'

The smirk on Aggie's face did not go unnoticed. She scraped back her chair, placed her tea and half-eaten breakfast on to a tray and started towards the parlour. 'Bring me a fresh brew in later.'

How rude of her, Eva thought. 'I'm sorry.'

'Ah! Sure begorra,' he chuckled. 'I don't like the woman any more than she likes me, so I don't. But tell me about yourself, Eva? How did you come to be working up here?'

Eva felt her face flush. She didn't want to talk about her life. There was nothing interesting about it.

'Ye have a surname, I take it?' he insisted.

'Well, yes, I do. It's Fallon.'

'Not a Cavan name then?'

She shrugged. She didn't know where she originated from, and she wasn't likely to find out.

'Sounds like a Dublin name.' He sat back down by the fire, placing his hands over the flames and rubbing them together. Then he took out his pipe and a pouch of tobacco. 'Yeah, it's a while since I've been up to the capital. Me late wife, Tess, used to love going up to Dublin – only on special occasions, mind.' He looked pensive. 'She were a bonny wee woman, so she was.'

'What happened to her?'

'She caught the consumption. Aye! Some years ago now. I never married again. As I was saying,' he chuckled, 'she'd get me to take her up to the big city just so she could look in them fine shop windows, Switzer's and Brown Thomas's department stores. Then we'd pay a visit to the ice-cream parlour. Aye! Them were the days. Have ye ever been yerself?'

Eva picked up the steaming clothes with the wooden tongs and pushed them through the wringer. 'No. But it must be exciting.'

With his penknife he cut pieces from the scented tobacco block, crushed the slivers in the palm of his hand and packed them into his pipe. He lit it and took several puffs. She liked the rich, pleasant aroma, so unlike Mr Blackstock's rather domestic whiff that caught the back of her throat and made her cough.

'I remember on one occasion taking her to a dressmaker, somewhere on the South Circular Road. Tess heard she had a good reputation, and she went again a few times for fittings and the like.'

Eva had this notion that her mother had been a seamstress, because she herself had a flare for sewing.

'Do you remember the woman's name?'

'Ah, sure no. I can't. It was a long time ago, and besides . . .'

Aggie stomped in and Eva turned back to the washing.

'Get that out on the line and stop wasting time.' She clicked her tongue. 'You still here?'

The old man appeared not to take any notice, and Eva wished she could adopt the same attitude. When Aggie had gone, and Eva had hung out the washing, she wet the pot and made fresh tea. After she had brought Aggie hers, she handed one to Finn.

'My mother ran a dress shop.'

Big Finn cupped his grubby hands around the tin mug.

'Ah, sure, it would never be the same woman, now would it?' He slurped his tea. 'You don't remember them then? Your ma and pa?'

'No, only vague snatches of my mother reading me stories.'

'Ah, sure there's many a young 'un brought up without a mother, and they grew up to be grand individuals. I've been bringing meself up all me life, so I have. And who else can ye depend on?' He chuckled. 'You'll be grand, so ye will. I can see it in your face.'

He made her smile. Later, as she collected the eggs and fed the hens, Big Finn sat at the door chatting to her. She loved having him around and she didn't want him to leave. She couldn't wait to tell Ma Scully all about her new friend on Sunday.

Chapter Nineteen

Big Finn stayed at the farm for four nights before he returned to his home. To Eva, working at the farm was dull without him.

In the village, people were talking about the plane crash for days. *The Anglo-Celt* carried the story, and she was not surprised to read in Mr Blackstock's discarded newspaper that a large section of the lake was prohibited to the public.

At the end of March, Mr Blackstock agreed to allow her the morning off to attend the requiem mass at the convent for the children who had died in the fire. Ma Scully accompanied her.

Inside the church she felt the stifling atmosphere dripping with sadness. She glanced towards the back where the nuns stood silently, shielded by a grille, their lips tight with indignation. Eva's stomach tightened. A row of girls sat with the adults. Many had now returned to the convent. Their sad eyes told her that nothing much had changed. It made her all the more aware of how lucky she was to have come across Ma Scully that night. Ma and Eva took their seats with the rest of the community who had come to pay their respects. The front pews were reserved for church dignitaries, councillors, the military and the Garda Shíochána.

Saying farewell to the only friends she had ever known brought a lump to Eva's throat. And when some in the congregation sniffed and cleared their throats, her lip started to tremble. Unable to stop her shoulders from shaking, she lowered her head and clasped her hands in front of her. Ma Scully passed her a handkerchief, and she blew her nose.

Ma patted her hand and murmured, 'You're doing grand, so ye are.'

Cathal walked in, accompanied by the chief fire officer. He wore a navy Dublin fireman's uniform, holding his peaked hat in front of him. Her heart raced. He nodded towards his aunt and smiled at her. He was a hero in her eyes, and she was proud to know him.

The bishop arrived with his entourage to officiate over the mass, and everyone stood. During the memorial service, the smell of incense caught the back of her throat; it always had that effect on her and made her eyes water. It helped to cover up the emotion she could no longer hide. The bishop paid tribute to all the major emergency services who had fed and looked after the children that night, and praised Cathal for his part in rescuing the orphans and recovering the remains of the dead. Loud sobs resonated around the chapel. He paid homage to the sisters for their love and tender care of the children, not forgetting their sense of emptiness at the loss of so many, ending with, 'Now let us kneel and pray for their tiny souls.'

Eva sucked in her breath. She could remember little love, or tender care, and she railed inside at the injustice of it all.

Outside, after the service was over, Eva let out a long breath and leant against the church wall, her arm covering her face to hide her distress.

'It's all right, child. It's over now.' Ma Scully, the nearest thing she would ever have to a mother, was beside her and Eva was glad of her company today.

Cathal, along with the chief fire officer, came across to speak to them. 'This is my aunt, Miss Scully. And this is a friend, Eva Fallon, one of the young ladies who escaped the fire.'

The chief took Ma's hand. 'A pleasure to meet you.' He smiled towards Eva, and she inclined her head.

Ma shook the proffered hand. 'You too, sir! It's a sad day.'

'Indeed it is, Miss Scully.' Then he stood aside to allow Cathal to speak further with his aunt.

'Glad you could come today, Ma.' Cathal turned to Eva. She glanced up into his handsome face and her fear subsided. 'You're a brave young woman. That couldn't have been easy for you.'

She shook her head.

He kissed his aunt's cheek. 'I'll be down on Saturday. I have something I want to put to you?'

'Oh. I'll look forward to that.' Ma smiled.

As Eva watched him retreat, her heart thumped. The pain of being here had been worth it to get a glimpse of Cathal again. How striking he looked in his uniform. He had called her a young lady, so he didn't think of her as a kid from the orphanage any more. His words would stay with her all day.

Inside a nearby public house parishioners had already

gathered. The first thing that hit her was the strong smell of smoke and stout. Men lined the bar, most of them wearing a black band on the sleeve of their jacket, while the women and children, in sombre colours, crowded into the snug. She had never been into one before. The room had two long wooden tables and chairs, and a hatch that opened where women ordered their drinks. Ma bought Eva a lemon soda and a sherry for herself. The group of six who joined them were quiet until a few glasses of stout loosened their tongues. Then they were as rowdy as the men at the bar.

'Hey, Ma,' one woman called. 'Why do ye think they took so long to open the convent gates that night?' She reached over, pouring more drink into her glass until it spilled over the top. 'Looks fishy, so it does.'

'What's going on, Ma?' another wanted to know.

Ma shifted in her chair. 'Look, I don't have all the answers, but mark my words it will all come out at the inquest.' She chortled. 'And wouldn't I like to be privy to that?'

'Course it spread so quick, there wasn't much left of the poor wee babes. Their screams echoed down the street.'

That started another discussion about the nuns and the delay in getting the children out until Ma, who by then had noticed Eva's discomfort, put a stop to their endless chatter. 'We're in here to get away from all that, so let's drink up and tonight pray for their wee souls.'

Silence fell, but the focus of attention turned to Eva. 'You're one of them orphans, aren't ye? How did you escape, love? Where were you when the fire broke out? What started it, do you know?'

Bombarded with questions, Eva was finding it harder to remain polite and she didn't like the woman's tone. 'I don't want to talk about it.'

'Shut yer gobs, the lot of ye, and leave the girl alone.' Ma Scully finished her sherry and ordered another.

And the conversation turned to husbands and children.

Later, when Ma walked Eva to the train for her return journey to the farm, she said, 'You know, Eva love, the worst is over and ye have to put this terrible business out of your mind.'

'I'll try. And thanks for being my friend today.'

Eva knew her life was changing, and her nightmares were becoming less frequent. In fact, she couldn't remember when she'd last had one. Now she dreamed of a brighter future.

Chapter Twenty

Cathal arrived in Cavan early on Saturday morning. Spring was in the air and he was looking forward to seeing Eva again. He loved coming to this part of the country when the fields were a lush green, lambs were bleating and everywhere was sprouting new life. Compulsory tilling was still taking place, and he wondered how much longer the war in Europe would continue. It was peaceful here after his hectic job in the city. He raised his hat to passing neighbours who reciprocated in sombre mood. The fire and then the plane crash had left its toll on the community. In fact, the whole country was gossiping about the cause of the orphanage inferno. Enquiry or no enquiry, it wouldn't bring back those little angels. Some of the small faces would live forever in his memory.

He admired Eva for the way she was coping with it all. She fascinated him, and he was glad his aunt had taken her under her wing. God knows, the girl needed all the help she could get. He knew little of what her life at the orphanage had been like, except for stray comments he had heard. And if it hadn't been for his aunt, his own life might have taken a different path. He supposed that was why he felt concern for Eva. 'There but for the grace of God go I,' he murmured. His aunt had made sure he wanted for nothing. He had benefited from a good education with the Christian Brothers and his aunt had beamed with joy when she discovered he'd passed his entrance exam for the brigade. It was his dream job. Although he had rooms in Dublin close to his work, he made a point of getting down to see his aunt at least every other weekend.

Today, he had something pressing on his mind he wanted to put to her. Unsure how she might take his suggestion, he hoped she would take it as a kindness regarding Eva.

He stopped by the general store to pick up a few provisions before going into the newsagent's. With the newspaper rolled and stuffed into his coat pocket, he carried a bag of groceries and walked towards the cottage where he was sure of a warm welcome.

'Ah, lad, it's great to see ye.' His aunt relieved him of the shopping. 'Been spending yer money again.'

'Just a few bits in case you run out.'

The smell of vegetable soup wafted through the room. He removed his coat and warmed his hands. She hadn't expected him so early, yet the table was already set with soup bowls and thick slices of his favourite oatmeal bread.

'No butter again then?' She put the milk, bread and dripping into the cupboard.

'You must start making it again, Ma.'

'Eva gets to make it at the farm, but that Aggie woman is too mean to part with her own spit.'

'How is she getting on?'

'Not sure I did the right thing sending her there, but jobs are difficult to come by.'

Cathal shook out his newspaper. 'She'll be fine. I dare say she'll tell you if she doesn't like it.'

'Aye, she will that.'

'Was the plane crash bad, Ma? Anyone injured?' He glanced through the paper. 'There's nothing in here!'

'An RAF plane, from what I heard. Sure, the two pilots who crashed it got away unscathed, so they did. Eva will no doubt be able to fill me in when she comes tomorrow.'

She poured the hot soup into the bowls, and he came and sat down.

'This smells delicious, Ma.'

'Get it down before it goes cold,' she said. 'Were there many on the train?'

'Just a few old farmers curious about the plane crash.' He broke the bread and ate it with the soup. 'So, you think Eva's getting on well at Blackstock's?'

'I dare say she finds Aggie tiresome and has had some run-ins with her.' She smiled. 'I've told her to keep a tongue in her head if she wants to continue working there. Sure, that woman would upset a saint, so she would.'

Cathal frowned. 'It's so far. Is there nothing doing in the town?'

She blew out her lips. 'She's a bright young thing, but there's not much around here. I doubt any of the shopkeepers would consider her. You and I know what folks are like about orphans. They don't have the trust.'

'This makes me sick. They tar everyone with the same brush. She needs a chance, Ma.' He swallowed. 'I hope they see that.'

'I know. But it's hard times and so few jobs suitable

around these parts.' She sighed. 'Anyhow! What's so important that you couldn't wait to come down to ask me?' She
moved her empty soup bowl to the side and leant her elbow
on the table. 'Nothing wrong, is there?'

He laughed and scooped up the last of his soup. 'No, I
wondered what you thought about me taking yourself and
Eva up to Dublin. A day trip to the capital would be a treat
after what she's been through. What do you think?'

A frown creased his aunt's forehead.

He glanced down at his hands, twirling one thumb over
the other, waiting for her to reply. 'It would have to be a Saturday. Do you think they would give her the day off?' He
glanced up. 'If you don't think it's a good idea, we . . .'

'No, I do. I don't think she's ever been. It's a lovely idea,
and it would do us both a power of good.' She shook her
head. 'But I can't see Blackstock changing her day off.'

'Why? It's only once. Surely it's negotiable.'

'We must wait and see.' She stood up and carried the
dishes to the small table where she washed the pots. 'Jacob
Blackstock, well, he's a funny begger.'

'What do you mean?'

'Look, I didn't want to say anything, and I've said nothing to Eva.'

'What is it?'

'That old goat has designs on her.'

Cathal was on his feet. 'No! The dirty old sod. Over my
dead body.'

'And mine.'

'And Eva doesn't know?'

'Sure, he came here to see me a week ago with the excuse
of thanking me for the elderberry wine, but he had an ulter-
ior motive. He sees a good wee worker in Eva and thought

124

it would suit him fine if she was to become his wife. Can you believe the cheek of the man? He only wanted me to give him my blessing.'

'The gall of the fella! I hope you showed him the door.'

'I did more than that. I told him a few truths and said that he should know better. And that if he lays a finger on her, he'd have me to deal with.' She chuckled. 'He went away with his tail between his legs.'

'Don't you think you should warn her?'

'There's no need to worry her. He'll not try anything.'

Cathal frowned and shook his head. 'His type won't give up easy.'

'Don't fret, I'll be keeping me eye on Jacob Blackstock, so I will. He won't dare put a foot wrong.' She straightened up. 'She'll be fine. It's lonely for a young one with no friends her own age. So, yes, a day out is just the ticket.' She moved across to the stove, pushed the poker through the bars and sparks flew up the chimney. She patted the seat next to her. 'Now come on, I want to hear all about your week.'

Chapter Twenty-one

'Are you sure Cathal wants me to come along?' Eva asked, her eyes wide with excitement.

'Yes, it was his idea, so it was.'

'Oh, that's grand. I've never been to the capital, although I feel I was born there.'

'What makes you think that, Eva?' Ma frowned.

Eva told her about Big Finn saying that Fallon was a Dublin name. 'I'd love to know where my parents lived before they died.' She shrugged. 'My memory is hazy. Do you think the nuns would know? They might have a record of the woman who left me at the orphanage ten years ago.'

'Well, now, sure, who knows? Best not to dwell on it. And tell Jacob Blackstock that I said you need to change your day off next week to a Saturday.'

Eva hadn't thought of that. 'I can't see him giving me Saturday off. It's one of the busiest days, but it would be lovely to look around the shops when they are open. Sunday is not much good for shopping for the things I need without having to ask Aggie, and she's always grumpy.' She pursed her lips.

'You tell him what I said. He'll let you have Saturday off, don't worry.'

Eva laughed. 'If only it was that simple, Ma. I'll try.' She didn't want to miss an opportunity to spend time with Cathal. He had asked for her to come with them and that must mean he liked her.

It was midweek before Eva could muster up the courage to approach her employer. She waited until the evening, when Mr Blackwell was relaxing and reading his newspaper. 'Can I have a word, sir?'

'Sure. What is it?'

'Ma Scully wants me to accompany her to Dublin on Saturday.'

He tapped his pipe out on the stone hearth. 'She does, does she?'

Eva nodded.

'What for? The woman's not sick, is she?'

'Oh, no, sir.'

He took a deep intake of breath. 'It's inconvenient. I must have a word with Aggie. I hope you won't be making a habit of this.'

'No, of course not, sir.'

He resumed reading his newspaper, and Eva carried on with her chores, amazed at how easy it had been. However, that night, when her day's work was done, and she wanted nothing more than to sleep, Aggie found more work for her. But Eva completed the task without complaining, determined not to let the woman see how tired she was. If Aggie thought she could induce her to leave, she did not know Eva Fallon.

It was the last minute on Friday evening when Aggie gave her permission to have Saturday off, telling her she was not happy with the sudden inconvenience when they were so busy. She placed a pile of darning on the table and insisted Eva get it done before going to bed.

It was late when Eva wound pipe cleaners around strands of her long hair to make it curl. At the orphanage she kept it tied back and, at one time, the nuns threatened to cut it. The curlers made her head ache and she couldn't sleep from excitement. It was surreal to her that Cathal had invited her to Dublin, and a fluttering started in her tummy.

The following morning, Eva was up with the lark. She prepared an early breakfast for Mr Blackstock and, once he had left the house, she had a bath and got dressed. It was the start of spring, and she wore a floral sundress with a matching bolero despite the unpredictable sky outside. When she brushed her hair out it fell around her shoulders and looked as if she'd had it crimped. She wasn't sure it suited her but it was too late now to worry. Then she pulled on her beige jacket that tied at the waist. If only she had a pair of fashionable shoes to wear instead of her old black ones – even if they were polished until they shone. She hated wearing thick stockings, but they were all she had; she imagined the Dublin girls walking about in the latest nylon stockings. It would be a while yet before she could treat herself to anything like that. She was grateful for all the second-hand clothes Ma Scully had given her and felt blessed to be handy with a sewing needle, as many of the outfits needed alterations to fit her.

She glanced outside. Grey clouds patterned the sky and a chink of sunlight struggled to get through. She didn't have an umbrella and hoped the weather would hold. In her excitement she kept listening for the sound of Ma Scully's trap to arrive. She slung her bag over her shoulder and stood by the door.

Aggie burst in. 'All dressed up, but ye can't disguise who ye are,' she sniggered. 'If ye ask me, you still look like a waif.'

Her words stung and knocked Eva's confidence. She fidgeted with the belt of her jacket and fought a strong urge to flee to her room just to make sure she looked all right. Instead, she bit her tongue and walked into the yard to wait.

Aggie followed. 'Where are ye going, anyway?'

'I don't think it's any of your business.'

'Oh, it will be if ye get yourself knocked up.'

Eva glared at her. She had heard the expression before; to stop herself getting upset by answering back, she sucked in her breath and hurried down the rutted track away from the house. Once out on the lane, she felt a surge of excitement when she saw Ma and Cathal coming towards her in the trap, and Aggie's words faded from her mind.

'Ah, there ye are. You all set then?' Ma said. 'You know you look grand, doesn't she, Cathal?'

'Yes, grand.' He smiled, reaching down to help her up on to the cart. 'You've done something different with your hair.'

'So, do I look okay to visit the big city?'

'You look bonny, so you do,' Cathal said.

A wry smile crossed Ma's face as she turned the cart round, and Eva felt a frisson of excitement sitting next to Cathal. He wore a long mackintosh and a striped scarf around his neck.

'I'm looking forward to the day,' she said.

'Well, make the most of it,' Ma said. 'You'll be back soon enough.'

'If the mistress had her way, I wouldn't have a job to come back to. She was in a right mood and said I looked no better than a waif.'

'Ah, the woman's jealous. Sure, I hope you held your tongue. Don't give her the satisfaction, or she could make your life even more difficult.'

'Well, I told her it was none of her business when she asked where I was going.'

Cathal laughed. 'Good for you.'

Chapter Twenty-two

In the village, Ma stabled the horse and trap at the livery. They walked towards the station on Bawnboy Road, where they caught the narrow gauge to Drumod. Ma glanced at her reflection in the waiting-room mirror and adjusted her hat with a brown feather in the side before climbing on board. Eva remarked on how smart she looked in a long brown coat and matching boots. 'Well,' she said, 'Dublin weather can be as unpredictable as anywhere.' She checked she had her umbrella tucked inside her shopping bag.

Once they were under way, Ma complained, 'I'd forgotten how uncomfortable this old bone shaker is.'

'The train to Dublin will have padded seats,' her nephew reminded her.

Eva enjoyed every bump in the track until they arrived in Drumod. The second leg of their journey was easier, and Ma dozed for most of the way until they arrived in Dublin.

Soon they were walking the streets of Dublin and Eva's

excitement mounted. The sun was shining and she looked around her, taking in the sounds and smells of a vibrant city.

Ships docked by the quayside and barges of merchandise floated along the river. Men sported cloth caps and older women wore headscarves, with ankle boots on their feet. People glanced in shop windows but few went inside. On the surface, life appeared normal. But with the war still on, she guessed it made them cautious about spending their hard-earned cash. They walked towards Nelson's Pillar. She saw no sign of fashion except on the mannequins on display in the shops. Irish songs blared out from music shops; one song struck a chord. It was elusive, hovering at the back of her mind, waiting, but she couldn't remember.

'What's that tune called, Ma?'

'"Kathleen Mavourneen". I think it's one of John McCormack's.'

Along O'Connell Street she saw young women, arms entwined, their clothes more refined and fashionable, wearing stylish coats over floral dresses and little cloche hats perched on top of their heads. People stopped to look at them and Cathal told her they were modelling for a magazine. She couldn't help wondering what it would be like to own a pair of wedge-heeled sandals with peep toes. One girl had a cigarette between her fingers. Cathal touched her elbow and pointed out places of interest: the General Post Office and Clery's department store. Ma paused by the cake shop. 'I'll just nip in here and buy a few fancies.'

'What's that over there?' Eva asked as they waited outside for Ma. 'Look there, in the middle of the street.'

'It's an air-raid shelter,' Cathal said. 'There's a few dotted around.'

'Are we safe in the city?' Her anxious expression made him smile.

'Hitler's not interested in our little cabbage patch. He has bigger fish to fry.'

Ma came out carrying a cake box tied with string. She stood staring, along with Eva, at the makeshift shelter. 'That's not very uplifting, Cathal. Is it necessary?'

'What about the bomb on Northside two years ago? It's just a precautionary measure.'

'Are ye sure?'

'Trust me, Ma.' Cathal took her arm. 'You're frightening Eva. Why don't you show her around the store? I have to be somewhere, and when I get back, I'll treat you both to afternoon tea, then we'll go to the top of Nelson's Pillar.' He laughed. 'You're not frightened of heights, are you, Eva?'

She shook her head, her mind still on the air-raid shelter. But whether she was or not, it would not stop her going anywhere with Cathal. 'I'd love that,' she said.

'You don't be getting me up there,' Ma said. 'I'll do a wee bit of shopping in Moore Street until you're back down again.'

'Okay.' He kissed his aunt's cheek. 'I'll see you both back here in an hour.' Eva's heart sank as she watched him weave his way towards O'Connell Bridge. Ma didn't question his motives and Eva guessed she already knew. Was he meeting a girlfriend? The more she thought about it, she knew it must be true, and her excitement waned.

'Come on,' Ma said. 'Let's go inside. With the war dragging on, most people are just looking.'

Cathal had said he would be back. So, pulling herself together, she smiled and followed Ma into the store.

If Eva thought the window displays were amazing, inside was just as magical, and her mood lifted when she saw several young people at the cosmetic counter trying on rouge and lipsticks. 'Can I try some, please?' she asked the assistant.

'Madam! This shade should suit you best.' The woman spread a little on Eva's hand. It was her very first lipstick and she couldn't wait to put some on later.

'Let me buy it for you,' Ma said. 'It looks nice, as long as you don't overdo it.'

'No, thanks all the same, Ma. I have money.' She opened her handbag, took out her purse and handed over the cash.

The assistant's hair was curled on top of her head and she wore earrings. Eva noticed her red fingernails as she placed the item inside a Clery's bag. She also bought a tortoiseshell slide and ribbons for her hair, and Ma insisted on buying her first pair of nylon stockings. Thrilled, Eva vowed to treasure them.

'Sure, they'll not last long enough. They ladder, so they do. I prefer my thick cotton ones.'

Everything she saw in the shop made her gasp – from fine materials, silks and nylon to the feel of the angora sweaters. A wide, majestic staircase led up to the tea room and more furnishings. Eva had never seen such beautiful things, except in the nuns' dining room. Ma took a great interest in the different-coloured yarns and bought some of the new shades for her quilt. Before they knew it, it was time to meet Cathal.

They were standing underneath Clery's clock when they saw him approach carrying a copy of the evening news, his face flushed.

Ma asked, 'Is everything okay?'

'Yes, it's fine.'

'Will I ever get to meet her, this mystery woman?'

'Soon.'

While this short conversation took place, Eva felt a dull ache in her stomach. Why should that be? She didn't want it to be true, but he was older than her, handsome, with a mop of dark curls and his self-assured manner; it was only natural he would have a girlfriend. A worry line creased his brow and she wondered what had upset him.

'Well now, Eva,' he said, breaking the tension. 'What do you think of Dublin so far?'

'Wonderful. I've never been inside a shop this big before.'

'Oh, this isn't the biggest, is it, Ma?'

'No, it's not. Brown Thomas is a lovely store, but rather expensive.' She sighed. 'Well, I'm wall fallin' and there's a pot of tea somewhere with my name on it.'

Cathal was smiling now and looking more like his old self. 'Come on, I'll treat you both.'

They went back inside and up the wide staircase. Eva kept looking upwards at the fresco design on the high ceiling. When they were all seated and handed a menu, the waitress said she would be over shortly to take their order. She had shapely legs, and she too wore her hair in curls on top of her head, making Eva's attempts look dated.

By the time Cathal had drunk his first cup of tea, his face had brightened and they laughed and chatted as they had done on the train. After a feast of small, delicately cut sandwiches and cream buns, Eva felt fit to burst. She couldn't remember when she had ever felt this full and enjoyed herself so much.

Cathal got to his feet. 'We have a lot more to pull in before we head back. So, let's go. How do you feel about going to see a film?'

'Sounds good,' Ma chuckled.

'Would you like that, Eva?' he asked.

'Oh, yes, please.'

'It looks like it will pour down any minute.' Ma glanced up at the gathering clouds. 'Where do you have in mind?'

'Laurel and Hardy are showing, and we could all do with a good laugh.'

Eva's eyes widened. This was a new experience. She had never been to a proper cinema, nor had she seen a movie – apart from the religious films *St Bernadette of Lourdes* and *The Children of Fatima* shown on a projector screen at the orphanage twice a year.

He guided them towards the cinema. She glanced up at the building's grand facade, much grander than anything she had seen before.

'This is a cinema?' she asked.

'Sure, it is. And this one has its own shelter down below, so, should anything happen, which is unlikely, we'll be safe.' He laughed at the uncertainty on her face.

'Oh, really!'

'Trust me. I won't let anything happen to you.'

She relaxed and her smile returned. 'Isn't it just grand?' Her feet sank into the plush carpet in the foyer. 'I could almost forget I have to go back to the farm.' She was mindful it was a means to a better life.

'Oh, don't worry.' Ma waved her hand. 'That old goat will have to wait for ye, if yer not.'

Cathal laughed. 'Too right he will.'

Eva wasn't too sure about that. It puzzled her as to their easy-going attitude. If she was late back, Aggie would make her pay with a lashing of her vile tongue. She was having such a good time and put any thoughts of work to the back of her mind. Inside the posh interior, they walked halfway down the aisle and Eva took a seat next to Ma, with Cathal on her other side. Her stomach did somersaults; to be sitting in a cinema next to the man she adored, watching the antics of Laurel and Hardy, was a dream come true. She and Ma were holding their sides with mirth, and she loved the sound of Cathal's laughter. It was masculine, husky and filled her ears and her mind. He passed her a bag of soft jellies, and at the interval he queued up to buy them all tubs of ice cream.

When they came outside again, it was dark. A group of American soldiers passed by, smoking cigarettes and laughing, a girl on each arm.

Eva turned to Cathal. 'Why are they here?'

'They're stationed in Belfast. You often see them down here looking for girls. Come on,' he said. 'We might just have time to go to the top of Nelson's Pillar. The queue is shorter now.'

Once his aunt was safely across O'Connell Street and heading for Moore Street, Cathal paid the man, and he and Eva ascended the narrow spiral staircase. Eva felt her heart thumping, being alone with Cathal in such a confined space. When they reached the top, he placed his arm across her shoulder and she wanted to stay where she was, enjoying the moment with him.

'Are you okay? It's not too cold for you, is it?'

'I'm grand.' She felt a flush to her face. 'How high up are we?'

'Hundred and twenty feet, I think.'

'Yes, it's wonderful.' Her eyes sparkled as she looked down at the crowd and Cathal laughed at her obvious pleasure.

It was turning out to be the best time of her entire life,

and being on top of Nelson's Pillar was a fitting end to their day out. They looked down on the streets below them, still busy with people.

'This is amazing,' she said.

The small platform held only six people at a time, and the couple on the other side of them looked cosy with each other. Eva felt a rush of cold air when Cathal removed his arm to point out places of interest. When they came back down, they waited by the foot of the pillar until they saw Ma struggling towards them with shopping bags full with vegetables and fruit hanging from her arms.

'Oh dear me,' said Ma. 'I was enjoying the banter of the women so much, I almost forgot the time. They're a law unto themselves, so they are. Tried to short-change me, so they did.' She was panting from the heavy shopping.

Cathal relieved her of her bags and they headed towards the train station.

When they reached Drumod, they alighted and caught the narrow gauge that would take them to Bawnboy. Ma and Cathal still had the long journey back to Cavan.

Before they parted, Eva said, 'Well, I'll be off now before Mr Blackstock locks me out.' On impulse, she planted a quick kiss on Ma's cheek.

'What's that for?'

Eva smiled. 'Thanks, I've had a wonderful time.' She turned towards Cathal – if only she could kiss him too! – and blushed at the thought. All too soon the day was over, and as she turned to go, Cathal touched her arm. It sent her heart racing.

'Hold on, Eva. Ma, can you wait at the livery while I walk Eva back to the farm?'

'Course I can. I'll pop into the snug and have a wee one for the journey.'

Then he remembered the heavy bags. 'Hold on, I can't leave you with all those bags.'

'I'll be fine. Meet me at the pub and you can carry them to the livery.'

'Well, if you're sure.'

Ma waved her hand for them to go.

Chapter Twenty-three

In spite of the rain that had threatened earlier, it was a clear night as Cathal walked Eva back to the farm. Eva felt as if she was walking on air and wished the day didn't have to end.

'If we'd had more time,' he said, 'we could have visited the Art Museum and Trinity College. Maybe another time, eh?'

There would be another time? His closeness made her heart race. Never had she experienced feelings like this before, but then she had never walked alone with a man at this time of the evening, or felt this safe. She glanced up. He appeared much taller now she was walking next to him. Their voices echoed in the silence.

'I've ... I've had a lovely day. Thank you.' She would always remember it. And whatever Aggie threw at her was of little consequence to her right now.

'It was a pleasure, Eva. I mean it. I'm proud to be walking the most beautiful girl in Cavan home. But I wish it wasn't to Blackstock's farm.'

Eva's heart soared. Did he mean that? And all she could think of to say was, 'You'd better not come any further, I'll be fine now, thanks.' She was fearful her boss might see them together and accuse her of all sorts.

'I'm walking you right to the door, young lady. You never know who's lurking about.'

She felt a flush to her face. He continued to walk alongside her, his hands tucked inside his pockets; her shoulder touching his arm sent a delightful shiver through her.

'It's quiet around here.'

'Maybe, but not so safe in the capital. Only last week a woman was thrown to the ground and her purse stolen.'

'Is she all right?'

'I guess so – shocked and shaken, the newspaper said.' He guided her towards the main entrance.

Eva paused. 'The front door is only used on Sunday. I have to go through the yard. But it's fine, honest.'

His eyebrows shot up and his laugh was so loud she was sure someone would hear. 'Are you serious?'

She nodded.

'There's no way you're walking through a muddy yard at this time of night.' He continued to steer her up the gravelled path.

'They won't open the door.'

'We'll see about that.' He lifted the knocker, letting it drop and making a terrible din.

She held her breath, waiting for the onslaught she knew would follow.

'You leave old Blackstock to me.' Straightening his shoulders, he knocked again.

The bolt slid back, and the door flew open.

Mr Blackstock looked from one to the other. Then his

eyes fixed on Eva. 'You know better than to come to the front entrance. And at this hour—'

'It was my fault,' Cathal intervened. 'I didn't think the young lady should have to walk through a muddy yard in the dark.'

'And who the bloody hell are you?'

'I'm Cathal Burke, Ma Scully's nephew.'

At the mention of his aunt's name, Jacob Blackstock appeared to shrink into the door jamb. He stood back. Eva thanked Cathal and slipped inside, going straight to her room. She heard the mumbling of voices but she was too happy to care. She lay on top of the bed thinking about Cathal and the wonderful day she had spent in his company.

If only he would take her seriously and ask her out on a real date. Sighing, she rolled off the bed, undressed, washed and got in underneath the covers.

The following morning, Eva wondered whether she should apologise to her boss for arriving back so late the previous night, but decided against it.

She was serving up his breakfast when his question took her by surprise. 'Are you walking out with this Cathal Burke then?'

She swallowed and looked up; she spilt tea into the saucer, mopping it up with a cloth. She didn't think it was any of his business and wanted to tell him so, but she kept a civil tongue in her head.

'He walked me back. Ma Scully insisted he did so.'

'So, he has no other agenda?'

'I'm sorry, sir. I don't know what you mean?'

'Course you do! Are you stupid?'

'Stupid! No, I'm not stupid, sir.'

Regardless of the consequences, he would not get away with calling her that. Furious, she made more noise than usual setting the table. 'Agenda' was a new word to her. Why didn't he say what he meant instead of using complicated words?

'I'm sorry. I didn't mean to upset you. Just get my breakfast, I'm late as it is.'

But for the rest of the morning she couldn't forget that he had called her stupid.

Chapter Twenty-four

Infused with happy thoughts of her day in Dublin, she refused to let Mr Blackstock's insulting remark overshadow it. With a world out there she had yet to explore, her dreams of working in one of the big fashion stores in the capital filled her days. For now she had no choice but to continue working at the farm.

It was the first week of April. Mr Blackstock and the men set off for the cattle market and wouldn't be back until evening. Eva wished she could go with them, but there was little chance of that happening. She took her time with the chores, daydreaming about Cathal and wondering when she would see him again. She was about to put water on to boil when she noticed the barrel was empty. It was so unlike John to forget, but in his excitement to get off this morning she guessed it had slipped his mind. Now she thought about it, he hadn't given her his usual friendly nod when he arrived. Pulling on one of the yard coats, she stepped into cold wellington boots. With a wooden pail in each hand, she was about to go outside.

'Where do ye think you're going?'

'The water barrel's empty, mistress.'

Aggie narrowed her eyes. 'What do ye mean?'

'John hasn't filled it this morning.'

'Well, be quick about it. These clothes won't wash themselves,' she barked.

The yard was quiet without the workers. In the distance Eva could see young boys of school age tilling the land. It was compulsory during the emergency and farmers who were duty-bound did their bit. She would rather be out there with them than stuck inside under Aggie's watchful glare. It hadn't taken her long to acknowledge that the men of this world had all the advantages. A gust of wind blew her sideways. The chickens ran towards her, almost tripping her up and clucking around her feet. Lucky, the farm cat, its fur raised in the wind, brushed up against her. These were her friends, the only ones she had at the farm. She put down the pails and bent to stroke the cat. 'You will work today and catch mice.' The cat meowed and followed her towards the well. She stopped to pat the donkey tethered to the side of the log shed – at least that was full. Then she looked into the cowshed. Mr Blackstock had said the baby calves were due. It was empty, but the smell of newborn animals and milk lingered. If only she could do this more often. As things stood, she was fortunate to be permitted a short stop to eat and use the privy.

A noise from behind the shed in the small orchard made her stop. Just some rabbits, she told herself, glancing up at the darkening sky. It was unlikely she would get to wash and dry the clothes before it rained. Lowering the buckets one at a time into the well, she carried them back, spilling water in the yard and over her boots. It was back-breaking work, and depending on how long the men would be away for, she would have to repeat this several times throughout the day.

She was right about the rain, and soon it was beating against the window. She chided herself for dallying and not getting the washing done earlier. Later, when she found the vegetable baskets empty, she was furious – another job the lads had neglected to do. She put the raincoat back on and went out. She placed as many potatoes, onions and carrots as she could carry into her basket. Field mice and vermin got to them first, and she took a while to find good ones. As she bent down to pick up the load, she heard a loud thud. Her heartbeat quickened, and she straightened up.

'Is . . . is someone there?' Telling herself not to be silly, it was just the wind.

First the orchard, now the barn. She was very much alone, and it made her jittery. With a farm like this, animals, stray dogs and rats ran around the place, and now rabbits were coming around more often. She couldn't blame them, they were always sure of something to nibble.

Lifting the heavy basket on to her hip, she heard someone call out, the voice weak. 'Help me!'

Startled, she dropped the basket and watched the vegetables roll across the barn.

'Who . . . who is it? What do you want?'

'I'm Matthew Blackstock. Come closer.'

Her eyes widened and she looked around and up towards the hayloft. She could see his head and shoulders, his hair tousled, as if he had slept in here all night. Could he be Mr Blackstock's younger son back safe from the war? If so, why was he hiding?

She couldn't risk going any closer. 'I'll find someone.'

How could she, with only Aggie in the house? Her hands shook as she gathered up what vegetables she could, leaving the rest in her haste to get away.

He stood up, and she could see he wore a British army uniform. She turned to flee.

'Wait, please! Don't go. Help me.' He started down the ladder.

Eva held the basket in front of her, and her whole body shook. He looked unkempt, and dirty. She nodded towards the house. 'The mistress will wonder where I am.'

'All I want is something to eat and a change of clothes. My father can't see me in these. Come on now! Help me! You're the only one who can. I've been here for hours, waiting for him to leave.' He stood at the bottom of the ladder, clinging to it as though he might keel over.

She wanted to help him. But how would she know if he was telling the truth?

'Please, I'm desperate.'

'I . . . I don't have the key to the food cupboard. I . . .'

'Some bread, anything will do. I'm starving. And for God's sake, don't say a word to Granny, not yet. I don't want to shock her.'

'I'll . . . I'll try.' Her heart racing, she ran from the barn, almost slipping in the muddy yard. At the door she took deep breaths before going inside.

Aggie had been dozing by the fire and started awake. 'Took your time, didn't ye?'

Eva tried to control her shaking limbs. 'The carrots were gnawed at, mistress, and I took ages to find half-decent ones.'

Aggie pointed to a neat pile of clothes on the table. 'There's some mending I want doing today. So ye better get a move on.'

How could she keep this to herself? Besides, where was she going to find clothes to fit Matthew without attracting attention? If she was caught sneaking about in Mr Blackstock's room, there was no telling what she might be accused of. The incident at Ma Scully's was still fresh in her mind. She couldn't chance it.

'What's the matter with you, girl? Daydreaming won't get the work done.'

'Yes, mistress.' Her concentration had gone; she was conscious of Matthew waiting out in the barn.

When Aggie stood up and went for a lie down, Eva searched through the clothes in the basket and pulled out a pair of trousers and an Aran sweater. Nerves churned her stomach. With the clothes tucked under her arm and two thick cuts of bread and cheese in the pocket of her apron, she put the raincoat back on and hurried towards the barn.

He shuffled out from behind a large crate and stood next to her.

She shrunk backwards. 'This is all I could find.' She placed the food, along with the clothes, by the door.

'What's your name?'

'Eva.'

'Nice!' He tore at the bread. 'It's just Granny in the house, is that right?'

She nodded. 'I must get back.'

'Remember, not a word. I'll break it to her myself.'

She couldn't relax. Jumping at every sound. Looking over her shoulder. What if he came in? She wanted to run to her room and lock the door. There had been something in his eyes that made her uneasy. Dear God! Why did he have to turn up today? What had enticed him to join up? she wondered. With so many already dead, the war was futile as far as she could see.

From what she had gleaned when listening to Big Finn, Matthew had defected from the Irish Free State army along with Thomas, Finn's grandson. That wouldn't sit well with most people, his father in particular.

She sat at the table, biting her thumbnail, and for the first time since working at the farm she longed for Aggie's company. With oil on ration she felt no guilt at turning up the wick on the lamp. As she did so, Matthew appeared in the doorway.

She froze. He was short in stature; Mr Blackstock's trousers were too long in the leg and the Aran jersey covered his hands. He was holding his crumpled uniform and moved closer.

Sick with fear, she lifted the mop and held it out in front of her.

'I won't bite. Get rid of this, have it burned or something.' He pushed it towards her.

She made no move to take it from him.

'What time is the old man back?'

Eva shook her head. 'I don't know.'

'Is Granny still here?'

'Yes.' She couldn't stop shaking. 'I think she's . . . she's in her room.'

He placed the uniform on the draining board and cupped his hands. Scooping water from the pail, he threw it over his face and hands and dried them with the towel. He glanced around at her.

She was holding the mop as if glued to the spot.

'Well, what are you waiting for? Go on! Tell her it's Matthew and be quick about it.'

She let go of the mop and rushed down the hall, knocking on the door before stepping inside.

'How dare you barge in here? What do you want?'

'It's . . . it's . . .'

'What's the matter with ye today, girl?'

Matthew stood behind her in the doorway. 'Hello, Granny.'

Eva saw Aggie's eyes light up. 'Oh, Matthew, lad. How did ye get here?'

They embraced while Eva stood in the doorway.

Aggie turned round. 'Go on, get out of here.'

Eva fled back to the kitchen. She scooped up the heavy uniform and bundled it underneath the sink, out of sight, until she had time to consider what to do with it.

It wasn't long before she heard raised voices. It would appear that after her initial delight at seeing her grandson alive, Aggie was screaming at him for his stupidity. Eva placed her hands over her ears to block out the torrent of abuse coming from Matthew towards his grandmother. When things had quietened down, Aggie unlocked her grandson's room and ushered him inside.

She handed him the key. 'Lock it, get some rest and leave everything to me.'

By late afternoon, Eva was longing for Mr Blackstock to return. She was sure he would know what to do.

They had just finished eating, and Aggie had taken food to Matthew in his room, when she said, 'You say a word to anyone and you'll find yourself without a roof over your head. Do ye hear me, girl?'

Eva swallowed. 'What . . . what about Mr Blackstock?'

'Not a word or you'll regret it. Go on, get out of my sight.'

'But . . . what about the master's supper?'

'I'll see to that.'

'Are you sure? What about the mending?'

'I said so, didn't I?' She flapped her hand. 'Just go!'

Eva hated leaving the kitchen with the chores undone. Aggie wouldn't wash up, and she would have to face it all in the morning on top of a day's work. As she lay in bed, unable to sleep, she wondered what would happen to Matthew when the authorities caught up with him. She feared things would only get worse at the farm once Mr Blackstock discovered his son was a deserter.

Chapter Twenty-five

When Eva woke, her mind flooded with thoughts of the previous day. She washed and dressed, feeling uneasy about Matthew hiding in the house. Had Aggie spoken to Mr Blackstock? She hoped so, and wondered how he had reacted. Despite her misgivings, she imagined the worry lines on his face relaxing once he discovered his son was alive. She knew the majority would shun someone in Matthew's position. Would Mr Blackstock make an exception for his own?

The sight of dirty dishes, mugs and breadcrumbs littering the table infuriated her as she passed through to the outside lavatory. At least the fire had been banked. She returned with an armful of logs, placing them by the hearth. While she waited for the kettle to boil, she scrubbed at the plates congealed with grease; she was conscious of Matthew's army uniform underneath the sink. Then while it was quiet, she took it to her room and stashed it away in one of her large suitcases until she had time to get rid of it. Why was it up to her to dispose of it?

She prepared the porridge, sausage, eggs and fried bread ready for Mr Blackstock. Keeping busy calmed her nerves. The men arrived in the yard and John headed straight for the sheds. She missed his friendly smile first thing in the morning and longed to confide in him.

Mr Blackstock came to the table, looking relaxed, and she placed his breakfast in front of him.

'Good morning, Eva. I trust you rested well last night? Aggie said you had a bad head.'

'I'm grand. I slept well, thank you, sir.' She felt a flush of guilt to her face.

He didn't know about Matthew, and her heart sank. It wasn't right she should be privy to news of his son's return when he knew nothing about it. Why in God's name hadn't Aggie told him?

When he had finished eating, he bent down to tie his boot laces and then straightened up. 'I'm sorry you had to fetch and carry yesterday. Those lads should have got all that done before we made off. It won't happen again.'

So Aggie had found time to tell him that – but not the most important news.

Eva wiped her hands down the sides of her apron. 'It's all right, sir. I managed.'

'The devil of all right!' An angry expression creased his brow as he pulled on his coat.

He was no sooner out the door and striding towards the sheds when Aggie trotted in, still in her dressing gown, slippers and hairnet. She picked up a plate and held it out to Eva.

'Fill this with as much food as you've got ready. And remember, not a word of this to anyone.'

'But, mistress . . . what about his father? Shouldn't he be made aware?'

153

'Mind your place, girl, or you'll be out on your ear.' Balancing a plate crammed with bacon, eggs, black pudding, sausage and fried bread in one hand and a mug of tea in the other, Aggie went down the passage and knocked on Matthew's door.

Eva stood rooted to the spot, looking after her. She had cooked the food Aggie had left out but hadn't expected her to take it all. Mr Blackstock would notice the provisions depleting and if he kept his accounts in order, which Eva believed he did, he would question Aggie sooner or later. She hated being party to their deceit. It was wrong! Why couldn't Aggie see she was making things worse by concealing Matthew? Eva had been looking forward to a nice piece of crispy bacon this morning but instead made do with bread and dripping.

When Matthew surfaced, she was rinsing the last of the washing. He lifted the lid on the cooking pot and sniffed the contents, then moved to the window. She tensed as he leant across her and drew the curtains.

'No one must see me before I talk to my father.'

Although relieved to hear that, she couldn't relax with him in the house.

He looked better dressed in his own clothes. He'd had a bath and washed his hair and was more his father's son. 'You've got rid of the army stuff then?'

She turned round with her back to the sink and nodded. At least it was out of sight for now. Aggie came in. She smoothed down Matthew's shirt collar like a mother hen. They both sat down at the table and Eva continued with the washing, her mind on what to do with the army uniform.

'Look, Granny, I can't stay cooped up here for much longer.'

'So, what do ye suggest we do? If your father finds out, he won't keep quiet. He'll kick up murder.' Agitated, she played with the ring on her finger.

'Sure, let him. He's no inkling of what it was like out there.'

'You're a deserter, Matthew. He won't be able to live with the shame.'

'Oh, to hell with him.' Matthew scraped back his chair. 'Can't you get rid of her?' he asked, gesturing towards Eva. 'She knows too much already.'

'Leave that,' Aggie snapped.

Eva glanced round. 'I'll just finish—'

'Do as you're told, girl! Go outside. Go on! You'll find plenty of work out there.'

'But I'm not finished in here, mistress. Besides, the master says, I'm not paid to work outside.' She knew she had gone too far when Aggie glared at her. And yes, she knew too much, more than she cared to. And if Aggie continued to treat her in this way, she had a good mind to tell Mr Blackstock what was going on.

Aggie sat back in her chair. 'Do ye see the cheek I get from this one! But will your father listen? Oh, no, he thinks she's God's gift.'

Matthew sneered.

Aggie got up and moved her face within an inch of Eva's. 'This is my kitchen. Now, get out and I won't tell ye again.'

For a few seconds Eva held Aggie's stare before removing her apron, pulling on her coat and stomping out.

The sun was shining, and she walked towards the village. If Mr Blackstock complained about her not being in the kitchen when he returned, she would tell him the truth. She didn't want to hide Matthew's army stuff. Why should it be her responsibility anyhow? The frame of mind she was in, she would tell him to burn the cursed uniform himself.

By the time she had walked to the shops she felt calmer. It was the first time she had been to the village when the shops were open.

Two small children playing on the pavement approached her for a halfpenny.

'A ha'penny,' she laughed. 'You cheeky rascals.' She shook her head and opened her purse. 'Here, you can have a farthing. Now, get away with you.'

The youngsters ran towards the store.

People rode on bikes, and it surprised her to see a car parked in the street with petrol on ration. A man in a long white apron arranging produce outside the grocer's smiled and bid her good day. She nodded. At least not everyone around these parts was as miserable as the Blackstocks. She paid a halfpenny for a rosy apple to take back with her.

The general store sold everything, from sweets to logs and paraffin, and she couldn't resist going inside.

'Nice day!' the shopkeeper called out to her.

'Yes,' she replied. 'Do you have any liquorice sticks?'

He picked up a jar. 'How many would you like?'

'Just one, please. And can I have two candles and some matches.'

Aggie insisted she buy her own. The man went behind the counter, brought out a brown box and peered inside.

'I'm low on candles. There's been a run on them, with oil on ration.' He stroked his chin. 'I could let ye have one. Will that do ye?'

'Thanks, sure, that will be grand.'

He placed the liquorice into a bag and did the same with

the candle and matches. 'Sure, can I get ye anything else now?'

'Yes, can I have a bar of Sunlight soap, please?'

'You seem like a nice wee girl. Are you the orphan working up at Blackstock's farm?'

She nodded.

'Well, sure, ye must feel lonely up there and I can't say I've seen ye about much.'

'No ... I get little time. Well, thank you, I must get back.'

Although the shopkeeper had been friendly, would she always be labelled an orphan?

Half an hour had flown past and the fresh air had improved her mood. If she hurried she might get back before Mr Blackstock came in from the fields looking for his dinner.

At the farmhouse door she took a deep breath and stood for a moment, then lifted the latch. It would not budge. She gave it a good shove, thinking it might be stuck, before she realised it was bolted from the inside.

'What are you doing out here?' Eva turned round to find Mr Blackstock behind her. 'I hope the dinner's ready?'

'I ... I can't get in, sir.'

He rattled the door. 'Why's the bloody door locked?' He looked to her for an answer.

'I ... I don't know, sir.'

When the door flew open and Aggie stood there, a defiant expression on her face, she glared at Eva, then at her son-in-law. 'Oh, what are you fussing about, Jacob? You're in now.' She narrowed her eyes. 'Girl, give the man his dinner.'

Chapter Twenty-six

The weight of the black iron made Eva's wrist ache as she struggled to get through a pile of clothes. Matthew insisted on having his shirts starched and pressed, despite being unable to leave the farm. The longer his movements were restricted, the more ill-tempered he became. She glanced up as he came into the kitchen in a white vest and pyjama bottoms, a naked woman tattooed on his forearm. Eva felt a flush to her face.

'Ah,' he mocked. 'Never seen a man without his shirt on before?'

She stopped ironing and placed the heavy iron on the hob to keep hot. He walked behind her and slid his hand around her waist.

'Get away from me.'

'Not so timid now, are we? I could have you thrown off this farm any time I want,' he smirked.

'Your father employs me, not you.' She bit her tongue.

'You dare take that tone with me?'

'I'm just speaking the truth.'

He stood glaring at her. 'I know what you convent girls are like, so don't play the innocent with me.' He kicked over a chair and snatched the shirt from her. There was no disguising the hate in his eyes.

'At least I still have my dignity.'

'Dignity!' he yelled, his cold stare boring into her. 'You wouldn't know the word unless it's explained to you. You're just a skivvy.'

Aggie rushed down the passage. 'What the hell's going on here! I can hear you in my bedroom. Do ye want him to find ye?'

Matthew shrugged. 'I don't care. And get rid of her. Like you said, she's the one causing trouble.'

Aggie placed her arm around him. 'No, we need her to keep her mouth shut.'

Talking about her as if she wasn't there infuriated Eva. 'Sack me, if that's what you want. But I promise you, I won't keep quiet.'

'Let her do her worst, Granny. I can't stay cooped up here. It'll drive me crazy.' He threw the shirt on the floor and stamped on it. So, he had a temper that matched his arrogance.

Eva looked down at her hard work, in a heap on the floor. When she glanced up, she saw a worried frown creasing Aggie's brow as she bent to pick up the shirt and placed it over her arm. Matthew stormed out, banging the door behind him.

'What are ye gawping at? Get that ironing finished before Mr Blackstock gets back.'

The clash with Matthew had left Eva shaky, but she was glad to have found the courage to stand her ground. If only her boss wasn't so blinkered, he might find out what was going on under his nose. She knew he wouldn't condone his son's behaviour, nor would he tolerate a deserter under his roof. No matter how cunning Aggie thought she was, they had both seen how volatile Matthew had become.

At lunchtime Mr Blackstock walked in, a thunderous expression on his face, as if he'd had a run-in with the labourers. He plucked a letter from the bundle he was holding and placed the rest behind the clock on the mantelpiece. 'Sit down a minute!' he commanded.

Surprised by his abruptness, Eva perched on the edge of a chair.

'I've a letter here addressed to you with a Dublin postmark.'

'For me, sir! Are you sure?'

'That's your name, isn't it?' He turned it towards her. 'Who would write to you care of this address?'

'I don't know, sir. Can I have it, please?'

He hesitated before handing it over. She fingered the cream manila envelope. Feeling a ripple of excitement, she hoped it might be from Cathal.

'Well, aren't you going to open it?'

She stood up. 'I'll do so in private, sir, if that's all right.' She placed it in the pocket of her apron and went to check the potatoes, carefully lifting one at a time. They resembled balls of fluff. She ladled the stew on top.

He pulled his chair closer to the table and picked up a spoon and fork. 'Is it from, what's his name, the young fella that brought you home the other night?' He tucked into his food.

Eva would not satisfy him with a reply. This letter was for her, and he had no right to pry.

'If it is,' he said, 'I won't have him coming round here while you're working. Is that clear?'

'Yes, sir.'

In her room, she sat on her bed and fingered the envelope. Excitement bubbled. It was the first correspondence she had ever received. Peeling back the flap, she extracted the single sheet of embossed paper. Her eye went to the Dublin address at the top of the page.

Dear Eva,

I trust you are well and that they are not working you too hard at the farm. It was very pleasant spending time with you and Ma in Dublin. We must do it again.

I'm hoping there won't be any objections writing to you here. Sure, my concern grew after I'd left you. Mr Blackstock sounded grumpy, and I hope you didn't get into trouble for coming back late. Remember, that's not the only farm in Cavan. You will soon discover there are more opportunities to suit a smart girl like yourself. In only a short time of meeting you, I can tell that you are an intelligent young woman, capable of doing whatever you put your mind to.

If you're happy where you are, please forgive my presumption.

Your friend,
Cathal

Smiling, she pressed the letter to her lips and hugged it to her. He was her friend, and nothing could upset her now. When John had turned his back on her, she had felt so alone, but none of that mattered any more. Cathal believed in her, and it gave her a new sense of worth. She wanted to reply, but she wasn't sure if he would expect her to. She could read and write, thanks to the nuns; she'd had her knuckles rapped enough times.

Her mind was full of the things she might put in her reply. She hadn't realised how long she had been sitting there holding his letter until she heard Aggie screeching.

'Eva! Where are you, girl?'

She kissed the letter again, placing it under her pillow before going back to the kitchen, deliberately dragging her feet.

Chapter Twenty-seven

On Sunday, Eva took the train to see Ma Scully, her mind made up to tell her everything. As she walked to the station, the sight of primroses and cowslips bordering the fields and hedgerows delighted her, and she picked a cluster to take to Ma.

Sister Catherine had once said primroses were a symbol of hope. And hope was what Eva clung to.

Cathal's letter had lifted her spirits, made her believe she could build a life for herself away from Blackstock's farm. Ma's kindness had given her a footing. Now it was up to her. She was in charge of her own destiny.

Ma Scully's cottage was a welcome respite after the dreary farm kitchen where she merely existed. Tucking into home-made scones spread with raspberry jam, she felt happy and relaxed.

'Well, aren't these pretty?' Ma placed the flowers in water and put them in the window. 'How's things at the farm?'

Eva brushed the crumbs from her skirt and took a sip of tea. She sat back in the chair and let out an audible sigh.

Cathy Mansell

'I can see something is troubling ye. What is it?' Ma leant her elbow on the table.

No longer was she able to pretend all was well. Eva took a breath and related everything, from finding Matthew in the barn to Aggie hiding him in his bedroom, stopping only to blow her nose.

'Holy Mother of God!' Ma's hand rushed to her face. 'And Jacob knows nothing of this?'

Eva shook her head. 'Matthew's not nice, Ma. He calls me names, and I wasn't standing for it. So I spoke my mind and said things that should have got me the sack. And I don't like the way he looks at me.' She glanced down at her hands, now folded in her lap.

'Has he hurt you?'

'No! But he has a foul mouth.'

Ma pulled her chair closer and placed her hand over Eva's. 'How long has he been hiding?'

'Three days. Will I be in trouble for not telling?'

Ma looked perplexed. 'I'm not sure, Eva, love.'

The tick of the clock sounded louder as she waited for Ma to continue, hoping she would suggest something to put her mind at rest.

Ma stood up, her hands on her hips. 'If I know Jacob Blackstock, he'll be furious with Aggie, and you too, for keeping this from him.' She pursed her lips. 'Sure, he's bound to find out. It will be worse the longer it goes on.'

'That's what worries me. I'm walking on eggshells every morning before he goes to the fields.'

Ma shook her head. 'As for Aggie, that one's as daft as a brush if she thinks she's doing her grandson any favours. And getting you involved . . .'

'I'm sorry, Ma. I'll tell the master as soon as I can.'

She fidgeted with the spoon, then stirred her tea several times.

'Yes, I think it's best, Eva, love. Once word gets out that Blackstock's son is hiding on his father's farm, sure there'll be a lynch mob out for him. Not only is he a deserter, but he left the Irish army to join the Brits. A double deserter won't bode well in these parts.'

Ma was right. Eva's anxiety returned and butterflies swarmed around in her tummy. Eager to return to the farm, she wondered how she would broach the subject and how her boss would react when she did.

'You enjoyed your day in Dublin then?' Ma punctured her thoughts.

'Oh, yes, I did, Ma. I had a letter from Cathal and he said he enjoyed it too. He was very encouraging.'

Ma took Eva's small hand in hers. 'I feel you may be sweet on my nephew, and there's nothing wrong in that. But you know he's a grown man with his own life. You need to meet young people your own age.'

Eva's face dropped, and she felt like someone had driven a tractor over her dreams. But it was more than that. Ma thought she was still a child, she didn't understand how deep her feelings went. Eva knew they were real, something she had never experienced before. Just thinking about him made her happy. Burying her hurt, she forced a smile. 'I don't get time to go out.'

'Look, Eva, you have looks most men are drawn to. I'd like to see ye going to a dance and enjoying yourself. You're only young once, ye know. A girl of your age has plenty of time to meet a nice beau.'

Eva shrugged, wishing she hadn't mentioned Cathal.

'Come on. It's too fair a day to stay indoors. I'll walk part of the way with you. I could do with some fresh air.'

Chapter Twenty-eight

Mr Blackstock sat by the hearth, smoking his pipe and staring into the fire. He was still wearing his Sunday clothes. Eva removed her coat and folded it across her arm. This was the perfect moment to tell him.

He glanced up. 'You're back then? I trust you found Ma Scully well?'

'Oh, yes, sir, quite well.'

Before she had time to utter a word, he said, 'Sit a minute, Eva.'

She sat down at the table.

'No, over here.' He patted the empty chair by the fire.

It was silent, apart from the hissing of the kettle hanging over the flame. Did he know about Matthew? She hoped that was why he had asked her to sit, and she placed her coat across her lap.

'Has something happened, sir?'

He removed his pipe, tapped out the used tobacco and dropped it down on the hearth. 'I'm not sure.' He turned to face her. 'Over the past few days, certain things have come to my attention.' He leant forward, smoothing down his thin moustache. 'I've been looking at the accounts. Aggie has ordered extra bread from the village store, along with other strange ingredients and food stuff.' He sat back. 'Aren't you getting enough to eat, lass?'

Surprised by the question, she met his gaze. 'That's nothing to do with me, sir. It's . . .' She almost blurted it out. 'You need to speak to the mistress.'

'So, this extra stuff is not for you?'

'No, sir. It's not my place to ask for more.'

'No. I'm sorry. I had to ask.'

Eva played with the button on her cardigan. 'Mr Black-stock, there's something I think you should know . . .'

He moved closer and reached for her hand. She withdrew it from his grasp and stood up. Her coat dropped to the floor.

She snatched it up and held it in front of her. 'I'm . . . good night, sir.'

'Don't go. I'm sorry. Sure, I didn't mean to startle you.' He cleared his throat. 'Please, sit down. There's something else I want to discuss with you.'

She remained standing.

'You must know how fond I am of you, Eva. You are the only sensible person around here.'

She froze.

'When Mary died, I thought I would sell the farm and everything in it, but Aggie persuaded me to keep it on. God knows why, as she shows no interest in the place.'

She edged away. 'I'm sorry . . . I have . . .'

'Just let me finish.' Talking faster, the words tumbling out. 'When you came here, looking for work, I was dubious at first. But after a short time I felt a new sense of purpose. Do you understand?'

'No . . . I'm not sure I do, sir.'

'Sure, you make a man feel alive, Eva, and I mean you no disrespect by saying so.'

Her body stiffened, and she glanced around. This wasn't going the way she had planned. She moved away from him, her heart thumping.

'Don't go. Not like this.'

'Hell's fire! What's going on here?' Aggie elbowed Eva and pushed past her into the room. 'What's she been saying?' She glared at Eva, her eyes wide.

'Nothing yet, mistress. But now you're here, you should tell the master the truth.'

'Tell me what? Why have you been ordering all this extra food?'

'Oh, take no notice of what she's said. This is a private matter.'

'Private! What's private about running up unnecessary bills? You'd better tell me what's going on, Aggie.' He stood up.

Aggie straightened her shoulders, drew her dressing gown around her and folded her arms. 'I'll not discuss anything in front of her.'

'I'm sure Eva would like to hear this as much as I would.'

Eva sat down at the table, eager to see how Aggie would explain the extra food.

'Don't take me for a fool, Aggie. I'm sensing some kind of conspiracy here. Out with it! Why do you need extra food?'

Aggie glanced across at Eva. 'It's all her doing, so it is.'

'Eva, if you know something, you'd better say.'

'I do, sir, but it's not for me to say what has been going on behind your back.'

'The business of this household has nothing to do with her.'

'I've had no sleep and I'm losing patience.'

Aggie threw an evil glare towards Eva before saying, 'Matthew's home.'

'Matthew's home, and you didn't think to tell me?' he yelled.

Aggie sat down, holding her head in her hands, while he continued shouting and blaspheming – something Eva had never heard him do before. As their angry words ricocheted between them, Eva slipped out of the room. She was creeping past Matthew's door when it opened, and he rushed at her, pushing her against the wall. She screamed out before he placed his hand over her mouth. 'Couldn't keep it shut, could you?'

She stiffened, terrified of what he might do, when his other hand fondled her breast. She lashed out, kicking him hard in the shin, until he loosened his grip. 'You'll pay for that, you . . .' He raised his hand to slap her when his father stood there, his tall frame rigid, his face red with rage.

'Well, if it's not the big man himself. Hit a woman, would you?' He grabbed Matthew's bare shoulders and pushed him up against the wall.

Eva rushed to her room, locking and bolting the door behind her, as a fierce row erupted between father and son.

Unable to control the burning anger inside him, Matthew's father paced the floor, his hands clasped in front of him. Had he not been preoccupied with thoughts of Eva, might he have noticed his son was hiding on the farm? And what he had just witnessed had both shocked and disgusted him. What sort of boy had he reared? He had never been a violent man, but right now he wanted to give his wilful son a good thrashing. Turning, he grabbed hold of Matthew, his fists curled.

Aggie screamed, pleading with him to be lenient with the lad.

Instead of hitting out, he shoved Matthew hard in the shoulder. 'You're no son of mine.'

'I knew you'd be like this. That's why I kept quiet,' Aggie yelled.

'You've no idea what you've done, woman. The authorities will be upon us once they find out he's here. You've done him, and yourself, no favours. But I'll be damned if I'll hide him in my house.'

Matthew sniggered and went to stand up, but his father pushed him back down.

'For the love of God, Jacob, he's family.'

'Huh! Keep out of this, Aggie. He should have thought of that before joining up with the British. Leave me to deal with things my way.'

'What are you going to do?'

He ignored her and glared at his son, who was slouched in the chair with his legs outstretched.

Matthew got to his feet. 'Let me explain. You don't know what it was like.'

'Explain? I warned you. But, no, you knew best. Despite the pleas from me and your mother, God rest her soul. You broke her heart. You selfish oaf.'

Matthew straightened his back. 'Please, Father, give me another chance. I won't let you down again. It was bad. You've no idea. It was carnage. I saw Thomas gunned down. I got scared, so I ran.'

'Thomas dead! That's shocking news. Does Big Finn know?'

Matthew shrugged. 'Help me, please, Father? I've nowhere to turn.'

'You'll get no help from me.'

The two men faced each other.

'You think I don't understand how abysmal it is out there? I read the bloody newspapers.' He banged his fist hard on the table.

'Just listen, will you? The Jerries were advancing on Italy, and it was obvious we wouldn't make it out alive. I was worried about you and Granny. I can work on the farm. No one need be any the wiser. You can silence the workers. Threaten them with the sack if they tell.'

'Think, Jacob,' Aggie cajoled him. 'It'll all blow over soon. What's the alternative? He'll be sent to one of them internment camps.'

'You're both mad, delusional. The answer is no!'

Aggie folded her arms, the evil glint returning to her eyes. 'If you won't, I will.'

'Now you listen! This is my farm and from now on you'll no longer hide in my house.'

Matthew glared at his father. 'You're throwing me out?'

Aggie pressed a hand to her face. 'No! Jacob, you can't.'

'I bloody well can! He'll reap the consequences of his actions by earning his own keep. And if I ever see you raise a hand to Eva again, you'll rue the day.'

Matthew kicked over the chair. 'Who is she anyway but a paid skivvy?'

Jacob moved closer and slapped his son's face, then undid his belt. 'I'll skin you for that.'

Aggie screamed and moved between the two men.

'Aye! Granny was right, so,' Matthew said, soothing his face. 'I see how it is for meself.'

'Get out of my sight. I can't bear to look at you. You're a disgrace to me and your country. Now put your clothes on and get out, before I take a whip to you.' He shoved Matthew towards the door.

Chapter Twenty-nine

There was no sleep that night. Weighed down with misery, Eva had overheard the row that had continued until dawn. She was glad it was all out in the open, but the cost to herself had been devastating. The master speaking to her in such a way had been upsetting, but what Matthew had done was far worse. How could she tell the priest in confession that a man had touched her breast? And how could she tell Cathal? He'd never feel the same about her if he knew. He might wonder why she hadn't stopped him, and how it had come about. It wasn't her fault. But it was still a sin. Grappling with her conscience, she reasoned how she might have prevented it.

Dawn arrived and light seeped through the thin curtains. She needed the privy. The house was quiet, and she was taken aback when she found Aggie and Mr Blackstock sitting at the table, a row of dirty mugs, glasses and a bottle of poteen in front of them, as if they had stayed up all night.

'Ah,' Aggie glanced round. 'So, you've graced us with your presence after all?'

If she thought Eva was here to cook their breakfast, she had better think again! Eva glanced around.

'It's all right, Eva,' Mr Blackstock said. 'You're in no danger from him.'

'This is all her fault!' Aggie poured more drink into her glass.

'What do ye mean?' Mr Blackstock asked, looking bleary-eyed.

'Hasn't she told ye that she knew Matthew was back afore anyone, even took him food and clothes out to the barn?'

Eva paused by the back door. 'No, it wasn't like that . . . I . . .'

'Stop blaming the girl. You've had too much to drink.'

' 'Tis the truth.' Aggie swayed on the chair, her words slurred. 'She agreed to keep it from you and washed his clothes in secret.'

Eva's face went hot. She wasn't standing for that. She had to defend herself from Aggie's spite. 'Is this true? Did you know Matthew was back?'

'Yes, but it wasn't my place to tell you, sir. I wanted to . . . but . . .'

'Ye're a liar!' Aggie said. 'The likes o' *you* can't be trusted around men.'

'I'm not lying! It wasn't my fault.'

Jacob stood up, his face red. He turned on Eva. 'Why the hell didn't you say something before?'

She swallowed. Nerves made her desperate for the privy, and she clutched her stomach. 'The mistress told me not to.'

'She's lying!' Aggie banged her glass on the table, spilling her drink.

'I'm not lying.'

'Someone is – and I'll get to the bottom of it, don't you worry.'

'Oh, that's right, side with her against me. You should throw the trollop out now, with no further discussion.'

Unable to wait a moment longer, Eva rushed outside.

Matthew was chopping logs. He sneered and muttered under his breath, hitting the log harder. She heard it split as she hurried into the privy, bolting the door. So, he was still here, even after his father had thrown him out. There was no way she would want to stay here now.

When she came in, she expected Mr Blackstock to have gone to work and Aggie to have taken to her bed. To her dismay, he was sitting by the fire with his head in his hands. He shifted his feet, and his big toe poked through his sock. She had a wicked urge to stamp on it. That was one sock she would not be mending. He had always treated her well, but now she doubted his motives – and more so, she feared and loathed his son.

He glanced up. 'Come and sit by me, Eva.'

'Sorry, sir, I'm leaving, and I've things to do.'

'Please . . .' He gestured to a chair next to him.

She remained standing.

'Sure, where will you go?'

She shrugged. Anywhere would be better than staying here. If he was looking for sympathy, she had no words of comfort to give. Her own world was caving in. He stood to place turf on the fire; it shifted and settled with a hiss and a lick of orange flame. Eva blinked, then swallowed. How could she relax around him now?

'Sure, don't go. Matthew's conduct was . . . it was unforgivable. If you stay, I promise you it won't happen again. I'll make sure of it.' He leant forward, warming his hands by the fire. Then he said, 'I . . . we need you. We wouldn't manage without you. I'm not blaming you for any of this, Eva.' He reached out to her, and she flinched. 'I'd never hurt you. You know that.' He rubbed his hand over his face. 'God help me, he's my son, but I won't condone what he's done, or have any part in concealing him. It's against my principles.'

'I . . . I have to go now, sir.' She moved away.

'If you insist on going, I'll not pay you a brass farthing. Do you understand?'

She ran to her room, her mind in turmoil. She lifted the case from underneath the bed – the one full of clothes she had never worn. The other suitcase hid Matthew's British army uniform. A shiver trickled down her spine. She packed only what she needed and placed the case by the window. She strip-washed and changed into a pleated woollen dress with a wide collar, then slipped her feet into sensible block-heeled sandals. Wearing her tweed belted jacket, she was ready to leave.

Eva undid the catch on her window and climbed out on to the grassy bank, pulling her case behind her. With no wages and little money in her purse, she would have to manage. Where she would go, she didn't know, but she had to get away.

The sun shone, and all around her workers were tilling the land, their heads bowed. They appeared happy, and she envied them. If anyone saw her hurrying across the fields, she was past caring. She couldn't help her dark thoughts contrasting with the landscape, where trees and hedgerows were bursting with new life.

As she turned the corner in the village, John was walking towards the farm, his hands in his pockets. Eva dipped her head and increased her pace.

'Eva! Eva, wait. Where are you going?'

She stopped, dropping her case by her feet. 'As far away from this place as possible.'

'Why? What's up?'

'It's all right for you to talk now, is it?'

He shifted his gaze. 'Look, I thought, you know! You and . . . the master . . .'

'Oh my goodness! If you thought . . . well, you believed a pack of lies.'

'I'm sorry.'

'And I believed we were friends.'

'We were. We are. I mean . . . he told me to stay away, because you and he had an arrangement.'

'He said that? And you didn't think to ask me?' She picked up her case.

'Eva, wait. He gave me no choice.'

'There's always a choice, I know now.'

'But where will you go?'

'That's my business.' She walked on without a backward glance.

As soon as he was out of sight, she sat down on a bench to regain her composure. Angry that John thought so little of her, tears gathered in her eyes. The master! It was unthinkable. He'd made a laughing stock of her, and no doubt the other men in the yard believed the same as John. Her decision to leave had been the right one, and she should have done it sooner.

Chapter Thirty

Unsure which way to turn, she walked towards the path that led to the lake where she had found solace with John on Sunday mornings. Now she felt his betrayal, and it hurt. She looked around; there were no fishermen in boats casting their nets. It was quiet, apart from the skylarks warbling overhead and cattle grazing nearby. In spite of the peaceful setting, she couldn't rid her mind of what John had said and what had happened back at the farm. No one saw her tears as she gave in to her pent-up emotions. She had been let down in the worst possible way. Was it her fault? Would Cathal and Ma think so? What a mess she had got herself into.

She stayed a while to ponder her situation. She could see St Mogue's island; part of it had wide strips of tape around the site where the plane had come down. Two boys were rowing towards it despite a large 'Keep Clear' notice.

No nearer to a solution, she picked up her case and walked further around the lake. In a nearby field, a farmer was yelling and waving his stick, a black collie by his side.

At first she thought he was shouting at her until she realised he was directing his anger at the youngsters who were dragging fragments from the water. The farmer's white beard, and the wispy hair sprouting from underneath his battered hat, caught her eye. She had not seen him since the night Mr Blackstock brought him home, but there was no mistaking Big Finn.

Eva threw her luggage over the gate and climbed into the paddock. Engrossed in what the boys were doing, he had not noticed her. Carrying her case, she stepped through the tall grass, wetting her bare legs.

As she approached him, he turned round. 'What the dickens do ye think you're doing tramping across my land?'

'Hello, Big Finn. It's Eva. We met at Blackstock's farm. Don't you remember?'

His eyes narrowed, and he moved closer. 'Ah, sure, I do.' He glanced down at her case. 'Are ye going somewhere?' Not waiting for a reply, he dragged his gaze back to the activity on the lake.

'What are they looking for?'

'Souvenirs! They won't be told, ye know. Sure it's dredged and raked over and still they keep coming. Like vultures, so they are.'

The dog licked Eva's hand and wagged its tail, and she bent to stroke it. 'I didn't know you had a dog?'

'It's a stray. He comes and goes. What brings ye here?'

'I ... I've ... walked out. I don't work at Blackstock's any more.'

'Ah, sure why is that now?'

Eva bit her lip.

He touched her elbow. 'Will ye come in a wee minute?'

He leant on his stick, and Eva followed him towards the

house, hidden by trees at the far end of the field. It looked neglected like its owner.

'How've you been?' Eva asked.

'Ah, middling, only middling. Me rheumatism gittin' worse, so 'tis.'

'Have you been to a doctor?'

'Ah, sure I have me own remedies.'

Before he could question her, she said, 'Did you get your roof mended?'

'Amin't I still waitin'. It's damn bothersome.'

Eva couldn't wait to see inside the old ramshackle house.

When Finn pushed open the door, the smell of raw fish was revolting, and a clutch of hens ran in pecking crumbs from the floor. He walked ahead of her into a room cluttered with newspapers tied with string, bundles of clothes and sacks of grain. She glanced up at the high ceiling. It was damp, the paintwork yellowed and blackened, and she tried to imagine what it might have looked like in its heyday. His bed was by the fireplace, covered in heavy blankets and coats. He put a match to the kindling in the cast-iron grate and threw logs on top. The room came alive, and the place warmed up. The collie ran across the floor, scattering the hens, and lay down in front of the hearth.

'Do you know when they'll mend your roof, Finn?'

'Ah, sure they came and looked, then went away and came back again, but said they needed to order special rafters. I'm gittin' fed up waitin'. I'd do it meself if I was a few years younger.'

She shook her head.

'Here yer are.' He pulled up a chair for her to sit. He perched on his bed. 'Look, ye'll have a mug of tae with me.' He got up and walked towards the kitchen.

Eva followed. A drink of any sort sounded good.

When she saw the state the kitchen was in, she sucked in her breath. A black pan had toppled on to its side, leaving a trail of some congealed yellow substance. Broken eggshells lined the edge of the worktop. Cracked dinner plates with food stuck to them were piled up by the sink. The smell of stale food and fish made her want to vomit. She would love to clean the place up for him, but fear of hurting his feelings meant she said nothing. The table was littered with empty whiskey bottles, tins, and an opened packet of Jacob's creams with green mould forming.

'How do you manage?' She tried to keep the alarm from her voice. 'Do you have a woman to cook for you?'

He laughed, pulled off his hat and scratched his head. 'What would I want with a woman when I can look after meself?' He lit a small Primus stove. 'Sure, since most stuff is scarce, I live a frugal existence.' He filled an aluminium kettle; his arthritic hand shook as he placed it over the flame. 'We should go back in and wait a while.'

In the room, Eva warmed herself by the fire and Finn sat down on his bed. 'Well, now. Whatever's caused ye to leave is your business, but I know Jacob will miss ye, so he will.'

Eva shivered; she didn't want to talk about it.

'You make the tae. See if ye can find two clean mugs and I'll cook us a nice fresh perch. How's that sound?'

'It sounds grand.' How he would make that happen, she couldn't visualise. But she was famished and hadn't eaten since the previous day.

By the time she came back with the tea she smiled to see he had cleared a space on a small table and was chopping vegetables and parsley, throwing them into the pot hanging over the fire. He went outside and Eva watched as he gutted the fish, removing the backbone and revealing the firm white flesh.

Soon the smell of an appetising meal cooking over a roaring fire eliminated any unpleasant odours, and she couldn't wait to taste it. He opened a cupboard and took out two plates. He dusted them with the sleeve of his jacket, then he pushed the table close to the fire. He asked her to sit while he ladled the food on to the plate and lifted the fish from the pan.

'Get that down,' he said, handing her a fork he had wiped on a piece of sacking. He filled another plate and sat on his bed opposite her. In spite of everything she had just witnessed, it made her mouth water. 'When yer belly's full ye can tell me what's troubling ye.'

His kindness touched her, and she relished every morsel, pulling at the white fish. It was delicious, and she licked her fingers. Afterwards, her hunger satisfied, she looked up. 'Thank you, that was a grand feast. You're a good cook.'

He rubbed his hands over his middle and burped. 'Ah, sure, there's no cooking in fish. Now, what's up? Ye have to talk to someone and it might as well be me.'

Happy to be here with Big Finn, she didn't want to spoil it by talking about the Blackstocks. Besides, Finn and Mr Blackstock were close friends. She fidgeted, lowered her eyes. A black cat wandered in and Finn scraped the leftovers on to a tin dish. It lapped up every morsel and then rubbed against Eva's legs while she stroked its fur. It reminded her of Lucky, the farm moggy.

'Come on now, better out than in. Ye're too fine a wee girl to have the weight of the world on your shoulders.'

'Oh, Finn, I don't know where to begin.'

'Well, sure, start at the beginning.' He stood up and moved the table to the side so he was looking straight at her.

She told him about Matthew hiding up at the farm, leaving out the embarrassing bits. Relieved to have got that off her mind, his reaction should not have surprised her, and brought a lump to her throat.

'Glory be to the name of God! Jacob's been beside himself with worry over that lad. And what about my Thomas? Did he say anything about him?'

'I don't know. I didn't hear everything.'

'But, didn't ye know it was wrong keeping it from Jacob?'

Tears coursed down her face. 'I had no choice.'

'Ah, there, there. Don't take on so. Sure, I know what Aggie's like.' He patted her arm, then scratched his head. 'There'll be murder now, so there will.'

'What should I do?'

'Get as far away from here as you can. These are dangerous times, and ye could find yourself tangled up in something that's not of your making.' He sighed. 'Jacob won't condone what his lad's done.'

'He's thrown him out, but he's still in the yard.'

Finn nodded. 'Aye! It was Matthew enticed Thomas to join up. He's sixteen. Too young to be fighting them Jerries. It's obscene, so 'tis.'

'I'm sorry.'

'My Thomas has a kind nature. I've cared for him since his mother died and tried to stop him from gittin' involved.' His shoulders shook.

Eva put her hand on his arm. 'Can I get you anything?'

'There's a bottle of the hard stuff in the cupboard. Bring it, will ye?'

He offered her some, but she refused. He drank from the bottle. She should be off, but how could she leave Big Finn drinking and muttering to himself? When he lay back on his bed and slept, she pulled a cover over him and settled down on the old sofa. The dog whimpered and jumped up beside her. 'Here now, fella. Sure he'll be right as ninepence in the morning.'

Running back to Ma Scully wasn't an option – not now, after what had happened with Matthew. Cathal had been so kind to her. How could she face him now? But she must let them know she had left the farm. While the room was still light, she opened her case, took out her copy book and pencil and wrote.

Dear Cathal . . .

Chapter Thirty-one

Eva woke with a crick in her neck. Big Finn was bent over the fire, cooking eggs. She looked across at this remarkable man whose kindness had helped her through some dark days and who, in spite of being eccentric, had touched her life in so many ways.

He glanced round. 'Sure, I'm glad ye waited till daylight, so I am.'

Stretching, she stood up. 'What's the time?'

'The dawn's upon us.'

'I hope you didn't mind me staying?'

'Not at all. Do ye like scrambled eggs?'

She nodded.

He scooped some on to a cracked plate and handed it to her. He ate his from the pan. 'Where will ye go?'

'Ballyconnell.'

'Aye, I guess it's best. You won't go back then, to Blackstock's?'

She shook her head. 'Never.'

'Well, you know best.'
'Please don't say where I've gone.'
'If that's what ye want. Ye'll come back sometime?'
She nodded. 'I'll make the tea and then be on my way.'

Ballyconnell was the nearest town, and she might be lucky in finding suitable work there. The morning was dry, and the sky was brightening as she walked through the village. She hurried past the dirt track that led to the farm as the cockerel crowed. It was peaceful, apart from sheep bleating and cows mooing, their udders heavy with milk. It was a long road, and she wondered if she could walk so far. She removed her shoes, her heels already blistered. She plucked a dock leaf and placed it on her throbbing skin, then soldiered on. Once she had secured a job, she would pay Ma Scully a visit.

She had not gone far when she saw a dishevelled figure staggering along the lane in her direction. Most people in these parts were friendly, but she wasn't sure about the man approaching her. He was unsteady, wobbling from side to side. On his way home after a night of heavy drinking, she assumed. As he drew closer, her heart raced as she recognised him, and her grip tightened on the handle of her case. She glanced about; the lane was deserted. A tight knot unfurled in the pit of her stomach as she tried desperately to think how to avoid him. But before she could do anything, he was swaying in front of her. She cowered away and leant against the hedgerow, its spiked leaves piercing her back.

'Well, if it isn't the bold wee Eva. Where would you be going at this hour? Shouldn't you be serving the master his breakfast?' He lunged forward, grabbing her arm.

She saw arrogance settle across his face. The smell of alcohol filled the air between them.

'Let me go, you drunken lout!' She hit out with her hand.

Her suitcase dropped to the ground, the contents tumbling out. Embarrassed, she bent to retrieve them.

'Allow me. I'd better make sure you've not taken anything that doesn't belong to you.'

Eva pushed him aside. He wobbled but remained upright. Her fingers shook as she gathered her possessions into the suitcase. He grabbed her around the throat. She felt the breath leave her body as she sank on to the grass verge. He dragged her to her feet and struck her across the mouth, sending her reeling backwards. He fell on top of her, his hands everywhere. She screamed at him to stop, lashing out with her feet. He was pulling at her clothes, his hands up her dress, his fingers probing.

'Come on. You're not fooling me.' His words were slurred. 'That place you came from is full of girls with loose morals.'

She yelled, pushing him off with all the strength she could muster. He gripped her shoulders, sitting astride her and pinning her to the ground.

She spat in his eye.

He paused a second to wipe it away.

She scratched his face.

'Slut!' He slapped her again.

Her head hit something hard . . .

The sound of horse's hooves and wheels on gravel alerted him and he jumped up, stamping on her arm with his heavy boots before he escaped through a hedge.

'Miss, miss, are you all right?'

Eva opened her eyes. A man she'd never seen before was kneeling by her side. He removed his jacket and placed it under her head.

She sat up, wincing, straightening her clothes and pulling her coat across her. Blood trickled from her mouth. She stayed where she was, shaking, bruised and sobbing. Her arm was throbbing, her belongings scattered in the ditch, her bag God knows where.

'Miss! Who was that?'

Eva's tongue refused to work, and she stared up at the man holding her arm.

'Don't worry, miss. The blighter wants reporting to the Gardaí.' He helped her to her feet, then gathered up her things.

Dizzy, she vomited into the ditch.

'Look, let me help you. Where do you live?'

She couldn't speak.

'My name's James. Just give me a second while I make room on the cart.' Leaving the empty milk churns by the side of the road, this gentle giant of a man, who looked to be only a boy, lifted her into his arms and placed her down in the wagon, covering her with his jacket. Then he placed her case beside her. 'You'll be grand. Sure, it's lucky I came along when I did. That drunken fool needs his head boxing.'

Unable to utter the smallest of words, not even 'thanks', left her angry and frustrated.

'It's all right,' he said again, while she cried in silence. 'I'll take ye to me sister's. She'll look after you.' When he got no reply, he gigged up the horse, and the cart rolled along the quiet country road.

Eva screamed inside, but no sound came from her lips. How could this have happened? She could still feel Matthew's hands on her skin, touching intimate parts of her body. Oh, dear God, she wanted to die!

Chapter Thirty-two

The cart entered a track with twists and turns, the wheels crunching the rough ground and the sound punctuated by the chirping of birds. It stopped in front of a two-storey house in a clearing surrounded by trees. Eva ached all over and the pain in her arm increased. No longer frightened of what else might happen to her, she forced herself into a sitting position.

'Don't worry, miss, I'll soon have you inside.' Her rescuer kept repeating himself, and she hoped that he had a sister.

The house was neglected; blistered brown paint peeled from the door. In too much pain to care where he was taking her, she wished she had died in the fire along with her friends. As the boy helped her down from the cart her legs buckled and she dropped to the ground . . .

When she opened her eyes, she was lying on a shabby sofa and a strong smell of stewed tea permeated the air. A woman with a pleasant smile was sitting next to her holding a basin of red-stained water and a towel across her knee. Eva jerked upright. The sharp pain in her arm was a reminder of what had happened and a blush coloured her face.

'It's all right, dearie. You're safe now.' The woman placed the basin on the table. 'I'm Kate. What's your name? Is there anyone we can get in touch with for you?'

Eva shook her head. What was the point? She couldn't tell her.

The boy glanced up from munching bread and dripping, and sipping tea. 'Sure, I'd better be getting back for the milk, so I had, and on to Ballyconnell.' He stood up, picked up his cap, rolling it tight between his fingers. 'Do you want me to get the doctor, Kate?'

'Yes, ask Pat to call this way as soon as he can.'

'Aye! Do ye need any messages bringing?'

'Just the doctor, James.' She turned back to Eva. 'Is it your arm that hurts?'

Eva nodded. Kate handed her two aspirins with a glass of water and she smiled her thanks. At least her facial muscles worked.

'I put ointment on your bruised face and lip as you slept. I hope it helps.'

Eva sent up a silent prayer for these kind people and reached out her hand in thanks, then winced in pain.

'If we can get your jacket off, I'll take a look.'

With Kate's help Eva removed the stained, muddied coat and rolled up the sleeve of her dress.

'Aye! It's a wee bit swollen. The doctor will be here soon.' Kate stood up. 'James is my wee baby brother.' She smiled. 'But don't tell him I said so.'

Eva shook her head. The tablets were numbing the pain.

'Perhaps you could eat a morsel now, dearie. I'll bring you a soft-boiled egg and bread, then you can try and sleep. After that, you must think about telling the Gardaí about the brute who attacked you. He can't have been from these parts. No one would do such a thing. The sooner he's caught the safer we'll all be.'

If she did that, everyone in the village would blame her and it would get back to Ma Scully. And what about Cathal? She couldn't bear for him to know. She had heard of men doing this kind of thing, and women ending up with babies. Was that what Matthew had tried to do to her? If James hadn't come along, he might have succeeded. The nuns explained nothing and, with hindsight, she wished she had attempted to find out for herself at the library. Now it was too late, her mind and soul defaced beyond absolution.

Kate carried in the food and helped her to eat, cutting the bread into small portions. Her throat was dry, and the tea too hot. Kate poured some on to a saucer to cool and held it to her mouth. All her vain attempts to speak brought nothing but tears of frustration.

She had lost her voice once before, when she became an orphan, and it was months before she regained it. Please God, don't let this happen again. Just one word would be enough, for now.

Kate appeared to sense her distress and patted her shoulder. 'Try not to worry, dearie. You've had a shock and you're welcome to stay until you feel stronger.' She continued to help her eat. 'We struggle like everyone else, but we'll share what we have.'

Desperate to say something, her only means of thanking this kind lady was to open her sad eyes, wet with tears, and nod her head.

191

'James grows vegetables out the back and brings bits home from the farm where he works. I do the washing and cooking. Since our mother and father died we have been on our own. We're used to it. Can't do with interference from well-meaning folk.'

Eva nodded. While Kate went about her chores, she tried to sleep. Thoughts of what had happened made her want to hide underneath the blanket and never surface again.

She must have dozed, for when she wakened, a man in a brown suit was talking to Kate. His black bag was open on the table in front of him. Her pulse raced. Had he come to take her away?

'I know only that,' Kate was saying. 'She hasn't spoken since James brought her here early this morning.'

'Do you know who she is?'

Kate shook her head.

'Aye, by God! Someone does, and too well by the looks of things.' He cleared his throat and glanced across to the sofa.

Eva lay gritting her teeth and seething at his words. She pulled the blanket up under her chin. She was wearing her petticoat minus her ripped dress. Her arm hurt. A bump had appeared on the back of her head and she felt light-headed.

'It's all right, dearie.' Kate walked towards her. 'This is Doctor Pat.'

Eva swallowed. She'd had no reason to see a doctor before, and she didn't like this one's unfounded insinuations. Cringing inside, she rolled one hand over the other.

He picked up a chair and brought it close to the sofa. Eva shrank backwards. His bright red tie had greasy stains on it.

He gave her a cursory glance. 'There's no need to feel agitated.' He lifted her hand, pressing his fingers against her wrist. She could hear her heartbeat. Glancing up at Kate, he said, 'Those cuts and bruises will heal.' Then with his stethoscope he examined her chest. Sighing as if annoyed, he placed it back in his bag. He straightened up. 'Does your head hurt?'

She nodded. And raised her hand to show him where, and winced.

'What's wrong with your arm?'

Kate moved closer and showed him where a dark bruise had formed.

He pressed it and she cried out. 'It's not broken. It'll heal. However, you've a nasty bump on the back of your head. Do you know when that happened?'

Tears welled in her eyes.

'Answer me, girl! Yes or no will suffice. Do you recall when it happened?' He was anything but sympathetic, and Kate intervened.

'I don't think she can speak, Doctor.'

'Either the girl's in shock, or this silence is wilful, and I'd say the latter. I'll leave her something to ease the pain and call in again tomorrow.'

Kate frowned. 'Are you sure, Pat? She is trying to speak.'

'I don't want to see you taken advantage of. I've seen this kind of thing before.' He measured out the tablets and handed them to Kate. 'Young women who get themselves in trouble and prey on decent folk like yourselves.'

'But James saw what happened,' she protested.

Unable to defend herself, Eva flung off the blanket and swung her feet to the floor. She banged her fist on the small table in frustration, shaking and willing the angry words inside her head to tumble out.

'Now, miss. I know what you're up to,' he said. 'You may have done this kind of thing before, but you'll find your tongue when you discover you're wasting your time.'

Eva glared at him, feeling sick. She wanted to strangle him with his stupid tie.

'And if things went too far between the man and yourself, you must come and see me, so that arrangements for your safety can take place,' he said. 'Do you understand?'

Her eyes widened. He was the last person she would see. He blamed her for what had happened and thought she was taking advantage of Kate. Her anger mounted until she thought her head would explode. The doctor turned to go and Kate followed. Eva saw her slip a silver coin into his hand.

'You've little enough for yourself,' he said, dropping the money into a dish on the window sill. 'Sure, you're too kind for your own good.' He left, closing the door behind him.

Eva knew doctors were expensive, and she didn't want to be beholden to anyone – least of all Kate, who, by the sound of it, struggled to keep body and soul together. If only her tongue would work, she could explain. She picked up her handbag and fingered her letter to Cathal. Taking it out, she held it close. How was she going to post it when she couldn't even ask for a stamp?

'Is that a letter to your family? Does it have your address?' Kate asked.

Eva shook her head.

'Would you like me to post it for you?'

Eva took a penny from her purse.

'I've got a stamp here.' Kate searched the drawer and found one.

Eva stuck the stamp on the envelope, then passed it to Kate along with the penny.

Kate shoved it into the pocket of her cardigan. 'When James gets back, I'll ask him to pop it in the postbox for you.'

Eva nodded her thanks. Then she opened her case and took out fresh clothes. Kate, reading her mind, showed her where she could wash and dress. Her smile appeared genuine, and Eva could only rely on her mercy until she could communicate. As she dressed she remembered the lined copy book. Why hadn't she thought of it before? Excitement surging through her, she struggled to finish dressing and went back out. The notebook was missing. Her heart sank. It must have blown away when her case flew open during the attack. She found the pencil stuck in the corner. Holding it between her finger and thumb, she made swirly movements in the air. At first, Kate watched, a curious expression on her face before she realised what Eva was trying to tell her. Then she rummaged in a drawer until she found writing paper. Eva sat at the table and wrote with fury the words that swam through her brain, scribbling as fast as she could to explain what had happened and how it had robbed her of her voice, omitting she knew her attacker for fear it would go against her.

Kate's hands covered her mouth when she read Eva's account.

Chapter Thirty-three

When James walked in, Kate was comforting Eva. 'How is she? Did Doctor Pat call?'

His sister nodded, passing Eva's jottings to him. He struggled with the words.

She took them back. 'It's high time ye learnt to read.'

'Don't need no reading to milk cows.' He sat down, spreading his long legs.

Kate shook her head. 'I'm just glad you happened along when you did. Eva is one of the girls who escaped the orphanage fire a few months ago.'

'Are ye sure, she doesn't look like an orphan?'

Eva smiled, pleased to hear him say it.

'Amn't I telling ye so, ye daft boy.'

'Sorry.' He sat down. 'That's terrible, so it is. And now that scoundrel has attacked you.' He scratched his head. 'I should have gone after him. Found out where he lived.'

'He won't be from round here,' Kate said. 'Probably

down from Dublin.' She turned back to Eva. 'Didn't you like the work at the farm then?'

Eva shook her head.

'How come I've not seen you afore?' James asked. 'I'm sure I'd remember.'

Eva picked up her pencil. *I didn't go out much, except to church on Sunday.*

'What church do ye go to, so?'

It was a relief to communicate even if it was on paper.

'Ah, sure we're Church of Ireland,' Kate said. 'We mix little with the villagers ourselves, do we, James?'

He shook his head. 'Sure, we eat what we grow and I earn a bit at the dairy. If Kate needs anything special, I go to Ballyconnell. Have ye ever been there, Eva?'

She shook her head.

James got to his feet. 'That reminds me, I'm away there now.'

Kate plucked Eva's letter from her pocket. 'Can you pop this in the post?'

'Do you want anything extra, Kate?' he asked.

'Just don't forget the flour and yeast.'

Days later, nothing had changed and Eva's frustration mounted. Would she be forever dumb? How could she support herself if she couldn't speak? These kind people had made it bearable for her but she needed to find someone who could help her talk again. She missed Ma Scully, and thoughts of Cathal made her heart ache to see him.

Eva was upstairs, resting on the straw mattress and wondering what she should do. The room was bare, apart from two large wooden boxes and a sack of meal leaning against the wall. She could hear muffled voices downstairs and sat upright.

Was it that doctor again? She got out of bed and dressed hurriedly, gritting her teeth as she pushed her arm into the sleeve of her dress. The small window looked out on to a vegetable plot and a hen house surrounded by trees and shrubs. The isolation had suited her, but now she was ready to leave.

She was sitting on the bed, her feet bare and unprepared, when Kate ushered the doctor upstairs. He stood facing her, his back to the window. She didn't like this man and if he thought he could lock her away somewhere, she would refuse to go with him.

He turned to Kate. 'Have we regained the use of our tongue, then?'

His scathing remark annoyed Eva. Had Kate not explained? Eva knew how the system worked and this man had the power to institutionalise her. She would not let that happen, not again.

He scratched his forehead. 'I hear you were one of the surviving orphans. How did you come to be working around here?'

She stared ahead of her, her eyes motionless.

He sighed.

Kate's hands were clasped in front of her. 'I've explained, Pat. Isn't there something you can do to help her?'

'Aye, maybe!' He moved closer, lifted her arm and held it upright. It hurt, but she wouldn't satisfy him by flinching. 'That appears to be much better. Now, there's someone I'd like you to see in Dublin. You'll be well enough to travel tomorrow. I'll leave details with Kate.' He got up and Kate followed him out, closing the door behind her.

Was that someone to help her speak, or something else? Eva didn't trust him. She listened through the door. Kate and the doctor were talking on the landing.

'Give her this card when she leaves. She must go there, the alternative is an institution. I'll drop a line to Mr Dummit today.'

'Will he be able to help her?'

'Depends.'

'What do you mean?' Kate sounded concerned.

'If it's selective muteness, and she's doing it to gain sympathy, then shock treatment might be the answer.'

'Does it work?'

'Aye, we must wait and see. Make sure she doesn't waste his time by not turning up. He's a busy man.'

When she heard the front door close, she pushed her belongings into her case. She smoothed her long hair with her hand, shuffled her feet into her shoes, and struggled into her coat. She checked her bag and counted the money she had. It wasn't a lot; she wished now that she had not been so hasty but waited for her wages from Mr Blackstock. If she had, she might not have found herself here in this situation. Would Kate try to stop her from leaving? She hoped not. Eva would have liked to repay her kindness, but all she could do was scribble a thank-you note and leave it on the bed.

Kate was down the garden by the hen shed, so this might be a good time. Carrying the case made her arm ache by the time she reached the hall. Struggling with luggage would only slow her down, so she left it behind. With her handbag over her shoulder she crept from the house.

Her heart heavy with anticipation, she ran back along the gravelled path, her eyes blinded by tears, too troubled to notice or smell the primroses, bluebells and forget-me-nots and the new life bursting forth on every tree, until she reached the road to God knows where.

Cathy Mansell

The world was becoming a more complicated place for Eva; she longed to communicate, to find employment somewhere she would feel safe. Was it only a week ago that she had spent time with Big Finn? She thought about Ma Scully, and in spite of her resolve not to trouble her, she was the only person who could help her now. If she didn't, she could end up at the mercy of hypocrites like Doctor Pat.

Cathal would probably never speak to her again. But one thing she was sure of – what had happened with Matthew would never happen to her again.

200

Chapter Thirty-four

Jacob Blackstock found it difficult to come to grips with his son's desertion and Eva disappearing like that. Aggie, who was doing the kitchen chores and making a hell of a din, made his head ache. Her disagreeable nature had worsened and early mornings hadn't sweetened her tongue. This morning she hadn't a good word to throw a dog. He did not trust her where his son was concerned and wondered what went on inside that head of hers. The porridge had been insipid, and he pushed aside his plate – with bacon burned to a crisp – and massaged his temples. Matthew deserting his post had turned their lives upside down and caused Eva to leave. She had been worth every penny he paid her, and more. He missed her sweet nature. If only he hadn't let slip his feelings for her! He should have been aware of how it might have appeared to a young convent girl. He had grown fond of her, more than he had any right to. And Ma Scully would have his guts for garters if she thought he had anything to do with her disappearance. Any day now, she would be down to find out what had happened.

He hadn't set eyes on his son for days and he hoped Matthew had taken his advice and given himself up. Aggie's vendetta towards him had continued, and she still believed they could keep Matthew hidden. Over his corpse would that happen.

His thoughts were interrupted by Aggie lifting dirty plates from the table and throwing them into the sink of soapy water, splashing the floor.

'Isn't it time you went to work?' Her tone was acid. 'You should be ashamed, turning your back on your own.'

His chair scraped the stone floor as he stood up. He pulled on his jacket and stepped into his boots.

Aggie waved her arm, her sleeves rolled up to the elbow. 'You and your principles. And another thing! You'd better get an honest woman from the village to skivvy for ye.'

Jacob glared at her. 'I'll not be setting on anyone. If you'd been kinder to Eva, she wouldn't have left. It's about time you did your share.' He went out, banging the door behind him.

On the way towards the fields, men glanced across at him. He was past caring what his workers thought. He knew he should have handled things better. Matthew had witnessed horrendous scenes at the front. As a father he should have shown sympathy, but the lad had irked him. Too damn cocky for his own good. Aggie would do all she could to discredit Eva, if it meant saving Matthew. She was a law unto herself. Angry to have lost Matthew for the second time, Aggie had taken to her room, wallowing in self-pity. More often than not, it was he who put a meal on the table.

Eva arrived in Cavan, her heart heavy. Her arm ached as she walked towards Ma Scully's cottage. She lifted the brass knocker and waited. There was no answer, and she tried the door. Ma always left it open if she was home. Despondent, she turned to go when a neighbour from across the street opened her window.

'Sure, if yer looking for Ma Scully, she's helping Lily Moran give birth to her first babby.' She chuckled. 'She could be a wee while now. Ye can come over and wait if you like?'

As much as she wanted to, Eva couldn't cope with her speech predicament so shook her head and smiled.

'Please yerself,' the woman yelled, shutting her window.

There was nothing she could do if the woman thought her unfriendly. Eva walked towards the cathedral – one place she would find sanctuary and rest a while.

Inside were two devout worshippers, their heads low in prayer. She knelt before the altar and offered her own silent prayer to God. The nuns used to say, 'Try listening to God's will and He'll speak to you.' This time she was sincere, and she hoped He would hear her. She sat a while but all she heard were the mutterings of prayers. She recalled the nun's words: 'When men do bad things, it's always the girl's fault.' If that was true, she would burn in hell's fire. She stayed a while, then genuflected and left the church.

Back at Ma's a group of women wrapped in shawls had gathered outside, chatting about the new baby girl.

Ma was saying, 'Anyone would think there'd never been a babby born in the street before.' When she saw Eva, she moved towards her and placed her arms around the girl. 'Where in the name of God have ye been?'

A sob choked in Eva's throat and Ma ushered her inside, away from the glare of curious stares. She pulled out a chair and Eva dropped on to it; her black hair fell over her face.

'Sure, I've not heard a jot from ye in over a week and now ye turn up like a lost penny.' She removed her coat and unpinned her hat.

Eva glanced up. Ma was flushed and looked tired. She must have been up most of the night and was ready for her bed. Now, here she was about to unburden herself.

Ma poured a glass of water and handed it to her. 'Have ye nothing to say for yourself?'

The glass slipped from Eva's grasp, leaving a pool of water on the linoleum floor.

'What's wrong with ye?' Ma retrieved the broken glass.

Eva stood up, then bent to mop up the water. She felt dizzy.

Ma helped her to a chair by the fire. 'I gather ye've not eaten.' She put broth into a mug and handed it to her.

Eva placed her hands around the cup and supped. In her hurry to get away she hadn't bothered to eat, and all the way to Cavan town she had worried about telling Ma what had happened.

'God in heaven, child, can't ye tell me where ye've been? I've been out of my mind with worry until Cathal told me about your letter. Sure, if it hadn't been for Lily Moran's baby, I'd a gone to the farm to see what had caused you to leave.'

Eva looked up, and her eyes pooled with tears.

'Perhaps after a sleep you'll feel like talking.' Ma patted her arm, and she winced. 'What's the matter? There's something not right, what is it?'

All Eva could do was cry.

'I can't help if ye don't tell me what's wrong.'

Eva got to her feet and opened the drawer where Ma kept writing paper, pen and ink. She sat at the table and wrote.

Tears cascaded down her face, and her fingers shook. When she had finished, her arm ached.

Ma, who had been glancing over her shoulder as she wrote, exclaimed, 'My poor wee girl. Do you know who it was? Was he one of the farm hands?' A worried frown wrinkled her brow. 'Did he . . . did he interfere with ye? I have to know. You don't want to land yourself in the family way, do you?'

It would be the worst thing she could imagine. She paced the room. She would never forget the evil in Matthew's eyes. But how could she say who, without adding to her distress? She sat down, twisting her hands in her lap. It was a bad thing he had done. But would that give her a baby? Oh God, her memory was patchy.

'You mustn't shield him if he has. Tell me, Eva.' Ma moved closer. 'Did he hurt ye down there? The drunken bastard.'

Eva choked on a sob, placed her head in her hands and wept.

Chapter Thirty-five

When Jacob Blackstock arrived, Big Finn was round the back chopping logs. The collie barked and growled.

'He's forgotten ye, Jacob. Where have ye been this past week?'

'Lost track of time.' Jacob stroked the dog.

It wagged its tail, stretched out on the grass, head on paws, and closed its eyes.

'Sure, I'm sorry, Finn. It's been difficult to get away. How have you been?'

Finn stopped working and wiped his hand across his forehead. 'Aye, they're sending back Thomas's personal effects.' He looked into the distance. 'Where did it all go wrong?'

'I've asked myself the same question. Hindsight is a wonderful thing. Sure, this war is taking its toll on our Irish boys as well as the Brits.'

Finn limped inside and Jacob followed. He moved a pile of newspapers from a chair and sat down. Finn poured whiskey into mugs and handed one to Jacob. 'I know ye don't partake but with the world the way it is.'

Jacob took the proffered drink. 'I've not seen Matthew in days. Can't trust that Aggie hasn't.'

'Well, sure, he's alive. Thomas is dead.'

Jacob felt sick. He knew he would have to take the flack for his son's actions for the foreseeable future. God forgive him, but he wished Matthew had never come back.

'I've heard he's been in the pub of an evening, his tongue loosened with the drink,' Finn said. 'Ah, sure they'll catch him sooner or later. He's a traitor and deserves to be court-martialled.'

Jacob sipped the whiskey. He took no offence. He'd have felt the same in Finn's shoes. He shifted in the chair. 'So, he's still in the village?'

Finn shrugged. 'Looks that way. And ye know folk round here won't keep quiet. I'm surprised you haven't turned him in.'

He had wanted to, but hoped Matthew would hand himself in, saving him the embarrassment. Now he had no choice. He should leave before an argument developed between himself and Finn. Fair or not, Finn blamed Matthew for Thomas's death. Neither boy would get much sympathy, he was sure of that.

'Ye've seen no more of the girl, Eva, then?' Finn broke the awkward silence.

'No, she upped and left without a by your leave. Why do you ask?'

'She called here a week ago, so she did.'

'And you never said? So, where is she now?'

'I don't know, Jacob. I don't think she'll be back. And if that lovely wee lass gits in bother over your lad's lies, you and I will have a serious fallin' out.' He shook his head. 'It's a right how-do-ye-do.'

Jacob nodded. 'Aye, 'tis.' He got up. 'It was good to chew the cud with you, Finn. I'd best be off. The farm won't run itself.'

After another sleepless night, Jacob drew back the curtains on the kitchen window and looked out at the muddy yard. He had hoped to have it filled in, but with the war on it became more important to grow crops and keep the farm ticking over. A streak of pink light in the sky made him think it might be a fine day until he glanced towards the footpath that led to the village. He could see the bright headlights of a car stopped in the road. A uniformed officer surveyed a map spread across the bonnet. The military! It hadn't taken them long. Someone had got there before him. He took a deep breath and braced himself before knocking on Aggie's door. 'Come on, get up. They're here.'

As he waited for her to emerge, he went into the front parlour. The car was now winding its way along the narrow lane towards the farm.

Aggie, her hair in curlers, her dressing gown dragged across her thin body, came in behind him. 'Who did ye say is calling at this hour of the morning?'

Jacob raised his eyebrows. 'The military police.'

Aggie ran back to her room and turned the key in the lock. Jacob straightened his shoulders before opening the door to two uniformed men who then barged inside without an invitation. 'Irish military police, and we believe,' one man began, 'that Private Matthew John Blackstock, who absconded his post in the British army, is at this address.'

Agitated by their attitude, Jacob stood aside. 'He's not here. Where did you get your information from?'

'We are not at liberty to say. Who are you, sir?'

'His father.'

'It states here,' he shook out a document, 'that your son has been absent without leave for over thirty days. If he had returned within the time limit, he may have received a lighter sentence, but as things stand—'

'Where is he?' the second man demanded. 'I'm obliged to inform you that you, and anyone else living in the house who knows of his whereabouts and doesn't report him, could be in serious trouble. Your son is a traitor who willingly joined the British forces fighting in the African campaign before he absconded.'

Jacob felt the life drain from him.

'Give him up now, or things could become complicated.'

Aggie emerged from her room, fully dressed. 'You heard my son-in-law, he's not here. And wherever he is, I hope you never find him.'

'Oh, we'll find him all right. He won't get far. We have men in the village.'

Aggie sniffed.

The two men searched Matthew's room, pulling out beds and moving furniture.

'What are you looking for?' Jacob asked.

'Evidence he's been here.'

'You won't find any,' Aggie sneered.

They continued to search leaving nothing to chance, opening drawers and cupboards.

'If you know his whereabouts or have been harbouring him, you will be charged with not only aiding and abetting but wasting army time.'

'We don't know,' Jacob said, but he knew they weren't convinced.

They opened the door to Eva's room, and he followed them inside.

'Who sleeps here?'

'Nobody.'

One of the officers picked up a bottle of lavender water from the window ledge. 'Who owns this then?'

'It belonged to the kitchen maid. She no longer works here.' Jacob noted how tidy she had left it. He glanced at the bike up against the wall and sighed.

'What's her name?'

Jacob hesitated. 'Does that matter?'

'It might, sir. Was she acquainted with your son? Maybe ran off with him?'

'No, no. It wasn't like that.'

Aggie, her arms folded, was listening at the door. 'I wouldn't put it past her.'

Jacob glared round at Aggie. 'She had nothing to do with this. She left of her own accord. Can't you see my son's not here?'

They continued searching. 'What's this?' Eva's large case was hauled from underneath the bed and flung open. 'Are you sure she's not here?'

Jacob looked on, astounded, when they held up the muddy khaki uniform.

'He's been here. And if the girl's innocent, why hide this in her room?'

Jacob shook his head. 'I've no idea how that got there.'

'Right then,' said the first officer, placing the uniform back inside the case. 'We'll take this as evidence. We'll need the name and address of this kitchen maid, so we can speak to her. You have her details, Mr Blackstock?'

'That's nonsense!'

'So, your son put it there, did he?'

'How should I know?' He went to his desk in the parlour and returned with Eva's details. 'This is all a misunderstanding.'

'We'll establish that for ourselves, sir.'

Aggie sniggered. 'I told ye she was no good, but would ye listen? Why else would she hide his uniform? She's as guilty as he is.'

'If you know that for certain, madam, you must go to the local station and make a formal statement.'

'Don't be ridiculous. I'm not going anywhere until I know my grandson's safe.'

'Look, officer,' Jacob said, 'will you let me know if you find him? I need to speak to my son.'

They walked to the door. 'Oh, we'll find him. And you'll be told when and where you can see him.'

Once they had left, Jacob turned on Aggie. 'You know full well that Eva's not involved with Matthew, and if you dare to make a false statement against the girl, you may have to refute it later in a court of law.'

Chapter Thirty-six

Ma Scully hadn't judged her and had shown her every sympathy – even prepared a hot tub for her in front of the fire, handing her a towel and soap. 'You have a wee soak now and call me if ye need anything.'

Left alone, Eva broke down, sobs shook her body. Having to write out what had happened to her had been embarrassing. And the thought of Cathal finding out filled her with despair.

As she scrubbed herself clean, she wished she could wash away the memory of Matthew Blackstock's hands creeping over her skin. She shivered, her mind full of dark thoughts. Praying for strength, she struggled into the clothes Ma had left out for her. Then she helped to drag the bath outside and empty the water.

Eva sat staring at the range, going over everything that had happened and what she had overheard at Kate's. What would she do if her voice didn't come back? She couldn't expect Ma to look after her forever.

'Sit to the table, Eva, love. I've made ye poached eggs on toast.'

Her negative thoughts interrupted, Eva pushed back a strand of wet hair and stood up. She hadn't eaten for hours and it looked appetising.

'That skirt needs a tuck here and there, but it's not a bad fit. Navy and white suits ye.'

Eva could tell that Ma was trying to make light of the situation. But once she knew who her attacker was, there would be hell to pay. Eva struggled to use the knife and fork.

'Is your arm still hurting?'

She nodded.

'Try to eat something and then, when you're ready, I'll take ye across to the hospital and have someone look at it.'

It was late afternoon when Eva walked with Ma Scully to the hospital. She wore white sandals and her thick black hair, still damp, cascaded down her back. As they approached, Eva tensed. The dull grey facade of the building reminded her of the orphanage. She paused, her pulse racing. Once she went inside, she might never see the light of day again.

'It's all right, Eva. Don't worry. I'll not be leaving ye here.'

Ma's words reassured her. But, just the same, she knew how persuasive doctors with authority could be.

Inside, the smell of disinfectant was overpowering. They were shown into a room where Ma explained to the doctor why they'd come. Eva sent up a prayer that the doctor could help her recover her voice.

After checking her throat and asking her to say, 'Ah!' which she could not, he said, 'Umm. This kind of thing is not unusual and can be caused by trauma. Has anything happened that might have contributed to your muteness?'

She sucked her bottom lip.

'Some drunken sod attacked her, and in broad daylight,' Ma interjected. 'Left her for . . .'

The doctor raised his hand. 'Let the girl try to answer for herself.'

'If she could do that, we wouldn't be here now, would we?' Ma sat back with an indignant look on her face.

'Miss,' he continued to address Eva. 'Yes or no will suffice.'

She did her best to form a word, any word, to no avail. Frustrated tears dropped on to her hands, folded in her lap.

'You must keep trying and don't give up, sounds will emerge. Start by practising the sound umm-umm instead of nodding your head, and try forming the letters of the alphabet.'

'Is that all ye can do?' Ma asked.

He nodded. 'Shock treatment can work for some but—'

'Ye can forget that,' Ma said.

'In that case, there's no more I can do. Time, patience and encouraging the girl to talk can help.' He cleared his throat, then said in a low voice, 'Has she been interfered with?'

Ma placed her arm across Eva's shoulders. 'She'll tell me when she's good and ready.'

'By then it could be too late.'

Uncomfortable, Eva fidgeted with her hands. She hated being talked about.

The doctor stood up and placed a gentle hand on Eva's arm. 'I will have to examine you.'

Eva eyes widened.

'No need to be frightened. I can call in a nurse if you'd find it easier.'

Ma was on her feet. 'If there's nothing you can do to help her regain the use of her tongue, we'll leave it there.'

The doctor sat back behind his desk. 'In view of the circumstances that have befallen this young woman, are you prepared to take responsibility for her?'

'I brought her here, didn't I? Now what about this X-ray?'

He walked ahead of them towards the X-ray department, where he left them. They were not alone, and sat down next to a row of people. A strong smell of antiseptic and other hospital smells Eva couldn't identify made her anxious; she couldn't wait to get outside again.

The X-ray showed she had a fractured bone in her elbow. 'You must be in considerable pain,' the nurse said and handed her a tablet with water.

Her arm was placed in a sling and she was handed a box of pills.

'Take one of these three times a day with water. They will make you sleepy. And try to rest it for a few days.'

That night, Eva slept in Cathal's bedroom. The tablets the doctor had given her made her drowsy and helped her to relax. Before she went to sleep, she prayed to all the saints she could think of, imploring them to help restore her voice. The wonderful day she had spent with Cathal in Dublin seemed but a distant memory, and she drew comfort from it as she drifted off.

In the middle of the night, loud screams woke her but she couldn't force her eyes open. Matthew was holding her fast, looming down over her, his face close to hers. A revolting smell of alcohol made her gag. He was crushing her to the ground. She couldn't breathe and was unable to stop herself from falling deeper and deeper into a long dark hole like a grave. Each time she clawed her way back up, his sinister face loomed before her, horns protruding from his head, and with his large boot he pushed her down, down until her screams echoed in the hollow grave.

A guttural cry erupted from deep within her throat and she shot upright, drenched in sweat.

Ma rushed in, her hair in curlers and her dressing gown hanging off her shoulders. She sat on the side of the bed. 'Hush now, hush. You were having a bad dream. You're grand now, so ye are.' She stroked Eva's hair.

'Oh, Ma, it was horrible. I . . .' Realising she was talking, her eyes widened. 'I'm talking, Ma. I can talk!' She was shaking and crying at the same time while Ma rocked her back and forth.

'So, ye can. Sure, you will be all right now, so ye will.'

Ma and Eva stayed up drinking copious cups of tea and talking. In fact, Eva could hardly stop herself.

'You know, Ma, it's a terrible affliction not to be able to speak. I'm so happy now. And I'm sorry to have woken you.'

'Sure, wasn't it worth it?' She turned towards Eva and took her hand. 'I know it's upsetting, but if you know who he was, tell me?'

Eva picked at the fluff on the blanket around her shoulders. She couldn't bear to say his name out loud. But what choice did she have? It was bound to come out.

'Eva, love. Do you know who he was?'

'Matthew Blackstock. It was Matthew Blackstock.'

The colour drained from Ma's face. 'Blackstock's son!' She sat upright as shock registered on her face. Then she reached out to Eva and held her.

It was late when they eventually went back to bed.

Eva woke to a chink of sunlight that brightened the room. Before stepping out of bed, she prayed the Hail Mary aloud to reassure herself she wasn't dreaming. Tears streaming down her face, she thanked God and all the saints for the gift of speech. Being dumb had made her vulnerable, but now she wondered if she should have told Ma the truth. There was no telling what might happen now.

She swung her feet out of bed when she heard voices in the outer room. There was no mistaking Cathal's broad Dublin accent. Her heart skipped a beat, and a nervous feeling settled in her tummy. She slipped her arm from its sling and washed. A light-blue summer dress with a belt hung on the back of the door, and she slipped it on. Then she pushed her feet into white sandals. If Ma had known Cathal was coming, she hadn't said. Feeling better than she had done in days, she brushed her hair, sprayed on a little cologne and pinched her pale cheeks. Her arm ached after her exertions, but it bothered her none. She stood for a second to quieten her heart.

Had Ma told Cathal it was Matthew? How would he feel about her now? Would he blame her? Would he look at her with distaste? Hesitating, she sat back down. It mattered a great deal to her what he thought of her.

Her excitement diminished, she lifted the door latch and went out to face him.

Chapter Thirty-seven

Cathal was sitting at the table, nursing an empty mug, a serious expression on his rugged face. He wore a blue shirt open at the neck to reveal a triangle of dark hair. He stood up when she came into the room. 'Hello, how are you doing?'

'Sure, I'm grand.'

'I'm so sorry, you know, about what happened. Do you have any idea who the blackguard was? He needs reporting.'

She swallowed and glanced down at her hands.

'Come and sit down, Eva,' Ma said, getting up and moving to the stove.

Although pleased to see him, she felt awkward, and wondered how much Ma had told him. She lowered her head and her dark locks fell across her face.

Cathal reached over and drew her hair aside like a curtain. His hand brushed the side of her cheek. The sensation made her want to weep. 'You've no reason to hide, Eva.'

She glanced up at Ma Scully, who was pouring her a hot drink.

'Now, try to eat something. There's not a pick on ye.'

Eva swirled the porridge around with the spoon. She had no appetite. And she couldn't think of a single thing to say.

Ma handed her a jar. 'Put a smidgen of honey on top, it'll taste better.'

Cathal turned his mug round and round in his hands. He looked pensive. 'Thanks for your letter. All we knew was that you'd left the farm. We didn't know where you'd gone and we were worried.'

Ma nodded. 'Sure, it's behind ye now.'

She bit her lip. 'I'm sorry to have caused so much trouble.'

'You're not to blame,' Cathal said.

She felt ashamed, confused; she couldn't cope with the emotions crowding her mind. Their patience and kindness made her feel worse.

'Isn't it grand you got your voice back?' Ma said.

She placed her hand to her mouth. If it hadn't been for the terror of the nightmare, she would still be dumb and feeling embarrassed, sitting with the man she loved, unable to speak.

He cleared his throat. 'You've been through a shocking ordeal but once I find out who the blighter is he'll rue the day.' He placed his hand on her arm. 'Eva, you're not alone. You're with friends.' He pushed back his chair and stood up, filled his cup and offered to fill hers.

She declined, sensing his unease. 'Thank you. I don't want to be a burden on anyone.'

Ma turned round from where she was putting tins and produce into a wicker basket. 'You're not a burden, child.'

She smiled. 'One day at a time. Thank the Lord yer safe, and ye can stay here until you feel ready to find work again.'

What could she say? Knowing that Cathal and his aunt were on her side, and neither of them at all judgemental, was a huge relief.

Cathal stood by the window, looking out, and turned round. 'Were they kind to you, the people who took you in?'

'Yes.'

'Sure, Kate Connell's place is the back of beyond, so it is,' Ma said, pushing her arms into her coat.

'Her brother, James, saved me from . . .'

'Aye, he did that. And Kate's a good sort, keeps to herself ever since she had that lad of hers.'

'Isn't he her brother then?' Cathal asked.

Ma shook her head. 'Few know it. The less said about that the better. They helped ye, that's how I measure a person's worth.'

'They were both kind.' Eva fidgeted with her hands.

'Look,' Cathal said, 'why don't I take Eva for a stroll? Would you like to, Eva?'

It was better than sitting here tongue-tied, as long as she didn't have to talk about what happened.

'Aye! You two get some air while the weather's good. I'm away up the street and see how young Lily Moran's getting on with that new babby.'

Eva, her heart all of a flutter, removed her uneaten food from the table and, apologising to Ma, put her cardigan on.

'Sure, happen ye'll have an appetite later.'

Eva glanced towards the orphanage, the memories of the fire still raw. Cathal steered her in the opposite direction.

The sky was a clear blue, and he unbuttoned his shirt cuffs and rolled up his sleeves. Eva walked next to him, her arm supported by the sling.

'Sure, isn't it a glorious day, now?'

'It is, Mrs Keogh,' Cathal said, as the woman slowed down to look at Eva, then shifted her shopping bag before moving on.

'I guess you know most people round here.'

He nodded.

As they walked, she asked, 'How long have you lived in Dublin?'

He scratched his chin. 'Oh, a few years now. I went up for an interview for the Garda Shíochána. I didn't get it and stayed a while with friends. Serving the public was what I wanted to do, and once I got into the fire service, I moved there.'

'Do you miss Cavan?' She was glad to have directed the conversation away from herself.

He laughed. 'Not any more. Although I miss the fresh mountain air.' He took a deep breath. 'And the peaceful scenery that the people of Cavan take for granted.'

'It can also be lonely.'

'Yes, I'm sure, but that's true of anywhere.'

They passed a field with a row of haystacks. Eva inhaled the scent of new-mown hay mingled with wild flowers. Not all country odours were as pleasant as this. Blackstock's farm yard came to mind.

Cathal turned towards her. His well-toned muscles glinted bronze in the sunlight. 'Eva, why did you leave the farm?'

Her heart raced as she walked close to him. If she was to tell him, she would have to think about Matthew Blackstock, and she wanted nothing to spoil this precious time with Cathal.

She shook her head.

'I'm sorry, Eva. You know you can talk to me, I won't judge you. Ma told me what happened. And if I could get my hands on the louse . . .' He drew a deep breath. 'I don't suppose you managed to see his face?'

She hated not being truthful with him, and swallowed, shaking her head. 'I'm so sorry, Cathal. You don't hate me?'

'Hate you? Oh, Eva. I think you're an amazing young woman.'

At his words, a sob caught in her throat. This was more than she'd hoped for.

Neither of them spoke until they came to a patch of grass next to a fallen tree trunk. 'Here, come and sit down.' They sat side by side. 'I didn't mean to upset you, bringing all that up.'

She sniffed and he passed her his handkerchief. Cows chewed the green grass and bluebottles swarmed on fresh cowpats.

'This isn't the nicest of places,' he said.

She smiled, hoping he wouldn't ask any more about her attacker. His nearness set her heart racing. The sun was hot and she removed her cardigan and played with the buttons. Her voice had returned, yet their conversation felt stilted. She couldn't tell him that she knew her attacker, not yet. She looked into the distance, across fields and craggy landscape.

'Cavan has stunning views, don't you think?' Cathal said.

'Yes,' Eva replied.

He smiled. 'Sometimes you have to go away from a place to discover what you miss.'

'Were you born in Cavan then?'

'No, I'm Dublin born and bred. My father died when I was three years old. He was in the brigade, and on a rescue mission, when he fell from a ladder.'

'I'm sorry. How did your mother manage?'

'The service awarded her a small pension. It went on necessities. My aunt helped pay for my education and sport.'

'What sport did you play?'

'I played Gaelic football for several years. Then my mother died when I was nineteen. I couldn't get back into anything. Then two years ago I took it up again, but not in the same league. I play when I can. Work is very demanding.'

'Yes, it must be.' Eva was in awe as she listened to him talk.

'Afterwards, I spent more and more time in Cavan with my aunt. It was she who encouraged me to apply for a job with the fire service, something I'd always dreamed of doing.'

'I'm so glad you did. We'd never have met otherwise.' She felt a flush to her face. She had no idea why she'd said that.

Nodding, he smiled.

From the moment she had set eyes on him, in spite of knowing nothing at all about him, she felt drawn towards him, saw a depth to him with his kind and caring ways towards her and his aunt. Lines furrowed his brow, and as he turned his arm brushed hers, making her heart race. A curly lock of his hair fell across his brow. To Eva, he was the most wonderful man in the whole of Cavan. She glanced down at her hands, picked at her nails and hoped he couldn't read her mind.

'You won't have seen much of Bawnboy while you were working?' he said.

'Just as far as Port Lake most Sundays after church.'

'When I was a teenager, I cycled over there with a pal. We even brought fishing rods with us.' He laughed, and it was music to her ears. 'We got soaked when a thunderstorm broke, and Ma had a face on her when I returned without a fresh perch.'

She laughed, imagining the disappointment on Ma's face. 'You know, it's where the plane came down.'

'I heard. Ma said you could hear the explosion for miles.'

As they chatted on, Eva found herself relaxing more and more, and the past few days were banished to the back of her mind.

'When your arm's mended, we could do something different. I'd love to take you for a picnic, we could make a day of it.' He smiled down at her.

She swallowed. 'Thank you, that would be grand.' Being here with Cathal, uninterrupted, was all she could think about until he stood up.

'I guess I'd better walk you back, Eva. I have to catch the train this afternoon.' He helped her to her feet. 'And don't worry, you'll soon pick up another job, something more fitting than Blackstock's farm.'

'Is there much work for women in Dublin?'

He paused and looked at her. 'There will be when the war's over. Is that where you'd like to work?'

She nodded.

'A girl like you can apply herself to any job that takes her fancy.'

She beamed. 'You think I could?' She hoped he couldn't hear the loud beats of her heart.

He nodded. 'You won't always be in the situation you find yourself in today, Eva. Give yourself time.'

The awkwardness between them had gone, and he had given her hope, and that was all she needed for now.

Chapter Thirty-eight

That evening after Cathal's departure, the two women sat by the range, hugging cups of creamy cocoa. No one could make it taste the way Ma could. Eva mused about her walk with Cathal, and she wondered how she would fill the time until his next visit.

'Ma, how much did you tell Cathal about what happened?'

'Everything you told me, except who it was. If he knew that, there'd be ructions. He'd go after him for sure. He'll find out soon enough.'

'Thanks, Ma. I think it's best he doesn't know.'

'These things never remain a secret. But don't you worry about it. Just get that arm better.'

'Thanks for looking after me. I don't know what I'd have done without you.'

'Get away with ye, I'm just guiding you in the right direction, that's all.'

Eva nodded. 'Can I ask you something? It's about Cathal.'

Ma looked questioningly at Eva. 'What about him?'

She hesitated, then decided she had to ask before she let her feelings for him run away with her. 'Is he . . . well, is he, you know?'

'He's not married if that's what yer asking. At least, not yet.'

'Is he going to?' Her heart missed a beat.

'Who knows? He's been friends with a librarian by the name of Isabel for a while now, and he keeps promising to bring her down, but so far I've not seen hide nor hair of her.'

'Oh, is he? A librarian.' How could she compete with that?

'You're still smitten, aren't ye?' Ma leant forward. 'Oh, Eva, love. It's just a crush. It will pass once you meet someone your own age.'

Eva swallowed the lump in her throat. What she felt for Cathal was no passing fancy. She brushed a tear from her face. If Cathal married Isabel, she would want no one else; she would end up an old maid.

Hoping she hadn't made a fool of herself in front of Ma, she stood up. 'I'm just being silly and I've kept you from your bed.' She leant in and kissed Ma's cheek.

'Come on now.' Ma got to her feet. 'You've been through a rough time and need your rest.'

A few weeks later, when Eva went back to the hospital, she was delighted to hear that the fractured bone in her elbow had knitted and she could remove the sling. Her arm may have healed, but the scars left by Matthew Blackstock would take longer. However, she refused to let him stop her from getting on with her life. She had searched for work but so far her attempts had come to nothing. She visited the library, where she borrowed books and sat reading and looking up words she didn't understand in the dictionary. She enjoyed the peace inside the building; no one interrupted her concentration except in whispers.

After an enjoyable few hours at the library, Eva returned to find Ma sitting at the table. Her expression was enough to set Eva's pulse racing. She was holding an opened letter in her hand.

Eva sat down. 'What is it? Is something wrong?'

'You tell me. This came addressed to me, Miss Scully.'

She hadn't seen that look on Ma's face since the day she had caught her snooping in Cathal's bedroom.

Ma pushed the letter towards her, her eyebrows raised. 'What's this then? Something you didn't think to tell me?'

Eva swallowed the bile rising in her throat as she scanned the letter. 'I don't know why the police would want to question me. I've done nothing wrong.'

'Don't ye?' The older woman stabbed her finger at the letter. 'Well, that says different. I think ye better tell me the truth, don't you? And ye can sit there until I get it,' she barked.

Eva read the letter again. None of it made any sense to her. It said she was suspected of perverting the course of justice by concealing a British army uniform in her room at Blackstock's farm.

'Well, I'm waiting.'

She choked back a sob, then anger rose in her like a stimulant. 'Okay, I . . . I didn't think it was important at the time, and when my voice came back I'd forgotten all about it.'

'Dear God in heaven.' Ma slumped forward and placed her head in her hands. Then she glanced up. 'Oh, Eva, this just gets worse. What else don't I know?'

'He bullied me,' she sniffed. 'I was terrified. He told me to burn it and when I couldn't, I hid it in my case underneath my bed.' She blew her nose. 'I was an idiot. I had to get away, Ma, and when Mr Blackstock—'

'What about him?'

Fearful of being accused of something else, she told Ma about Mr Blackstock's outburst of affection for her, another reason she had to leave.

Ma stood up, her face a mixture of anger and frustration. 'Well, he wouldn't have stopped there either. The randy old swine. Oh, Eva, love. This letter is serious and you can't ignore it.' Sighing, she sat down again. 'There's two issues at stake here. The assault on you in broad daylight, that won't get house room. Not that I agree. It's the way of the world. But what will be more important is that you aided and abetted a deserter and hid his uniform. Can you see how it looks? The army won't let this go.'

'Oh, I'm sorry. I'd never have come back if I'd known this would happen.'

'You've been taken advantage of, Eva. Sure, it's no wonder ye ran away.' She straightened her shoulders. 'Look, pet, put the bolt across the door. I want no one walking in, or getting wind of this, until we've had time to think.'

Eva did as she was asked and looked round at Ma, her head bowed, her chin resting on her hands. Eva noticed the grey in the woman's neat wavy hair.

She placed her hand on Ma's arm. 'This is my problem, Ma. I'll just tell them the truth.'

Ma's smile was tight. 'You've no idea what yer dealing with. These are dangerous times, and no matter what you say, they'll look at ye and believe you were in cahoots with him.'

Eva's eyes widened. 'But that's not true.'

'You and I know that, but there's no accounting for what the army will believe.'

Eva gasped. 'Do you think it will go that far?'

'Look, we're clutching at straws here.' She reached over and touched Eva's hand. 'They know you're here. Black-stock will have given this as your last known address. I'll drop Cathal a line and get it in the post. He'll advise us on what you should do.' She went across to a small writing table, took out a pen and ink and began her letter.

It was brief. She addressed and stamped it, then she asked Eva to post it. Anxiety gripped Eva's heart as she slipped it into the green letter box.

Chapter Thirty-nine

It was Friday; the station was crowded. The weather forecast was good, and everyone had the same idea to get away for the weekend. Cathal took the train from Dublin to Cavan, on the Leitrim line, lucky to find a seat. He sat in the carriage pretending at reading the evening newspaper, his mind flitting from headlines about the war in Europe to his aunt's brief letter.

She would never write to him unless it was urgent. Did she know who had molested Eva? Reading between the lines, he assumed it had something to do with the Blackstocks. What was it all about? He couldn't wait to find out.

Eva had been on his mind ever since their walk in the country two weeks ago. She had, in only a few months, blossomed into an amazing young woman. Her calm beauty belied the passion he saw inside. She had the most kissable lips, and he had felt a pang of guilt to have entertained the thought in view of the ordeal she had endured. He was growing fond of her, and for someone to hurt her in any

way made his blood boil. He vowed that the lowlife, who-
ever he was, would be brought to justice.

He had plenty of time to mull things over at the inter-
change. His mind flipped back to his date with Isabel this
week. After the cinema they had walked along O'Connell
Street. He had been subdued, thinking about the actress
Merle Oberon in *That Uncertain Feeling*. It was how he felt
about Isabel, uncertain. Merle Oberon had a startling
resemblance to Eva: the eyes, and her long black hair. The
sensual curve of her lips.

'What are you dreaming about?' Isabel linked her arm
through his.

'Sorry.' He turned to face her. 'The woman in the movie.
She has such beauty.'

'You really think so?' she laughed. 'She's not that beautiful. But she's a good actress.'

'Oh, she is, beautiful, I mean.' He felt unable to stop the
emotion building inside him, making his eyes water.

Isabel paused and removed her arm. 'Jesus, Cathal, you
sound like a schoolboy with a crush on Merle Oberon. Is
this something you do often?'

'What do you mean?' He frowned.

'Go all soppy over a movie star! Only, if one day we were
to marry, I'd need to know these things.' Her lip curled in a
slightly mocking smile.

He laughed. 'Marry!'

'Oh, don't look so worried.' She shoved him with her
elbow. 'After we've both sown our wild oats.'

Cathal couldn't believe she'd said that. For a woman she
was very broad-minded.

'So, do you?' she insisted.

'No, not since I was a kid.' He'd cried at his mother's

funeral, and he recalled how he had wept when he failed to save all of the children at the orphanage.

'Cathal,' she shook his arm. 'Why tonight?'

He spread his palms. 'Beats me. I've no way of explaining it.'

'Don't forget Friday night,' she interjected. 'We're invited to a party in Foxrock. It's my friend Gloria's twenty-first.'

Isabel was far too racy for his liking. He was fond of her, but he had never intended to have a future with her. They were just good friends who enjoyed an occasional meal or cinema outing together. But when he got Ma's letter he had no choice but to cancel their date. He felt bad about letting her down at the last minute and had scribbled her a note of apology, posting it through her letter box so she got it in time.

When his train hissed into Cavan station, Isabel was well and truly wiped from his mind. He walked the short distance to his aunt's, lifted the latch and called out to her. He could smell bread baking in the oven. There was a half-empty bottle of elderberry wine on the table, a sign something serious had gone on.

Ma walked in from the yard, her face flushed. 'It's good to see ye, lad. I hope you can stay the weekend.'

'Sorry, Ma, I have to go back early tomorrow morning.'

She pulled out a chair. 'That's a shame. Anyhow, I'm glad you're here. Sit down.' Unsteady on her feet, she went to the oven, whipped out the soda bread, wrapped it in a tea towel and stood it up on the window sill to cool.

He realised his aunt was a little tipsy. He glanced around.

'Where's Eva?'

'She's gone to the shops. And I told her to take her time. I wanted to have a wee chat with ye afore she gets back.'

'Sounds serious?' He frowned. 'Is . . . is she all right?'

She sat down and leant forward. 'Yea, well, no. Listen, Cathal, you wouldn't fathom it.'

'What?'

'Things have taken a turn for the worse.'

'Ma, for God's sake, stop shilly-shallying and tell me?'

She glanced up, her eyes glazed.

'You've had too much wine.'

'No, I've not. Well, maybe! She needs your guidance, Cathal.'

'You mean Eva?'

'I wouldn't ask . . . only you know more about . . . this kind of thing.'

'What kind of thing?' Exasperated, he ran his hand through his curly locks. It was a long time since he'd heard her slur her words. 'Will you talk sense, Ma?'

She took the letter from the pocket of her apron and handed it to him. 'This came . . . a few days ago. Read it!'

Flummoxed, he leant back in the chair, frowning as he read.

'This is a serious accusation. It has Dublin Castle printed on the top.' He lifted the bottle of wine and poured himself a glass. 'What has Eva said?'

Ma blew out her lips.

'You'd better tell me what's going on.'

During the telling, he felt a mixture of emotions before pushing back his chair and standing up. 'That's ridiculous!' He ran his hand across his brow. 'After all she's been through. I don't believe she had any part in hiding that blither, or his uniform. Do you?'

Ma shook her head. 'I hate having to tell ye this, but it was him who attacked her and left her for dead in a ditch.'

'No!' He paced the room. 'That little weasel. God forgive me, I'll kill him with my bare hands. He can't get away with this. Has she reported him?'

'Humiliate herself! What good would it do? They wouldn't believe her, but turn everything on her. You know how the law works against women. That's what's so damn maddening. The army will do for him when they catch up with him.'

'But where's the justice for Eva?'

'I don't know, lad. He put pressure on her to get rid of his uniform and she, in desperation, shoved it underneath her bed.' She sighed. 'Sure, she was bullied and cajoled by the lot of them.'

'He'll pay for what he's done to Eva.' A dark expression clouded his rugged face. 'Do you think Jacob Blackstock knew what was going on?'

Ma shook her head. 'It's unlikely.'

'Well, I'll not let it rest, Ma. You know how I hate injustice.'

'Look, sit down, will ye? Don't go making a big thing of it. Not in front of her.'

'But it's against any good Christian's principles, Ma!'

'I know, sure don't I know. Let the military deal with the scoundrel.' She heaved a sigh. 'Sure, I was the one who trusted Blackstock to give the girl a chance, only to have his son abuse her. When she gets back, say nothing. On Monday she's going down the local Garda station, and she hasn't a clue what it'll be like. You could explain a few details to her. She thinks if she tells the truth they'll believe her. But you and I know better.' She sighed. 'Now let me open another bottle.'

Cathal shook his head. 'You've had enough wine, Ma.

You need to sober up before she gets back. I'll make you a strong mug of coffee.'

'Sure, it's not like me to let things get under me skin. But this business with Eva's upset me more than I thought. I'm glad you've come down, lad. Talk to her, will ye? I'll have a wee lie-down.'

Cathal sat with his hand under his chin. He couldn't remember feelings of anger like the sort that tore through him right now. And he vowed, there and then, to do all he could to get justice for Eva.

Chapter Forty

Eva's heart raced when she walked in and saw Cathal sitting at the table. Had she known, she would have come back sooner. He stood up to greet her. 'Hello, Eva. It's good to see you.'

'You too,' she smiled. 'What brings you to Cavan on a Friday evening? We didn't expect you so soon.'

'When I read Ma's letter I came down earlier. I want to help in any way I can, if you'll let me.' He remained standing, looking awkwardly at her.

As their eyes met, she knew Ma had spoken to him. 'Thank you. I can't believe what's happening.' A flush coloured her cheeks in the knowledge that he now knew everything. She glanced around the room. 'Where's Ma?'

'She's having a lie-down.'

'That's not like her. Is she sick?'

'She's fine.'

Being alone with Cathal in other circumstances would have delighted Eva. He was so nice, so handsome. The way he was studying her made her face flush more. She pulled at the sleeves of her dress. 'You must be weary after your journey. I'll move my things out of your room.'

Cathal waved his hand. 'Don't do that, Eva. I'll sleep on the settle. It's only for one night. Come and sit down. I'd like to talk to you.'

She couldn't look him in the eye. Talking about it would only compound her shame. 'I'll brew us a fresh pot of tea.'

He reached out, not far enough to touch her. 'Please, Eva.'

She sat down, avoiding his gaze.

He placed both hands on the table and looked across at her. She wasn't sure if what she saw in his face was compassion or pity.

'You can only stay for one night, then?' she said in a soft voice.

'I've things to sort out back in Dublin.'

In spite of how she felt, she wished he could stay longer. She couldn't help her downcast expression. He took a small notebook and a fountain pen from his inside pocket, gave the pen a shake. Then wrote something down.

'This is my station's telephone number. Put it somewhere safe and phone me any time you feel you want to talk.'

She stared at the six digits. 'Thank you.' She picked up her handbag, undid the zip and placed it inside. 'I'm sorry to be so much trouble.' She dropped her gaze.

'You've no need to feel embarrassed. This is not your fault, Eva. Me and Ma will see you get justice. But hard as it might be, we have to talk about this.' Without realising what he was doing, he poured her a glass of wine and another for himself.

Holding her hands in front of her, Eva said nothing.

He swallowed some of his drink. 'We know you've done nothing wrong, Eva. Substantiating evidence can be conflicting.'

A tear trickled down her face.

He placed a comforting hand on her arm. 'It's okay.'

It brought a lump to her throat, and she sat back in the chair. 'Ma doesn't think the Gardaí will believe me. You don't either, do you?'

He leant his elbows on the table. 'The truth can sometimes be hard to prove. That is why you need to have your story straight in your head before you go down there on Monday. You must stay strong and not let the sergeant on duty sway you. And trust me, he'll try. They'll want this cleared up fast. And will try to get you to confess and make their job easier.'

She looked up at him, shock registering on her face.

'I'll confess to nothing but the truth,' she retaliated. 'I won't be pressured into anything.'

'Good!' Cathal smiled. 'That's the reaction I was hoping for.'

'I'm sorry. This whole thing has made me jumpy, and I can't wait for it to be over and done with.'

'You can't do this alone. We'll be with you all the way. I want to see that swine get what he deserves.'

'Thanks, Cathal, but I'll be grand. Don't you see? I have to do this myself. Once they know the truth, I can get on with the rest of my life. Matthew Blackstock will not ruin my life, not any more.'

She knew he had heard the quiver in her voice, knew she was nervous. Despite that, she hoped he knew she hadn't lost her fighting spirit. He touched her hand and when she looked into his eyes, the depth of her feelings made her heart race.

Ma drove the trap with purpose up the gravelled pathway to the front door of Jacob Blackstock's farm. She could see workers across in the fields but the yard was quiet. She knocked on the door that Eva said they used on Sundays and for special visitors. Well, she was a special visitor. No way was she taking her trap into that filthy yard.

When she got no response, she hammered on the door until a sheepish-looking Aggie peered out, holding on to the door frame. 'Who are you, calling here at this hour of the morning?'

'Who I am is not important. I'm here to see Jacob Blackstock. And ye can drag that grandson of yours out from his hiding place while you're at it. I want to wring his neck, so I do.'

Aggie's lips curled. She pulled her brown dressing gown across her chest, her hair in pipe cleaners. 'Well, neither of them are here, so clear off.' She shoved the door to, but Ma wedged her foot in the crack and pushed it open. 'How dare you barge in here uninvited?'

Ma now stood in the hall, hands on her hips.

Aggie cowered back against the wall. 'Haven't I said there's no one here.'

'Well, I don't believe a word that comes from yer lying mouth. Now, are ye going to get him, or do I have to go through the house?'

Aggie's eyes widened, and she glared at her. 'I know you! You're that Scully woman who brought that troublesome orphan girl here, aren't ye? Well, she's gone, and good riddance,' she sneered.

'You never gave that young girl a chance, did ye? Ye miserable cow.' Ma made her way down the corridor.

'Where do ye think you're going? You're not welcome!'

'Welcome or not, I'm not going anywhere until I see Jacob Blackstock.'

Grumbling underneath her breath, Aggie went into her room.

Ma stood in the doorway to the kitchen. The place was worse than she had imagined. The smell of stewed tea, tobacco and burned food in the pan wrinkled her nose. She hesitated before walking on the muddy floor. Dirty washing and plates were piled up by the sink. The only glimmer of brightness in the gloomy room came from the fire. Ma pulled out a chair, wiped it down with a cloth and sat down. She thought about Eva working here, keeping this place spick and span every day, as she knew she would, and felt a pang of regret to have brought her here, where she must have felt isolated and trapped.

Aggie returned, dressed but with her cardigan incorrectly buttoned and her hair still in pipe cleaners.

Ma shook her head. This woman was something else.

'You still here? Now out, afore I call the men.'

Ma leant back in the chair. 'Oh, please do. I'm sure they'll be interested to hear how your so-called grandson attacked a helpless young girl and thinks he's gotten away with it.'

'He's done no such thing. She's made it all up.'

'We'll see who's making up stories. Now, get Jacob, because I've had enough of your spiel. And put peat on that fire, ye lazy good-for-nothing.'

'Who do ye think ye are, telling me what to do in me own house? And,' she sneered, 'if ye think I'm making tea, you can forget it.'

Ma chortled. 'I wouldn't touch a utensil in here with a bargepole. Now, are you going to get him?' She pulled her shoulders up to her full height. 'Or, do I have to take the place apart to find him.'

With that, Aggie ran from the kitchen like a scalded cat.

Jacob stomped into the kitchen, Aggie at his heels. 'What's all this about?'

Ma got to her feet. 'Oh, I think you know full well, Jacob Blackstock.'

Aggie's eyes flicked from one to the other. 'Ask her to leave, Jacob?'

'Shush, woman.' He waved his hand. 'Show Ma Scully into the parlour. I'll join you there when I get cleaned up.'

Ma settled into the only comfortable chair that overlooked the view outside. In the fields, workers were gathering the crops; she knew it was a busy time for farmers, with certain essentials still on ration. The room was neat and just how Eva had described it.

Within minutes, Jacob walked in. He wore the same beige jersey and blue shirt he'd had on when he called at her cottage begging for Eva's hand in marriage. The thought sent a shiver down her spine.

'Where's that no-good son of yours?'

'They've taken him to the Curragh detention centre. They'll show him no mercy there.'

'He deserves everything coming to him,' she huffed. 'And that won't be enough.'

He lifted a mahogany dining chair, moving it closer, and sat down with his hands knitted in front of him.

Ma stared at him. He was a decent type, and she could well understand his loneliness living here with that Aggie woman. But making a play for Eva! No, she couldn't condone that.

'Aye, you've come about the girl, Eva. I know nothing of her whereabouts, haven't seen her since she walked out of here.'

Ma leant forward and wagged a finger at him. 'I warned you, Jacob Blackstock. And if it gets out, your name will be mud. You should be ashamed of yourself.'

'I . . . I regret that, and I intended to apologise before she absconded.'

'Now, you listen, Jacob Blackstock, and listen good. You know what happened to Eva, and don't pretend otherwise.'

He looked confused. 'What? I swear I don't know what you're talking about?'

'Well, let me refresh your memory, shall I?' She leant in closer and looked him in the eye. 'Your Matthew tried to put her down and left her for dead in a ditch. He bullied her into hiding his uniform and keeping his whereabouts from you.' Her face was red with rage. 'What ye got to say about that then?' She went on. 'And as for Aggie, I could swing for her. She showed the girl no mercy.' She took a breath and sat back.

Jacob buried his face in his hands. 'Dear God Almighty, I knew none of this. I've been a fool.' He scratched his head.

'Well, you'd better do something about it. Have the decency to tell the military police she is an innocent victim in all this conspiracy, before she has to appear in court for something she didn't do.'

'I condone nothing Matthew's done, but, God help me, he's my flesh and blood. And Aggie, well, she meant well. Sure, she loves the bones of that lad.'

'I'm not interested in excuses, Jacob. Just do right by that innocent girl.'

He stood up. 'I'll see what I can do.'

'You'll do more than that. She deserves none of this, and you know it.'

'I'm sorry it's come to this.' He looked contrite.

'Your being sorry won't help Eva. She's appearing at the local Garda station on Monday morning at eleven. And you'd better let them know the truth afore then.'

'Well, sure, how am I going to do that? I've a visitor's order to see Matthew on Monday.'

She stood up. 'Let me down, Jacob Blackstock, and your name will be mud in these parts, not just because of your deserter son, I can assure ye of that.'

She swept out of the house the way she came in and climbed into the buggy. She gave the horse a light tap with the whip and it trotted away from the farm, out of the village towards Cavan town.

Chapter Forty-one

Monday morning was sunny when Eva, wearing a bright floral dress and a jacket with a buckled belt, walked down the street. Feeling only a modicum of fear, she passed the convent where men were working on the site. One workman startled her with a wolf whistle. She paid him no heed, her mind focused on where she was going. The sooner she got this over with the better. After all, she had done nothing wrong, and the sergeant on duty would soon realise that. She had had a hard time convincing Ma Scully that she would be grand on her own.

She glanced up at the small building with the sign Garda Shíochána above the door. Taking a deep breath, she went inside. Sun shone through the window, hitting the high counter and showing a coat of dust. She resisted the urge to rub it clean with her sleeve. There was no one else in there, apart from her and the sergeant behind the desk. He was writing in an open ledger, his pen making a scratchy sound. He was so engrossed in what he was doing, he hadn't seen Eva standing there. She waited, glancing about her. It was the first time she had been to a police station, and now a fluttering settled in her tummy. Would they arrest her? She straightened her back and swallowed when the tall policeman closed the book and looked up, placing his hands down on the counter. He blinked twice, removed his pipe and his moustache twitched.

'Well, now.' He smiled. 'It's rare we get a young girl coming in here. What can I do for you, miss?'

She relaxed a little. 'I've been asked to come here.' Taking the official letter from her bag, she moved a step closer. Reaching up, she passed it to him.

'What's this then?' As he read, his face reddened and his expression turned to alarm.

Eva thought he would have a heart attack.

He looked down at her, his bushy eyebrows knitting together. 'So, you're the young woman, are you? I'd never have believed it. You look like a well-brought-up convent girl.'

Eva felt her face flush.

'I hope you know this is a serious matter. You'd better sit over there while I make a telephone call.'

'Can't you deal with it?'

'No, I can't.' He picked up his pipe. 'This is far too important. It's out of my jurisdiction.'

'What do you mean? I've done nothing wrong, and if you'll just listen I—'

'Take it easy, miss.' He came out from behind his post, placed his hand on her arm. 'Please sit down. This could take a while.'

She thought she would be sick. The sun was beating through the window, making her hot. She unbuttoned her coat, put her handbag on the table and sat down. A clock ticked on the green painted wall and an eerie feeling swamped her. This was not what she had imagined. A large public information poster read: *Report Any Minor Disturbances Here.* Had she been fooling herself? This wasn't any petty annoyance, she was in big trouble. She swallowed and nervousness tightened her stomach. Why couldn't he deal with it? And who was he telephoning in the back room?

She thought about Cathal, his kindness towards her, and how he had encouraged her to stay strong. If only he was here now to support her.

When she looked up, the sergeant had returned, a grave expression on his face. 'This way, miss.' He lifted the counter flap and beckoned her to follow him into a back room where she had to sit and wait.

With no window, there was no sun. A table faced the door and four chairs were lined up against the wall. She sat on the chair nearest the filing cabinet with a wilting marigold plant on top. She bit her thumb-nail, and the silence unnerved her. With hindsight, she wished she had refused to do Matthew's bidding when he first arrived at the farm, but it was too late for regrets. If the truth wasn't enough, what else could she say to defend herself?

She had been waiting in the depressing room for over half an hour, with nothing but her own gloomy thoughts for company, when an army officer walked in and closed the door behind him. His uniform had two white stripes, the material similar to the uniform Matthew had asked her to burn. His buttons were polished to a high standard, as were his shoes. She wasn't familiar with army ranks. He looked hot and removed his hat, leaving a red rim across his forehead. He placed the hat on the table. Eva felt a tremor run through her. Her heart was now beating faster than a bird's wings. Without speaking, he moved across to the cabinet and plucked out a file. He lifted a chair and placed it in front of the desk.

'Come, sit here,' he said.

She stood up, her limbs shaking, and perched on the edge.

'My name is Officer Sherwood, Military Police. I want to ask you a few questions.'

Eva nodded, then lowered her eyes. Confused, fear gripped her, and she hoped she wouldn't lose her powers of speech.

He opened the file containing sheets of paper with rows of words and lines underneath. Her resolve to stay strong already weakening, she held her hands in front of her to stop them shaking.

'Your name?'

'Eva Fallon.'

'Address?'

His tone was cutting, and she didn't like his unfriendly manner. 'I don't have one,' she said, without flinching.

'Indeed! Well, it says here . . .' He inspected the duplicate letter in the file. 'You are living with Miss Scully, Main Street, Cavan. Is that correct?'

Eva swallowed. 'Yes.'

'And before that?'

She didn't want to tell him any more. His attitude irked her, and she wanted to get up and leave.

Before she got the chance, he bellowed, 'The sooner you cooperate, the sooner we can be on our way. Now, where were you born?'

'I don't know.' She sniffed. 'I think it was Dublin.'

'So what brought you down here?'

'When my parents died, I was taken to an orphanage in Cavan.'

He scribbled something down, then he glanced up. She thought he would mention the fire, but he didn't. 'So, when did you first come into contact with Matthew Blackstock?'

'Last month, when I found him hiding in the barn at his father's farm in Bawnboy.' She took a deep breath and bit down on her lip.

'Were the two of you sweethearts?'

'Goodness me! No, of course not.'

'How soon after he deserted did he get in touch with you?'

Eva's head hurt. 'No, he didn't. I'd never set eyes on him until that day. He's nothing to me.'

'Right, that will be all for now. We'll continue this interview in Dublin.'

Chapter Forty-two

Jacob Blackstock was dressed in his Sunday best, his morning newspaper tucked under his arm, and his prison pass in his top pocket. Anger raged through him. The farmer was under no illusions about his younger son. He had disgraced his family and his country and he couldn't miss this opportunity to make him understand the consequences of his actions. Discovering Matthew was a deserter had been a huge shock, and he wasn't dealing with it as well as he might. Farmers and gentlefolk alike showed their disgust by turning their backs whenever he came into contact with them. Today, he wasn't surprised by the looks of contempt that followed him as he walked towards the narrow gauge on the Bawnboy Road.

Aggie had begged to come with him, but he was adamant he was going alone. He had urgent business to discuss with Matthew; if what Ma Scully had told him was true, he had not only disgraced the family name but committed a vile act against an innocent woman he so admired. His plans to ask

Eva to marry him had backfired. It had been a huge mistake, no more than a lonely old man's fancy. But he had never meant her any harm.

Deep in thought, he had not noticed where he was, until the train hissed into the station. From Dromod he caught the connection to Dublin and then Kildare.

He had no idea where the Curragh was, so he took a cab and arrived just before eleven, his appointed time. It was a large open area with army huts and red-brick buildings like rows of flats. Each block was separated by small areas of patchy grass. Soldiers marched in groups while officers barked orders. It was a sprawling place in the middle of nowhere. With so many individual buildings, he hoped he was in the right camp. He looked again at the letter. Military prison, Tintown. At least it wasn't Spike Island, he thought, where he'd heard of the terrible conditions prisoners experienced. A uniformed officer in a jeep raced towards him, the wheels throwing up dust as he pulled up next to him and rolled down the window. 'You know this is a specified zone. What are you doing here?'

Jacob removed his hat and wiped sweat from his brow. 'I'm here to see my son, Matthew Blackstock. I believe he's detained here.'

'Have you permission to visit him?'

He produced his pass.

'You've come in through the wrong entrance, but if you carry on, it's the glasshouse at the top of the hill,' the man grunted. 'Talk to the CO in charge.'

Jacob's impression of the place was dire. Feeling daunted, he carried on through the camp, noting the harsh regime meted out to the prisoners, and wondered how Matthew was coping. Men in heavy khaki trousers and white vests were being made to exercise in the scorching heat, sweat pouring from their bodies. Perplexed, he continued towards the glasshouse, a strangely constructed building. Dust settled on his black polished shoes and the hot sun bore down on him, but he vowed not to weaken when he came face-to-face with his son; he would stick to his principles.

He arrived at the prison; it was mainly glass, constructed as a harsher punishment unit and well away from the rest of the camp. Jacob looked up at the barred windows and swallowed. The camp depressed him, and this place was worse.

Before he was allowed in, he was frisked and witnessed a visitor's bag being confiscated. He was asked to follow a guard down a long corridor with faded green cell doors on either side. The low ceiling was oppressive. He could hear the shouts of the men inside rattling their tin mugs against the bars. Finally, he was taken into a room with a prison warden on the other side of the door. He nodded but didn't speak. A line of tables and chairs ran the length of the room. Most of the visitors looked relaxed, as if they were used to coming here, but Jacob was mortified and sat at one of the vacant tables. No one spoke, and he felt the tension like a razor blade. A nerve in his jaw twitched, and he folded his arms. Then he heard the rustle of keys as the prisoners were brought in from a side door. Chairs scraped the stone floor as each prisoner sat opposite his visitor.

Matthew stomped in and sprawled on to the chair. A guard stood close by.

'How are you?' Jacob placed his elbows on the table.

'How do you bloody well think?' Matthew sneered. 'What have you brought me?'

Jacob glanced around. He saw no one handing over packages to the detainees.

'Is that all you have to say?'

'Hasn't me granny sent me anything?' Matthew's mouth tightened.

'Don't be an idiot! It's not a holiday camp.'

'I want a comb, soap and razors. Do you hear me, Father?'

'You can want all you like but you won't get it from me.' In spite of Matthew's haggard appearance, Jacob would not give him an easy time. 'Now, you listen here, boy! I know what you did to Eva. And I'm not the only one who knows. So, whatever the length of your confinement, you can add a charge of attempted rape.' He leant in close. 'No matter what you think of the law, lad, the army will take a dim view.'

Matthew laughed. 'And you think they'll take the word of a whore!'

'As unrepentant as ever! No, Matthew, the word of an innocent young woman whom you took advantage of.' He looked across the table at his wilful son, who had been a bitter disappointment to him, and wondered what life would have been like had his eldest son, Luke, lived. 'You can make amends for what you've done to that girl by admitting that you forced her into concealing your uniform.'

Matthew swore underneath his breath. 'Never! She got what she deserved.'

His father looked at him with contempt. 'You're a lost cause.'

'And you'd have me hanged, your own son.'

'You're no son of mine. Now, you've heard what I came to say.' He got to his feet. 'If that wee lass is charged with conspiracy, you won't see me visit here again.' He stood up, glancing across at the guard. 'Can you take me to the officer in charge?'

Matthew kicked over his chair, pushed past his father and stalked out.

On his way home Jacob replayed the scene that had transpired between himself and his son. He didn't regret a word of it. However, he felt a tear sting the corner of his eye. He couldn't let him away with what he had done. That boy had to learn the hard way.

When Matthew joined up, Jacob had convinced himself that he wouldn't survive – not only the harsh regime, but the front line. However, he had to end up here in this godforsaken place! The only hope was that he would come out a reformed character. Although he wished it, it was unlikely to happen in a place as terrible as this. For now, he had no choice but to do the Christian thing and report what he knew to be the truth to Matthew's commanding officer.

Before returning to Bawnboy, Jacob made a detour to Cavan town's police station. He was relieved to find no one waiting. He tapped on the counter and a young man popped his head up.

'Right! What can I do for you, sir?'

'Can I see the sergeant in charge?'

'Ah, sure, Sergeant O'Malley's not here, so he's not,' the young fresh-faced garda said.

'Where is he then?'

'Ah sure, I'm not allowed to say. He's away on important business, so he is.'

'Well, when will he be back?' Jacob was in no mood for riddles.

The garda doodled on his notebook. 'Sure, that could be any wee time. He's away in Dublin.'

'Dublin!' Jacob blew out his lips. Just his luck. He was about to leave, then turned round. 'Did a young woman come in here this morning?'

The younger man straightened his back and held the lapels of his uniform. 'Now, you know I can't divulge that kind of information, sir.'

'Drat! Write this down. Tell O'Malley that Jacob Blackstock of Blackstock's farm wants to see him as soon as he gets back. Have you got that?'

He scribbled in the ledger. 'Yes, I have, Mr Blackstock.'

Outside, Jacob breathed fresh air into his lungs. Had O'Malley taken Eva to Dublin? Dear God! If that was the case, he was already too late. An unsettled feeling churned his stomach. He should get back to the farm. Things were a mess. He wasn't sure who he could trust. Not those two young layabouts, John and Mick. The loss of respect amongst the men had been noted once it was known that Matthew was a deserter. But there was nothing he could do about that. Once he got home, he would, somehow, have to convince Aggie to drop her statement against Eva. If he was truthful, he missed Eva around the place; her honest, lovely face. He missed Mary too, and loneliness had made him think he could win the heart of a young lass.

He was about to catch his train when he thought about Ma Scully. She would know what had transpired at the station that morning when Eva called in. Should he pay her a visit? He was virtually on her doorstep. He hated being at loggerheads with a long-time neighbour. Turning round, he headed towards Ma Scully's.

Chapter Forty-three

Eva sat on the back seat of the car next to Sergeant O'Malley, rigid with fear, while Officer Sherwood drove them through the streets of Cavan towards Dublin. No amount of pleading enabled her to get in touch with Ma Scully, and she knew from the expression on his face it would be pointless to plead further. Alone with her fears, she bit down on her lip to stop tears forming in her eyes. All she had done was hide the uniform until she could think of what else to do. Was that such a terrible crime? The secrecy of her being whisked away without a word to anyone worried her. The sergeant stayed tight-lipped, but gave her a cursory glance now and then.

While Eva, who had never driven in a car before, felt bewildered as green fields and roads rushed past. Sherwood kept his eyes on the road ahead. It was raining, the awkward silence broken only by the windscreen wipers swishing back and forth. Soon they were passing grand houses with neat front gardens. Traffic was building, and the car slowed down. Just as she entertained the thought of escape and reached for the door handle, the sergeant placed his hand across hers. 'I wouldn't, miss.'

Frustrated, she sucked in her breath. How much further was it? Her stomach churned. How embarrassed she would feel if she had to ask for the privy. Where in Dublin were they taking her? What if she was thrown into a cell? How would she get word to Ma and Cathal? Would they ever find her?

Soon they were in the city with trams, carts, lorries and bikes that criss-crossed the busy streets. She glimpsed Dame Street and before she knew it they were pulling up outside tall gates. It looked like a prison, with soldiers standing to attention. Her heart thumped, and she gasped. They were taking her to gaol.

Sherwood let down the window, his arm resting on the door frame, to speak to a soldier in uniform. Rain splashed on to the upholstery and Eva felt the spray on her face. Once identification was approved, the gates were swiftly opened. The car drove through and stopped outside a red-brick building. The plaque above the door read Guard Room. Why had they taken her here? Too nervous to ask, she could not stop herself shaking.

'Out you come, miss.' The door was held open for her.

An army soldier slipped into the driver's seat and drove the car away. Eva stood, shivering in spite of the humid weather, her arms folded, her head bowed.

'This way, miss,' Officer Sherwood said.

Taking a deep breath, she followed him into the room. It smelt of artillery and leather. Old fusty ledgers lined the bookshelves. A man in uniform put his head round the door, nodded to Sergeant O'Malley who went out. Left alone, Eva felt numb. How did she get to be in this terrible situation? It was all happening too fast for her mind to comprehend. If only she'd known, she would have welcomed Ma's offer to come with her. She could kick herself now. At least Ma would know where they had taken her. What was this place?

The door opened and a stout man in uniform walked in, followed by O'Malley who stood guarding the entrance. Did they think she would try to escape? The uniformed man stubbed out his cigar and sat down. Smoke curled up from the ashtray, creating a halo of gloom. The middle-aged military man with three pips on the shoulders of his jacket removed his hat to reveal a tight haircut. He was clean shaven. Clearing his throat, he opened the folder in front of him and studied it for a few seconds. Eva thought she might be sick and placed her hand across her mouth as bile rose up her throat. She felt small and inadequate with only the truth as her defence. Her resolve not to let them intimidate her well and truly evaporated. She gripped her shaking hands. The glare of the single light above her made her head ache. She was being treated like a criminal.

The man glanced up. 'I'm Captain McLaughlin, head of security. You are Eva Fallon. Is that correct?'

'Yes, sir.' She felt the quiver in her voice and took a deep breath before asking, 'What is this place? And why have I been brought here?'

'This is Dublin Castle. The security section for the military police.'

She sat forward. 'I've done nothing wrong.'

'The army will be the judge of that, miss. Private Blackstock has been questioned, and we have taken his signed statement. All you have to do is answer the questions truthfully.'

She nodded and her hair fell across her face. That's all she wanted to do.

'You are a temporary guest with Miss Scully, of Cavan town. Where did you live before that?'

'I . . . I lived at the orphanage in Cavan.'

His face remained expressionless. 'Umm, well. You are accused of a serious offence. Do you realise that?'

She hadn't, but she was beginning to. She nodded.

'Miss, you may or may not realise that absconding from the army for whatever reason is desertion and a punishable crime. Now if Private Blackstock did it for love.' He raised his bushy eyebrows. 'I can understand that. You are a pretty young woman. And, had you persuaded him to return voluntarily within a period of time, both your sentences might have been lighter.'

'What . . . what do you mean? There's nothing between Matthew Blackstock and myself. I hardly know him,' she stressed. 'He . . .'

She was about to mention the attack on her when the captain tapped his fingers on the desk.

'Now, look here, miss. We know you hid him at the farm, did his washing, cooked for him and stashed his uniform in your room.'

'But I . . .' She felt herself sway. How could she contradict him? She had done all those things. She looked down and played with the hem of her jacket.

'I'm sure you are aware, young lady, that withholding information about a person who has gone AWOL is very serious indeed.'

She wasn't sure what that was. 'Please, Captain! Can I tell you the truth?'

He sucked in a breath and leant across the desk. 'That's

what we're here to establish.' His eyes flashed. 'But don't waste my time by lying.'

Eva looked round at Sergeant O'Malley, hoping he might somehow intervene on her behalf, but he continued to stand upright, a frozen expression on his face. Fighting back tears, she retold her story. This time, even she couldn't make it sound credible. The captain sat back, lit a cigar, and Eva could tell her efforts were in vain.

Annoyed at being interrogated with no one to defend her, she stood up. 'You don't believe me, do you? But you'd take the word of a man mean enough to attack me, fracture my arm and leave me for dead in a ditch.' She was trembling, and her tears came as fast and as furious as her anger.

'Sit down, young woman!'

Her pulse raced. Eva sat back in the chair and blew her nose into her handkerchief.

'Is there anyone who can testify to what you've just said?'

She looked up, her eyes wide. 'Yes. Yes, there is.'

'Are you prepared to take the oath?'

'What do you mean?'

'I mean, are you prepared to swear in a military court of law that everything you've told me here today is the truth, the whole truth and nothing but the truth?'

'Yes, yes,' she said, her voice shaking. 'I am, sir.'

He sighed. 'That will be all. You're free to go.' He beckoned to Sergeant O'Malley. 'Take the girl away, release her for now.' Then he pushed back his chair and left the room.

Chapter Forty-four

Jacob Blackstock arrived in Cavan town. He knew that Ma Scully was well known for her good deeds around the county, always out and about, helping lost causes. In Eva's case it was a deserving one. He straightened his shoulders and lifted the knocker. On the second attempt the door opened, and she stood before him, dressed in her outdoor clothes.

'Oh, it's you,' she said. 'I'm just off out. What can I do fer ye?'

He removed his hat. 'I wondered how Eva got on at the station?'

'Well, ye better come in a wee minute.' She closed the door behind him. 'I'd offer ye some hospitality only, as ye can see . . .' She placed her hat on her head and secured it with a pin. 'Eva's not back from the Garda station and I'm away down there to find out why it's taken her so long.'

'I've just come from there, and she's not there.' He held his hat in front of him.

'Where in God's name is she then?'

'The young upstart behind the counter wouldn't tell me anything. Sergeant O'Malley's in Dublin.'

'You don't think! God and his Holy Mother. You don't suppose he's taken Eva with him?' Ma threw up her arms, and he thought she would burst a blood vessel. 'I should a known better than to let her go alone. I've been at the hospital all morning and when I got back, she wasn't here. That poor child.' She sat down and unbuttoned her coat, her breath coming fast. 'Get me a wee dram from the cupboard. I've come over giddy. You'll find a glass on the dresser.' She unpinned her hat and laid it on the table.

Jacob poured the whiskey and handed it to her.

She took a swig. 'You know what them Dublin Jackeens are like. They'll drive her into the ground to get a confession out of her. She's innocent. I know it and so do you, Jacob Blackstock. If it hadn't been for your son ...' She paused.

Jacob hung his head. 'I'm truly sorry.'

Ma finished her drink, stood up and looked out of the window.

'Can I ask what you plan to do?'

'That's my business. I will not stand by and see her rot in a cell for your son's sins.'

'I may have had my head turned by the girl – who wouldn't? – but I never meant her any harm. You've got to believe me.'

'Aye! That's as may be, but your son had other ideas,' she snapped. 'And I hold you and that Aggie woman responsible.'

She picked up his hat and handed it to him. 'I've things to be getting on with, so, I'll bid ye good day.'

* * *

Cathal returned to the fire station after rescuing a cat from the attic roof of a house on Haddington Road. The little girl's face when she held her pet in her arms was worth the time and effort it had taken. So, feeling good, he had just removed his outer garments when the call came through. His first thought was Eva as he hurried to the office and took the phone from the chief.

'Sound's urgent, Cathal. I'll give you some privacy.'

Nodding, he placed the receiver to his ear. 'Ma! What's up?' He listened until she had finished talking. 'You go home, Ma. Stay put in case she comes back. I'll see what I can find out. My relief is due in half an hour. Ring me again tomorrow morning. Stop worrying, Sergeant O'Malley will bring her back safe.' The pips went, and he replaced the receiver.

On the walk to his digs, he pondered what might have happened at the Garda station that morning. He was furious with O'Malley for taking her anywhere without informing his aunt. Eva was bound to be frightened by it all, and who wouldn't be? He had a fair idea how the Gardaí worked; if they got their teeth into someone whom they suspected had harboured a deserter, they would be relentless in their questioning.

He opened the bottle of Johnnie Walker he had been saving for times in his career when he'd had a particularly bad day and someone had died in a rescue. Like that terrible night when the orphanage caught fire. The memory still haunted him. He poured himself a generous helping, took a sip, sat down and rubbed his temples. His attraction for Eva had grown over the past months. Concern for her welfare and safety went well above and beyond the call of duty, and he couldn't deny his feelings for her were growing. Now he was desperate to get justice for her.

Downing the rest of the liquid, he had a quick wash and changed his clothes, then glanced at his watch. He was due to meet Isabel after work; as far as he was concerned, for the last time. His feelings had never been more than friendship and now that he realised she was looking for more, he had to speak with her face-to-face. He knew Isabel; she was, and always would be, a free spirit who liked to play the field. He also knew she had other admirers. So, why she wanted to entertain marriage to him made no sense. He enjoyed her company, her intelligent conversation, but that was all. Anything else had never entered his mind. Their friendship had gone on long enough. It was time to let her know how he felt. He must do it now, then devote all his spare time to helping Eva prove her innocence.

He rounded the corner into Mary Street, arriving at Arnotts tea room in plenty of time. Inside, it was still busy with individuals and couples canoodling at tables. He had a splitting headache and ordered a strong coffee and sandwiches.

'Any preference, sir? We have . . .' The waitress reeled off a selection.

'Anything will be fine, thanks.'

Ten minutes later, Isabel sashayed through the door. She had just finished work at the city library and looked happy, and he felt bad about what he was about to say to her. She sat opposite him, and a tray of neatly cut sandwiches and steaming coffee was placed in front of them.

'Good, you've ordered,' she smiled.

'How was work?'

She shrugged. 'Busy as usual.'

He cleared his throat. 'Isabel, we need to talk.'

'Why do I feel there's something ominous afoot?' Frowning, she sat upright.

'You're far too perceptive, Isabel.'

She cut into a sandwich, popped a piece into her mouth and leant back in the chair. 'Well, let's have it then. Better still, let me help you. You want to end our relationship.'

'Relationship now, is it? I've enjoyed our friendship, but you appear to want to take it further and . . .'

'Is that why you've been avoiding me lately?'

'No, of course not.' He sipped his hot drink. 'It's been busy at work, and . . .'

'You've met someone else. Is it Gloria?'

'Gloria! Good God, no. What makes you say that?' He swallowed.

'She's had a crush on you for ages. Haven't you noticed?'

Dumbfounded, Cathal shook his head. 'No, why would I? I was walking out with you.'

'So!'

'Look, Isabel, I'm not that kind of person. And don't think I don't know how flippant and carefree you are with relationships, casual and innocent as they may be.' He paused and touched her arm. 'You and I, we want different things.'

'Oh, don't be such a killjoy, Cathal. There's a war on and anything might happen. I want to experience life before it's too late.' She pouted. 'What's wrong with that?'

'Nothing, if that's what you want.' He leant towards her. 'You're beautiful, clever. But if that's your view of life, it's not mine.'

She ran her painted finger down the side of his face. 'Poor baby, all work and no play . . .'

He removed her hand and finished his coffee. 'I have to go.'

'Oh, can't you stay? I want to show you off,' she whined. 'I'm meeting friends at the pub later.'

He smiled. 'Sorry. Early shift tomorrow. I'll see you around, though.'

'You certainly will. I don't give up that easily.'

Outside on the street again, he blew out his lips. That was easier than he had first expected. He felt tired and drained as he walked back to his flat. Thoughts of Isabel were replaced with his longing to see Eva again. He wondered where she could be, and if she had returned to Cavan. He couldn't wait for morning when Ma would ring and let him know.

Chapter Forty-five

Eva was escorted out into the Castle grounds by Sergeant O'Malley. 'Aren't you taking me back to Cavan, then?'

'Yes, but I can't leave just yet. Take a look at the sights and meet me outside the gates at,' he glanced at his watch, 'say five o'clock.'

'But that's ages. What am I supposed to do until then?'

'I'm sure you'll find something, miss.' With that, he turned on his heel and went inside.

The army captain hadn't believed her story, and Sergeant O'Malley had given her no support in there; he too thought her guilty. Shocked by the treatment meted out to her, she walked out of the courtyard, through the security gate to find herself on the streets of Dublin. It had stopped raining, and the sun had come out, but the air was humid. In different circumstances a walk around the shops would have been inviting, but with only pennies in her purse, she was dependant on the sergeant to get her back to Cavan.

Happy shoppers went about their business with smiling

faces, and yet, she couldn't raise a smile. The interrogation had left her numb and humiliated. Bustling city life with trams, horse and carts, bikes and noisy traffic everywhere made her head ache. Not looking where she was going, she stepped into the road almost under the wheels of a tram.

'Are you trying to kill yourself?' the angry driver shouted.

Aware of cursory glances coming her way, she hurried into the doorway of a confectioner's where she glimpsed her downcast image in the glass door. She looked a sorry sight. But worse still was the old gentleman standing on the corner playing the violin. His clothes were in tatters, and his toes protruding through his boots. She wondered what had brought him to this, and dropped one of her pennies into his tin. He smiled and bowed as if he was onstage. Although Eva didn't recognise the cheerful tune, she felt uplifted.

The numbness and shock of her ordeal were wearing off but in their place a rising anger brought tears to her eyes. Avoiding the city centre, she stuck to the area around the Castle. A row of shops faced on to the Liffey wall, selling many goods, from second-hand furniture to old books, but she couldn't raise any interest. The sweet smell of hops wafting on the air from the Guinness Brewery reminded her of her visit to the pub in Cavan with Ma Scully after the memorial service. Feeling hot and sticky, she went into a small quaint tea room and asked the portly woman with an apron and short bobbed hair if she could have a drink of water.

'Is that all you want then?'

Eva nodded and sat down. The dryness in her throat eased as she drank, then asked if she could use the washroom.

'It's outside,' the woman told her.

Eva locked herself in, leant against the door and wept. When she came out, she washed her hands and threw cold water on to her face, ran her comb through her hair and powdered her nose. The tea room was empty, apart from a young couple, and Eva sat down by the window. People rushed past on the pavement, intent on where they were going, and somehow the thought of sitting next to O'Malley for the journey back to Cavan sounded less inviting. She poured herself another glass of water, ordered a cup of tea and sat nursing it for as long as she could. With half an hour before meeting the sergeant, she let her thoughts wander. Ma Scully would wonder why she hadn't come back, and Eva hated to be the cause of her worry. The strain in the older woman's face hadn't gone unnoticed. And if today was anything to go by, there was more to come. If she could find work in Dublin, it might solve some of her problems and relieve Ma of the worry. She would also be closer to Cathal. The more she thought about it, the more plausible it seemed. She would phone Cathal and ask him to let Ma know she was all right and would be home tonight.

'Are you all right, dearie?' the woman behind the counter asked. 'You look lost, so you do?'

'I'm grand, thanks. I'm meeting someone at five. Is the water free?'

'Ah, sure, help yourself. There's no charge for water. It's very humid out there.' The woman wiped the surrounding tables. 'Were you meeting your friend here? Because I'm closing soon.'

'No, not here.' She poured herself another glass of water. 'Is there much work in Dublin?'

'Ah, sure, there's not a lot going. The war has made people wary of hiring at the moment. The theatre on Dame Street were looking for cleaners the other day. You could try them.'

'Thanks.' Eva was glad she had asked the question.

'Ah, sure, a pretty girl like yourself won't want to do cleaning, will you?'

Eva shrugged. 'Beggars must.'

The woman wiped crumbs and tea stains from the oil-cloth on the table next to Eva. 'It's almost five. What about your friend?'

'Oh, I'm sure they'll wait.'

'Well, I wish you luck.'

Eva's stomach rumbled as she walked in the direction the woman had told her. The theatre was nothing special on the outside, but it had an impressive foyer with framed posters of artists. There was no one about, so she opened the door and glanced down at plush seats all the way to the stage. A man and woman were rehearsing from scripts.

The man hurried towards her, an indignant expression on his rosy face. 'What are you doing here?' He waved his hands about. 'The box office is not open for ticket sales.'

Feeling like an intruder, she struggled for words. 'I . . . sorry I . . . Is the vacancy for the cleaner's job still available? I'm . . .'

He chuckled. 'I've absolutely no idea.'

He spoke in a posh accent, and she felt silly to have asked. 'Now can you please leave.'

Turning, she fled from the theatre, annoyed with herself to have entertained such a ridiculous notion. What choice did she have but to return to Cavan with Sergeant O'Malley and await her fate?

She hurried back the way she had come, passing City Hall with Christ Church Cathedral to her right. Arriving at the Castle with its impressive gates, where he had arranged to meet her, she braced herself for a tongue-lashing for keeping him waiting. Out of breath after her exertion, she found he wasn't there. At the gatehouse she made enquiries and was informed that the sergeant had already left for Cavan.

Finding herself alone and hungry in the capital without a roof over her head churned her insides. Only now did she feel justified in phoning Cathal, and she thanked God she had his telephone number with her. The first free phone box she came across she went inside. She had never used one before but after reading the instruction, she lifted the receiver and placed the coins into the slot. Her fingers shook as she dialled. There was no ring tone and her money was swallowed up. She stared into the mouthpiece and then realised the phone was out of order. 'Oh no! Oh no! God, no.' That was every penny she had; she wished now she had not given one to the violin man. She stayed where she was for a few seconds, her face in her hands.

Disappointed, weak from hunger, her shoulders hunched, her gait slower, she walked along South Great George's Street and Aungier Street, until she came to a church, always a place of sanctuary. Hefty pillars framed the entrance with doors that looked strong enough to withstand any storm. Ignoring the begging pleas from women outside wrapped in shawls, she went in, genuflected and with a grateful sigh lowered herself on to a seat. People knelt in prayer, while others prayed in front of statues. Her stomach ached. How long she could stay here depended on what time the doors were locked at night.

The smell of candles burning always evoked a sense of belonging in her, and right now she wished she was back at the orphanage. With no stamina to kneel, she sat to pray. 'God! It's Eva. Please tell me what to do?'

In spite of the number of people visiting, no one paid her any heed, too busy mumbling into their rosaries.

Having made her pleas to God, she looked down the line of confessionals on both sides with a different priest's name on each door. As the church emptied, she chose one and slipped inside. The kneeling cushion was the only comfort, so she sat down. The box was stuffy and smelt of old prayer books, and she wondered how many sinners the priest had forgiven in here over the years. What kind of things did other people confess? She herself had plenty to repent. She wanted to clear her conscience in confession, and she knew she would have to do it sooner or later. If only she had got through on the phone to Cathal, he would have helped her. Thinking about him brought tears, and she placed her head in her hands and wept.

Chapter Forty-six

Once Cathal discovered that Eva had not returned to Cavan, he asked his superior for an extended lunch hour. At Pearse Street Garda station nobody appeared to know anything about a girl called Eva Fallon. The garda on duty showed not the slightest interest in Cathal's request for information and left him waiting before showing him to the sergeant's office.

'I'm sorry to have kept you, Mr Burke, but this is a very busy station. We have to be sure you're not just wasting police time.'

'Wasting police time, is it?' Cathal stood glaring at the man. 'I've wasted ten minutes of my time trying to convince your bodyguards out there to let me see you, and I'm in no mood to wait any longer.'

The sergeant stood up and proffered his hand. 'Sergeant Cooney. I'm sorry about that. Please, sit down.' He gestured to a seat. 'I needed to catch up on important issues and asked the boys not to disturb me.' He coughed and cleared his throat. 'Now, what can I do for you?'

Cathal pulled over a chair and sat down, loosening the button on his jacket. 'I'm enquiring about a young girl by the name of Eva Fallon.'

The sergeant shifted in his chair. 'What has she done?' He frowned. 'And what makes you think she's here?'

'I believe she may have been brought from Cavan to Dublin for questioning. If she wasn't taken here, one of the biggest stations in the city, then you have the means of finding out where.'

'Well, Mr Burke, I've been on duty most of the day and I can assure you, there are no women in the cells – at least, not yet. And I don't like your attitude.'

'Your feelings don't concern me, Sergeant. My concern is for this young woman and what has happened to her.' Cathal sat upright and looked the man in the eye. He knew the type, full of his own importance; he would delight in taking him down a peg or two. 'If I don't get answers, Sergeant Cooney, I won't hesitate to take this further. Now, if she's not here, where would they have taken her?'

Sergeant Cooney sat back in his chair. 'I've no idea. On what charge was she detained?'

'I'm not willing to discuss that with you. Let's say it was a miscarriage of justice and a punishable offence if found guilty. So,' he leant forward, placing his elbows on the table, 'where would she have been taken?'

'If you would wait outside a while, Mr Burke. I'll make a few enquiries.'

Less than half an hour later, Cathal was on a bus taking him to Dame Street and the Castle. Refused admittance at the gate, he stood arguing with the guard when an army officer walked towards them.

'You can admit Mr Burke,' he said, once he had established Cathal's credentials as a fire officer.

Escorted into the guard room, he could only imagine how terrified Eva must have been in a place like this, swarming with military, and he would not leave without answers. A broad-shouldered man sat behind a desk. The name Captain McLaughlin was pinned to his decorative uniform. Cathal settled himself on the seat opposite him.

'What is it you want to know, and why does it concern you, Mr Burke?'

'A young dark-haired girl by the name of Eva Fallon was brought here for questioning. She lives with my aunt and we're concerned for her welfare. I want to know where she is.'

'Oh, yes, Miss Fallon.' McLaughlin reached across to the filing cabinet and plucked out a folder, then paused for a moment to read the notes. 'Got herself involved in a conspiracy to conceal the whereabouts of a deserter, Private Blackstock.'

'She's innocent.'

'People rarely get mixed up in this kind of thing by accident, Mr Burke. For a young woman as attractive as Miss Fallon it could only have been for one reason.' He smiled. 'I can—'

'Can I stop you there, Captain? You're barking up the wrong tree. It's a clear case of injustice.'

'Can you prove that? Were you living at the farm at the time of the alleged incident?'

Cathal took a deep breath. 'No, but I know a convent full of nuns who can vouch for her good character.'

The captain tried to suppress a snigger. 'You seem sure about this young woman's integrity. Convent girls aren't the most reliable. And better men than yourself have fallen into the trap of a cunning woman.'

Furious and ready to explode, Cathal took a deep breath and kept his dignity. Why, he thought, were army personnel so pompous? 'Where is she? Can I see her?'

'She left here yesterday afternoon. Sergeant O'Malley took her back to Cavan.'

Cathal was on his feet. 'Well, that's rather strange, Captain, because she never arrived back last night.'

'Well, there you go then. She must have stayed in Dublin. Besides, we will need to talk to her again once we've questioned Private Blackstock further.' He pushed back his chair. 'I'll have someone show you out.'

'I'll see myself out!'

Chapter Forty-seven

Eva sat on the confessional kneeling pad all night, listening to the creaks and groans of the empty church, until it was safe to come out. With cold and hunger gnawing at her insides, she stretched out on a wide bench at the back of the church and tried to sleep.

The rattle of keys and the sound of someone unlocking the sacristy woke her in the morning, and she fled back to the cubicle. Footsteps echoed down the long aisle, then paused close to her hiding place. For a second her heart almost stopped. There was a brief exchange of voices before someone walked back towards the altar and all was quiet. She crept from the box, her stomach rumbling. Her legs wobbled. She must find food before she collapsed. She stood in the entrance, surprised to see beggars gathering up their belongings from behind pillars where they had spent the night. They glared at her as she walked past them.

'Hey!' one man called. 'How come you got to sleep inside?'

Eva couldn't get away fast enough and tried to close her ears to the rest of the man's quips about her and the priest. The church bell rang eight times and she hoped the tea room would be open.

She half walked, half ran until she arrived. She prayed the woman would take pity on her and give her something to eat. But the closed sign was still on the door, and her heart sank. Unable to put one step in front of the other, she lowered herself down in the shop doorway. If people thought she was a beggar, looking dirty and unkempt, their hostility washed over her. As soon as she heard the key turn in the lock and the bolt being pulled back, she got to her feet.

'Oh, I didn't expect to see *you* again. What brings you out so early of a morning?'

Eva was embarrassed and felt tears gathering. 'I'm sorry. Can I come in, please?'

'I'm not open yet.' The woman held the door ajar. 'Oh, you'd better come in before you collapse.' She wrinkled her nose. 'Where have you been? You look queer, so ye do. Are ye all right?'

Eva swallowed and her tongue moved over her dry lips. 'Can I use your ...?'

The woman nodded. 'And while you're out there use the tap and tidy yourself up. I don't want you putting me customers off their breakfast.'

Eva used the privy and gulped down the tap water, letting it run over her face and hair before using the soap provided. When she came back out, she felt fresher. If only she had a change of clothes. A weakness came over her and when the tea-room lady beckoned her to sit down, she was glad to do so. Two dockers wearing caps sat by the window, eating toast and drinking tea; the smell made her mouth water.

'Look, love. Whatever your problem is, I'm not a charity. So, unless you buy something, I must ask you to leave.'

Eva glanced up, her eyes wide. 'I have no money. Please can I have a sweet tea? I'll . . . I'll pay you back, I promise.'

'Sugar's rationed, or have you forgotten there's a war on?'

How could she forget? It was due to the war she found herself in this predicament. But how could she tell a complete stranger how she came to be in such a low place.

The tea arrived, with a Marietta biscuit on the saucer.

'I gather you had no luck at the theatre then?'

Eva shook her head, picked up the cup and blew on the hot tea before taking a sip. The woman busied herself serving a customer. Eva was unable to wait for the drink to cool, so she did what the nuns would have rapped her knuckles for: she poured a small amount on to the saucer and sipped it. She bit into the biscuit, which tasted delicious. The telephone rang out from a room somewhere behind the counter and the woman went to answer it. When she came back, Eva had finished the last of her drink and stood up to leave. The two dockers raised their caps as they tucked into their cooked breakfast.

'Thank you. I'll be off now.' She buttoned her jacket and moved to the door.

'Hang on a minute,' the woman said. 'I gather you're still looking for work?'

'Yes, yes, I am. Do you know of somewhere?'

'I might have a few hours here, if you're interested.'

Eva bit down hard on her lip to stop herself from crying.

'Bernadette, my regular, has just phoned in. One of the kiddies is sick. So, I could do with the help. It might only be for a day.'

'Thank you, thank you very much.'

'Bernadette covers the lunch from eleven to two. But as you're here, you could wash up. It will pay for the free tea you've just had.'

Eva took off her jacket, rolled up her sleeves and in spite of her hunger washed a pile of dirty dishes, cleaned the small kitchen and mopped the floor.

'Well, that's impressive,' the woman said. 'By the way, I'm Doreen.'

Smiling, she offered her hand. 'I'm Eva.'

'Where're you from?'

'Cavan. But I'm trying for work in the capital.'

Doreen gave her a quizzical look. 'What about your friend?'

'They let me down.'

'I'll see you at eleven then.' Doreen put a sticky bun into a bag and handed it to her. 'Don't be late.' More people came into the tea room and Doreen went to serve them.

The cake was a godsend. No sooner was she out the door when she devoured it, licking the icing from her fingers to the disapproving stares of passers-by. But Eva couldn't afford to be proud.

A few hours' work might be enough for her train fare to Cavan. So with new hope lifting her spirits, she walked back towards the church. The entrance was now clear of vagrants. Two women with small children dipped their fingers into the holy water font. Eva blessed herself and followed them inside.

Mass had started. She bobbed to the altar before taking a seat in one of the pews. Joining her hands, she looked up at the tabernacle. 'God, it's me again,' she murmured. Then she sat contemplating her uncertain future while the priest's incantations echoed around the half-filled chapel. She thought about Ma Scully, the only friend she had in the world, and Cathal's kindness towards her, and a tear slipped unchecked down her face. If she could talk to him, let him know where she was, her worries would soon be at an end. The bell chimed at the consecration and the priest elevated the host, bringing her out of her reverie, and she knelt in adoration. She felt guilty for allowing her thoughts to stray, but her head was all over the place. And God forgive her, she was only killing time before she could return to the cafe.

While people lined up to take communion, Eva left quietly. Her conscience would not allow her to partake while she felt she was in the state of mortal sin.

She took a slow walk down the narrow lane by the side of Christ Church Cathedral towards Wood Quay and walked along the pavement by the Liffey wall until she arrived back early at the tea room.

Chapter Forty-eight

Pleased not to be on call-out, Cathal sat at his desk willing the phone to ring. He had given Eva his number, so he hoped she would get in touch.

'You seem troubled, lad. Is there anything I can help with?' Andy Baxter, his superior, asked.

'No, thanks, Andy. I'm expecting an urgent call from my aunt in Cavan. Once I speak to her, I'll be fine.' How could he unload this on him? Besides, Eva might phone and the problem would be solved.

When the telephone rang, Cathal jumped to answer it. It was the chief fire officer. 'It's for you, sir,' he shouted. Disappointed, he sat back down to finish writing up reports.

Half an hour later, it was Ma Scully who phoned. Andy was on his way out of the office to join the rest of the crew for elevenses.

'Stay alert, Cathal. You know what it can be like. One minute nothing and the next all hell breaks loose.' He knew his boss wouldn't be happy about the line being tied up, and he didn't want to be the cause of an urgent call not getting through.

'Thanks. I won't be long.' After a brief conversation with his aunt, he discovered that Eva hadn't returned. 'Try not to worry, Ma. I'll find her.' He replaced the receiver, knowing he had set himself an impossible task.

That afternoon, he confided his worries to Andy, who agreed for him to take two days' leave. 'You're due a break, lad. No one has worked harder these past few months.'

Andy had been a mentor to Cathal since the death of his mother, guiding and advising him in his career as a fire officer. When Cathal was twenty-one, Andy had written him a character reference and put in a good word for him at the station. There was a mutual respect between the two men. Andy had instructed him well. It was thanks to him that Cathal now had a good career in the service.

Two call-outs that day had kept him focused. A small fire that started in the canteen of a glove factory could have been worse, had they not got there in time before it spread to the workplace. The other was in a sacristy, when two young altar boys experiencing their first cigarette knocked over a lighted candle. No one was seriously hurt in either incident. Had it been a bomb alert, could it have made his day any more harrowing? As it was, he refused to be anything but optimistic in his quest to find Eva as he walked back to his flat in Pearse Street.

According to his aunt, Eva had taken nothing with her apart from her handbag and the clothes she stood up in. And Ma couldn't say if she had any money with her. It was now two days since she had gone to the Garda station in Cavan, and he was none the wiser where she might be.

Anything could have happened to her. He blamed O'Malley, and if he could get his hands on him . . . he gritted his teeth. How the man could have left without her was beyond belief.

He washed, shaved, changed his clothes and pulled on his mac. He shoved a warm scarf into his pocket for Eva, if he was lucky enough to come across her. The evening had turned chilly and the blue sky was now a dull grey. He hoped the rain would keep off as he walked into town. It could be a dangerous place in spite of the night patrol. He hoped to God that she had found a safe shelter last night. Crossing O'Connell Street to the air-raid shelters, he recalled how worried she had been that day in Dublin. He glimpsed inside the smelly shelters but there was no sign of her. Homeless beggars now used them to smoke and drink.

He popped his head around the door of every public house within the city's boundary. The town was full of drunks, the military, and American soldiers with girls hanging off their arms. He visited all the Garda stations in the centre, but no one had seen a girl of Eva's description, nor were they interested in helping him to find her. Exasperated with his efforts, but determined not to give up, he tried the hospitals in the Dublin area, but none had anyone by the name of Eva Fallon. Cathal wasn't sure whether to feel relief or disappointment. Where in God's name could she be?

Exhausted, he returned home, but thoughts of her alone somewhere, frightened and in danger, worried him.

'Oh, Eva!' he murmured. 'Where are you?'

That night as he lay sleepless, with the rain beating against the window, he conjured up every possible scenario, imagining what might have happened to her. Had she been swayed by some smooth-talking guy? There were plenty of them out there ready to pounce on a defenceless young woman. Maybe she had lost her way, or was lying hurt somewhere? He felt the knot in his stomach tighten.

Early the next morning, he caught a tram to the top of Grafton Street and stepped off at the park. It was a popular place, peaceful by day and frequented by dog owners, families, and women wheeling babies in perambulators. Had she come here and stayed the night after closing? He was horrified at the thought of her sleeping rough. He meandered through the park, searching behind hedges and under the bandstand in hopes of finding her. It was like looking for a fish in the ocean.

He cut through the narrow lanes that brought him back to the Castle gates and down Lord Edward Street, past City Hall, assuming she might have gone towards the town rather than away from it. He looked down every alley as he walked. He continued past the theatre, with South Great George's Street on the right. Where would she go for help? He cut through to the Ha'penny Bridge, lined with beggars, searching their faces and hoping to see Eva's. He questioned an older woman, but all he got was a shake of the head. He crossed her palm with silver and she called down blessings upon him and his children. If only he had a photograph. He could have had copies made and distributed them.

It rained, wetting his curly mop. He pulled the collar of his mac snug around his neck as the rain beat down on his shoulders. The streets were grey and miserable, with most people running for cover, but Cathal, as relentless as the rain, carried on calling at every convent, church and orphanage within the limits of the city until, soaked through to his blue shirt, he admitted defeat and called into the nearest public house for a stiff drink.

Chapter Forty-nine

Eva was almost on her knees by the time her three-hour shift finished. If she'd had food in her belly, the work would have been a drop in the ocean to her. Doreen had said she could have a snack afterwards, and she hoped she wouldn't faint before that. Eva had cooked and served up scrambled eggs, bacon and sausage to that many customers she had to drink water to stop herself drooling. She was even tempted to eat a portion of sausage before taking it to the table but stopped herself when her boss chivvied her on. 'These men won't wait all day, you know. They have to get back to their jobs.'

By two o'clock, her energy depleted, she rushed out back as her stomach pains contracted. Doreen gave her a suspicious look. Eva knew she would have to tell her the truth, or lose the few hours' work she had been offered. It was wrong to lie, and since leaving the orphanage she had covered up so many things. Doreen didn't know her and would think

286

all sorts, but how much should she tell? If she mentioned her arrest, she would be shown the door sharpish. Please God, help me. She splashed cold water on her face before coming inside.

The cafe was quieter and Doreen was wiping down tables. She glanced round at Eva. 'What's the matter with you?' Her tone was harsh. 'No, don't tell me.' She straightened up. 'If you've gotten yourself in trouble, you can leave my establishment now, young woman. This is not a refuge for the likes of you.'

Eva's legs buckled, and she sat down. 'I'm so sorry.' She buried her head in her hands.

'Aye! You thought you'd try to hoodwink me. Tell it to the fella who filled your belly.'

Eva's head shot up. 'I'm not . . . I mean . . . You've got it wrong. I'm just hungry.' Her mind went back to what Matthew had done, and the thought made her heart beat so fast she wanted to run from the tea room, but her legs wouldn't carry her as far as the door.

'Hungry!' Doreen sat down next to her, the dishcloth in her hand. 'When did you last eat a decent meal?'

Eva shook her head, her eyes full with unshed tears.

'You'd better be telling me the truth, or I'll not only throw you out, I'll call the Gardaí.'

'Please, don't do that.' She must justify her actions by revealing part of the story: that she had come to Dublin looking for work with only three pennies to her name; she hadn't eaten since Monday morning and stomach pains were making her sick. 'Can I have something to eat? I'll work for it.'

Doreen sat back and looked her in the eye. 'Okay! I'll

give you the benefit of the doubt. But, if I find out you've been lying . . .' She got to her feet and rustled up a breakfast that Eva had been drooling over all morning.

Eva tucked into the egg, dipping the thick slice of bread into the runny yolk, crunching the crispy bacon and then mopping up every morsel before sitting back and holding her tummy. Doreen shook her head, then went to serve a customer who only wanted tea and cake. Eva was clearing the table with renewed energy and taking the dirty crockery to the kitchen when Doreen followed.

'That was grand, so it was. Thank you.'

'So, with only pennies in your purse where have you been sleeping?'

Eva placed the dirty dishes into the sink of soapy water. 'Well, I . . . I slept in the church last night.' She felt embarrassed when she saw the shocked look on the woman's face.

'You what? You're codding! Sure, that's a terrible thing to do. Did the priest know?'

Eva felt colour flush her face. 'I had no choice.' Tears threatened. 'I hid inside a confessional.'

'Glory be to God!' Doreen's hand rushed to her face. 'It's no wonder you're dead on your feet. So, what plans have you made for tonight then?'

Eva dropped her gaze.

'Look, love! I'm not sure this will work out. You can't work when you've not had a good night's sleep.'

Eva eyes widened. 'What can I do? I've nowhere to go and no money.'

'Did you not think about that before you left home?'

'I . . . I . . . had no choice.'

Doreen's eyes softened and Eva hoped she would help her.

'Look,' she said. 'I hope I won't regret this. You could

sleep here tonight. There's a box room upstairs where I keep the stock and there's a small couch, looks about your size.' She shook her head. 'It's the best I can offer.'

Eva let out a sigh of utter relief. 'Thanks, I won't let you down.'

Doreen poured tea into a mug and handed it to her. She sighed. 'I can't let you roam the streets without a bed in these troubled times.'

Eva, more grateful than Doreen could possibly know, continued washing the dirty plates, while her boss served tea to the afternoon ladies who frequented her establishment. It was a busy little cafe and if things had been different, and she didn't have the troubles of the world hanging over her, she would have loved to work here.

Now she had somewhere to lay her head tonight, she thought about Cathal. If only she had the money to phone him. After all Doreen had done for her already, she couldn't muster up the courage to ask her. At five o'clock, Doreen closed the tea shop and bolted the door.

'Would you like me to mop over the floor and wipe the tables?' Eva asked when she saw the tired look on Doreen's face.

'Well, if you're up to it.'

'Oh, I'm fine. Much better now I've eaten.'

'Okay then. I'll find you a spare pillow and a blanket.'

When Doreen returned, the chairs were upside down on the tables, the floor clean, and the kitchen spick and span. 'My, you're a quick worker. Sure you've never worked in service?'

Eva smiled. 'I'm glad to be of some help.'

'Look, lovey! I can only keep you on while Bernadette's off. And the money I pay you won't get you far.' She knitted her fingers across her abdomen. 'Jobs are scarce, and my advice to you would be to go home. Your family will be worried.'

Ma and Cathal were the only family she had. 'Well, yes, I guess it might be best. I thought there would be plenty of work here.'

'Yes, if you have qualifications. Sure, the war has changed a lot of things, lovey. Aren't we the lucky ones in Ireland not to have been drawn into it?'

Eva nodded. She was in the thick of it, and being inter-rogated at Dublin Castle would remain with her forever.

'Look, I'll pay you for today,' Doreen said. 'You should ring or write and let your family know you're all right.'

A smile brightened her face. Doreen gave her some writing paper and that evening, in the privacy of the small room upstairs, she wrote a brief letter to Ma Scully, explaining what had happened and where she was.

The next day she posted her letter then made her way to the nearest pay phone, making sure it worked this time by listening for the dialling tone before placing her money into the slot. Her hands trembling, she dialled the number and, as directed, pushed in the required amount. It rang several times and her heart raced. And when she heard the voice, she pressed button B.

'Yes, Dublin fire service. How can I help?'

'Might I speak to Cathal Burke, please? It's ... it's urgent.'

'He's off duty for a few days. Who's calling?'

Eva's heart sank into her sandals and she almost dropped the receiver.

'Who is this?'

She heard irritation in the man's voice and it rendered her speechless. She replaced the receiver. Tears gushing down her face, she fled back to the cafe. Off duty! Why hadn't she asked when he would return? For all she knew, he could have left the country. Where could she turn for help now?

'Oh, Cathal,' she murmured. 'Where are you?'

Chapter Fifty

That evening, Cathal sipped a Guinness and concluded that without help he would never find Eva. Angry and frustrated to have failed her, he caught the train to Cavan. When he arrived, he was spitting feathers. The connecting train from Drummond was delayed, and he had to stand around waiting for a replacement to take him into Cavan. His aunt's gas lamp was still on, but the door was locked. He tapped on the window and called her name. Nothing. He could hear the wireless muttering. He knocked on her neighbour's door. Annoyed to have been woken from their sleep, they relented once they recognised Cathal and allowed him to go through to the back. To his relief, he found his aunt snoring in her rocking chair. The room was cold. He raked the ashes and twisted old newspapers to encourage the embers and threw turf on top. Then he made tea before waking her.

'For the love o' God, Cathal! Are ye trying to stop me ticker all together?' She placed her arm across her chest and blew out her lips.

'I'm sorry, Ma, but I couldn't get you to hear me at the door.' He passed her the tea. 'Maybe it's time for you to have your ears tested.'

'Nothing wrong with me hearing, lad.' She sat upright and sipped her drink. 'What do ye expect, calling midweek and at this hour?' She put her tea down on the side table. 'Anyhow, I'm pleased to see ye, mind.'

He hunkered down next to her and took both her hands in his. 'I've taken time off work to look for Eva and I've searched all over Dublin.' He stood up, paced the small room, and ran his fingers through his wavy hair. 'Where in God's name can she be? I could throttle O'Malley for his treatment of her.' From the look on his aunt's face, he realised he may have revealed too much of his feelings towards Eva.

'Look, will you stop prattling? Anyone'd think ye were sweet on the girl. And if ye'd give us a wee chance I'd tell ye.'

His aunt was too perceptive by far. He sat down and turned to her. 'You know where she is?'

Ma prised herself out of her cushioned chair and reached up to the mantel shelf. 'This came in the afternoon post. Read it, why don't you?' She thrust it towards him.

'Is she okay?' He plucked the letter from the envelope, scanning its contents. Sighing, he felt his shoulders relax. 'That's a relief.' He folded the note and pushed it back inside the envelope.

'Sure, I was worried sick myself. But that girl would find her way out of a paper bag, so she would.' A smile curled his aunt's lips, making him smile.

'Yes, I'd forgotten how resourceful she could be. Do you think she's still there?'

'Sure, where else would she go? She has no money and

the tea-shop owner has given her a few hours' work for a day.' She raked the fire and hooked the poker back on the wall. 'I've grown fond of wee Eva. But you seem very taken with her yourself.'

'Well ... what would you have me do, Ma? With O'Malley deserting her like that? The city's not a safe place at night.'

Ma shook her head. 'Aye. That useless lump of a man didn't think. I've already given out yards to him. If he had a daughter of his own, he'd never leave her to wander the streets alone, during wartime, without checking she first had a brass farthing to her name.' She paused. 'He's had a lashing with me tongue, so he has. Says he waited and when she didn't come back, he thought she'd gone to visit a friend and would be all right. I told him, should anything happen to her because of his stupidity, I'd report him, so I did.'

'He took her to Dublin, Ma, and he should have escorted her back. He should be disciplined.'

Ma narrowed her eyes. 'I agree with ye. Now, what's this Isabel got to say about you chasing all over Dublin looking for Eva?'

'She and I are no longer walking out. We want different things from life.'

'Aye, I see!'

'What does that mean? I thought you'd be pleased.'

'Why? I've never met the woman. I'm not blind, Cathal.'

He shuffled to his feet. 'Oh, give over, will you, Ma?'

'Aye! It's late, but we need to talk about this, Cathal, whether you like it or not. And ye know I'm right.'

He bent and kissed her cheek, then he strode towards his room.

* * *

The next morning, he was hoping to be away before his aunt surfaced and asked awkward questions he had not yet processed in his head; he was surprised to see her sitting at the table, scrambled egg and bacon warming on the hob.

'You shouldn't have troubled. I have to get back.' He had a towel over his shoulder and went outside.

When he came back he got dressed in his room. He could not recall a time when he had felt embarrassed talking to his aunt, but this was about his feelings for Eva, an innocent orphan girl, too young to know what love was, and it was difficult to admit his feelings to himself. He knew he would always want to protect her, make sure she was safe. But was that all? Who was he kidding? She had gotten right under his skin and he knew he could never forget her. Had she any idea how she made his heart race? It was foolish, yet the most sane feeling he'd ever had. Thoughts of her wandering around alone had made him frantic to find her. And he couldn't wait to see her lovely face again.

The clatter of the letter box broke his thoughts. He dragged a comb through his curly locks and pulled on his jacket. Taking a deep breath, he went out to face his aunt.

'It's still hot,' she said, placing the plate of food on the table in front of him. 'So, eat that afore ye go chasing back up to Dublin.'

The smell was too good to resist. Smiling, he tucked in.

Ma Scully, her elbow on the table, was looking at him.

'What's wrong?' He shoved down his food and popped the last piece of bacon into his mouth before glancing up.

'A letter has just arrived for Eva.'

Cathal reached for the letter. He turned it over in his hand. 'It'll be from Dublin Castle.' A frown puckered his face.

'Should we open it?'

Cathal shook his head.

'If we don't . . . It might be important.'

'Leave it here until I bring her home. She won't be able to deal with that until later.' He pushed his plate away. 'If it's about Blackstock, the military will be like a pack of dogs with a bone.'

"Tis a disgrace, if you ask me.' Ma stood up and cleared the table. 'She'll need a defence lawyer.'

'Let's not get carried away until we know what's in the letter. I'll not stand by and see an injustice done. The captain at the Castle said he would question Eva again after they'd spoken to Matthew Blackstock. I hope his conscience prods him to tell the truth. He'll try to save his own scraggy neck at all costs.'

'Aye, he will that, lad.' She heaved a sigh. 'You'll see she gets back okay, won't ye?' She picked up a small case. 'And bring her this change of clothes, she'll be mangy by now.'

'Yes, I will.' He kissed her on the cheek and dashed for the train.

Chapter Fifty-one

By Thursday, Eva felt optimistic. With the means of getting back to Cavan tucked inside her purse, she was excited, and nervous at the same time. She had not slept a wink and hoped Ma Scully had received her letter. She couldn't wait to see her, tell her everything that had happened and find out where Cathal was. Had he gone away or, worse, was he with Isabel, the librarian?

Doreen insisted she ate breakfast of bacon and egg in the busy tea room, served up by Bernadette, before she left and told her if she came up to Dublin again to be sure and pay her a visit. Doreen had been a good friend to her over the last few days. She liked Bernadette, felt they would have hit it off had there been enough work for them both.

'I'm sorry things haven't worked out for you in Dublin,' Doreen said. 'Perhaps when the war's over things will change.'

Eva thanked her and promised to come back one day. It had only been days since she last saw Ma and Cathal but it felt like weeks. She was about to leave the tea room when she gasped to see Cathal's broad figure filling the doorway, his head bent to accommodate his height. She stood transfixed. Was she dreaming? Her heartbeat resounded in her ears. Then, blinking a few times, she fought the urge to rush towards him. He wore a dark jacket with a white open-necked shirt and grey trousers. She smiled and then, embarrassed, she touched her hair, wishing she had washed it.

'Eva, thank God! Until Ma got your letter with this address, we had no idea where you were, or what had happened to you!'

At the sound of his voice, she swallowed the lump in her throat. She couldn't believe he was here in front of her. He carried a small suitcase. Was he going away? She didn't want to ask and have him confirm her fears. How could she bear to lose him now?

'It's so good to see you, Cathal.'

Could he hear her heart beating? He took a few steps towards her.

She could feel Doreen's eyes on her back and she turned round. 'This is . . . this is my friend, from Dublin.'

'Pleased, I'm sure.' Doreen rushed over and offered her hand while Bernadette tore herself away to take orders.

'Nice to meet you, and thanks for looking after Eva.'

'Pleasure,' she said, smiling and hurrying back to serve a customer at the counter.

Eva couldn't drag her eyes from him. He moved closer and for the first time she noticed the tiny flecks of gold around the edges of his brown eyes. She wanted to touch him, make sure he was real and not a figment of her imagination.

He held up the case. 'Ma sent it, she thought you might need a change of clothes.'

She could have cried. So, he wasn't going away. He was

here to see her. 'Thank you. How thoughtful. Why don't you stay and have a cup of tea while I go upstairs and change?' She glanced over at Doreen, who gave her a conspiratorial wink. Eva ran her hand down her dress, which was sorely in need of a wash. 'I . . . I won't be a tick.'

Cathal sat down and Bernadette came over to take his order. Eva couldn't stop smiling. Her troubles were far from over, but with Cathal to help and advise her, she was ready to face the world.

She opened the case, and lifted out a pink floral dress and undergarments, a towel, Pear's soap and talcum powder. There was also a pair of Lisle stockings and a suspender belt. 'Oh, Ma!' A tear trickled down her cheeks. What would she do without her? She held the soap to her nose and inhaled the scent. The dress, although freshly ironed, was old-fashioned when compared with what the Dublin girls wore. But right now, it looked amazing. Hot and excited, she stripped off, poured water into the basin and washed her body, lathering her hair with the soap. When she was dry, she dressed in the fresh clothes and combed her hair, leaving it loose to dry. She wasn't used to the luxury of silk stockings against her skin and she took a while to get the line straight on the backs of her legs. Pushing everything into the case, her jacket over her arm, she went down.

Cathal was sitting cross-legged reading one of Doreen's newspapers. When he saw her, he stood up, folding the paper. 'You look gorgeous, so you do. It's so good to see you.'

'You too.'

'Are you . . . were you going somewhere when I arrived? Only . . . I mean, would you take a walk with me?'

She placed her bag over her shoulder. She would love to walk with him into eternity. 'Yes, I'd like that, but I'm catching a train to Cavan.' She gave Doreen a wave, picked up her case and followed him outside.

'I'll carry that.' He guided her down the street towards the Ha'penny Bridge. The sun was shining and she was pleased he was here by her side.

'What a lovely day,' she remarked.

'It's just perfect.' He smiled down at her. 'Do you have any idea how worried we were?'

Pausing halfway across the bridge, Eva glanced down at the Liffey. 'I do, and I'm sorry. I thought I'd never see you again.'

People walked around them where they stood.

'I . . . I phoned your station. You weren't there.'

'When? When did you phone?'

'The other morning, as soon as Doreen paid me.'

'I took time off to look for you.'

'You were looking for me?' She choked back a sob.

He paused by the Liffey wall. Barges, laden with barrels, sailed towards the docks. He turned to her. 'Eva, I said little to Doreen. I wasn't sure how much you'd told her.'

'Not much.'

'She must have thought it strange, you turning up with no luggage?'

Eva smiled, then nodded. 'Yes, she did. I told her I was in Dublin looking for work. It was lucky I came across her. I said I'd left Cavan in a hurry, and she formed her own opinion.'

'She believed you?'

'It wasn't a lie. Besides, I needed to survive.'

'You're extraordinary, Eva Fallon.'

She blushed. 'No, I'm not, Cathal. I'm accused of hiding an army deserter. I've been foolish. And when I'm forced to think about that man, it makes me angry.' Her heartbeat quickened as he moved closer to allow people to filter past them.

'Eva, none of it was your fault. You can be as vexed as you like. I'm sorry for what you've been through. I wish I could have gone with you to the station on Monday.'

'No, it was best I went alone. I know now the truth wasn't enough. They didn't believe me, and think me guilty.' She swallowed. 'They believe I was his girlfriend. It was horrible!' She shuddered.

'I promise you, it will all be sorted. And I still think you're a remarkable young woman.'

She stepped sideways when she heard the angelus bell ring out. 'I'll miss my train, and I want to see Ma Scully. Explain everything to her.'

He placed his hand on her arm and his closeness made her tremble. 'I've just come from there, Eva. She's expecting you.'

'Oh, that's grand.' She glanced up at him. 'Don't you have to be at the fire station?'

'Not until tomorrow. I'm coming to Cavan with you. We'll catch a later train. I'm not letting you out of my sight.' He laughed, and she laughed too, feeling like she was in a wonderful dream. 'We'll make time for lunch first.'

She looked down at her clothes. 'If you don't mind being seen around town with me?'

'You're beautiful, and I'd be proud to take you anywhere.'

'Now you're making me blush.' This wasn't a dream. Cathal was here by her side, offering to buy her lunch. Just two days ago she had almost died of starvation. Unable to express her feelings, she smiled and allowed him to escort her downtown.

They strolled along, at ease in each other's company. They passed many shops selling books, second-hand clothes, shoes and dresses. But they held little interest for her right now. She was walking side by side with Cathal, the man she loved and admired. He placed his hand on the small of her back as they darted between trams and crossed over O'Connell Street.

Eva looked around her. 'Why are the air-raid shelters still up? Is the capital under threat?' Her eyes widened and a worried frown wrinkled her brow.

'Ah, sure, don't worry, Eva. They're precautionary while the emergency lasts.' The sound of an aircraft flying over-head caused her to duck down. He touched her arm, and she stood up. 'It's just a passenger plane. Although some Americans are still based in Belfast.'

She knew cities were most at risk and she wished to be back in Cavan, safe from Hitler's bombs.

'Let's not think about the war, or anything associated with it for an hour,' he said, as if reading her thoughts. 'We'll find somewhere quiet where we can talk. I've not eaten and I'm wall fallen, so I am.' She knew only too well what that was like. Although Doreen's breakfast had satis-fied her hunger, she never wanted to experience that hollow feeling in her stomach ever again. They walked in silence, a discreet distance between them.

'Let's go in here.'

The waitress brought the menu; she had a lovely smile and Eva imagined she must have a wonderful life.

'What are you thinking about?' Cathal asked, removing his jacket and draping it across the back of his chair.

'How nice it would be to have a normal existence, like most people. Maybe I'm fooling myself and it will never happen.'

'Now who's being silly?'

'Well, since the orphanage fire nothing has gone right for me. I wonder why I bother.'

His face clouded. She had said the wrong thing. He must think her most ungrateful.

'Yes, you've had a rough time of it, Eva. But I never had you down as a quitter.'

She tossed her head. 'Who said anything about quitting? Just saying.'

He smiled at the determined jut of her chin.

'Look, let's eat.' Their food – two ham salads, crusty bread and butter, and a pot of tea – was placed before them. He leant forward. 'Now eat up, and then I have something important to discuss with you.'

Chapter Fifty-two

The train back to Cavan was empty, and they had a carriage to themselves. Eva wasn't surprised to hear there was a letter for her at Ma Scully's. The captain at the Castle had said he would want to speak to her again. Had it not been enough that she had answered all the questions put to her? She had nothing more to add. Cathal reassured her that, whatever the outcome, she would have his full support. And for that alone, she was thankful. But she couldn't help the butterflies that floated around in her tummy.

'What will happen if they still don't believe me?'

He placed his arm across her shoulders. 'Try not to worry. It might be nothing. Put it out of your mind. We'll face it together once we know what we're dealing with.'

'Do you think I'll go to prison?' She looked up, her eyes dark with despair.

'That won't happen,' he said. 'Remember, Eva. You're not the one on trial. All the army are interested in is nailing that louse for desertion.' He smiled.

She knew he was trying to cheer her up, and she wanted to believe him. He had been a rock of strength to her ever since that first day she escaped the orphanage fire.

'If it comes to it, and you need someone to defend you, I know of a good solicitor who might help. You'll be told how to plead and what to say. Don't worry. Trust me.' He removed his arm.

She wanted him to keep it there. It made her feel safe, and she wondered what it would be like if he was to kiss her.

'Eva, whatever you're thinking, get it out of your head because you've done nothing wrong.'

She smiled up at him. 'I know, and I'll try to be more positive.'

'Good, that's settled then.'

For the rest of the journey, they spoke of Ma Scully and laughed at everyday things.

'Feeling better now?' he asked.

'Yes, much.'

By the time they arrived in Cavan, Eva was ready to stand up in court and fight to clear her name of any wrongdoing.

Ma Scully clasped her in a hug. She had a sprig of lavender pinned to her dress and Eva buried her face in her ample chest, so pleased to see the older woman again. Tears gathered in her eyes.

'Sure, you're home now and that's all that matters.' Ma patted her shoulder. 'Ye've had a rotten time of it, so ye have. And I want to know all about it.' There was a delicious smell of rabbit stew wafting around the room. 'I have everything ready. Ye must be famished.' She took Eva's jacket and hung it up.

Cathal remained standing. 'I won't be staying, Ma. Once I know what's in Eva's letter, I'll be on my way.'

'Ye've time for a morsel first. It'll sustain ye for the journey back,' Ma cajoled. 'Now sit down. There's enough here to feed a horse.'

Smiling, her nephew pulled out a chair. 'Well, I can't argue with that, Ma. The smell has given me a right appetite. But I must leave straight afterwards. I've someone to see.'

Eva felt a stab to her heart. He was seeing someone, and the girl must wonder where he'd been. He looked tired, and she felt responsible for him chasing around Dublin looking for her. She had mistaken his acts of kindness for something else, letting her imagination run ahead of her as usual.

As Ma spooned out their hot meal, Eva said, 'I should open that letter.'

'Oh, it can wait. I want nothing to spoil the enjoyment of the food.'

'I agree.' Cathal tucked in.

Eva lowered her head. 'I thought I'd never see either of you again.'

'It's been a worrying few days. But, sure, I'm glad you're back safe.' Ma smiled towards Eva. 'It might be good news, so it might.'

The food smelt delicious. Cathal ate without speaking until he had finished. Eva was struggling with hers, feeling fuller with every spoonful. Ma pushed hers to the side, stood up and plucked the letter from the mantel shelf. 'Here, get it over with.' She handed Eva a letter opener. 'Put us all out of our misery.'

The three of them sat waiting as Eva lifted the important-looking letter from the envelope.

Cathal sat back in his chair. 'Would you like me to read it, Eva?'

She shook her head and unfolded the stiff paper.

Tribunal: District of Dublin
Name: Private Matthew Blackstock
Address: Blackstock's farm, Bawnboy, in the county of
    Cavan. Residing at the Curragh Camp, Co Kildare.
Date: 29th June 1943
Notice of hearing

Notice is hereby given that the case of the above-named soldier of which details are stated below will be considered at the place and on the date shown.

APPLICATION FOR REVIEW OF CERTIFICATE OR EXEMPTION FROM COMBAT SERVICES.

Case to be considered at Military Headquarters, Dublin.

Date: 29th July at 11 a.m.
Signed: Captain McLaughlin, Military Police

The silence was tangible.

Seconds passed before Eva spoke. 'There's another letter enclosed.'

Cathal reached across and covered her hand with his. He then removed the letter from her trembling fingers. Ma brought her chair closer.

Tribunal: District of Dublin
Name: Eva Fallon
Address: Care of Primrose Cottage, Main Street, Cavan

Date: 29th June 1943
Notice of hearing

Notice is hereby given that you attend the case stated below at the place and time shown to give evidence and answer questions on alleged offences. You are honour bound to attend under a court of law.

Review of the alleged offence: Concealing the whereabouts of deserter Private Matthew Blackstock at Blackstock's farm during wartime and perverting the course of justice.

Case to be considered at Military Headquarters, Dublin.

Date: 29th July 1943 at 11 a.m.
Signed: Captain McLaughlin, Military Police

Eva choked back a sob. She would come face-to-face with the man who had tried to ruin her life. His hearing was scheduled for the same day and time as hers. It couldn't be worse. She was charged with a serious offence and there was nothing she could do. Her word had no standing.

Cathal placed his hand on her shoulder. 'We have a whole month to prepare, so, you mustn't let it get to you. Stay strong, we'll fight this.'

Her resolve was already weakening. 'Defence lawyers are expensive.'

'Eva's right, Cathal. Who have ye got in mind?'

'Leave all that to me.' He smiled across at Eva, then glanced at his watch. 'I'm sorry but I have to dash.'

Eva's heart sank. She didn't want him to leave. He instilled confidence in her, and that would ebb as soon as he disappeared. 'I'm sorry to leave now, Eva, but I have no choice.' He buttoned his jacket. 'I'll be in touch.' Then he kissed his aunt's cheek and made for the door.

Eva watched him through the window until he was out of sight.

Observing her, Ma said, 'Come and help me wash up this lot, then you can tell me what they said to ye at Dublin Castle.'

Chapter Fifty-three

Matthew Blackstock sat in his darkened cell, not knowing what time of day it was, cursing the injustice meted out to him since his internment. He had railed against the decision to place him in with IRA prisoners, serial rapists and other deserters but it had got him nowhere. The conditions, overcrowding and lack of privacy had overwhelmed him until he had rebelled, landing himself in detention, and isolation.

After yet another beating, he lay on his bunk. Any movement aggravated the pain in his legs; otherwise he would have lashed out at the walls of his tiny cell. No one heard his whimpering. No one cared. He was regarded as insubordinate and a coward. Regretting none of his outbursts, he wanted to die rather than face any trial. He wrapped his arms tightly across his body, as if squeezing out his despair.

That skinny bitch who worked at the farm would give evidence against him. The army wouldn't care about what he had done to her. Punishing him for desertion was all they were interested in. He had wanted to ruin her, stop her messing with men like his father, and he would have succeeded if that idiot from out of town hadn't happened along. His father didn't treat her like a skivvy; he had seen him pander to her treating her as if she was a member of the family and not a scullery maid. It disgusted him, and his mam not cold in her grave. This chit of a girl had taken her place in his father's affections. He clenched his fists and winced at the pain in his knuckles.

An old black-and-white photograph of his mother sent to him by his granny was stuck to the wall, taken before she became sick. She wore a long-sleeved blouse and a dowdy brown skirt. He gazed at the picture. How appalled she would be to see where he had ended up. His father had blamed him for her death. It wasn't true. He left because he'd never liked working on the farm. But he would not let that slut get her hands on it. And the way he was feeling right now, he'd give anything to be back there on his father's farm.

He moved on to his side and cried out in pain. No one would come until morning. Dreading the long night ahead, he couldn't remember the last time he'd slept. This was a hellhole far worse than what he had experienced in the North African Campaign. No one could sleep in this godforsaken place, and when he drifted off, he dreamed he saw the faces of his comrades – limbless, lying in the mud. He could smell the stench of dead bodies, then someone was playing the mouth organ, and the world appeared sane and normal for a short time before the next barrage of artillery shattered the peace and he awoke in a sweat. He hadn't wanted to die, had begged for leave of absence to go home to see his mother. Being refused had made him run. With hindsight, it would have been better if he had stayed and died like his friend Thomas.

A shard of light shone under the door. He braced himself. There was the sound of footsteps outside on the landing. The COs were checking the spyholes. Heavy steps pounded closer to his cell. Were they going to do him over again? Numb with pain, he was past fear. If they beat him he'd be dead by morning. The bolt was drawn, followed by the hiss of a key turning in the lock. He saw the polished toecaps and glanced up to see the well-pressed uniform of his CO who hadn't given him a kind word since being locked up here. The orderly placed a bowl of water on the table with carbolic soap, a towel and a grey, loose-fitting tunic.

'On your feet, traitor,' the CO bellowed. 'You've got ten minutes to clean yourself up.'

Matthew remained silent.

'Are you deaf? I said, on your feet, *traitor*!'

If his jaw didn't hurt so much, he would tell this piece of shit where to stick his orders. He rolled off the bed and tried to stand, but his legs gave way and he collapsed in a heap at the CO's feet. The orderly rushed in.

'Go for the medic and be quick about it. I'm not taking the rap if this gobshite kicks the bucket.'

Chapter Fifty-four

Ma's fingers had become painful and swollen and Eva was glad to be of some help around the house. She did the washing, went to the dairy and made herself useful. But it bothered her that she could only repay Ma in kind. Most folks were struggling to make ends meet and although she tried for local work, there was nothing going.

She spent time at the library. And with help from the assistant she found her way around the bookshelves. She spent as much time as she could in the reading room, and the more she read the more she realised what a sheltered life she had led. Looking up various aspects of the law and court procedure that might be helpful to her later, armed her with knowledge she would otherwise not have known. She felt anxious about taking the oath, and she could not wait to see Cathal again and go over everything with him.

She was desperate to find work and, experienced at sewing and embroidery, she wondered if she should approach the nuns.

Ma discouraged her. 'Don't do that, Eva. Sure, them nuns will want ye to work for nothing, so they will.'

'But I have to do something. I can't live off you. It's not fair.'

Ma puckered her lips. 'Well, I said nothing before but the dairy are looking for a reliable milking maid. Old Simms was telling me the other day he can't get anyone who's not frightened of milking a few cows. If ye think you could do it?'

'Why? How many cows are there?'

'Oh, there's a whole herd of them, so there is. And you'd be there from dawn till dusk, shepherding them back and forth from the field to the sheds.'

'I'll do it, Ma. Can't be any worse than working for Blackstock.' Besides, she needed something to keep her from dwelling on the trial, and the long hours would suit her fine.

'Shall I tell him you'll call in then? He'll only pay two bob.'

'Yes, please, Ma. It's more than I have now.'

Eva discovered that Mr Simms was a kind, rosy-faced farmer who was fond of his herd.

'Have you milked cows before?'

'No, but if you show me how it's done, I can learn.'

He frowned, lifted his straw hat and scratched his head. 'So, you're willing to have a go then?'

She nodded.

'They need careful handling.'

'It'll be grand. Honest,' she said, with conviction. Now she had to convince herself.

'Can you start the morra at six? I'll do the weekends myself like.' He looked down at her sandals. 'What size feet have you?'

'Oh . . .' She didn't know. Most of her shoes were hand-me-downs and sometimes too big. 'Size four should be grand.'

'I doubt I have any that small, but, sure, I'll have a wee look and see if I can find a pair of rubber boots. You might have to stuff the toes with newspaper.'

She nodded. 'How big is the herd?'

'Two dozen. Each one knows their own name. A list is pinned up in the milking shed. And if you talk to them, call them by their names, they'll give creamy milk. That's important, you understand.'

'Yes, Mr Simms.' Was he serious? Eva suppressed a giggle. It was just what she needed to take her mind off her own concerns.

'Right, I'll see you the morra, bright and early like.'

When she got back, Ma greeted her as she walked in. 'How'd ye get on?'

'I start at six in the morning.'

'Well, good for you, love. And it's only down the way.'

Eva smiled, filled the kettle and hung it over the hob.

'Oh,' Ma said. 'This letter came for ye while you were out.'

They both sat at the table. Eva recognised the handwriting and a wobbly, excited feeling stirred in her stomach.

'What's he say then?'

Eva scanned it first, then read it aloud.

Dear Eva,

I'm sorry I can't get down this weekend. I'm on duty and I'm not even sure about the following weekend.

315

Tell Ma not to worry. It's all in the line of duty. A known gang of kids with nothing better to do are setting fires in the Wicklow hills and we are flat out trying to stop it from spreading.

She paused and glanced up at Ma. Disappointment brought on a dull ache that settled in her stomach.

'Go on. What else does he say?'

I'm also working on your behalf and you should get correspondence any day now from a Dublin solicitor, Mr Kelly, with a date to come and see him at his office. He's a decent sort who has lived a time in England.

I'll be there to meet you. Let me know when it arrives. The sooner I know, the sooner I can arrange leave.

I trust all is well with you both and that you are keeping busy. It will help to pass the time.

All the best,
Cathal

Eva clutched the letter to her. Two whole weeks. She missed him so much. Ma got to her feet. 'Right then! That's good news and the quicker all this is cleared up the better.'

Eva nodded while reading through the letter again. There was no sign of anything other than friendship in it. She frowned. For all she knew, he could still be seeing the librarian.

'And you can stop worrying.' Ma's words broke into her thoughts. 'Cathal won't let you down. Sure, the lad's sweet on ye.'

Eva's cheeks coloured. 'What makes you say that, Ma?'

'Ah, it's as plain as the nose on his face, so it is.'

Eva's hand covered her mouth. Cathal had intimated nothing of that to her. 'Is . . . I mean is he, you know. Is he still seeing the librarian?'

'Sure, hasn't he said?'

'No! Not to me.'

'Well, he told me they were no longer walking out. And that this Isabel, whom I've never met, and he weren't suited.'

Eva's face brightened. A gush of words came into her mind but she held back, fearful of revealing too much of her feelings in front of Ma. He would suit her fine, she thought. Then on impulse, 'I'd be proud to walk out with him.'

Ma glanced up from setting the table. 'What's that?'

'I'm sorry.' She felt hot. 'I shouldn't have said. Cathal would never want to, not with me—'

'Will ye give over and let me get a word in? I'd like nothing better than to see me two favourite people walking out together. I'll admit at first I had me doubts but . . . I've watched ye grow into a strong, confident young woman. Never let it be said that Ma Scully stood in the way of true love.'

'Oh, Ma. Thank you.'

'Sure, me only concern was that you'd seen nothing of life, pet, and that you were too young to know your own mind.'

'That's not true, Ma. By the time the trial is over I'll have experienced enough, more than most girls my age. I've loved Cathal from the first moment I saw him. There'll be no one else.' She gushed, then lowered her eyes. Had she revealed too much?

Smiling, Ma sat down while Eva cut bread and buttered scones.

'That's quite a declaration, Eva, love. And aye! Happen yer more mature than I give ye credit for. I think we'd better keep this to ourselves for now. Men are slow to show their true feelings, and Cathal's no different.'

Next morning, Mr Simms was waiting when she arrived at the milking shed. Kitted out in rubber boots and plastic apron, she sat on the three-legged stool and watched while he instructed her on how to warm her hands before touching the cow's udders. The cowshed was hot from the animals and she could smell the fresh milk as it squirted against the sides of the galvanised bucket.

'Now you try,' he said.

Eva settled herself, pulling the seat closer, her head close to the cow's stomach. As soon as Eva put her hand on the cow's udder, it was obvious the animal didn't like it and she kicked the bucket over. Luckily it wasn't full.

She expected Mr Simms to tell her off but instead his laugh was hearty. 'Daisy's not the most compliant, but once you get to know her, she will be more cooperative,' he assured her. 'Come on, Daisy, be a good girl.'

Eva thought she would never get the hang of it, but Mr Simms encouraged her. When the milking was finished, he instructed her how to herd the cows outside, two at a time. It took ages.

And it took days of trying and failing before Eva came to look forward to seeing her friends the cows, and got to know each of them by name.

Talking to them like they were children at first seemed a crazy idea. But once she did, they trusted her – apart from Daisy, who refused to cooperate unless Mr Simms milked her.

On occasions, Eva helped Mr Simms with household chores and he increased her money to five shillings. She still had time to visit the library and help Ma Scully in the evenings. The week flew past and, apart from missing Cathal, Eva found she had less time to dwell on her fate regarding the trial. She was finding a new contentment.

Chapter Fifty-five

It was a wet Saturday morning when Eva stepped from the train. Her eyes scanned the crowded platform for Cathal. When she couldn't see him, her stomach lurched. Had he forgotten? Perhaps he was delayed at work. It was eleven thirty, and her appointment with the solicitor was at noon. She sat down on the wooden bench to wait and opened her handbag to retrieve the letter. She had no idea where Merrion Square was, or what the solicitor would cost.

A cold breeze swept along the platform. She tightened the buckled belt of her tweed coat that Ma had insisted she wore. 'The weather in Dublin can be as contrary as the folk who live there,' she had said. Now Eva was glad she had heeded her, and she pushed her hands inside her pockets. A poster advertising the latest fashions read: 'You might as well be out of the world as out of fashion.' It made her smile. She was never more conscious of it than when she came up to Dublin. None of the young women had long, straight hair, and she wondered what it would be like to have her own cut in a fashionable style.

She was just about to go outside and look for Cathal when he arrived, windswept and out of breath.

'Sorry, Eva. I got delayed at work. Hope you haven't been waiting long?'

Her face brightened. 'That's okay. You're here now.'

He opened his black umbrella, drawing her underneath. 'It's not far. Are you all right to walk, or would you prefer to take the tram?'

'No. I don't mind walking.' She liked being this close to him and inhaled the clean crisp smell of his masculine scent.

He placed his hand on her waist as they flitted between the traffic.

'Is it me, or are there more cars in the city today?' she asked.

'You're not wrong there, Eva. And I find that surprising, in spite of the war.'

They arrived outside the solicitor's office. He guided her up the few steps to the front door and placed the wet brolly in the receptacle. Eva felt anxious thinking about the cost, and although Cathal had told her not to worry, she couldn't help her feelings of inadequacy regarding her financial situation.

Cathal placed his hand on her arm. 'Eva, before we go up, Mr Kelly is offering his services free of charge.'

Her face clouded. 'Cathal . . . I don't want to be seen as a charity case.'

'He's doing this because, like me, he's a man of integrity and he wants justice for you. He asked me some questions I couldn't avoid answering. I'm sorry if it makes you feel uncomfortable, Eva. But we can't look a gift horse in the mouth, can we?'

'No. I'm sorry. I don't mean to sound ungrateful.'

'It's grand. Just be yourself and it'll be fine.' He smiled and escorted her upstairs.

Clearing his throat, he knocked on the door. The solicitor, a fat portly man, shook both their hands and gestured for them to sit.

Eva folded her hands in her lap and composed herself.

'Mr Burke has explained the situation you find yourself in, Miss Fallon. The hearing is in two weeks, is that right, on the 29th of July?' He glanced down at his diary.

Eva nodded, then raised her head. 'I've done nothing wrong, and I told the truth but . . .'

'Unfortunately, the truth is not always the most convincing story. Remember, Miss Fallon, that you are not the one on trial. But it would be advisable to get yourself a defence lawyer.'

'But . . . why?'

'I have to warn you that these trials can be intimidating to most. But for a girl like yourself, with little experience of these things . . .'

Cathal touched her hand.

Mr Kelly cleared his throat. 'To my knowledge the outcome of court cases, including court-martials, are determined within a day or two, so you should only have to attend the once.'

'You mean it could take longer?' The idea knotted her stomach.

'It's unlikely in this case, Miss Fallon.'

Cathal leant forward. 'Mr Kelly, would you say Eva's guilty of perverting the course of justice?'

'Only if they can make it stick.' He turned towards Eva, who was feeling out of her depth. 'My advice to you, young lady, is to get as many witnesses as you can to back up your story. And someone to vouch for your good character will help.' He stood up and went to his files.

Eva's vulnerability returned, and her stomach tightened. The solicitor handed her a card. 'Ring this fellow. He's sterling. Tell him I've sent you, and with him on your side, I'm sure it will turn out okay.' He remained standing.

Cathal got to his feet and proffered his hand. 'Thanks for seeing us, Mr Kelly. What you've said is most helpful.'

The solicitor shook both their hands and wished Eva good luck.

The following week, Eva and Cathal were in Dublin again. Each time they met up, a closeness grew between them. When they were together, nothing could douse her confidence, but when they were apart she felt as if she was drowning in a whirlpool she couldn't break free of. Today they were going to see a defence lawyer.

It wasn't until they were walking towards his rooms, around the corner from Fitzwilliam Street, that Eva's courage ebbed. 'What if he doesn't believe me?'

'The truth is the truth, Eva, no matter how it's interpreted by others. Don't lose heart. Sure, you haven't met him yet, and Mr Kelly wouldn't have suggested him if he didn't think you had a chance.' He gave her hand a little squeeze.

It was enough to boost her self-confidence. She would do this, otherwise she would not only be letting herself down but the two people who had believed in her the most.

Once inside the lawyer's office, introductions were made, and they all relaxed before they got down to business. Eva had imagined lawyers to be unapproachable. However, Mr Timmons, a tall thin man in his thirties, possessed an air of friendly authority in spite of being dressed in casual cords and a sloppy-looking navy jersey. But then it was the weekend and good of him to give up his time. Passing them each a mug of coffee, he sat down behind his mahogany desk. He placed a cigarette between his lips, leaving it unlit and dangling. A stack of papers, held together with a large paperclip, and a pile of folders were moved to the side before he opened his diary. He dipped his fountain pen into the inkwell and drew ink before glancing up.

'Now, Miss Fallon,' he removed the cigarette to drink his coffee, 'my colleague, Tim Kelly, has informed me of your situation and I'm ready to defend you.' He jotted something down. Looking up, he smiled at her. 'If you could tell me in your own words what happened from your first encounter with Blackstock junior in the barn?'

She glanced towards Cathal, and his smile reassured her. Taking a deep breath, she began her story, pausing only when she got to the bit about hiding his army uniform. What an idiot she had been not to have realised the consequences.

'Take your time. It is crucial we get your side of things straight.' The solicitor continued to scribble down notes and replenish the ink in his pen. 'Is that everything, Miss Fallon?' He cleared his throat. 'Please hold nothing back. If there is anything at all that might come to light on the day of the trial, I'd rather hear it now. Otherwise it could discredit you and weaken my case. You understand?'

How could she recount to a complete stranger what Matthew had done to her? And for Cathal to hear it from her own lips would be worse. She felt the bile rise in her throat. What if Matthew brought it up, blaming her? How would she feel then? She fidgeted with her hands.

'Miss Fallon, is there anything else I should know?'

She glanced up and tears gathered in her eyes.

Cathal reached for her hand. 'It's all right, Eva.'

Eva took a deep breath and then, her face hot with embarrassment, she held nothing back. Cathal passed her his handkerchief, and after mopping her eyes she sipped the water Mr Timmons had fetched for her.

'I appreciate how difficult that must have been, Miss Fallon. Thank you for telling me.' He finished writing and leant his elbows on the desk. 'However, he won't be tried for his abhorrent attack on you, and will get away with it even though he set out to discredit your reputation from the word go. What you've told me will help me to get justice for you in the trial.'

Desperate to stop her limbs trembling, she nodded her thanks.

'Will Eva have to talk about this in court?' Cathal asked, returning his handkerchief to his pocket.

'It's unlikely, but if this scoundrel brings it up to dishonour Miss Fallon, I'll be forewarned.' His elbows on the desk, he linked his fingers. 'The army will try him for desertion. His CO will try to defend him. All they're interested in is finding him guilty of shunning his duties in the face of the enemy. When you're questioned, just be truthful.' He put the cigarette back between his lips and stood up. 'If I were you,' he turned towards Cathal, 'I would take the young lady somewhere nice and leave the trial aside until the 29th.' His handshake was firm. 'I'll see you in court, Miss Fallon. In the meantime, if you think of anything you need to tell me before then, you can get me on this number.' He handed her a small white card.

Chapter Fifty-six

Eva found that milking cows made her less anxious. But as the date of the hearing drew nearer, she couldn't sleep and even her visits to the cathedral to pray and light candles did nothing to dispel the knots that each day formed in her stomach. Cathal sent her letters of encouragement, telling her he would support her all the way. Each night when her eyelids closed, all she could see were Matthew's cold eyes staring at her, his mouth twisted in a sneer.

When Ma Scully caught her staring at nothing in particular, she chided her. 'You've got to keep strong, Eva. Ye want to win, don't ye?'

'I do, Ma. But the waiting is what's getting me down.'

'Sure, it'll be here before you know it, so it will.' She rocked back in her chair. 'If I'm called as a witness, I'll give them what for, you see if I don't.'

'Oh, Ma. The lawyer was doubtful about that. The only witnesses are the Blackstocks, and they're out to blacken my name.'

'Well, I know little about the law, Eva. But you didn't escape that fire to end up accused of something you didn't do, now did ye?'

Ma was right. She had to fight her corner. Her reputation was at stake. 'If only . . .'

'What?'

'There won't be anyone in that courtroom, apart from the lawyer, defending my good name and vouching for my honesty and integrity. So, I've been thinking of asking the nuns for a character reference. What do you think?'

'I think ye've swallowed the dictionary.'

'I've been reading about the law, Ma.'

'Aye! Well, too much learning's not always a good thing.' She folded her arms. 'I suppose there's no harm asking them nuns. What about that Sister Catherine? You said she was fond of ye.'

The following morning, Ma walked with Eva as far as the convent on her way to a meeting at the Town Hall. 'Go on now. Good luck.'

Eva, having rehearsed what she would say, had a sudden attack of the shakes and fought the urge to change her mind. Straightening her shoulders, she reminded herself that she was no longer a child in their care, and the nuns had no hold over her any more. She was a woman in charge of her own destiny and in desperate need of their help. She took a deep breath and rang the bell.

The convent door was opened with caution at first, then wider, by a young nun she didn't recognise.

'Would it be possible to speak with Sister Catherine?'

'She's teaching. Is she expecting you?'

Eva shook her head. She would hate it if she had to come

back another day; her courage would have deserted her by then. 'Can I wait?'

'Come in while I find out.'

She stepped into the hall with polished quarry tiles, the centre covered with a square of Axminster carpet. There was a light mahogany table and chair by the wall, and above it a statue of Mary. The wide staircase and the familiar smell of lavender polish brought a lump to her throat. In the silence the ticking of the grandfather clock set her nerves on edge. Through the open door she could see furniture she had polished many times, and thoughts of her unhappy life here came flooding back. So many silly rules, like running in the corridor, warranted a detention. How hard she had to work, looking after the infants, being wakened at night to attend to them. And then being punished for falling asleep throughout her afternoon lessons. Apart from Sister Catherine, she didn't think the nuns were holy; some of them were cruel, the way they beat her for the smallest misdemeanour. The hours spent kneeling, praying for forgiveness, when she felt she had done nothing wrong. No matter how bad her life was now, she would miss none of this.

She remained standing for some time before Sister Catherine bounced in and greeted her with a smile.

'Bridget! It's good to see you again. Shall we?' She guided her into the refectory and asked her to sit.

'My name's Eva, Sister. The name my parents gave me.'

The nun smiled and inclined her head, then she looked up. 'What's troubling you, child, and how can I be of help?'

There was a tap on the door and the young nun who had admitted Eva entered with a tea tray and placed it on the low coffee table.

'I have often wondered what became of you.'

Sister Catherine poured tea into small cups and Eva sat back in the chair. There was no mention of the orphanage fire.

'So, what brings you back?'

'It's complicated, Sister.'

The nun was looking at Eva's floral summer dress and white cotton jacket. 'You're working then?'

'Well, yes, at the dairy. I live with Ma Scully at the far end of Main Street.'

Sister Catherine leant forward, crunched a custard cream and sipped her tea. 'You're turning into a fine young woman.'

'Thank you, Sister.' Eva fidgeted with her hands and hoped she wouldn't ask her too many details about her life.

'I hope you're not neglecting to say your morning and night-time prayers and attending the sacraments?'

Eva would not lie to the nun, as she wanted her to say good things about her in court. 'I do my best, Sister Catherine.'

'Well, now, what's wrong, child?'

An anxious feeling knotted her stomach. Her fingers played with the folds of her dress and she swallowed.

'Are you in trouble?'

'Yes, and no, Sister Catherine. I've somehow got myself tangled up in a dilemma.' She bit her bottom lip. 'I was wondering if you would give evidence in court as to my good character?' There, it was out.

The nun shifted, placed her cup back on the saucer. Shock registered on her face. 'Do you realise what you are asking? No one has ever asked such a thing of me before.'

'I know it's unusual, Sister.'

'What have you done to warrant you going to court?

And even if I could help you, the Mother Superior would never allow it.'

Eva leant forward. 'Sister Catherine, please reconsider. You've known me from the first day I entered the orphanage. And in spite of my frustrations when I lived here, you know I'm not a bad person. Please say you'll help me.' In the past, the nun had come to her aid and got her out of many scrapes, bringing her bread and milk when she was in detention. Surely, she wouldn't let her down now.

Sister Catherine fiddled with her rosary beads.

Eva's bottom lip trembled as she reached for her tea. 'I promise you I've done nothing wrong, and you are the only person I can turn to.'

The nun studied her. Then she put her hands together, as if in prayer, and settled back into her chair. 'Well, so, I think you had better tell me what this is all about, don't you? Then we'll see what Mother Superior has to say.'

Mother Superior sat stony-faced in front of her. In spite of Eva's appeal for mercy, she was adamant. 'Whatever trouble you've got yourself into, I will not allow you to bring this establishment into disrepute. Is that clear?'

'Please, let me explain. I've done nothing wrong. I—'

'Silence, girl!'

Eva had no choice but to listen to a litany of good and bad behaviour and how she should have thought about her Catholic teaching and the consequences of her actions. Had she done so, she wouldn't have found herself in such a predicament.

Sister Catherine, who had sat poker-faced throughout the litany, intervened. 'Far be it from me to questions your authority, Mother, but we can't let one of our own young women go to prison. She did what she had to do under great duress and with no knowledge of the consequences.'

The Mother Superior glared at Sister Catherine, who glanced down at her hands. In the brief silence that followed, Eva crossed her fingers.

'No, no, I can't allow it.' The older woman stood up and walked across to the window.

Eva closed her eyes in a silent prayer.

'Is there nothing we can do,' Sister Catherine asked. 'The girl's innocent. She was coerced by intimidation and threats.'

The Mother Superior came back and sat down, her hands joined in front of her. 'To appear in public is out of the question. However, Sister, if you feel it will help the girl, you may write a letter to the court, outlining Bridget's character, her good Catholic upbringing and anything else to help her case.' She stood up and made a swift movement towards the door.

Later that evening, Eva found it hard to relax. She paced the room, going over everything she needed to say at the trial, until she couldn't think straight.

'Sure, will ye stop pacing about? Ye'll wear a hole in the lino, so ye will.'

'I'm sorry, Ma, you must be fed up with all this.'

'Here,' Ma handed her the evening newspaper, 'it'll take your mind off things. I'm tired. I'll read it the morra.' Ma had been grumpy all day and Eva wondered if her rheumatism had worsened.

Bored reading about the war, she was about to put the paper down when a notice bigger than the usual obituaries caught her eye.

The funeral arrangements for the repose of the soul
of the late Finbar McCreedy will take place at Templeport Church, on 29th July 1943. After which his
body will be interred in the family plot on St Mogue's
Island.

A sadness enveloped her. No, please God, don't let it be
true. A sob caught the back of her throat. She turned to Ma,
who had her eyes closed. 'Oh, no. I can't believe it, Ma?'

'Sure, what ails ye now?'

'Something awful's happened. Big Finn ... he's ...
he's ...'

'Ye've gone white as a sheet. What are you reading?' Ma
took the paper from her, and after a few seconds declared,
'Ah, the poor old crater. May the Lord have mercy on his
soul.'

The times Eva had meant to call on him, but now it was
too late. Tears fell in large drops on to her hands. 'Oh, I feel
terrible. So wrapped up in my own problems, I've let him
down. I should have gone back to see how he was after he
lost his grandson.'

'Stop fretting. He's in a better place, so he is.' Ma patted
her hand. 'Sure, ye've had no time to think with all this
other stuff going on. Put it from your mind and say a wee
prayer for his soul.'

Eva couldn't forget. 'I'll go to his funeral, it's the least I
can do. Would you come with me?'

Ma picked up the paper. 'It's this Thursday.' She shook
her head. 'Ah, sure, that's sod's law, so it is.'

'So I can't even pay my last respects.' She sat down and
blew her nose. 'I wish you'd known him, Ma.' A little smile
wrinkled her face. 'He was funny, made me laugh, so he did.'

'Aye! Well, you can visit his resting place later on, but for now, ye've enough to concentrate on.'

Ma was right, she needed to focus on the trial. But in bed that night she thought about Big Finn who had befriended her, made her a meal and listened to her troubles.

Chapter Fifty-seven

The day before the trial, Eva arrived back at the cottage to find a letter addressed to her, which confused her more.

Dear Miss Fallon,

I am writing to update you on the case. Since we were last in contact the following key events have taken place.

Due to unforeseen circumstances, Private Matthew Blackstock's court appearance has been postponed.

A copy of this letter has been filed. In light of this, I plan to inform you of a revised date and time for the new hearing.

Mr C. Timmons,
Defence Lawyer

She sat and pondered what this meant. After all the waiting, when she had lived with the inevitability that it would happen, it had been cancelled. A mixture of annoyance and relief swept over her. Why? And how much longer would it drag on, keeping her in limbo? She wanted to move on – but how could she, until this episode of her life was over? She read the letter again. Had something happened to him? Cathal had booked the day off to support her. She must let him know as soon as possible. And Ma had rearranged her appointments to accompany her.

Checking she had Cathal's phone number in her bag and enough money in her purse, she hurried down to the local store. She was both nervous and excited to be phoning him. Two customers in the shop bid her good day, then lingered, ears cocked to find out who she was ringing.

'Move along now, ladies,' the storekeeper said. 'You're blocking the doorway.' Shrugging and muttering, they left. He raised his eyebrows. 'I'll be out the back. Give me a shout if anyone wants serving.'

The phone rang three times before being picked up.

'Hello, how can I help?'

'Can I . . . is Cathal Burke there, please? It's Eva Fallon.' She took a breath.

'Hello, Eva. I'm Andy Baxter. I'm sorry but Cathal's out in Bray on fire duty.'

'Oh!'

'You could call back later, or leave a message?'

'No, thank you. Can you tell him I called and that it's important?'

'Sure.'

The phone clicked and purred in her ear before she replaced the receiver.

When she arrived back, Ma was home, and she told her about the letter.

'And they left it this late to let ye know!' Ma was furious.

'It's a bother for everyone.'

Ma nodded and passed the letter back to Eva. 'Put it in a safe place.'

'Why do you suppose he can't attend?'

Ma shook her head. 'There could be many reasons. Not your worry. Now what about Cathal? He must know.'

'He's out on call. This is such a mess.'

'It'll be grand. One door closes, another opens. The three of us can pay our last respects at Big Finn's funeral.'

She hadn't thought of that. 'Are you sure Cathal will want to come?'

'Aye! I guess he will. I'll go down in a wee while and phone him.'

Eva's face brightened.

Ma stood up and moved across to the stove. 'Sure, let's get the bit of dinner afore it turns to mush.'

In spite of the downpour, the church at Templeport drew a crowd for Big Finn's funeral service. It transpired that Finn had no living relatives, but he had many friends willing to give him a good send-off. Two neighbours, along with Eva, Ma Scully and Cathal, weathered the storm and crossed the lake by boat to the family burial plot on the island.

Mr Blackstock raised his hat and came across to where they stood, wearing waterproof capes and hats. 'It's a rum day for a funeral,' he said. 'Good to see you again, Eva.'

Eva couldn't bring herself to look at him; she had not seen him since she'd left the farm months ago.

'I want a word with you, Jacob Blackstock.' Ma's tone was cutting.

Cathy Mansell

'You're not the only one,' Cathal said. 'But this is neither the time nor the place.'

'Indeed! We can talk later at the wake.' Ma shrugged, then pulled the strings of her waterproof hood tighter under her chin.

The rain was relentless. They moved to the side while the men loaded Finn's coffin on to a flat-bottomed boat. Cathal took Ma's arm and helped her into the rowing boat, and then Eva. She had never been in a boat before but somehow the lake held no fear for her. The air was humid in spite of the rain. Cathal edged closer to Eva and held her hand. In her other hand she held a bunch of wild lavender, tied together with blue ribbon.

'Right then,' the boatman said. 'There's room for two more in here.' Mr Blackstock stepped in and sat next to Ma. The boat wobbled from side to side. 'Can you sit in the back, sir?' the man told him.

Again the boat swayed and Eva stiffened, letting go of Cathal's hand to grip the side of the boat. 'It won't sink, will it?'

Cathal smiled. 'Sure, if it does, I'll save you.'

She gave him a shy smile and relaxed her shoulders. When they were ready, the man took up the oars and eased the boat out from the landing station and made steady pace behind the cot that carried Finn to his resting place. It was a solemn crossing, during which no one spoke apart from the mutterings of prayers.

Eva couldn't help a sob that caught the back of her throat. Again, she regretted not going to see him. He had been a true friend to her. But she was here now, and she hoped he knew.

When they arrived, the rain stopped and a chink of light

brightened the sky. Wild flowers covered the small island, and some family tombs were hidden beneath brambles and ivy. Cathal, Eva and Ma stood together while Mr Blackstock and two neighbours stood a few feet apart.

Eva had wanted to visit the island but never imagined it would be to bury her dear friend. Prayers were said over the coffin as it was lowered into the ground. In spite of the sadness of the occasion, from where they stood, the view was stunning.

'I'm not surprised Big Finn wanted to be buried here,' she whispered to Cathal.

'Shame the residents can't see it.'

She smiled at his humour.

Soon they were back across the water and shedding their rainwear. Mr Blackstock striding along beside them made Eva feel uncomfortable. With so much left unsaid, she hoped that would be rectified before the end of the day. However, as a mark of respect, no one spoke until they were inside the wake.

The meal of hot soup and sandwiches was a welcome sight. Eva hated the confrontation that was sure to take place and wished it didn't have to happen at Finn's funeral.

Then, as if reading her mind, Ma said, 'Why don't the two of you get off? I'll stay a while longer. See what I can find out from Blackstock.'

'I need a word with the father of that evil scoundrel,' Cathal said.

'No, Cathal. If you get his goat, he'll become obstinate. And we don't want to risk him changing his mind about giving evidence on Eva's behalf. Now, you take Eva back to mine. She's had enough for one day. I'll find out what's going on.'

The look of annoyance on Cathal's face didn't go amiss but Eva knew he would not go against his aunt in a public place, so she linked her arm through his and steered him outside.

Back at Ma's cottage, Cathal and Eva waited for her to return, and later they all sat round the table.

'Jacob Blackstock is worried.'

'And so he should be,' Cathal said. 'He better come good for Eva, or—'

'Listen,' Ma interrupted. 'The rogue is in the military hospital with injuries, but no one will say who put him there. Sure, that's why the hearing was called off. Jacob believes his son was battered while in solitary confinement.'

'It's only what he deserves.'

Eva wasn't surprised and knew how stubborn Matthew Blackstock could be.

'Yes, I agree, Cathal. Few will feel any pity for the blighter.'

'Do they know how long he'll be in hospital?'

Ma shrugged. 'Anyone's guess.'

Eva was quiet, mulling over how much longer she would have to endure the agony of waiting. Tears gathered in her eyes.

Ma reached over and patted her hand. 'Don't waste your tears on that scoundrel.'

'Oh, I'm not. I'm angry with myself. He's guilty of desertion but the other stuff . . . if I hadn't . . . if I hadn't left that morning.'

Cathal placed his arm around her shoulders. 'Stop talking like that, Eva. When are you going to stop blaming yourself? You must stay positive. This trial is Matthew Blackstock's, not yours.'

'I'm sorry. I can't pretend I'm not worried and frightened about it all.'

'It's only natural,' Ma said. 'No matter, we'll get through it together.'

'Would you mind if I go for a lie-down? I've a splitting headache?' Eva massaged her temples.

'It's been an upsetting day. You go ahead,' Ma said. 'I'll see to things here.'

Eva stood up and so did Cathal. He placed his arm around her. 'You did well today.' Then he gave her hand a reassuring squeeze.

Cathal helped clear the table and dry the dishes. 'I hope all this isn't getting too much for her.'

'She's stronger than we give her credit for. Underneath all her anxieties she's determined to clear her name.'

'Ma?' Cathal asked, placing his aunt's best plates upright on the dresser. 'Do you think Eva would come back with me tomorrow?'

Ma glanced up. 'Well, the only way to find that out is to ask her.'

'I thought about it earlier, but then . . . I wasn't sure.' He stoked the fire. Then he came and sat by Ma.

She gave him a stern glare. 'Was I wrong in thinking your feelings for Eva are more than concern?'

Cathal lowered his head into his hands.

'If you don't feel that way towards her, ye've got to tell her.'

Glancing up, he blew out his lips. 'My feelings for Eva far surpass anything I've ever felt for any other woman. I don't want to scare her off. She's so young and . . . well, you know . . .'

'Aye, I do, lad, but isn't Eva the one you should talk to?'

'There's never been a right moment, and I thought a day in Dublin might give us a chance to get to know each other better. I'd like to do something nice for her, show her around. She needs distracting from the trial.'

'I dare say it will do no harm.' His aunt shook her head and got to her feet, smiling. 'Well, anyone with a bed is in it.' Picking up her drink, she headed for her room.

Chapter Fifty-eight

While Cathal was at the store picking up the newspaper and some groceries for his aunt, Eva washed her hair and took extra care over her appearance, sorting out what she wanted to wear. Ma told her she looked grand in a bright floral skirt that swung out from the hips, teamed with a white blouse with tiny pearl buttons down the front. It was the middle of August and she wore a light tweed jacket and her best peep-toe sandals. Ma wound Eva's long black hair into a chignon and Eva liked how it elongated her slender neck. She dabbed a small amount of Lily of the Valley scent behind her ears, like Ma suggested.

Cathal wore the same beige twill trousers and tweed jacket he had come down in. He slung his mackintosh over his arm. 'Are we ready, Miss Fallon? I feel shabby next to you. Are you sure you want to be seen out with me?'

She laughed and gave him a playful nudge.

The journey flew past, and before long they were walking through the Dublin streets. She observed his summer tan, and how his black curly hair flopped down over his forehead when he turned his head towards her. And her heart swelled with love for him. She knew what she felt was real, and it was the one thing that got her through each day. Shoppers were out in full force, but most of them appeared to be browsing. However, the sight of a patrol officer's arm-band brought home the reality that the war was still a threat, but most people carried on with their everyday business.

'You haven't told me where you are taking me?'

'When you were here before, I never got to show you the good things about Dublin – and the not so great. I'd like to make up for that today with a few surprises.'

'Wow!' She was excited to be here with him and there was so much she wanted to talk to him about.

They crossed over Butt Bridge towards Tara Street and when he paused outside the fire station, she glanced up at the splendid red-brick building with its tall clock tower. It stood in total contrast to the run-down area of tenement houses and alleyways. A tram clanged past with an advert for Bovril across the front. In the streets round about, women wrapped in shawls chatted at the doorways while feeding babies. Children ran barefoot.

'This is the real Dublin, Eva,' he said when he saw her frown. 'Poverty lurks everywhere. The capital is no different to any other part of Ireland.'

'I realise that.' This could have been her life, begging on the streets, had she not been taken to the orphanage. 'Is this where you work?'

'Yes, it is. I'm not going in. Sure to get collared for something. Today I want you all to myself.' Taking her hand, he carried on walking.

She felt his closeness and what he had just said made her

pulse race. If only he knew how happy he made her feel. Now might be a good time to ask him the question she had been wondering about.

'So where do you live then?'

'I rent rooms around the corner in Pearse Street. It's nothing to write home about. It suits me and is close to work,' he said. 'You can take a look at it later if you like.' He steered her towards College Green, pointing out Trinity College and talking above the noise of trams, horse and carts, bikes and vehicles roaring past.

Eva marvelled at the beautiful Georgian buildings. The Bank of Ireland with its blackened exterior remained as evidence of the 1916 conflict.

'They were fighting for our independence,' Cathal told her.

'Why do wars have to happen?' She paused. 'How do you feel about the war in Europe, Cathal? Do you believe we should have stayed out of it?'

He took her elbow and guided her across the busy traffic on to Suffolk Street. 'At first I didn't agree with De Valera keeping Ireland out. Now, I'm not so sure.'

'Why?'

'Because most of the Irish men joined up, anyway. Haven't you noticed the lack of males in the city?'

'Yes, I have.'

'I love my job. Being a fire officer has kept me from thinking about it too much. But I'm not a pacifist, Eva.'

She frowned. She was naive about military matters.

'I mean . . . I'm not against it.' They walked side by side. 'Sometimes it's a necessary evil. I would fight to save my fellow countrymen, once I'd weighed up the pros and cons and felt it was fundamental to our well-being.'

She nodded. 'You're not a patriot?' Although she asked the question, she knew little about the country's politics. But she'd read in the library about heroics and patriotism.

His face clouded. 'Would you prefer that I was?'

'Oh, no, not at all.' She was glad he was here with her and not God knows where, fighting the silly war.

'Enough of them are trampling each other to death without me adding to it. There's nothing romantic about it.' He looked sad, and she was sorry she had mentioned it. 'Let's forget the war.' He was smiling again. 'I want you to experience the city and most of what it offers.' He took hold of her hand.

It delighted her and they walked up Grafton Street. Eva stopped at every shop to gaze in wonder at its merchandise: gowns, exquisite clothes, sweets and chocolates of fine quality. They passed jewellers and tobacconists until they came to Brown Thomas, a splendid department store that made her gasp at the fashions displayed in the window.

'Do you want to look inside?'

'Oh yes, can we?'

He opened the door, and with his hand in the small of her back guided her inside where she could only stand and stare. The smell of scent and luxury soaps invaded her senses. The assistants wore black dresses with white lace collars. Eva walked towards the ladies fashions where she examined the latest styles in skirts and blouses. Most of the clientele being served spoke as if they had marbles in their mouth. She stifled a giggle. A shop assistant kept looking across at her as she moved from rail to rail, fingering the texture of the different materials. She picked up a slim skirt. How hard could it be for her to make one like this for herself?

'I'd love to work here.'

'There's nothing to stop you.'

With no qualifications she knew she had no chance. Realising that there was only so much browsing they could do before the woman came across to see if they wanted to buy anything, she glanced at Cathal and smiled, then they hurried from the store. Holding hands, they moved along the pavement, passing flower sellers, whistle players and fiddlers. With music floating on the air, they turned down Wicklow Street where Cathal surprised her by buying her a multicoloured silk scarf and placing it around her neck.

'Oh! It's beautiful.' Her hand touched the delicate soft material. 'But you shouldn't have.'

'My pleasure! I'm taking you to Bewley's for lunch. They serve the best coffee in Dublin. You'll love the taste.'

Her stomach rumbled. It had been a while since they left Cavan.

'Is it far?'

'You'll smell it in a minute.'

It wasn't long before she found herself seated opposite him, being served by the waitress. While they tucked into a choice of sandwiches, followed by cream buns with coffee, Eva asked, 'Have you always wanted to be a fireman?'

'Most lads follow in their father's footsteps. I was no exception, despite his death in the line of duty.'

Eva put down her cup. 'I'm sorry.'

'My mother, God rest her soul, didn't want me to be a firefighter, and after she died it was my aunt, Ma Scully, who encouraged me to follow my heart.'

People were milling around looking for a seat, but she hardly noticed.

'So now you know my life story. Have you had enough to eat?'

Eva leant back in the chair. 'I'm fit to burst. That was a treat, thank you.'

'You won't mind if I have that last cake then?'

Smiling, she shook her head.

He bit into the bun and cream oozed on to his chin. He mopped it up with his napkin. 'Eva, how much can you remember of your life before . . .'

'Before the orphanage, you mean? Not a lot. I wish I could.' She rested her elbow on the table. 'Does it bother you that I lived in an institution and come with no known parentage?'

'No, not in the least. Your parents died. Just like mine. Not a lot we can do about it.' He leant in close. 'I knew how much you meant to me after I spent days searching for you.'

'Oh! That is the nicest thing anyone has ever said to me.'

He reached for her hand. 'Eva, some of the greatest people started their life in a home.'

'That's what Big Finn said.'

'It's the truth. However, it won't matter a jot. I'm just glad I found you.' He glanced at his watch. 'Come on.' He got to his feet. 'I have a surprise for you later.'

He helped her on with her jacket and she followed him outside. The streets were still busy with people. Holding hands, they caught a tram into the city.

'Where are we going?'

'You'll soon see, but first, I need to change my clothes.'

They got off the tram in College Street and walked along Pearse Street. The women and children had gone indoors and, apart from the noise of traffic, it was quieter. His bedsit was on the top floor of a tenement and they had to climb countless flights of stairs to reach it. Curious, she followed behind. She could hear arguing and crying babies on the way up.

'Don't you find it noisy at night?'

'I'm used to it. Besides, I have a wireless.' He produced a box of matches from his pocket. 'Be careful. Stand still a minute. When they fitted the gas lamps, the top landing was overlooked.' He struck a match to light their way.

'How long have you lived here?' Eva felt guilty that he lived in a shabby area of the city while she enjoyed the comfort of his aunt's cottage. It didn't seem right.

When they reached the top floor, he unlocked his door and her eyes widened as she stepped inside. The two rooms Cathal occupied were decorated to a high quality, anything but shabby.

'Please, sit down. I won't be long.' He disappeared into the other room, which she assumed was the bedroom. She could hear him pour water into a basin.

She sat down on the grey sofa. A heavy-curtained sash window overlooked the street. She couldn't believe how little sound penetrated from below. A paraffin heater stood in the corner. She got to her feet and walked around. A picture of Cathal receiving some kind of award hung on the wall, together with other photos of the fire service crew. She moved around to look at scenic pictures of Cavan hanging on the wall. A sideboard had individual framed photos, and one of a man and woman; the man had Cathal's broad shoulders and his smile. A Philips wireless sat on a table nearby.

She drew back a curtain in the corner to reveal a small scullery with facilities to make tea; two gas rings and two saucepans. She guessed the privy was in the yard; it was a long way down if you were taken short. She felt glad now that she had used the convenience at Bewley's. Before she could sit back down, Cathal was in the doorway. She observed the neat single bed before he closed the door. 'Well, what do you think? It's nothing special but it fills a need.'

'It's lovely, really it is.'

He came and stood next to her. He had on a grey suit and white shirt.

Aware of his closeness, the clean crisp smell of his after-shave, she glanced down at her own dress. 'You still haven't said where we're going. Am I okay in this?' She ran her hand over her hair.

'You look beautiful, Eva.' He touched her cheek and tilted her chin.

She felt her colour rise and her heart galloped.

Again, she was wondering what it would be like if he were to kiss her when he said, 'We had better be off, or we'll be late.'

Chapter Fifty-nine

They hadn't walked far when he placed his arm around her. The sun had gone in, and there was a chill in the air, but the warmth of Cathal's arm was comforting.

'Have you ever been to a variety show, Eva?'

'No, never. Why?'

'Look over there?'

She could see the lights above the Theatre Royal. 'Is that where we're going?' Her eyes were bright with excitement.

He produced two tickets from his inside pocket.

She looked up into his eyes and her heart skipped. She clapped her hands. 'Oh, how wonderful! If I'd known, I'd have worn something more appropriate.'

'You look fine. Besides, it wouldn't have been a surprise – and it was worth it to see your face.'

'I should hate you, Cathal Burke,' she said, smiling.

He paused. 'You don't, do you?'

'No! Of course not.' She wanted to say, I love you with all my heart. But she would never be so bold.

He guided her across the street and they joined the queue.

Inside the plush auditorium, an usherette showed them to their seats and Eva couldn't help gazing about her as the hall filled up. Some of the women wore their hair crimped, some with wavy curls on top. Eva's chignon had stayed in place, thanks to Ma Scully.

The show was non-stop music hall comedy and variety. An orchestra ascended on an electric lift, to come level with the stage. The songs were catchy, and they sang along with the rest of the audience. Eva laughed so much she thought her sides would split. The Royalettes danced in a line across the stage. She had seen nothing like this and after her initial shock at their long bare legs, she settled back and enjoyed it.

Soon they were running towards the train, still laughing, oblivious to the late hour until they arrived to see the back end of the train puffing out of the station.

'Oh, no,' Eva gasped.

'Sorry, Eva. I was sure we had enough time.'

'What can we do?'

They sat down on a bench. Cathal lowered his head and she could see he was trying to sort something out.

He looked up. 'Ma will have my guts for garters. I'm sorry,' he said again. 'Don't worry.'

How could she not? Ma Scully would be livid.

'Is there no other way of getting back?'

He shook his head. 'I know someone who can put you up.'

'But . . .' She didn't relish being separated from him.

'It'll be grand. My boss, Andy Baxter, lives down the road on Amiens Street. He's on duty but his wife, Ethel, will be more than happy to help us.'

Eva wondered why he hadn't suggested staying at his place. She would have slept on the sofa. But then maybe he wouldn't want to cause a scandal, knowing how people gossip.

A light was showing in the fanlight above the door when Cathal pressed the bell. When the door opened, the woman at first looked startled, until she recognised Cathal. 'Is there something wrong at the fire station?'

'No, Ethel. I'm sorry to call at this late hour, but we've missed the train to Cavan, and I was wondering if you would give Eva a bed for the night?'

'Come in, please.' She held open the door. 'Sure I will. She's welcome to stay in the spare room.' She took their coats and told them to go through, then rushed off to put the kettle on.

'Don't look so worried,' Cathal said. 'You'll be fine here. I'll be back first thing, and we'll get back to Cavan.'

When Ethel returned, they were still standing awkwardly in the middle of the room.

'Sit yourselves down. The tea won't be long.'

It was a cosy room with a small three-piece suite and a coffee table. Ethel smiled across at Cathal, who was fidgeting with his tie.

'You'd better introduce me to this lovely girl, then.'

'Forgive me. This is Eva Fallon.'

'I'm Ethel Baxter,' the portly woman said, shaking her hand.

'It's kind of you to take in a complete stranger.'

'But you're not a stranger. I've heard all about you from Andy. Now, I'll get that tea. Make yourself comfortable, and when you've had something to eat, I'll show you upstairs.'

* * *

Next morning, Eva was up and dressed when Cathal arrived. After a quick piece of toast and marmalade, she thanked her host before they left. They caught the first available train out of Dublin for the connection to Cavan.

'Do you think Ma will be cross with me for not getting back last night?' Eva asked.

'She'll blow her top at me, that's for sure. If, when we arrive, she has her rolling pin in her hand, she'll skelp me alive.' When Eva frowned; he said, 'Only joking, but you know she'll worry.'

'Oh dear! But I had such a wonderful time,' she said as they boarded the train and found an empty carriage. 'I hope she will understand, once we explain what happened.'

'Leave me to deal with Ma.' He turned to face her. 'There's something I've been wanting to say to you.'

Eva's heartbeat quickened.

He shifted round, so he was looking into her eyes, and took her hand. 'Eva. Do you think you could . . . I mean.'

She had never seen him this flustered.

'How would you feel if I was to ask you to be my girl?'

Releasing her hand from his, she covered her mouth to stop her lip trembling.

'I . . . I didn't mean to upset you. Forget I said anything.' He sat back and played with his watchstrap.

'I don't want to forget it.'

'You don't? You're not upset?'

'No. Not at all.'

'Eva, I'm hopelessly in love with you.'

Stunned, she stifled a sob. Could this be happening? He wanted her, after she had been abused by another man. 'Cathal, I . . . I love you too, and yes, I would love to be your girl.' Her tears fell in large drops and landed on his hand, which was now covering hers again.

'That's settled then.' He smiled.

Eva recovered her composure as more people piled into the carriage, and some stood in the aisle. For the rest of the journey they talked of everyday things, until Eva whispered the question that had been bothering her for a while.

'Cathal, are you ... are you still seeing Isabel?' She needed to hear it from his own lips but regretted asking when she saw the hurt in his eyes before he glanced out at the passing countryside. Eva felt her pulse quicken. What had she done? Why did she have to spoil such a wonderful moment?

People were getting off the train when he turned back to her.

'I'm sorry you had to ask me that, Eva. Isabel and I parted weeks ago. Do you think I'd have said what I did otherwise? We were never more than friends.' He swallowed. 'I thought you knew.'

She shook her head. 'You never said. I love you and I don't want to share you with anyone.'

He ran his fingers through his hair and the smile returned to his face. 'You won't ever have to. You have my word on that, Eva.'

She moved closer to him. He placed his arm around her shoulders and she glanced up at him. 'Can I ask you another question?'

'Fire away! I don't want us to have any secrets.'

'This is about Ma Scully.'

A puzzled expression puckered his handsome face. 'What about her?'

'Did she ever marry?'

'No.'

'Who's the man with the moustache in the photo hanging on your bedroom wall at Ma's?'

'Oh, that's my Uncle Bert, my aunt's brother. He was a butcher. Died when I was a boy.'

'Oh, that's a shame. Do you remember him?'

'Yes, he used to take me for long walks when I came to Cavan for my holidays. My aunt and I used to visit him at the butcher's shop. I never liked the smell of the raw meat.'

And so, chatting happily, they arrived in Cavan.

Chapter Sixty

Holding hands, they were walking down Main Street, when Eva said, 'What do you think Ma will say when she finds out how we feel about each other?'

'Let's see what happens after I've had the chance to explain about last night.'

Eva swallowed. 'She's bound to be cross.'

'Oh, hump it,' Cathal said when he saw Eva's downcast face. 'She must take us at our word.'

All the same, Eva couldn't help feeling a knot in her stomach. It wasn't the done thing. She was prepared to be chastised, and took a deep breath before going inside.

'So, there ye are. Come home, have ye? Now, you can tell me what kept the pair of youse out all night.' Ma glanced round from where she was sitting in her chair by the range.

'We missed the train and Eva stayed with Andy's wife, so you've no need to fret.'

'Who's fretting? I wondered, that's all.'

'I'm sorry, Ma,' Eva said. 'There was no way of getting word to you.'

'It was irresponsible of you, Cathal. Didn't ye check the train times?'

He glanced across at Eva. She stifled a giggle.

'It's not funny, miss. This mustn't happen again.'

'It won't. I'll make us a drink?'

'First, ye better take a look at this.' She stood up and plucked a letter from behind the clock on the mantel. 'This came yesterday. It might be important.'

Eva looked at Cathal, then sat down. 'It'll be a new date for the trial?'

'Well, open it then.' Ma folded her arms.

Eva read it and wrinkled her nose. 'I don't understand.'

'What is it, Eva?' Cathal touched her arm.

'A solicitor by the name of Duffy from Bawnboy wants me to come and see him as soon as possible.'

'Does he say why?'

She sat back and handed the letter to Cathal. Ma leant in to look.

'He doesn't tell you much.'

Eva sat forward. 'Can it be anything to do with the Blackstocks?'

'Well, there's only one way to find out,' Ma said.

'I'll see him first thing in the morning.' She placed the letter into her bag and set about making them all a drink.

Cathal glanced at her and winked. She smiled back at him.

When they were seated round the table, he said, 'Ma, we have something to tell you and we hope it'll make you happy.'

Ma's head shot up. 'What is it now?' Her brow wrinkled.

During the telling, a smile spread across her face.

'Well, I won't say I hadn't noticed.'

'You knew?' Cathal asked.

Ma chuckled and glanced at Eva. 'So, you're courting then?'

Eva beamed. 'Yes, I guess we are. Are you all right? I mean . . .'

'Yes, why wouldn't I be? When's the wedding?'

Cathal glanced at Eva. 'I've not asked her yet.' Then he reached for her hand. 'We're not rushing anything.'

'Just as well. I need time to save up for a new hat.'

They all laughed.

Eva arrived in Bawnboy and walked through the village towards the address in the letter. In spite of the beautiful landscape surrounding her, a shiver ran through her as she passed the road where Matthew Blackstock had attacked her; with the trial still looming, it was giving her sleepless nights. The solicitor's office was in the middle of a row of cottages. She took a deep breath and composed herself before knocking on the red door.

A thin woman with a severe expression opened it. 'What's your business?'

Her abrupt manner was unexpected, and Eva wondered if she had knocked on the correct door. 'I'm here to see Mr Duffy. I received a letter asking me to call.' She realised perhaps she should have made an appointment.

'Oh,' the woman said, stepping back. 'Come in. What's your name?'

'Eva Fallon.'

The room had a low ceiling and was simply furnished with a table and a chair.

'You can sit if you wish,' she said brusquely and walked away, as if on eggshells, into another area of the house.

The tick of the clock was loud and set Eva's nerves on edge, reminding her of standing outside the Mother Superior's office for one of her misdemeanours. She couldn't wait to find out what it was all about. If by any remote chance she had a relative she knew nothing about, she would feel cheated not to have known about them before.

The woman returned and asked Eva to follow her into a back room with an even lower ceiling. Eva had to bend her head as she entered. A stout man raised himself from behind a desk. The skin underneath his chin wobbled as he shook her hand.

'Won't you sit down, Miss Fallon?'

Eva perched on the edge of the wooden chair. 'So, you are the young lady? I don't recall ever seeing you in these parts.' He coughed to clear his throat and sat back down. 'I'm sure I'd have remembered a pretty girl like yourself.'

She fidgeted with her hands and waited while he appeared to be in no hurry, moving papers from one spot to another on his desk, pulling open drawers, keeping her in suspense.

She shifted in the chair. 'Why have you asked me here?'

'All in good time, miss.' His eyebrows shot upwards. 'And you've no idea why you are here?'

She shook her head.

'Well . . .' He sat forward, his elbows on the table. 'I'm always intrigued to see how complete strangers react when they inherit money.'

'Inherit! What are you talking about?'

'Who do you know in the village who liked you enough to leave you a small fortune?' He ran his tongue around his lips.

She took a deep breath. Were the Blackstocks trying to buy her silence?

She got to her feet. 'I . . . I . . . think you may have mistaken me for somebody else.'

'Well, if you're not Eva Fallon, then there's been a big slip-up.' He was toying with her.

She sat forward. 'I can assure you, sir, I am Eva Fallon. And I have a job to get back to. So, if you don't mind telling me why you've asked me here?'

He chuckled. 'Feisty too.' He appeared to be enjoying her unease. 'I don't think you'll have to worry about work for some time, miss. Now you're a woman of, shall we say, reasonable means?'

'What are you saying, Mr Duffy?'

He opened a folder. 'I'm delighted to inform you, Miss Fallon, that you have come into money. Seven hundred and fifty pounds, twelve shillings and sixpence, to be precise. What do you think about that?'

Her heart raced, she gasped and her hand flew to her face. She felt faint, and she gripped the desk.

'Are you all right, miss?' He called out to his assistant, who came rushing in. 'Get her some water.'

Relieved she hadn't fallen off her chair, Eva sipped the cool drink. 'Thank you! I'll be fine now.'

'It's the shock. It has that effect,' he said.

The woman removed the glass from Eva's shaky hand and left them alone.

'Who . . . who would leave me this kind of money? I . . .'

'Finbar McCreedy. Goes by the name of Big Finn. He knew you, even if you don't remember him.'

Tears gathered in her eyes. 'Remember him! Of course I remember him, quite fondly.'

'He has no known relatives and stipulated his estate was to go to none other than yourself, Miss Fallon.' He passed over an envelope. 'Read the instructions.' He coughed. 'Do you have a bank account?'

'No. No, I don't.'

'Well, I would advise you to open one. And if I can be of further help, let me know.' He peered over his spectacles.

Her legs shook as she got to her feet. Thanking him, she left with her thoughts in a whirl.

She should feel excitement, but instead she felt numb. Why had Big Finn singled her out? He had other friends in Bawnboy. She had done nothing to deserve it. Thomas had been the rightful heir. Dazed from the shock, she couldn't wait to get back to Cavan town.

Chapter Sixty-one

Ma Scully clapped her hands with delight when Eva told her the news. 'Old man Finn, well that's a turn-up for the books,' she said, unpinning her hat and shrugging out of her coat. Eva was scrubbing potatoes and scraping carrots to put into the stew pot. 'Leave that and sit down. You've just come into a fortune. Aren't you pleased? What's up with ye?'

She sat down. 'But, Ma, it's not rightfully mine. I barely knew Big Finn, and I feel guilty I didn't visit him before he passed on.'

'Aye, sure you weren't to know, and you were in no position to, now were ye? Thomas is gone, and he had no other living relatives. You must have made quite an impression on him, Eva, love. You can't turn it down. There's many a one who'd jump at the chance.'

'Yes, I know. I'm more than grateful, it's just ... I still can't believe he left me all his money.'

'Well, he did. And it couldn't go to a more deserving person. Big Finn wanted you to have it.'

Eva cried and Ma handed her a handkerchief.

'Ye daft creature. Laughing and dancing ye should be, not bawling yer eyes out. Anyone'd think ye'd lost a fortune not gained one.' Ma got to her feet and lifted the black pot from the range. 'Get your glad rags on, we're going out to celebrate. And you can phone Cathal with the good news.'

Although Cathal had congratulated her, she sensed the lack of excitement in his voice. The money would mean nothing to her if it came between them, and she couldn't wait for the weekend when she could discuss it with him face-to-face. Her dreams of working in Dublin close to Cathal were now possible. He wouldn't want to live off her money, she knew that. Rather than embarrass him, she was prepared to give it away. Ma Scully came to mind. She had done so much for her, and it would be her way of repaying a debt of gratitude. But first, she would discuss it with Cathal and find out how he felt. With her mind settled, she was now counting the days to his visit.

Each morning as she milked the cows and herded them back to the paddock, she sang to herself. She almost forgot she had a trial hanging over her head. The trauma she had experienced at the hands of Matthew Blackstock would never leave her. But she was stronger now, prepared and ready to fight her corner and clear her name. Her days spent at the library, reading up on court procedure, had given her an insight into what she might have to face. Her resolve to tell the truth was still her motto and if things went against her, she would hold her head high, knowing there were two people who would be there for her when it was over.

Cathal arrived in Cavan early on Saturday morning. They

walked out together, stopping at a grassy bank by a stream where they sat on a bench. There was no one to overhear their conversation, apart from the cows in the fields. The water was clear as it gurgled over stones smooth with age.

Eva was the first to speak. 'How do you feel about the money Finn left me?'

Cathal leant forward, skimming pebbles into the fast-flowing stream. A few heartbeats passed before he responded. He turned towards her, his face pale. Eva held her breath.

'It's not for me to say. You must do what makes you happy, and if you change your mind about getting wed and want to make other plans . . . well . . .'

'But I have no plans, Cathal. Not without you. The money changes nothing as far as I'm concerned. Can't we decide together?'

He placed his arm about her shoulders. She swallowed. Not so long ago, she had nowhere to lay her head. She twisted a lock of her hair around her finger. Sitting here with the man she loved was still surreal, and each time she glanced up at him her heart swelled. 'What do you think I should do?' she persisted.

'Eva, you don't have to decide right now. I'd like you to take your time before making any decisions.'

'Don't . . . don't you want to marry me now?'

He held her close, looking into her eyes. 'Of course I do. Eva, love, this money can transform your life.'

'I know that, Cathal.' She smiled. 'I don't want to change my life unless it's with you.'

'All the things you've dreamed of from your time in the orphanage are now possible.' He held her away from him. 'I want you to experience them.'

'Can't you see? You are what I've dreamed of.' A tear

trickled down her face. 'Our life together is all that matters to me.'

He shook his head. 'I have an irresistible urge to kiss you, Eva Fallon.'

And before she knew what was happening, his lips were on hers; gentle at first, like summer rain, then with desire and passion. Warmth spread through her deep in her belly and she responded as if it was the most natural thing in the world. Astounded by her boldness, she pulled away, her face hot, her lips tingling. How could she have acted that way, with every fibre of her being?

'Cathal, I . . .' She moved further along the bench.

He shifted closer. 'Didn't you want me to kiss you?'

Her pulse quickened. It was just a kiss, but it was the most wonderful feeling in the world and left her shaking and lost for words. How she had longed for him to kiss her, to feel his strong arms around her, but she had not expected it would pleasure her so much.

'Eva, I couldn't help myself. I'm in love with you and no one ever made me feel this way before.'

'Oh! Cathal. You must think me such a baby.'

'Why? Why do you say that?'

'I've never been kissed before and I feel giddy and silly.' She giggled.

'Oh, Eva.' He gathered her to him. 'That's how it should be when two people love each other as we do.'

'In that case, I like it very much.' Cathal's arms around her were so gentle, so loving and protective in comparison to Matthew Blackstock's brutality that had terrified her and left her feeling unworthy.

He kissed her again, and she melted against him. Time stood still and Eva floated on air.

'Isn't love wonderful?' she murmured.

'I want to marry you, Eva. I promise not to rush you into anything, but when you're ready. What do you say?'

If he only knew how she had longed for this moment?

'Is that a proposal?'

'I guess it is.'

A smile brightened her face. 'I'd love to marry you. Next year, after my eighteenth birthday.'

'Sure, in that case, I'll hold you to it. And one day we'll both have a family of our own to love and cherish.'

He pulled her to her feet, and she placed her arms around his neck as he swung her round.

Chapter Sixty-two

Cathal's proposal of marriage far exceeded the excitement of the legacy, and Eva walked about in a daze. Weeks later, with no word of the trial, she put it out of her mind. Her newfound happiness with Cathal took over her thoughts. She opened a bank account in her name and said no more about it. Ma Scully's painful joints were getting worse so Eva insisted she rest more and let her see to the everyday running of the household. When the money was in her account, she bought a whistling kettle. It boiled faster than the big black one Ma hooked over the stove.

Ma wasn't that impressed. 'I've had me life and I need none of them fancy gadgets. Once you make plans for your wedding, ye'll be needing every penny. You'll need a house for starters.'

But Eva took no notice, and when Ma was out she put a substantial amount into her money jar above the mantel and said no more.

One evening, Eva pulled out a chair and sat next to Ma.

'Cathal won't talk about the money. I want us to decide what to do with it together.'

'I'm not surprised. He wouldn't want to be kept by a woman. He's a proud man and will have saved a fair bit himself.'

'I don't want it to come between us.'

'Ah sure, just let it lie for now, Eva. It'll be there when ye need it. That kind of money can't be sniffed at. Have you decided where ye'd like to live after ye's wed?'

Eva shook her head. 'I guess Cathal will want to continue living in Dublin, close to his job. I don't mind, Ma, apart from leaving you.'

'Ah, sure I'll miss you, so I will. But, once ye marry you make your life where ye have to. Sure, ye'll be down every other weekend with Cathal and I'll look forward to that.'

'I guess so.'

For now, her days were full with happy thoughts and she was ill prepared when the letter she was expecting popped through the letter box.

Dear Miss Fallon,

I wish to inform you that the revised date for the new hearing is Monday 27th September 1943 at 11 a.m., McKee barracks, Dublin.

Mr C. Timmons,
Defence lawyer

Her stomach did a flip. She had a week in which to prepare. How silly of her to think she could compete with the military. The fact she had, without realising it, broken army rules wouldn't stand up in a court of law. She vowed to stay positive in spite of the nerves and anger she felt returning along with a resentment towards Matthew Blackstock. She would never allow herself to be manipulated in that way again.

That night, as she began her nightly ablutions, brushed her teeth and slipped on her cotton nightdress, she went over her defence as instructed by her lawyer. Her mind too active for sleep, her thoughts drifted to happy times with Cathal.

The day before the hearing, she was a bag of nerves and couldn't eat her supper. Ma Scully gazed over at her strained face. 'Now, will ye stop frettin' or ye'll be like a wet rag the morra?' Giving her an encouraging smile, she said, 'Sure, this time the morra, it'll be all over.'

Eva nodded, but still the negative thoughts got the better of her. This time tomorrow she could be locked away in a darkened cell.

Ma folded the towels and put them in the cupboard; her heavy gait as she walked didn't go unnoticed, and Eva felt guilty to have caused her worry. Ma had been a tower of strength and the least she could do was show her determination to win, even if she didn't feel it.

'I'm sorry, Ma.' A tear trickled down her face.

'Ah, sure, will ye give over? Haven't I told you, none of it's your fault?'

Eva bent down and planted a kiss on her cheek.

'Get away with ye now.' However, there was no disguising the smile that brightened Ma Scully's face.

A mixture of fear and anticipation knotted Eva's stomach as she stepped from the bus with Cathal and Ma for support. Desperate to hide how terrified she was, she smiled up at the man she loved. He took her hand and gave it a squeeze.

She took a long breath. Today was her chance to clear her name. And she would do it, no matter how frightened she felt. She owed it to the man she loved. With him by her side, her confidence returned. They walked towards the barracks, each subdued, preoccupied with their own thoughts.

Inside, they were told where to wait in a long corridor until someone came to fetch them.

Cathal placed his arm around Eva's shoulders. 'Just be yourself and you'll be fine,' he smiled. 'Whatever happens, I want you to know I love you very much.'

His words brought a lump to her throat. 'I'll be grand.'

The barrister, Mr Timmins, walked towards them and shook Eva's hand. 'You will wait here until you're called, Miss Fallon.' He turned to Cathal and Ma. 'You can enter the courtroom, but you must remain silent, no matter how much you might feel like intervening. Otherwise, you could be held in contempt of court. Do you understand?'

They both nodded.

'Don't worry, Miss Fallon. I'll do my utmost to get you acquitted. And I may have forgotten to say, you must refer to the prosecution as "sir", not "your honour", or anything else.'

At that moment Matthew Blackstock arrived at the far end of the corridor, flanked by two officers. He glared down at Eva before being guided towards a seat. She gripped Cathal's hand and her body stiffened. He looked nothing like his former self and walked with a limp.

'Don't let him intimidate you, he can't harm you any more,' her lawyer said. 'He'll be tried in a separate courtroom, and from what I've heard he'll be charged with defecting from the Irish army and then sent back to his commanding unit in the UK to answer charges there.' His words reassured her, and she regained her resolve. 'You may have a short wait before being called.'

'Thank you, Mr Timmins.'

Mr Blackstock, accompanied by Aggie, came in next. He raised his hat in a half-hearted greeting, then sat opposite his son. Aggie, dressed in sombre clothes, hid her face under her wide-brimmed hat and sat next to her grandson, muttering to him. Matthew kept his gaze on the wall in front of him and made no gesture towards his father.

Ma patted Eva's hand and Cathal kept his arm across her shoulders. 'Remember what we said, Eva. You are not the one on trial.'

She nodded, but she knew Aggie would lie under oath to protect Matthew, and she couldn't help her feelings of uncertainty.

'I wish they'd get on with it,' Ma said.

An usher in army uniform walked past them and stopped in front of the Blackstocks. He spoke to Matthew before escorting him into a room. His family were asked to stay where they were. Relieved he was no longer feet away from her, Eva released a heartfelt sigh.

'You're doing grand, so you are,' Cathal said. 'He won't be so cocky once he gets in that courtroom, and it looks like he's had a tough time at the camp.'

She nodded.

'Remember to stick to your story. We'll be nearby. We're not going anywhere.'

Eva, still holding Cathal's hand, found she was gripping it tighter the longer they waited. And she asked herself how she would let go of it and walk into a den of military personnel who would crucify her with highfalutin questions? She closed her eyes and prayed for courage.

Chapter Sixty-three

Eva's head was resting on Cathal's shoulder when she heard her name being called. She sat upright. Fear, mingled with a dozen other emotions, flooded her mind. She had waited too long for this moment not to do it justice, for her own sake. Bracing herself, she stood up and brushed her hand over her hair and down the length of her skirt, smiled at Ma, then held her head up and walked without flinching behind the usher into the courtroom. She was followed by Cathal and Ma, who were directed where to sit.

Eva stepped up on to the witness stand. Facing her, three military officials sat at a long bench draped in green. The Irish Tricolour hung on the wall behind them. She recognised one man as Captain McLaughlin who had interrogated her at Dublin Castle. There were no white wigs, stiff collars or black cloaks as she had imagined. The prosecution were dressed in smart army uniforms and red sashes with stripes and pips – one, two or three, according to rank – on the shoulders of their army uniforms.

The Bible was placed in her hand. 'Do you swear to tell the truth, the whole truth and nothing but the truth, so help you God?'

She nodded.

'Please answer.'

'Yes, I do.' She was surprised not to hear a quaver in her voice.

'Can you state your name and address?'

'Eva Fallon, Primrose Cottage, 43 Main Street, Cavan Town.'

'Who lives with you?'

She glanced over at Ma and Cathal. 'Miss Scully.'

'I know this is a daunting experience for someone so young, Miss Fallon. However, we are here to help you, and to establish the truth.'

The truth was all she wanted.

'You work at Blackstock's farm. Is that correct?'

'Not any more, sir.'

'Yes, or no, will suffice.'

'No, sir.'

'Why is that? Were you given the sack?'

'No, sir, I left because I was frightened of Matthew Blackstock.' An all-round intake of breath ensued. However, the remark was overruled, and the dismissal of her feelings in the matter strengthened her resolve.

'So, you left of your own free will.'

Forcing back her annoyance, she answered, 'Yes.'

'How long were you working there before the alleged offence occurred?'

'Six weeks, sir.'

'Did you know the prisoner, Matthew Blackstock, before you came to work for his father?'

'No!'

'Why then were you so willing to help him, hide his uniform and keep his whereabouts secret?'

'The mistress said I'd lose my job if I didn't keep my mouth shut.'

'But you knew you were doing wrong?'

'Yes, I did. I was in fear of Matthew Blackstock. He attacked me and left me for dead in a ditch.' Her anger rose.

'Just answer yes, or no, Miss Fallon.'

'Yes, sir.'

'Were you aware that by concealing the whereabouts of a deserter you were breaking the law and perverting the course of justice?'

'No. I didn't know.'

'That'll be all for now. Thank you, Miss Fallon.'

At this point Mr Timmins stood and took a slow walk to the centre of the courtroom, and a hushed silence descended. He looked at Eva and smiled. His confident air helped her to relax. He offered her a glass of water before beginning. Her throat was dry and, thanking him, she sipped it.

'Miss Fallon, you lived at the orphanage for girls in Cavan until the age of seventeen. Can you tell us what that was like?'

Recalling her life at the orphanage brought back memories she wanted to forget. She took a long breath. 'It was tough, and I saw little of the outside world.' She took another sip of water.

'So, in that case, Miss Fallon, being segregated at an early age meant you would not have come into contact with men, or boys, is that correct?'

'Yes, sir.'

'In your own words, can you describe how you felt when you encountered Private Blackstock in the barn at his father's farm in April of this year?'

'I was terrified. The men were away at the cattle market and I was alone with the mistress.'

'What did you do, Miss Fallon?'

'I turned to run, but he asked me to help him. I was shaking so much I dropped the basket of vegetables.'

'What happened then?'

'He was starving and begged me to bring him food and a change of clothes. He said he was Matthew Blackstock and when I hesitated, he promised not to hurt me.'

'And we know he never kept that promise.' Mr Timmins paused and glanced towards the prosecution. 'Did you do as he asked?'

'Yes, sir, I had no choice. He was my boss's son.'

'Did you tell anyone?'

'No, not then.'

'Go on.'

'He asked me not to and said that he would tell the mistress later. After I brought the food and clothes, he asked me to burn his uniform. I couldn't do it and he kept on asking me about it so in desperation I hid it in my room.'

'What happened then?'

'He came in the house. I shook with fright. I heard him row with his grandmother and then she hid him in his bedroom.'

'Thank you, Miss Fallon; that will be all.'

Aggie was called in next and Eva sat down next to Ma and Cathal. Aggie glared at her as she walked to the stand. Taking the Bible in her right hand, she swore to tell the truth and Eva prayed that she would.

'You are Mrs Aggie Curran and live at Blackstock's farm, is that correct?'

'Yes.' Her eyes were downcast, her arms folded, a stance she often took when she was in a mood with Eva.

'If you could please speak up, Mrs Curran.'

'I said yes.'

'Why did you not inform your son-in-law that Private Blackstock had defected from the British army?'

'Because I knew what he'd do.'

'You mean he would have reported him.'

'Yes.'

'Were you aware that you were committing a crime by concealing him?'

'Yes, I bloody well did. I wouldn't rattle on me own grandson.'

'Any more of that and your statement will be void. Do you understand?'

Aggie grimaced. 'Yes.'

'In your original statement, you said Miss Fallon was to blame for hiding your grandson's uniform, when I put it to you that you in fact conspired with your grandson to frighten Miss Fallon into doing so. Is that not true? And in fact you were willing to lie and hide him from the authorities for as long as you could get away with it?'

'I've nothing more to say.'

'May I remind you that you are still under oath?' Mr Timmins said. 'How did you get along with Miss Fallon?'

'I didn't.'

'Why was that, Mrs Curran?'

Aggie's mouth was as taut as piano wire. 'She's a magnet around men. Encouraged Matthew by feeding him extra food and washing his clothes and then when he . . . well, you know what her sort are like.'

Aggie's words rankled and Eva had to force herself not to retaliate.

'Would you like to explain what you mean by "her sort", Mrs Curran?'

'Out of the convent and into the world, she makes a play for the first man in trousers.'

Cathal stood up. 'That's a blatant lie, and you know it!'

Mr Timmins raised his eyebrows and shook his head. Ma put a staying hand on his arm, and he sat back down.

Mr Timmins continued. 'That will be all, Mrs Curran. You may step down.'

The prosecution then called Mr Blackstock. After he had answered the preliminary questions, Mr Timmins asked, 'In relation to Miss Fallon, what was your overall opinion of the girl?'

Jacob cleared his throat and ran his fingers round the edge of his stiff shirt collar. 'Hardworking, honest and easy on the eye.'

'Did you see her as someone who would break the law?'

'No! Otherwise, I wouldn't have taken her on. She came recommended.'

'Yes, or no, will suffice.'

'No, sir.'

'Do you believe she set out to keep your son's whereabouts a secret?'

'No.'

'Do you believe Miss Fallon and your son colluded, or conspired together, to keep his desertion secret and pervert the course of justice?'

'No, sir, I do not.'

'Thank you, Mr Blackstock. That will be all. You may stand down.'

Captain McLaughlin called for a recess of fifteen minutes.

Mr Timmins stood at the table, talking to the prosecution, before speaking to Eva. 'You did extremely well, Miss Fallon.'

'Is that it now?' Ma asked. 'Can she go?'

'I'm afraid not.' He cleared his throat and sat on the bench next to them. 'You'll be called again for the verdict.' He smiled. 'Try not to worry. I'm hoping I can turn this around. However, the army may want to justify your actions with an appropriate form of punishment.'

'What does that mean?' Cathal wanted to know.

'Let's wait and see. It won't be long now.' He turned and went back into the courtroom.

Eva, her insides churning, rushed into the toilet. She heard Aggie whimpering in the next cubicle and for a second wanted to comfort her. Instead, she washed her hands and hurried out. 'I think Aggie's upset. I heard her crying.'

'Don't waste your pity on her, Eva,' Cathal said. 'She'll get her comeuppance.'

'Do you think I'll go to prison?'

'Don't talk daft,' Ma said. 'But I still think Jacob Blackstock could have said more in your favour.'

Eva turned to them both. 'If . . . if things don't go well for me, will you . . . ?'

'Stay positive, my love. Don't lose confidence now.' Cathal placed his arm around her shoulders. 'You've come this far, and you told the truth. Let's wait and see what Mr Timmins can do. Okay?'

She nodded, but her stomach was in knots.

Back in the courtroom, when Eva stepped up to the witness box she tried to remain optimistic. It was easier without Mr Blackstock and Aggie sitting opposite her. Mr Timmins sat down, and the three army officials were reading a document and muttering to one another. It made her anxious, and she glanced over at Cathal. His smile reassured her.

Captain McLaughlin cleared his throat and stood up. 'We have in our possession a letter from Sister Catherine, counter-signed by the Mother Superior of the orphanage where Miss Fallon grew up.' He looked at Eva. 'The reputable sisters who brought you up have plenty of good attributes to add to your character. They include honesty, a strong sense of right and wrong, and a willingness to care for sick children above your own needs. Never failing in your duties to fulfil your religious obligations . . .' He paused. 'It states you are a talented girl whose exceptional needlework went beyond what was expected from a girl of your years. All commendable, Miss Fallon, but she also said you could be wilful, with a tendency to rebel and disobey rules, a childish trait they hoped you would now have outgrown.'

Eva lowered her head. That wasn't what she had wanted to hear. She hoped it would not go against her? She held her breath.

'We have looked at all the evidence given here today, and I'd say the good sisters would be upset if one of their own charges were to – how shall I say? – bring their good reputation into disrepute. It was naive of you to have allowed yourself to be manipulated into committing an act that could have resulted in a much harsher sentence, Miss Fallon. However,' the Captain added, 'you will pay this court a fine of five pounds to cover costs and administration and consider yourself lucky. You're free to go.'

Eva let out a gasp and a smile lit up her face. The lawyer rushed to shake her hand as Cathal and Ma hurried across the courtroom.

'Thanks, Mr Timmins,' Eva said. Her eyes were brimming with joyful tears. 'You can't imagine how it feels to be cleared at last.'

'I never doubted you would be. However, I think the nuns' character reference might have swung the verdict in your favour. And no one would argue with the nuns, now would they?'

He laughed. And she knew it was true.

'I suppose they have their uses,' Cathal said, placing his arm around Eva.

'What will happen to Aggie?' Eva asked.

'Due to her age, it's hard to know. Not your concern any more, Miss Fallon.'

Ma Scully buttoned her coat and pinned her hat in place. 'That grandson of hers will not thank her for sticking her neck out for him.'

Mr Timmins turned to leave. He nodded towards Cathal and Ma before saying, 'All the best for the future, Miss Fallon.'

'Thank you.' Shaking with relief not to have a prison sentence hanging over her, Eva blew out an audible sigh. 'I can't believe it's over, Ma.'

'Me neither. Why don't we do something special?'

'Alas, I have to get back to work.'

The smile slipped from Eva's face. She hated to be parted from Cathal.

'Sure, there's enough time for a quick bite to eat and a glass of something to celebrate,' he said. 'I know a popular place down the road.'

The three set off, Cathal's hand in Eva's and his other arm around his aunt.

Chapter Sixty-four

With the trial now over, Cathal was on his way back to Cavan, proud of how Eva had handled the court case and looking forward to seeing her. He had to admit to worrying about how the ordeal of giving evidence might affect her, but his concerns were unfounded. He recalled how his heartbeat had quickened when he heard her name called out. And when she walked to the witness stand, she had looked as fragile as porcelain, but there was a rod of steel running through her slender backbone. And throughout the hearing he had struggled to stop himself from shouting out her innocence. She was vulnerable and yet strong when she had to be. He loved that about her.

He couldn't wait to make her his wife, but she was still so young; she'd seen nothing of life. In truth, he wanted her to enjoy a little independence before tying her down. He had sown his wild oats, at least as much as he had wanted to, but Eva . . . he sighed. What he didn't want was for her to feel rushed into marriage.

The money she had inherited from Big Finn had messed up his plans; taken the wind out of his sails. He would never begrudge her. He was planning a surprise for her, wanted to take care of her, give her things she never had, and now . . . now she had the means of making a life for herself without him. She could go to America. The possibilities were endless. Yet she seemed happy when they were together. And her happiness was all he cared about. If she changed her mind, it would drive him crazy. Hadn't she said herself that she wanted to marry him when she turned eighteen? And he had seen the love in her eyes when they were together. By the time he stepped from the train in Cavan, he was feeling more positive.

In the town he called into the local store and picked up a bottle of sherry and a few provisions for his aunt before walking to the cottage. As soon as he stepped through the door, he knew something was wrong. There was no familiar smell of bread baking. His aunt was hunched over the fire coughing, a blanket draped across her shoulders, but there was no sign of Eva. A neighbour was making a hot drink.

He dropped the shopping on the table. 'What is it, Ma? Are you sick?'

'Ah, it's nothing. Sure, don't go jumping to conclusions.'

'Where's Eva?'

'The girl's at the dairy,' the neighbour said. 'I came in to see your aunt, noticed she wasn't the best, so I'm making her a hot toddy.'

'Why didn't you let me know, Ma? I'd a come down last night. Does Eva know?'

'No. She'd left before I got out of me bed. Now stop fussing. It's only a sniffle and me rheumatism playing up.'

'Ah, it's more than that, so it is,' the neighbour said. 'She should get herself down to the quack.' She passed Ma the drink, with a generous dollop of whiskey, and gave Cathal a concerned look. 'Is there anything else I can do now I'm here? Young one won't be back for a while, will she?'

Eva seldom milked on Saturday, and he wondered if she had forgotten he was coming?

'It was good of you to drop in, we'll be fine,' he said.

'Well, if you're sure!'

She was reluctant to leave, so he placed his hand on her arm, steering her towards the door.

'You'll give me a shout if ye need anything?' she asked.

'I will, and thanks.' This was one neighbour he knew his aunt could do without right now. He boiled water and poured it into a water jar, then pushed it underneath her bed quilt. When he guided her towards her bedroom, she didn't protest. He made her comfortable before removing his coat, then put more peat on the fire and brewed himself a pot of tea. He wondered how long Eva would be? His aunt had a fever and, in spite of her protests, she needed a doctor.

It was sometime later when Eva came in, humming. She looked surprised to see him. 'Hello, Cathal.'

He drew her to him and kissed her. 'You smell of milk!'

She laughed. 'Do I? I didn't expect you this early.' She glanced around. 'Where's Ma?'

'She's having a lie-down, she has a temperature. I'm going for the doctor.'

'What's happened? Is she bad? I should have checked her before I left, but I thought she was asleep and didn't want to disturb her.'

'Don't worry.' He kissed her cheek. 'You stay here, I won't be a jiffy.'

* * *

The doctor knew about Ma's rheumatism and how hard she worked on behalf of the community. He pulled a chair closer to her bed and took out his stethoscope. When he had finished examining her he said, 'Now, you and I have known each other a long time, Miss Scully, and there's none of us getting any younger.'

'Oh, stop fussing and just leave me the medicine.'

Cathal glanced at Eva and shook his head. 'She's as stubborn as a mule, Doc.'

'Sure, don't I know it?' He scribbled something down. 'The tablets and this tonic mixture should do the trick. They will dispense them for you at the local chemist.' He turned back to Ma Scully. 'When you're on your feet again, you must cut back on the gallivanting. Think of yourself for a change. That old ticker of yours is struggling to keep up with you.'

'We'll make sure she does,' Cathal said and smiled at his aunt.

'Get him out of here.' Ma dismissed the doctor with a wave of her hand.

Cathal knew the man would take no offence. Thanking him, he paid the fee and saw him to the door.

Cathal stayed for the whole of the weekend and helped to look after his aunt. Insisting she stay in the warm, he only let certain people in to see her for short periods as she tired easily. On Sunday evening, Eva didn't want him to leave. He held her close and kissed her, and she clung to him, then watched him through the window as he hurried off to catch the train.

Ma Scully stayed in bed for two days and made no attempt to get up. Eva watched over her and prayed for her recovery. Ma was not a good patient; she was cranky, and nothing Eva did was right, refusing to take her medicine, telling Eva to stop fussing. But Eva, just as stubborn, continued making a fuss until Ma was better. She informed Mr Simms that she couldn't do the milking for a few days and devoted her time to looking after Ma.

By the end of the week, Ma decided she'd had enough of lying in bed and got up. 'Are you sure you're strong enough? The doctor said plenty of bed rest.'

'Ah, sure, what does he know, child? I'm as right as rain, so I am.'

Eva didn't argue. She sat Ma by the range and placed a rug across her knees, then went to make her a hot drink.

'Did Cathal say when he'd be back down?'

'Friday evening, if he's not on duty.' Eva was glad to hear Ma chatting as normal, her grumpiness gone.

'Now that court business is over, I want to see you and Cathal settled before I kick the bucket.'

'Oh, Ma, don't talk like that!' Eva put the hot cocoa into her hand. 'You're on the mend.'

'Aye, I am that, but I can't live forever, so what plans have ye got going on inside that head of yours? Ye can't be thinking of staying here looking after Simms' cows for the rest of yer life.'

Eva knew her future was in Dublin with the man she loved, but she refrained from saying so. Leaving Ma would be a wrench. She had grown to love her. No one had done more to nurture and care for her since the fire. And Eva didn't intend to forget.

'We've not discussed it proper yet, Ma. There's no rush.'

'Has Cathal said any more about the money?'

Eva shook her head.

'He'll come round to it, you'll see.' She sighed. 'He's a

man and ye know they like to be the ones looking after the coffers. Talk to him again and decide what ye want to do. And I don't want either of ye worrying about me.'

Eva leant down and kissed her cheek, then pulled a chair closer. 'Would you ever consider leaving Cavan, Ma?'

'What for?'

'Could you live in Dublin, do you think?'

'Why would I? Sure, haven't I lived in Cavan all me life?'

'I know. It's a silly question but—'

The knock on the door stopped her in her tracks and she hesitated before opening it. Eva recognised the woman as one of Ma's friends from her Town Hall meetings.

She breezed in, wearing a woollen coat, fur boots, gloves and a headscarf. 'There's a wind out there that would cut you in two.' She moved towards the fire. 'Sure, I heard you'd been ill so I've called to see how you're doing?'

Eva glanced at Ma to gauge her reaction.

'Shut that door afore I catch me end, and set another place at the table.'

Chapter Sixty-five

Eva had wanted a heart-to-heart with Ma about the birds and the bees, and in particular about the feelings that coursed through her when she was with Cathal. The thrill she experienced when he held her close. But whenever she broached the subject, someone knocked on Ma's door, or called in to see her. The moment lost, Eva decided there would be plenty of time later once they decided on a date for their wedding.

When Cathal arrived back in Cavan the following weekend, he smiled to see his aunt up and about again.

'Well, thank the Lord for that.' He turned to Eva. 'Sounds like you had a good nurse.'

'Aye! I did that, lad. And before ye start, I won't be told what I can and can't do. I'm away to a meeting at the Town Hall.' She buttoned up her fur-collared coat, pinned her hat in place and pushed her hands inside a pair of gloves.

'But, Ma! It's freezing.' Eva's words fell on deaf ears as the door closed. Shaking her head, she laughed and went to fill the kettle.

Cathal removed his mackintosh and hung it up. 'That's Ma for you. She'll never slow down. Thanks for looking after her.' He held his hands out to the fire, rubbing them to get heat into them, then he came up behind her and kissed the back of her neck.

It sent a delightful sensation down her spine. Her voice shaky, she said, 'I'll bring the tea.'

He took hold of her hand. 'Leave that. Come and sit beside me.'

'Is something wrong?' Her eyes widened.

'I hope not.'

She sat down. 'Is it about the inheritance?' She needed to know how he felt.

His face clouded, and he stood up, then reached out and took her hands. Pulling her to her feet, he wrapped his arms around her. 'Eva, the money is immaterial. It's yours and you must spend it how you wish.'

'Oh, Cathal, I've been so worried. You don't mind then?'

'No, as long as you allow me to look after you finan-cially as a husband should.' He looked down at her. 'It's just my way. Are you all right with that? I have saved money and have plans to put a deposit down on our future home once we're married.'

She relaxed against him. 'So you don't want me to help with anything?'

'You can buy whatever you like for the house and your-self. Why don't you and Ma have a spending spree in Dublin?' He kissed the top of her head.

Her eyes brightened. 'Would you mind if I put some of it away for our children's education?'

'Children, eh? You are forward thinking.'

She felt her cheeks hot. 'Well?' she asked.

'I'd be more than happy with that. In that case, I had better hurry up and put a ring on your finger.' He laughed, and kissed her with passion.

When he released her, she was breathless. 'I think I had better see to dinner before Ma gets back.'

'That's a good idea. I'm starving.'

She nudged him with her elbow. 'Oh, you!'

After their meal of mashed potatoes, sausage, onion and home-grown garden peas, Cathal patted his tummy. 'That was delicious, thank you.'

'Aye, that was grand, so it was,' Ma said. 'And it's revived my appetite.' She stood up and cleared the dishes until Eva stopped her. 'I'm not an invalid. And ye can stop trying to wrap me in cotton wool, because it won't work.'

Cathal raised an eyebrow and pushed back his chair. 'I'm away down to the store. I won't be a minute.'

Both women looked up as he pulled his coat on and disappeared out of the door.

'What's he up to?' Ma narrowed her eyes. 'Hope he doesn't have to dash back to Dublin yet. Has he said anything?'

'No, but we spoke about my inheritance, and it's all sorted. Like you said, Ma, he's a proud man.'

'Good. And what do ye plan to do with all that money then?'

'Cathal suggested that you and I spend it in Dublin. I can buy things for my bottom drawer. I'm so excited, Ma.'

'Did he now? Well, that's a start, isn't it? I'll look forward to that, love.'

Eva was washing the plates when Cathal burst in, carrying a bottle of red wine and a cake box. A gust of wind followed him and he kicked the door shut with his foot. He placed the items on the table and removed his coat, smoothing down his hair.

'What's this then?' Ma, sitting in her chair by the fire, glanced up.

Eva dried her hands and removed her apron. 'Is it someone's birthday?'

'Not that I know of.' He took down three glasses from the dresser, uncorked the wine and poured them each a glass.

Eva gave Ma a quizzical look and sat at the table.

Cathal, a huge smile on his face, got down on one knee. 'I know I've asked you before, Eva, but I didn't have a ring.' He plucked the small black velvet box from his pocket and flicked it open. 'Eva Fallon, will you marry me?'

She gasped, and tears gathered in her eyes. Speechless, she nodded.

'Well, is it all right? Do you like it?'

'It's beautiful, Cathal. Of course I like it. I love it.'

He got to his feet and she threw her arms around him. Then he placed the sparkling diamond on to her slim finger and gathered her into his arms. 'I love you, Eva Fallon.'

'And I adore you, Cathal Burke.'

Ma stood up and Eva drew her into their circle. Tears glistened in the older woman's eyes. 'I couldn't be happier for my two favourite people. But tell me, have ye set a date?'

Cathal and Eva looked at each other. 'A few months from now, when I'm eighteen,' she said.

'Oh, that long then?' Ma chuckled.

Smiling, they raised a glass to their future. And whatever happened, they would both make sure that Ma Scully was part of it.

Epilogue

One Saturday morning at the end of October, Eva stepped off the train in Dublin.

Cathal was there to meet her. 'You look lovely.'

She wore her new cream trench coat, belted at the waist, over a blue twinset and slim black woollen skirt, and her black boots to keep out the cold. Her long hair was swept up under a red woolly hat. Her previous concerns about what to wear, and why he had asked her to get here so early, melted away with his kiss. And before she could catch her breath, he hurried her towards a waiting cab. His message had been vague and her curiosity could wait no longer.

'What's going on, Cathal? You're acting very strangely,' she said as he helped her into the cab and sat next to her. 'Where are we going?'

'You must wait and see.' He held her close, kissing her lips whenever she tried to persuade him to tell her.

Eva didn't know Dublin well. As the cab headed south

out of the city, she sat back, content to let him take her to their destination. After a short ride, the cab came to a stop alongside a row of shops. While Cathal paid the cabby, Eva stood on the pavement surveying her surroundings. It was a busy little place with a church spire towering in the distance. A tram clanked past and a woman pushing a pram, a little boy at her side, hurried by.

'Where are we?' she asked him, when Cathal joined her.

'Donnybrook village. Haven't you heard of the famous Donnybrook fair?'

Eva shook her head.

'Remind me to tell you about it sometime, but now . . .' He took her hand and walked further along before turning a corner on to a row of red-brick cottages. 'I'm meeting someone at number sixteen. It's at the end of the row.'

Two young girls played hopscotch on the pavement and stopped to look at Eva. She smiled, and they turned back to their game.

'Is it a friend of yours?'

He laughed. Then he hugged her close. 'I want to buy it, if you like it.'

'Buy it!' Eva swallowed. 'That's grand. Why didn't you tell me?'

'I wanted to surprise you.'

And before she could reply, the door flew open and a tall, thin angry-looking man in a black overcoat, a drip hanging from the end of his red nose, stood before them holding a clipboard. He glanced at his watch. 'We said ten, Mr Burke. It's now gone half past.'

'I'm sorry. We're here now.'

They stepped into a spacious room with a strong smell of paint. It was empty, apart from a mirror hanging from a chain above the fireplace. A brown rug lay on the floor with spots of green paint. Eva glanced to a door on her right.

'That's the bedroom,' the man said. His voice echoed. 'There are two more towards the back.'

Eva smiled at Cathal. Already she was planning where she would put everything. 'Can we . . . ?'

'It's a solid little place with no damp,' the agent cut in, then he sniffed and blew his nose so loudly that Eva suppressed a giggle and Cathal squeezed her hand. 'You two look around. I'm going to the pub to thaw out. I'll be back in half an hour. If you have any questions, you can ask me later.'

'Thanks, Mr Sweeney.' Cathal rubbed his hands and turned back to Eva, who was already exploring the rest of the cottage. 'What do you think?'

'It's perfect.' She thought about what it would be like when it was furnished, with a roaring fire in the hearth. A home of their own! She wanted to cry. 'But, is it not too soon? I mean . . .'

'Not at all. If you like it. Sure, I can live here until we're married. By then I'll have decorated it throughout and have it nice for when you join me.' His voice was high with excitement.

The other two rooms were small but adequate. The scullery was clean, the walls whitewashed.

'We'll need a new gas cooker.'

Eva nodded. She saw herself making dinner for Cathal when he returned home from work, and her heart soared. The back yard had a washing line and a small garden with neglected rose bushes climbing the back wall. Tears welled in her eyes.

'Well, shall I buy it? It's a bargain and won't be on the market long. It's no distance from my job in the city, and . . .'

To stop him talking, she reached up and kissed him.

'Is that a yes, then?'

'I love it. And I can't wait to tell Ma.'

He kissed the tip of her nose. 'And there's a room for Ma when she comes to visit.'

Wrapped in each other's arms, they shared a passionate kiss before he released her.

'That's settled then. I'll sign on the dotted line when Grumpy gets back. Might put a smile on his face.'

On the way back to the city, Cathal answered all Eva's questions. His boss, Andy, had gotten wind of the property from a friend and he knew Cathal was looking for a place. He had to act fast before it went on the market. 'Keeping it from you was hard, but,' he laughed, 'it was worth it to see the surprise on your face.'

'Well, I forgive you this time.' She leant in and kissed his cheek.

'Let's get off here, Eva. I could murder a mug of tea. How about you?'

'Yes, we can go to Doreen's cafe. I want to invite Doreen and Bernadette to my wedding. And would you mind if I asked Sister Catherine?'

'I think that would be nice, Eva. She was instrumental in getting you acquitted at the trial. Have you got a date in mind?'

They were walking by the Liffey wall when Eva paused.

'My birthday falls on the anniversary of the orphanage fire. I can't get married on that day.'

With his arm around her shoulders, he pulled her closer. 'I'm sorry, Eva. And Lent follows. We can't marry during Lent.'

She fell against him, her head resting on his chest, unaware of irritated shoppers pushing past them on the narrow pavement. He pulled her closer.

Why hadn't she thought about that?

Her eyes wide, she looked up at him. 'What are we going to do, Cathal?'

'We can't wait until after Easter. It's too long.'

They walked on, arm in arm, when Eva said, 'Let's get married a week before my birthday.'

'Are you sure?'

'Yes, yes, I'm sure.' She smiled.

'Where would you like to get married?'

'Can we marry in the church at Donnybrook?' She moved her body closer to him. 'It's where we will be living.'

'I'll make the arrangements. And once I've got the house in order, you and Ma can go shopping and make our house a home.'

She had to restrain herself from kissing him right there in the street. They were laughing as they walked into the small cafe where Doreen was busy making sandwiches and Bernadette serving tables. As soon as Doreen saw them, she stopped what she was doing and came over to welcome them.

'Well, you're a sight for sore eyes,' she said. 'What's this then?' She was looking at the sparkling diamond on Eva's finger. 'I'm happy for you both.'

After a brief chat, Bernadette served them steaming hot tea and home-made scones. Before they left, Doreen and Bernadette congratulated them both on their forthcoming marriage and said they would be delighted to attend the wedding.

When Eva and Cathal took their vows at the church in Donnybrook village, Eva looked radiant in a long, white chiffon gown, decorated with lace, made by herself with the help of Ma Scully. Her long hair, styled by Bernadette, framed her face and a veil with a coronet resembling a daisy chain crowned her head. As she walked up the aisle on Andy's arm, Sister Catherine sitting next to Ma Scully smiled her approval. Then, as Cathal took her hand, there was no mistaking the love that shone from his eyes.

Afterwards, the small party of eight celebrated at the home of Andy and his wife, Ethel, with hot broth, sandwiches, bottles of stout and glasses of sherry, plus a small wedding cake made by Ma.

'May all your troubles be little ones,' she said, toasting the happy couple.

That evening, Ma stayed with Andy and his wife to give the young couple privacy on their first night together as man and wife.

When Cathal carried Eva over the threshold of their new home, Eva, overwhelmed with love and gratitude, looked into the eyes of her husband whom she had loved and admired from the moment she first set eyes on him. He had stood by her, despite the trial and Matthew Blackstock, and she would stand by his side for the rest of their lives, in their very own home, in the place where she belonged.

Acknowledgements

My thanks go to:

The wonderful people of Bawnboy, Co. Cavan, too many to mention by name, who helped in various ways while I was researching *A Place to Belong*. Their hospitality, generosity and sharing of historic facts helped enormously. I was taken by rowing boat across Templeport lake to St. Mogues island, a historic burial ground, to see where the Beaufighter crashed next to the island in 1943.

Jonathan Smyth and County Cavan library, Farnham Street; Kildare library; Cavan Walking History; Bawnboy & Templeport Development Association's website; my amazing critiquing group, Just Write, in Leicester, UK; The Romantic Novelists' Association for their friendship and encouragement over the years; author, Jean Chapman, for her insightful constructive advice while writing the synopsis; Leicester Writers' Club who were my first critics;

Lutterworth Writers' Group; my wonderful agent, Vanessa Holt, for believing in me. Last but not least, my remarkable editor, Kate Byrne, for her meticulous editing, and the team at Headline Publishing for bringing *A Place to Belong* to fruition.

Finally, a huge thank you to everyone who pre-ordered a copy of *A Place to Belong*. I'm hugely grateful, and I hope you will enjoy reading the story as much as I loved writing it.

A Place to Belong

Bonus Material

Cathy Mansell Shares Her Favourite . . .

Book:
Wuthering Heights.

Film:
Gone with the Wind.

Food:
Sunday roast with the family.

Drink:
Red wine.

Place:
My office.

Season:
Spring when the first daffodils appear.

TV Programme:
Vera.

Song:
'Candle In The Wind'.

Possession:
An owl carved from wood sitting on two books. It was given me by my grandson when Headline offered me a two-book deal.

Item of Clothing:
A grey tailored trouser suit my husband bought me years ago that I can just about squeeze into. Could never find another one like it.

Colour:
Buttercup yellow.

Flower:
The rose-coloured fuchsia.

Perfume:
Knowing by Estée Lauder.

Place:
Ireland.

Way to spend the day:
Writing, reading, spending time with my grandchildren, and a bit of gardening.